THE VERDANT GATE
THE SKYREND PROPHECY BOOK TWO
JOSHUA J. WHITE

BERSERKER BOOKS

Stay Connected with Joshua J. White

Before you begin...

If you're drawn to myth, mystery, and stories that echo long after the final page,

I invite you to join me on the journey ahead.

This world — and the ones that follow — are part of something much larger. By joining my mailing list, you'll get early access to new books, hidden lore, exclusive behind-the-scenes notes, and the occasional dispatch from the quiet woods where I write.

Sign up here: www.JoshuaJWhiteBooks.com/TheSkyrendProphecy

No noise. No spam. Just stories worth sharing!

— Joshua J. White

Author & Founder, Berserker Books

CONTENTS

PROLOGUE

The memory-bloom unfurled like a wound in the air. Three ancient druids stood equidistant around it, their breath freezing in the twilight air of the hidden grove. Hawthorn, eldest of the Verdant Wardens, reached forward with gnarled fingers to trace the shifting images within the bloom's gossamer petals.

"There," she whispered, her voice a rustling of autumn leaves. "The flame-bearer walks the northern paths."

The memory-bloom pulsed crimson, revealing a man with golden marks spreading across his chest. He trudged through snow, a bronze sword at his hip gleaming with inner light. His eyes flickered between human blue and something molten, inhuman.

"Asvarr Skyrend," murmured Rowan, the youngest of the three, though her youth was relative—her face was lined with a century of watching the worlds break and mend. "The first Root claimed him, just as the signs foretold."

Ash filled her palms—gray remnants gathered from a northern village where clan-blood had soaked the earth during the Shattering. She cast it into the circle before them, where it formed runic patterns that shifted like serpents chasing their tails.

The third druid, Oak, maintained the binding circle around them. His voice was deep as old roots. "The second Root stirs. It recognizes the flame in his blood." He pressed his forehead against the silvery bark of the ancient tree at the grove's center. "It calls to him, though he doesn't yet understand."

Around them, Vanaheim's broken beauty sprawled in verdant dusk. The grove existed in a fold of reality—neither fully in the fertile realm of the Vanir nor entirely in Midgard. Stones bleached white as bone formed three concentric circles around the central tree, each ring carved with sigils older than gods. Many had cracked during the Shattering; others had been deliberately broken by the druids themselves in rituals of unbinding.

Hawthorn's fingers, twisted like the roots she tended, traced the images flowing through the memory-bloom. "Show me the second Root," she commanded.

The bloom shuddered, its petals contracting before expanding outward in a shower of golden spores. The vision within shifted—revealing a twisted gate formed of living wood, branches contorted into an archway threaded with veins of golden sap.

"The Verdant Gate," Oak whispered with reverence. "It's awakening after nine cycles of silence."

"Because it feels him," Hawthorn said, eyes narrowing. "The Root knows its kin."

Rowan's brow furrowed. "But Asvarr comes from warrior stock, not our bloodline. The old treaties gave guardianship of the flame and storm to the northern clans. Root and seed belonged to—"

"The Hrafn clan," Hawthorn finished. "Yes. But something has crossed the boundaries. The Root wouldn't respond to him otherwise."

She thrust her staff into the earth. The soil responded, rippling outward like water. At the circle's edge, tiny saplings erupted, growing in moments to saplings with leaves shaped like hands reaching skyward.

"We must proceed," Oak urged, his voice tight with restraint. "The spore count rises. If we don't complete the location ritual before moonrise, the Root will shift again, and we'll wait another season before attempting contact."

Hawthorn nodded grimly. They had already waited too long. Nine of her twelve apprentices had withered in the past month, their bodies reclaimed by the soil as the Root demanded sacrifice. Only these two remained beside her—the strongest, but still fragile compared to the power they sought to contain.

"Begin the circle-singing," she commanded.

The three druids raised their voices in a chant that seemed to come from the earth itself. Their song had no words a human tongue could form—it resonated at the frequency of growing things, of cells dividing and roots spreading through dark soil.

The ashes from Asvarr's destroyed village swirled faster, forming intricate patterns that spiraled toward the grove's center. The memory-bloom responded, its petals spreading wide to reveal more fragments of vision:

Asvarr kneeling before a pool of golden sap. A crown of tangled roots upon his brow. A woman with raven-black hair and an arm of living wood, watching him from shadows. A child born during the Shattering, existing partially in multiple realities. A broken oath-stone, its pieces scattered across bloodied snow.

"The bloodlines have crossed," Hawthorn murmured, her eyes wide with understanding. "That shouldn't be possible unless..."

She thrust both hands into the memory-bloom, her skin absorbing the golden light. The veins in her arms glowed as the vision-sap coursed through her.

"Hawthorn!" Rowan moved to intervene, but Oak held her back.

"She seeks deep-knowing," he warned. "Interrupt, and her mind will shatter."

Inside the memory-bloom, Hawthorn's consciousness traveled backward through twisted roots of time. She saw a northern village generations ago. A trader from her own lands with Verdant blood in his veins. A winter storm, a lonely hearth, a union that should never have happened. And nine months later, a child born with mixed bloodlines, who would eventually become the grandfather of the man now called Asvarr.

The root of the northern clan intertwined with a branch from the Verdant line.

Hawthorn gasped as she pulled free from the vision, golden sap leaking from her eyes like tears. "He carries both bloodlines," she rasped. "Flame and Root. He was never meant to be the vessel, but fate has twisted around him."

Rowan's face paled. "Then who was intended?"

"The Hrafn girl," Oak guessed, his expression grim. "Brynja. The one who escaped when her clan was slaughtered."

Hawthorn nodded, wiping the sap from her cheeks. "The Root would have chosen her, had the Shattering followed its proper course. But the breaking was too violent, too widespread. And now..." She gestured at the memory-bloom, which showed Asvarr standing before the Root with his sword raised, golden light flooding from his chest.

"Will the second Root accept him?" Rowan asked, her voice barely audible over the wind that had begun to swirl through the grove, lifting fallen leaves in tight spirals.

"It's already reaching for him," Hawthorn replied. "But the connection is... unstable. Dangerous." She pressed her palm to the earth, feeling the resonance below. "The second Root seeks what it recognizes, but finds the flame mixed in its essence. It both desires and rejects him."

Oak's expression darkened. "Then we must intervene. Guide the Root toward its true purpose."

"Or sever the connection entirely," Rowan suggested, earning sharp glances from both elders.

"We are not Root-killers," Hawthorn snapped, though uncertainty flickered in her ancient eyes. "We are its guardians, its tenders."

"Even if it chooses the wrong vessel?" Rowan challenged. "One who carries storm and flame alongside Root-essence? The mixture could corrupt it entirely."

Oak raised his staff, thumping it against the ground. "Enough. We haven't survived nine cycles of breaking to abandon our oaths now. We must complete the location ritual and prepare the way for whichever vessel approaches."

Hawthorn nodded slowly, though doubt now threaded through her resolve. She reached into a pouch at her belt, withdrawing seeds of various shapes—some round as tears, others twisted like tiny animal horns, and one perfectly formed in the shape of a key.

"We'll bind the memory-seeing to these seeds," she instructed. "When the vessel—whichever one reaches the Verdant Gate first—arrives, they'll guide them through the trials."

She placed the seeds in the center of the ash pattern, which had formed a perfect replica of Yggdrasil in miniature, its roots and branches forming the boundaries between realms.

"From ash to seed," she intoned. "From death to life. The cycle turns."

"The cycle turns," Oak and Rowan echoed.

***

Hawthorn cut her palm with a sliver of white bone, letting seven drops of blood fall onto the seeds. Each droplet hissed upon contact, the seeds absorbing the offering greedily.

The memory-bloom convulsed suddenly, its petals darkening from gold to crimson to black. Inside, the image of Asvarr vanished, replaced by a woman's face—sharp-featured, with eyes like frozen amber and hair black as a raven's wing.

"Brynja Hrafndottir," Hawthorn whispered. "She comes."

"But how?" Rowan asked, her voice tight with alarm. "She walks with the Ashfather's servants. She shouldn't be able to perceive the Root at all."

Oak's expression hardened. "The bloodlines call to each other. Even across realms. Even through the barrier of broken oaths."

Hawthorn stared into the bloom, watching as Brynja's face twisted in pain or rage. Behind her loomed a shadow with a single golden eye.

"The Wanderer guides her," Hawthorn said. "He's found her. Just as he found Asvarr's grandfather."

"Then we've already failed," Rowan whispered.

"No." Hawthorn straightened, her ancient frame suddenly rigid with purpose. "The Root still chooses. And now it must choose between them—the unintended vessel or the one corrupted by shadow."

She pressed her bloodied palm flat against the earth beside the seeds. "We'll anchor the Verdant Gate to this grove. When either seeker approaches, they'll find their way here first."

"That will drain what little strength we have left," Oak warned.

"We have no choice." Hawthorn glared at him with eyes now fully golden, her pupils swallowed by sap-light. "The second Root must be claimed before the Wanderer twists it to his purpose. Whether by Asvarr's flame or Brynja's shadow, the binding must happen soon."

The ground beneath them trembled. Around the grove's edge, the trees began to groan, their bark splitting to reveal pulsing veins of sap. The seedlings Hawthorn had sprouted earlier twisted unnaturally, their limbs elongating into something more animal than plant.

Rowan stepped back, alarm spreading across her features. "Something's wrong."

Oak extended his senses toward the earth. His eyes widened. "Something comes. Something that walks between Root and shadow."

Hawthorn clutched the key-shaped seed tightly, her knuckles whitening. "Complete the ritual," she commanded. "Quickly."

But the memory-bloom was already collapsing, its petals withering as darkness filled its center. The ash patterns shifted, forming new shapes—thorns and teeth and eyes that blinked with malevolent awareness.

"It's too late," Rowan whispered. "We've drawn its attention."

The central stone of the inner circle cracked with a sound like bones breaking. Soil erupted upward as something pushed through from below—something that had once been human but had merged with root and thorn until it became a twisted mockery of both.

Hawthorn stepped back, clutching the key-seed to her chest. "Verdant preserve us."

"The Gate opens for none but blood," the spriggan rasped, its voice both masculine and feminine, threaded with the creaking of breaking branches. Its face was a tangled mass of thorns, but its eyes glowed with amber light.

It spoke with Brynja Hrafndottir's voice.

"And he carries mine."

Blood sprayed across Hawthorn's face as Oak fell, his throat torn open by a whipping tendril of thorns. The spriggan lurched forward on limbs that bent at impossible angles, its body a grotesque fusion of human skeleton and invasive rootwork. Moss and lichen draped its exposed ribs like rotted flesh. The center of its chest housed a pulsing amber knot that glowed with each labored movement.

"Protect the seeds!" Hawthorn commanded, backing toward the tree at the grove's center. Her gnarled fingers clutched the key-shaped seedpod against her heart.

Rowan stood her ground, thrusting her staff toward the advancing horror. "By root and branch, by seed and soil—"

The spriggan's laughter cut through her incantation, wet and terrible. It raised what had once been a hand but was now a mass of flexible thorns. "The old words hold no power here, tender."

With frightening speed, it lashed out. Thorns pierced Rowan's chest, lifting her from the ground. Her staff clattered into the ash circle, disturbing the careful patterns they'd worked hours to create. Blood dripped from her mouth as the spriggan pulled her closer, bringing her face inches from its own twisted mass of brambles and teeth.

"Tell me, child." The creature's voice shifted, becoming feminine, yet resonant with multiple tones simultaneously. "Does it hurt to die among your precious growing things?"

Hawthorn's voice rose in a desperate chant, invoking the deepest protective magic of the grove. The ground rumbled in response. Thick roots erupted around her feet, forming a partial barrier between her and the abomination.

"You cannot hide from me, elder," the spriggan said, dropping Rowan's twitching body. It tilted its head, an eerily human gesture from something so monstrous. "I've walked with Root and flame both. I've tasted the sap of gods and men."

Hawthorn pressed backward into the tree's embrace, feeling its bark part slightly to cradle her ancient frame. Sap trickled down to mix with the sweat on her brow. "What are you?" she whispered, studying the creature more carefully.

The amber knot in its chest pulsed faster as it approached. "I am the vessel you abandoned," it said, the voice now distinctly female. "I am the branch you failed to tend."

Recognition flooded Hawthorn's awareness. "Brynja Hrafndottir."

The spriggan's thorny mockery of a face contorted into something like a smile. "The girl is no more. And yet..." It flexed its thorn-fingers before its face, examining them with curiosity. "She persists. Her flesh houses me poorly. Her will resists even now."

Hawthorn's mind raced. This was no true spriggan, but something worse—a possession, a merging of corrupted Root essence with a living host. The Verdant Five had whispered of such abominations in the oldest texts, calling them "the broken bloom."

"Listen to me," Hawthorn said, pressing herself more firmly against the tree. She felt the key-seed pulse in response to her elevated heartbeat. "The Root you seek isn't meant for—"

"For me?" the spriggan finished, stalking closer. Dead leaves crunched beneath its twisted feet. "I know. You intended it for him. The flame-bearer with the mixed blood." It spat a glob of sap that sizzled when it hit the ground. "My blood."

Understanding crystallized in Hawthorn's mind. "Then it's true. Your lineages are connected."

"More than connected," the spriggan growled. "We were kin before the breaking of clan borders. Before the oaths were severed." It paused, head tilting again. "She knows this, somewhere deep in memory. Fragments of truth passed through generations. The betrayal that split Root-tender from Flame-keeper."

Hawthorn's fingers tightened around the key-seed. "Then there's still hope for balance. If both bloodlines flow in Asvarr and Brynja—"

The spriggan lunged forward with shocking speed, its thorn-hand closing around Hawthorn's throat. "There is no balance, elder. Only survival." With its free hand, it reached for the key-seed. "The Gate opens for none but blood. His or mine."

Hawthorn gasped for breath, feeling her ancient windpipe beginning to collapse under the pressure. She summoned her remaining strength and pressed the key-seed into the bark behind her. The tree shuddered, absorbing the precious object into its living wood. Golden sap oozed down its trunk, marking a spiral pattern that glowed briefly before fading.

The spriggan howled with rage, tightening its grip. "What have you done?"

"Secured the way," Hawthorn wheezed. "Neither light nor shadow can claim it now. Only the worthy."

The creature's amber core pulsed rapidly. It lifted Hawthorn until her feet dangled above the ground. "Then I will take it from your flesh," it snarled, driving thorns deep into her chest.

Pain blossomed throughout Hawthorn's body, sharp and clarifying. She felt her lifeblood flowing outward, feeding the hungry roots below. As her vision dimmed, she fixed her gaze on the memory-bloom, still floating at the circle's center though now withered and dark. Within its dying petals, she glimpsed Asvarr once more, trudging across a snowy landscape with golden light leaking from the mark on his chest.

The flow of visions shifted, showing Brynja—the real Brynja, her face untouched by corruption—watching the same snow-covered mountains from a different vantage. Between them pulsed the living gate, calling to both with promises of power and purpose.

With her final breath, Hawthorn made a decision. She pressed her bloodied palm against the tree trunk, leaving a crimson handprint. "Let them both seek," she whispered. "Let them both be tested."

The spriggan ripped its thorns free, and Hawthorn's body crumpled to the ground. Blood pooled around her, soaking into the soil, feeding the earth one final offering. The creature bent down, rifling through her robes with clumsy, thorn-encrusted fingers.

"Where is it?" it growled, frustration mounting. "Where is the key-seed?"

A voice whispered from the tree, though its leaves remained still in the windless air. The voice was Hawthorn's, though her body lay motionless at its roots. "Gone where you cannot follow, broken one. Not until you are whole again."

The spriggan's roar shattered the memory-bloom, sending fragments of golden light spiraling into the night sky. It slammed its thorny appendages against the tree trunk, tearing at the bark where the key-seed had disappeared. Amber sap leaked from its chest as it raged, matching the golden tears that wept from the wounded tree.

"I will burn this grove to ash," it threatened, voice shifting between Brynja's natural tone and something ancient and twisted.

The whisper came again, fainter now. "Then you will never find the Gate."

The spriggan froze, thorns still embedded in the tree bark. Something in its demeanor changed—a subtle shift in posture, a momentary softening of its jagged silhouette. When it spoke again, the voice was purely Brynja's, though cracked with pain.

"I need the Root," she pleaded. "It's my birthright. My clan guarded it for generations before—" She doubled over suddenly, thorns erupting from her shoulders as the corruption reasserted control.

"Before they were slaughtered," the darker voice finished. "Yes. As were all the guardians when they outlived their purpose."

The spriggan straightened, amber core pulsing evenly once more. It surveyed the destruction around it—three dead druids, broken stone circles, scattered ash that had once formed sacred patterns. The ritual ground was tainted now, rendered useless for future workings.

Yet something remained. A faint golden spiral marked the tree where the key-seed had vanished, barely visible in the deepening twilight. The spriggan approached it cautiously, running a thorny finger along the pattern. The spiral responded with a quick flash of light before settling back into dormancy.

"Blood," it murmured. "Of course."

It pressed its thorns into the soft wood, drawing forth golden sap. Where the sap touched the spiral, new symbols appeared briefly before sinking back into the bark—stars, roots, flames, gates. A map, encoded in patterns only the Root-connected could perceive.

The spriggan stepped back, absorbing what it had learned. Then, with sudden violence, it tore at its own chest, ripping the pulsing amber knot partially free. Sap and blood mingled as it held the living core against the spiral. The tree shuddered, branches swaying though no wind blew.

"Show me," the spriggan commanded.

The spiral blazed to life, projecting a golden map into the air—nine realms arranged in familiar pattern, but with new paths marked between them. At the center of the configuration floated a gate of tangled wood, its edges flowing like liquid. The Verdant Gate.

The spriggan's thorny face split in a grotesque approximation of triumph. "There you are."

It pressed the wounded amber core back into its chest, where thorn-veins quickly secured it in place. With one final look at the dead druids, it turned toward the edge of the grove. Each step left a blackened footprint in the soil, killing the grass beneath.

"The flame-bearer seeks the Gate as well," it muttered, Brynja's voice briefly dominating. "He doesn't understand what he carries."

"Neither do you, vessel," the darker voice responded through the same twisted mouth. "But you will. When the Root claims you fully."

At the grove's boundary, the spriggan paused, looking back at the scene of carnage. For a moment, something like regret flickered across its features—a ghost of Brynja Hrafndottir, watching through eyes that were increasingly less her own. Then the moment passed, and the creature slipped into the shadows between trees, leaving the grove to its deathly silence.

Behind it, the central tree continued to weep golden tears. Within its bark, the key-seed pulsed with patient rhythm, waiting to be discovered. The spiral glowed faintly, visible only to those with eyes to see—a beacon calling to those with the right blood.

Blood that flowed in two veins, separated by betrayal, now converging once more.

The spriggan's final words lingered in the empty air. "The Gate opens for none but blood. And he carries mine."

CHAPTER 1

THORNS IN DREAMS

A svarr stopped short at the ridge's crest. His left boot sank ankle-deep in snow that shouldn't exist in this season—white powder that crumbled under his weight like calcified bone. The sigil on his chest throbbed, a hot pulse of warning that drew his fingers to the hilt of his bronze sword.

Something was wrong here.

Below, the valley stretched like an open wound between the mountains. Three months since claiming the first Root Anchor, and still Asvarr found places like this—locations where reality had thinned, where the Shattering had torn deeper than elsewhere. The boundary markers of a half-dozen farms remained, but the structures they once protected had been replaced by twisted growths. Spires of wood and bone jutted from the earth at impossible angles, their surfaces alive with moving patterns that made his eyes ache.

Asvarr exhaled slowly through his nose, watching his frosty breath drift in a breeze that shouldn't have been able to carry it upward. His body had changed in these months of wandering. The leather armor that had once fit snugly now hung loose on his leaner frame. The bronze sword, however, seemed heavier—its blade drinking in the weak sunlight, veins of golden sap pulsing beneath the metal's surface.

"Something hunts here," he murmured to himself, voice rusty from disuse.

The only answer came from the sigil on his chest. The Grímmark had expanded since his binding with the Root Anchor, spreading across his torso in patterns resembling both roots and flame. Now it leaked a single drop of golden sap that trickled down his skin, warm and sticky against the cold mountain air. He wiped it away, only for another drop to form immediately.

He'd need to cross the valley to reach the pass beyond. The mark urged him onward, pulling him northward with the insistence of an embedded hook. Since binding with the Anchor, Asvarr had learned to trust these urgings—they led him to places where the breaking between realms required mending, where his presence could help stabilize fractures in reality.

Descending the slope, he noticed small blooms sprouting in his footprints—golden flowers that grew to maturity in moments before wilting just as quickly. The Root's influence, working through him. These momentary growths had marked his path across the fractured lands for weeks now, a trail any skilled tracker could follow.

The valley floor greeted him with wrongness. The air tasted metallic, like blood on a blade. What had appeared to be low-lying mist from the ridge revealed itself as something far stranger—a knee-high layer of transparent filaments, pulsing with faint light, spreading outward from the corrupted growths. Asvarr's boots crunched through them, sending ripples of agitation across their surface.

"Like walking through spider webs," he muttered, slicing his sword through a particularly thick patch. The filaments recoiled from the bronze blade, curling away with an audible hiss.

When he reached the first of the twisted growths, Asvarr paused to study it. Up close, he could see it for what it was—a farmhouse transformed. The wooden frame had grown like a living thing, walls pushing outward, floors buckling upward. Windows stretched into screaming mouths. The hearth stone had cracked, revealing a mass of root-like tendrils that pulsed with steady rhythm.

Asvarr pressed his palm against the transformed wood. Images flooded his mind—a family gathered around the hearth, singing winter songs though the season was spring. A child's laughter cut short. Eyes rolling back as bodies contorted, becoming part of the structure that had sheltered them. The Root, hungry and confused, consuming what it once nurtured.

He recoiled, sweat beading on his forehead despite the cold. These visions had grown more frequent, more vivid, since the binding. The sword in his hand hummed in response to his distress, the sap-veins brightening momentarily.

"I'm not here to judge," he told the twisted house, uncertain if anything remained to hear him. "Only to witness. To remember."

The structure creaked, wood bending subtly toward him like a flower tracking the sun. The Grímmark on his chest warmed in response. Recognition, perhaps. Or hunger.

Asvarr continued through the valley, giving the other corrupted structures a wide berth. Some had grown tall enough to block the weakening sunlight, casting long shadows that seemed to move independently of the fading day. In those shadows, he glimpsed movement—scuttling, low to the ground, too quick to track properly.

The stillness felt deliberate, expectant. The entire valley held its breath, watching him pass.

Near the center, where a stone well had once served several farms, Asvarr found a circle where nothing grew—not the golden flowers that trailed his steps, not the filament layer that covered everything else. Just bare, blackened earth radiating outward from the overgrown well. The hairs on his arms stood rigid.

A clean-edged boundary encircled the well—growth on one side, emptiness on the other. The mark on his chest pulsed with increasing urgency, matching the quickening of his heartbeat. He knelt at the boundary, pressing his fingers to the scorched soil.

The vision struck like lightning—a woman with raven-black hair standing beside the well, one arm transformed into gnarled wood, her face twisted in rage or pain. Brynja. The same woman who haunted his dreams nightly, watching him through tangles of roots, never speaking but always present. Around her, the earth burned in a perfect circle, charred by power he recognized—Root essence, corrupted by shadow.

The vision shifted: Brynja reaching toward him with her wooden arm, fingers elongating into thorns. Her mouth opening to reveal teeth filed to points. A voice that wasn't hers speaking through her lips: "Blood calls to blood."

Asvarr lurched backward, gasping. The bronze sword leapt into his hand without conscious thought, blade angled toward the well. The mark on his chest blazed with golden light visible through his leather armor.

Nothing moved in the valley, yet he felt observed from every direction.

"Show yourself!" he called, voice echoing across the emptiness.

Only silence answered him, though the filaments trembled across the valley floor, responding to his agitation. The shadows seemed to lengthen despite the sun's position remaining unchanged. Night would come soon, and Asvarr had no desire to face the valley's darkness.

He rose, sheathing the sword with reluctance, and continued toward the far slope. Each step left a bloom that died more quickly than the last, golden petals withering almost instantly now. The Root itself seemed eager to leave this place.

Half-way up the opposite ridge, Asvarr paused to look back. In the dimming light, the corrupted growths resembled massive thorns thrust upward from below, as if something enormous slumbered beneath the valley floor, its spined hide barely concealed by soil. The well at the center appeared darker somehow, a hole in reality rather than merely stone and earth.

His hand drifted to his chest, where the mark pulsed steadily. Three months ago, he'd bound with the first Root Anchor, accepting its power to continue his journey. He'd sacrificed memories, identity, certainty, free will—pieces of himself traded for the ability to mend what had broken during the Shattering. The bargain had seemed necessary, unavoidable.

Now, staring at the corruption below, Asvarr wondered if the exchange had been worth it. The sigil spread further each week. Sap occasionally leaked from the corners of his eyes while he slept. His dreams had become foreign landscapes populated by figures from ages past, their voices speaking words he understood but couldn't quite remember upon waking.

All except Brynja. Her appearances in his dreams remained vivid upon waking—her raven hair, her cold amber eyes, her arm of living wood. Always watching. Always reaching for something he carried.

As darkness swallowed the valley, Asvarr turned away and continued climbing. He needed shelter before nightfall. The corrupted land below was stirring to life as sunlight faded, the filaments glowing brighter, beginning to sway though no wind disturbed them. In the shadows between the twisted growths, larger shapes now moved with purpose.

The pass at the valley's end opened onto a plateau dotted with stands of pine. Asvarr found a sheltered hollow beneath an overhanging rock, partially blocked by fallen trees. He gathered dry branches for a small fire, working quickly as true darkness descended. The flame caught easily, almost eagerly, dancing with unusual intensity when he fed it pine needles from his pack.

He kept his sword unsheathed beside him, its sap-veins providing additional light. The fire's warmth barely penetrated the chill that had settled in his bones. It was not a physical cold, but the lingering unease from the valley. The sensation of being watched persisted, even here.

Sleep stalked him cautiously, circling like a predator uncertain of its prey. When it finally pounced, Asvarr descended into the same dream that had haunted him for weeks:

A forest of thorns, its canopy blocking all light. Roots writhing beneath his feet with deliberate movement, seeking purchase around his ankles. Trees with bark that resembled human skin, stretched taut over knobby wooden limbs.

He walked a narrow path through this forest, following a distant sound—rhythmic, like a heart beating. The bronze sword led the way, its sap-veins pulsing in time with the distant beat.

The path ended at a gate formed of living wood, branches twisted into an archway that seemed to breathe. Golden sap leaked from its joints, pooling at its threshold. Beyond the gate, something massive pulsed with power that called to the mark on his chest.

And always, watching from between the thorns, Brynja. Her raven hair tangled with roots and leaves. Her amber eyes reflecting golden light that had no source. Her mouth forming words he couldn't hear.

Tonight, something had changed. She stood closer to the path than ever before. Close enough that he could see tears of sap running down her cheeks. Close enough to hear her voice for the first time:

"The Gate opens for none but blood," she said, extending her wooden arm toward him. The limb elongated impossibly, thorny fingers reaching for his chest where the mark burned. "And you carry mine."

Asvarr lurched awake, a scream dying in his throat. The fire had burned to embers that cast just enough light to reveal a figure standing at the edge of his camp. Small, humanoid, motionless.

The bronze sword was in his hand before he'd fully processed what he was seeing. The sap-veins flared brilliantly, illuminating the intruder.

A child stood watching him. No more than seven or eight winters, with hair so pale it appeared white in the sword-light. The child's clothes were ragged, caked with dried mud. In one small hand, clutched with white-knuckled intensity, was a stone that seemed to absorb the light around it.

Not just any stone. A runestone, identical to the one Asvarr had found in his own hearth all those months ago, before the first binding.

The child tilted its head, studying Asvarr with unnerving focus. Its free hand lifted slowly to point beyond the camp, back toward the corrupt valley.

"She comes," the child whispered, voice barely audible above the night winds. "She walks the Root-path between realms. She hungers for what you carry."

The mark on Asvarr's chest blazed with sudden heat. Golden sap leaked through his tunic, dripping onto the ground where it sizzled against the cold stone. The child's eyes reflected the light, revealing pupils like liquid gold.

"Who are you?" Asvarr demanded, rising to his feet.

The child simply pointed again, this time toward the east. In that direction, just visible above the treeline, a column of darkness rose against the night sky—something more solid than smoke, more purposeful. The distant trees around it writhed like tentacles, reaching skyward as if pulled by an unseen force.

"The Gate opens," the child whispered, backing away from the camp. "Blood calls to blood."

Asvarr took a step toward the retreating figure, but his legs buckled as the mark flared with crippling heat. He fell to one knee, cursing through clenched teeth. When he looked up again, the child had vanished into the darkness beyond the dying firelight.

Only the lingering words remained, echoing in the cold night air: "Blood calls to blood."

Dawn broke with reluctance, light filtering through a screen of pine needles to dapple Asvarr's weathered face. The fire had died to ash hours ago. Of the pale-haired child, no trace remained except for a set of small footprints leading eastward—the same direction as the column of darkness that had now faded with morning's arrival.

***

Asvarr rolled to his feet, wincing as the mark on his chest throbbed. Gold-tinged scabs had formed where sap leaked during the night, cracking as he stretched. Three moons since binding with the Root Anchor, and still his body rebelled against the foreign power he'd welcomed into his flesh.

Following the child's tracks proved simple enough. Fresh impressions in dew-softened earth led down the plateau's eastern edge where the vegetation thickened into proper forest. The bronze sword hung ready at his hip, yet Asvarr found his hand straying repeatedly to the mark beneath his tunic. Something pulled at him through the child—a connection similar to what he'd felt near the anchor, though weaker and less focused.

The tracks ended abruptly at a stream bank, pointing toward a village nestled in a shallow valley below. From this distance, Asvarr could see smoke rising from at least a dozen points, yet something about the pattern struck him as wrong. The plumes didn't rise with the steady consistency of hearth fires, but sporadically, in bursts and spirals.

Drawing his sword, Asvarr descended the slope. The mark pulsed faster with each step, golden light spilling between his fingers where they clutched his chest. His approach to the village wall revealed blackened timbers and shattered stone—defenses broken from within rather than without. Gaps in the palisade revealed glimpses of destruction beyond: buildings split open like overripe fruit, streets littered with debris, objects strewn in patterns suggesting panic rather than organized resistance.

The gate hung askew on a single hinge, allowing Asvarr to slip through without effort. Inside, the destruction revealed itself fully. What had once been a prosperous settlement—large enough to support carpenters, blacksmiths, and traders, judging by the specialized structures—now resembled a nightmare excavated from fevered sleep. Broken wagons lay overturned in the central square. Buckets lay scattered around a well clogged with what looked like living roots that twisted slowly, searching for moisture.

The village retained no survivors—only evidence of their passing. Blood spatters dried on walls. A dropped doll with carefully embroidered clothing. Doors left hanging open in mid-flight.

And everywhere, signs of what had taken them: gouges in wood and earth made by thorns and roots, buildings split from within by growths that had since retreated, leaving only hollow shells behind.

"The Root," Asvarr murmured, trailing his fingers over a wall marked with spiraling patterns that matched those on his chest. "Corrupted, hungry, confused."

He stepped into what had been a mead hall—the village's largest structure—and stopped short. The central hearth had been transformed into a nest of twisted roots and branches, forming a lattice that cradled dozens of objects: wooden carvings, metal implements, fabric scraps, all placed with deliberate care. At the nest's center sat the pale-haired child from the night before, cross-legged with the runestone clutched in both hands.

Asvarr approached cautiously, sword held low but ready. The massive firepit-turned-nest emanated a subtle humming that made his teeth ache. The child didn't look up, attention fixed on patterns he traced in dirt between his feet. With each completed pattern, the runestone pulsed dully, absorbing light rather than emitting it.

"I've found you," Asvarr said, keeping his voice measured. "Are you hurt?"

The child's hands stilled. Slowly, he raised his head. The eyes that had seemed golden in last night's firelight now appeared normal—gray-blue like a winter sea. When he spoke, his voice emerged as a whisper, as if long unused.

"You came."

Something in the tone sent a cold prickle along Asvarr's spine. The bronze sword hummed in his hand, sap-veins brightening. "What happened here?"

The child returned to his tracing, dragging one finger through the dirt with painstaking precision. "The root-mother came. The thorned ones took everyone." His finger completed a pattern—a spiraling gateway formed of interlocking branches. "All except me."

Asvarr crouched to examine the drawing, muscles tensed for quick movement if needed. "Why did they leave you?"

The child's lips quirked in an expression too old for his young face. "I'm not here. Not really." He held up the runestone. "This is more real than I am."

The stone was unnaturally black, drinking in the dim light that filtered through the mead hall's broken roof. Runes marked its surface—not the familiar Futhark that Asvarr knew from his childhood, but something older, carved in spiraling patterns that resembled the Grímmark on his chest.

"Where did you get that?" Asvarr asked, recognition flooding him with unease. The stone resembled the one he'd found in his own hearth before his first binding—the stone that had led him to the Root Anchor.

The boy tilted his head. "It found me. When the world broke and remade me." He extended the hand holding the stone. "You should take it. It belongs with your mark."

Asvarr hesitated. Memories of the first runestone's power—how it had burned into his mind, flooding him with visions—gave him pause. But the mark on his chest pulled toward the stone like iron to a lodestone. His hand moved almost without conscious thought.

"What's your name?" he asked, fingers hovering above the offered stone.

"Leif," the boy said, the single syllable emerging with effort. "At least... that's what she called me. Before they took her."

Asvarr's fingers closed around the stone.

Vision crashed through him like a wave breaking against cliffs. The mead hall vanished, replaced by a forest of impossibly tall trees with bark that spiraled upward in complex patterns. Golden sap bled from their trunks, pooling on the forest floor to form reflecting puddles. In each puddle, a different image—fragments of past, present, future, all existing simultaneously.

And before him stood the Verdant Gate.

The living archway from his dreams towered at the forest's heart, branches intertwined to form a structure taller than ten men. Sap leaked from its joints, dripping into a shallow pool at its base. The entire construction breathed—expanding and contracting in rhythm with Asvarr's own heartbeat.

Standing before the gate, her back to him, was Brynja. Her raven hair hung loose, tangled with small blossoms and thorns. One arm remained human; the other had transformed completely into gnarled wood, fingers elongated into curved talons. Her hands—both flesh and wood—dripped with something dark that steamed where it struck the pool of sap.

Blood.

She pressed both palms against the living arch, leaving crimson handprints that the wood absorbed eagerly. The gate shuddered, its breath quickening. Cracks appeared in its surface, leaking more golden sap that mixed with the blood at its base.

"The Gate opens for none but blood," Brynja intoned, voice resonating with multiple tones simultaneously. "Our bloodlines joined and severed, flame and root, now converging again."

She turned, and Asvarr recoiled from eyes that contained entire forests, swirling with green-gold light. Recognition flickered across her features, followed by rage or pain—impossible to distinguish in her transformed face.

"Flame-bearer," she hissed. "Thief of my birthright."

Her wooden arm extended, stretching impossibly, reaching for his chest where the mark burned beneath his clothing.

"Blood calls to blood."

The vision shattered.

Asvarr found himself kneeling on the mead hall floor, gasping. The rune-stone now burned hot in his palm, no longer absorbing light but emitting it—pulsing with golden radiance that matched the glow from his chest. Leif stared at him with wide eyes, now unmistakably gold-flecked.

***

"You saw her," the boy said. "The root-mother."

"Brynja," Asvarr managed, throat raw as if he'd been screaming. "She stands before the Gate."

Leif nodded solemnly. "She seeks to open it. To claim what waits behind." He pointed to Asvarr's chest. "The same thing you seek."

The floor creaked beneath them. Roots that had been dormant now stirred, pushing through dirt and stone, reaching toward the pulsing rune-stone. Asvarr lurched to his feet, pulling Leif up beside him.

"We need to leave," he growled, sliding the stone into a belt pouch. "This place isn't safe."

Outside, the village had changed in the short time they'd spent in the mead hall. Mist clung to the ground in patches, billowing from cracks in the earth where more roots pushed upward, seeking something. The earlier smoke plumes had multiplied, rising from every collapsed building. The light had dimmed despite the morning's advance, as if the sun itself hesitated to illuminate what grew here.

With Leif's hand clutched firmly in his own, Asvarr headed for the broken gate. The bronze sword led the way, its sap-veins pulsing a warning cadence. Behind them, wood groaned and split as something massive pushed through the mead hall's roof—a tangle of branches and thorns that twisted skyward in a mockery of a tree.

"They're coming back," Leif whispered, tugging at Asvarr's hand. "The thorned ones. They feel the stone awakening."

At the gate, Asvarr paused to study the surrounding landscape. The forest to the east now teemed with movement—branches swaying against the wind, undergrowth rippling as if alive. From that direction came a sound like breathing, magnified a thousandfold.

"How far to the next settlement?" he asked, scanning the horizon for safe passage.

Leif pointed north, toward distant mountains partially obscured by mist. "Three days' walk. If the paths stay solid."

The boy's phrasing struck Asvarr as odd, but the approaching danger left no time for questions. He hoisted Leif onto his shoulders, the child weighing almost nothing—as insubstantial as his earlier claim suggested.

They fled northward, toward higher ground where the corruption might not have spread. Behind them, the twisted tree-thing continued to grow, reaching heights that no natural growth could achieve in such time. Its branches extended outward, grasping at air as if searching for something—or someone.

The mark on Asvarr's chest burned with increasing intensity as they put distance between themselves and the village. The runestone in his pouch vibrated in counterpoint, both objects seemingly responding to each other's proximity.

By midday, they reached a ridge overlooking a river valley. The corruption had spread here as well, though less severely. Trees along the riverbank grew at unnatural angles, their branches reaching toward the water rather than the sky. The river itself ran cloudy, choked with fallen leaves that moved against the current.

"We'll follow the ridge," Asvarr decided, setting Leif down on a flat stone. "Stay above the waterline."

The boy nodded, eyes fixed on something in the middle distance. "She knows you have the stone now. She'll come faster."

"Brynja?"

"The root-mother," Leif corrected, as if the names held different meanings for him. "The thorned-vessel."

Asvarr frowned, recalling his vision at the village well the previous day. Brynja with her wooden arm, standing in a circle of scorched earth. "What happened to her?" he asked. "Why do you call her that?"

Leif traced patterns on the stone, similar to those he'd drawn in the mead hall. "She opened herself to the Root when she shouldn't have. Let it in too deep." His finger completed a circle. "Now it wears her like a glove."

A chill ran through Asvarr. He thought of his own binding with the Root Anchor—how it had changed him, spreading through his body like slow poison or powerful medicine, impossible to distinguish which. The mark on his chest throbbed as if in response to his thoughts.

"Am I becoming like her?" he asked, voicing the fear that had haunted him these last three moons.

Leif looked up, golden flecks swirling in his irises. "Everyone who touches the Root changes. The question is whether you change it back." He pointed to the pouch containing the runestone. "That will lead you to the second Anchor. The verdant one."

Asvarr's hand moved to the pouch. "How do you know these things?"

"I told you. I'm not really here. Not all of me." Leif's expression remained unnervingly serious. "I was born when the Tree shattered. Part of me is there, where it fell. Part is here. Part is..." He waved a hand vaguely. "Elsewhere."

The child's words aligned with Asvarr's experiences since the binding—his dreams of places he'd never visited, knowledge he'd never learned bubbling to the surface of his thoughts. The Root connected all things, past and present, real and imagined. Perhaps Leif existed at one of those connection points, spread thin across multiple realities.

A distant sound interrupted his contemplation—a groaning of wood under immense pressure, echoing across the valley. On the far bank, trees bent unnaturally, their canopies dipping toward the ground before springing back. The pattern repeated, approaching their position with steady rhythm.

"She's found our trail," Leif said, standing. "The roots tell her where we've walked."

Asvarr drew his sword, though he knew it would provide little protection against what approached. The Grímmark blazed beneath his tunic, golden light spilling through the fabric.

"That stone," he said, gesturing to the pouch. "If it leads to the second Anchor, then we need to find it before she does."

Leif nodded solemnly. "The stone shows the way, but only blood opens the Gate." He stared directly into Asvarr's eyes. "Your blood. Her blood. The same blood, from before the sundering of your lines."

The trees across the river bent nearly horizontal, their roots partially tearing free of soil. Between them moved a figure—neither fully human nor fully plant, but something merged uncomfortably between states. Even at this distance, Asvarr recognized Brynja's raven hair, now intertwined with leaves and thorns. Her wooden arm had grown, extending into a network of smaller branches that dragged along the ground beside her.

She paused at the riverbank, head tilting upward to fix them with a predator's stare. When she spoke, her voice carried unnaturally across the distance, simultaneously whispered directly into Asvarr's ear and booming through the valley.

"Flame-bearer," she called. "Thief of my birthright. Return what you carry."

The mark on Asvarr's chest flared with blinding pain. The runestone in his pouch pulsed in response, growing hot enough to sear through leather. Together, they created a resonance that vibrated through his bones, drawing him toward the twisted figure across the river.

Blood calls to blood.

Asvarr staggered backward, fighting the pull. He grabbed Leif's hand and turned northward, away from the river, away from Brynja.

"We run," he growled through clenched teeth. "Now."

Behind them, Brynja's scream tore through the valley—rage and hunger and something like grief tangled together in a sound no human throat could produce. The trees along the ridge shuddered in response, their branches reaching toward the fleeing figures with grasping, hook-like twigs.

The forest had awakened. And it hungered for what Asvarr carried.

Chapter 2

The Memory Keeper

Asvarr crouched at the forest's edge, one hand pressed against Leif's thin shoulder. They'd spent the night sheltering beneath a stone outcropping, both too exhausted to move further. Dawn revealed what darkness had mercifully concealed—a woodland grown wrong in ways that chilled Asvarr's blood.

Trees jutted sideways from reality itself. Trunks emerged horizontally from thin air, their roots splayed like desperate fingers, branches reaching downward toward earth rather than sky. Leaves grew on the undersides, creating a canopy that hung like stalactites in a cave. Between these impossible growths, normal trees stood intermittently, though their bark spiraled in unnatural patterns.

"Stay close," Asvarr murmured, drawing his bronze sword. The weapon's sap-veins pulsed with fitful light, responding to the wrongness that pervaded this boundary zone.

The Grímmark on his chest throbbed painfully. Three days of hard travel since fleeing the ravaged village had left him weary and increasingly aware of how the Root-power within him responded to the altered landscape. Each morning, he woke to find the mark had spread further across his torso, golden patterns extending toward his shoulders like reaching branches.

Leif nodded silently, clutching the runestone in both hands. The boy had barely spoken since their escape, though his eyes tracked their surroundings with unnerving intensity. Occasionally, he would stop to trace patterns in dirt or snow—always the same interlocking branches forming a gateway.

"The forest isn't natural," Asvarr said, testing Leif's understanding. "It's grown across the boundary between realms."

"Sideways," Leif whispered, his face expressionless. "Like me."

Before Asvarr could question this cryptic response, movement flickered between the trees—a splash of emerald and copper amid the distorted woodland. He tensed, angling his body to shield Leif while raising the sword defensively.

"Come no closer," he called, voice carrying in the unnatural stillness. "I bear the Grímmark and Root-fire."

A woman stepped from behind a horizontally growing oak. Copper-red hair spilled over emerald robes adorned with spiral patterns of silver thread. At her waist hung multiple pouches, each sealed with different colored wax. Her skin was sun-darkened, marked with faint lines suggesting long years spent outdoors. Around her neck hung a crystal pendant that caught the filtered light, refracting it into dancing patterns on the forest floor.

"I know exactly what you bear, Asvarr Flame-Tongue," she replied, stopping at a respectful distance. Her voice carried the lilt of eastern settlements, softening hard consonants. "Just as I know what pursues you across the fractured lands."

Asvarr's grip tightened on his sword. "How do you know my name?"

The woman smiled, reaching into one of her pouches to withdraw a small cloth bag. "I've tracked you since your first communion with the Root. Since you claimed the first Anchor. The Tree remembers, and through it, so do I."

She knelt, opening the bag on the ground between them. Inside were clumps of pale green moss, their surfaces mottled with darker spots that resembled eyes.

"I am Yrsa Ninevane," she continued, focusing on her task. "Some call me the Memory Keeper, though that title belongs more properly to what I gather." She gestured to the moss. "This grows only where realities have thinned. Where memories leak between worlds that should remain separate."

Leif edged forward, peering at the moss with fascination. The runestone in his hands pulsed faintly, absorbing light rather than emitting it.

Yrsa looked up, studying the boy intently. "So it's true," she murmured. "You found an untethered one."

Asvarr stepped closer, placing himself partially between Yrsa and Leif. "What do you mean, untethered?"

"Born during the Shattering," Yrsa explained, returning to her collection of moss. She pulled a small silver knife from her belt, carefully scraping growth from an exposed root. "Existing partially in multiple realities."

The moss emitted a faint, high-pitched sound when her blade touched it—a scream almost too high to perceive. Asvarr winced at the noise, while Leif showed no reaction.

"The boy walks the boundaries," she continued, placing the screaming moss in her bag. "Like these trees that grow sideways from one realm into another, he exists in fragmented states across multiple worlds."

She rose, dusting her hands on her robes. "That's why the thorned ones didn't take him in the village. They couldn't fully perceive him, just as they can't fully perceive me when I walk the boundaries." She gestured to the woodland around them. "This is my domain—the spaces between spaces. The seams where reality was torn and imperfectly mended."

Asvarr lowered his sword slightly, though wariness still tensed his muscles. "You said you've been tracking me. Why?"

"Because you carry what I've sought for nine cycles of breaking." Yrsa's hand moved to the crystal at her throat. "The path to the second Root Anchor."

Leif looked up sharply at her words, the golden flecks in his eyes brightening momentarily. Asvarr noticed the reaction and filed it away—further evidence of the boy's connection to the Root.

"If you know so much," Asvarr challenged, "then you know what follows me. What hunts me."

"Brynja Hrafndottir," Yrsa nodded, face grim. "Or what remains of her beneath the corruption. The Root-vessel. Thornmother."

She pointed to a nearby tree—a normal one, though its bark spiraled unnaturally. "These woods offer temporary protection. The boundary-state confuses her senses, makes tracking difficult. But it won't stop her for long." She fixed Asvarr with a penetrating stare. "Nothing will, until she claims what she believes is her birthright."

The Grímmark on Asvarr's chest flared with sudden heat, causing him to wince. He pressed a hand over it, feeling the raised patterns through his tunic. "You know about our shared bloodline."

"The flame-keepers and the root-tenders," Yrsa confirmed. "Sundered generations ago by betrayal and oath-breaking. Now converging again through you and her." She gestured for them to follow her deeper into the distorted woodland. "Come. We shouldn't linger at the edge where the boundary is thinnest."

Asvarr hesitated, torn between caution and the pull of answers this strange woman might provide. The mark on his chest throbbed insistently, urging him forward—whether in warning or encouragement, he couldn't tell.

"Why should we trust you?" he asked, making no move to follow.

Yrsa paused, turning back with a sad smile. "Because unlike every other power in the fractured realms, I don't want either you or Brynja to claim the second Anchor." She tapped the crystal at her throat. "I want both of you to claim it—together—as it was meant to be before your bloodlines were severed."

This unexpected answer left Asvarr momentarily speechless. He studied her face for deception but found only weariness and what might have been hope.

"The boy is fading," Yrsa added, her gaze shifting to Leif. "His connection to this reality weakens each day. Soon he'll slip completely into the in-between, lost to all worlds. I can help anchor him, but only within the boundary-forest where my power is strongest."

Asvarr glanced down at Leif. The woman was right—the boy seemed less substantial in daylight, the edges of his form slightly blurred as if poorly focused. The runestone he clutched remained solid, however, its black surface drinking in surrounding light.

"We'll follow," Asvarr decided, sheathing his sword but keeping his hand near the hilt. "But I'll bind you by blood-oath if you attempt treachery."

Yrsa inclined her head. "I would expect nothing less from a flame-keeper." She turned and walked deeper into the forest, her emerald robes catching on jutting roots and branches.

The further they ventured, the stranger the woodland became. Trees grew at impossible angles, their trunks bent into spiral patterns. Some passed entirely through one another, creating lattices that defied natural law. Light filtered differently here—sunbeams splitting into colors Asvarr had no names for, casting shadows that moved independently of their sources.

"The memory-moss grows thicker here," Yrsa explained, stopping beside a particularly dense patch coating a tree growing parallel to the ground. The moss pulsated gently, its eye-like markings blinking at irregular intervals. "Each growth contains fragments of what was lost during the Shattering—memories, knowledge, even pieces of souls torn from their owners."

She carefully harvested several clumps, ignoring their faint screams as her silver knife separated them from the bark. "I preserve what would otherwise dissolve into nothingness. The collected memories help me map the boundaries, track the anchors, understand the patterns of breaking and remaking."

Asvarr watched her work, questions piling up behind his reluctant silence. Finally, he could contain them no longer. "You knew about me before we met. About the mark, about Brynja. How?"

Yrsa placed the harvested moss in one of her pouches, sealing it with green wax from a small pot at her belt. "I walked with the Norns before they cut fate's thread. I witnessed the first Shattering, and each one that followed."

Leif suddenly spoke, his voice clearer than Asvarr had yet heard it. "She's like the trees. Growing between worlds." He pointed to Yrsa's crystal pendant. "Anchored by memory."

Yrsa's eyes widened slightly as she studied Leif with renewed interest. "The untethered sees clearly." She touched her pendant thoughtfully. "Yes, child. I exist partially between states, bound to this reality only through what I carry."

She led them deeper still, to where the forest's distortion reached its apex—a clearing where trees from multiple realities converged, creating a canopy of impossibly intermingled branches. At the clearing's center stood a small hut built into the massive trunk of a horizontally growing oak. Its door and windows followed the tree's orientation, making it appear that one would need to climb up to enter.

"My dwelling," Yrsa explained, approaching what from their perspective was the side of the structure. "The boundary-forest shifts constantly, but this tree remains fixed—an anchor point between realms." She pressed her palm against the bark beside the perpendicular door, murmuring words too low to catch.

The tree shuddered. Reality around it rippled like heat waves above summer stone. Gradually, the hut rotated until its door faced them properly, gravity reorienting to accommodate the change.

"Perception shapes reality here," Yrsa said, pushing the door open. "Remember that. What you believe affects what is possible."

Inside, the hut was larger than its exterior suggested—a single circular room filled with shelves containing hundreds of moss-filled jars. Each was labeled with symbols Asvarr didn't recognize, though they resembled the runes on Leif's stone. A central hearth burned with blue-white flame that consumed no visible fuel. Above it hung bundles of drying plants that filled the air with sharp, medicinal scents.

"Sit," Yrsa instructed, gesturing to cushions arranged near the hearth. "Rest. The boundary-forest will shield us temporarily, though no place is truly safe now that Brynja has merged with corrupted Root-essence."

Asvarr remained standing, the hut's ceiling barely accommodating his height. "You still haven't explained why you've been tracking me. What you want from us."

Yrsa moved to a shelf containing larger jars, selecting one filled with amber liquid. "I track you because you carry the only power capable of breaking the cycle of shattering and remaking that has trapped us for nine turnings." She poured three cups of the liquid, offering one to Asvarr. "I want what few others in any realm desire—true transformation rather than mere restoration or destruction."

The Grímmark throbbed at her words, an answering resonance that sent warmth spreading through Asvarr's chest. He accepted the cup cautiously, studying the contents—a tea that smelled of pine and something sweeter, like the sap that occasionally leaked from his mark.

"Drink," Yrsa urged, offering a smaller cup to Leif. "It will help organize the Root-memories that overwhelm you, and strengthen the boy's connection to this reality."

Asvarr sniffed the liquid once more, then took a careful sip. Instantly, heat spread through his limbs, followed by clarity that sharpened his senses. The constant background whispers of the Root—the fragmented memories and knowledge that had plagued him since the first binding—suddenly organized themselves into coherent patterns. He gasped at the sensation, nearly dropping the cup.

"What is this?" he demanded, even as he took another deeper drink.

"Memory-tea," Yrsa explained, watching Leif sip from his own cup. "Brewed from forest boundary-moss and sap from the first Root Anchor. It helps integrate what the Root has given you."

Leif drained his cup, his form seeming to solidify slightly as the tea took effect. The golden flecks in his eyes grew more pronounced, swirling visibly within the blue-gray irises.

"I can feel him," the boy said suddenly, voice stronger than before. "The other me. The part that waits by the Verdant Gate."

Yrsa nodded as if this made perfect sense. "The untethered exist in fragments. The tea helps reconnect what was scattered." She turned to Asvarr. "The boy is crucial to your journey. He exists simultaneously here and near the second Anchor. He can guide you along paths others cannot perceive."

Asvarr finished his tea, marveling at how it calmed the constant storm of Root-whispers that had haunted him for months. For the first time since the binding, he felt fully himself again, the foreign memories and knowledge settling into accessible patterns rather than overwhelming his thoughts.

"You know where the second Anchor is," he stated, setting down his empty cup.

"I know where all five are," Yrsa corrected, refilling his cup. "But knowing their location and reaching them are separate challenges. The second Anchor—the Verdant one—lies behind a gate of living wood, grown from time-locked trees that predate the gods themselves."

Leif nodded eagerly. "The gate from my drawings. The one from your dreams."

Asvarr recalled his recurring nightmare—the forest of thorns, the archway of twisted branches leaking golden sap. "Brynja stands before it in my visions. Her hands covered in blood."

"Because blood opens the Gate," Yrsa confirmed grimly. "Specifically, the blood of those who bear the original bloodlines—flame-keeper and root-tender." She glanced between Asvarr and Leif. "Your blood and Brynja's share an ancient connection. Before the sundering of your clans, you were one people—the guardians of Yggdrasil's balance."

She touched her crystal pendant, which glowed faintly in response. "The Verdant Gate requires both bloodlines to open properly. One alone—flame or root—creates imbalance, corruption." Her gaze fixed on Asvarr's chest where the Grímmark pulsed beneath his tunic. "That's why you carry aspects of both bloodlines, diluted through generations of separation. And why Brynja seeks what you have—she senses the flame essence she lacks."

The implications settled heavily in Asvarr's mind. If Yrsa spoke truth, then his recurring nightmares of Brynja were more than dreams—they were glimpses of a possible future where she reached the Gate first, using blood that shared aspects of his own lineage.

"Why should I seek this Anchor at all?" he asked, voicing the doubt that had gnawed at him since fleeing the village. "The first binding changed me, took pieces of me. Each subsequent Anchor will demand more."

"Because the alternative is worse," Yrsa said softly. "If Brynja claims it alone, the corruption will spread. If no one claims it, the fractured realms will continue to decay until nothing remains but void." She leaned forward, her expression intensely serious. "And because you've already begun the process that cannot be halted—only guided toward the least destructive outcome."

Leif suddenly stood, moving to one of the hut's circular windows. Outside, the boundary-forest had darkened, though no sun was visible to mark the passage of time. The moss on nearby trees glowed faintly, illuminating twisted branches with eerie blue-green light.

"She's found our trail again," the boy announced, pressing one hand against the glass. "The thorned ones search the forest's edge."

Yrsa rose swiftly, gathering items from various shelves into a travel sack. "We must move deeper into the boundary. Where the forest grows most sideways, her perception will fail entirely."

Asvarr joined Leif at the window. In the distance, at the woodland's periphery, trees bent unnaturally inward, branches reaching toward a central point like countless grasping hands. Though too far to see clearly, he knew what was approaching. The mark on his chest burned in recognition, responding to its counterpart.

Brynja had found them. And with her came the corrupted Root-essence that threatened to consume them all.

Yrsa moved through her hut with practiced efficiency, gathering supplies into a leather pack while keeping one eye on the window. Outside, the boundary-forest had darkened further, moss-light casting eerie blue patterns across twisted branches. Asvarr stood by the door, sword drawn, the sap-veins pulsing with increasing urgency as Brynja's presence grew closer.

"We must travel deeper before nightfall," Yrsa said, sealing a pouch of memory-tea leaves. "The boundary thins with darkness, allowing more of her essence to penetrate."

Asvarr glanced at Leif, who sat cross-legged near the hearth, eyes half-closed as if listening to distant music. The boy's form had solidified somewhat after drinking the tea, though his edges still blurred when viewed from certain angles.

"You still haven't told me everything," Asvarr challenged, turning back to Yrsa. "The second Root Anchor—where exactly does it lie? How do we reach it?"

Yrsa straightened, slinging her pack over one shoulder. The crystal pendant at her throat caught the hearth-light, refracting it into dancing patterns across her face.

"The second Root—the Verdant one—lies beyond a gate of living wood," she explained, her voice taking on a storyteller's cadence. "A door grown from time-locked trees that existed before the first gods drew breath. Unlike your flame Anchor, the Verdant one cannot be claimed through direct confrontation. It must be approached through indirect paths—the grief-trails left when Yggdrasil shattered."

She moved to a shelf containing maps drawn on bark. Her fingers traced one that showed nine spiraling lines converging toward a central point.

"When the Tree broke, fragments scattered across all realms. Each piece carried memories, power, and pain. Wherever they fell, they left trails of excess sorrow—wounds in reality that connect to the Root directly." Her finger tapped the map's center. "Follow these grief-paths, and you'll find the Verdant Gate."

"And behind it, the second Anchor," Asvarr mused, studying the map. The pattern reminded him of the Grímmark on his chest—roots spreading outward from a central trunk.

"Yes. Though 'behind' isn't precisely accurate when discussing something that exists partially outside normal space." Yrsa gave him a measured look. "The Gate exists simultaneously in multiple locations, accessible only to those who understand its true nature."

Leif spoke suddenly, his voice clearer than before. "It breathes. Opens and closes with the cycles." He opened his eyes, the golden flecks swirling visibly. "I've seen it. From the other side."

Yrsa nodded, as if this made perfect sense. "The untethered perceives truly." She turned back to Asvarr. "This is why the boy is crucial to your journey. His fragmented existence allows him to see paths hidden to those fully anchored in a single reality."

A sharp crack from outside interrupted their discussion—the sound of wood breaking under immense pressure. The hut trembled, dust shaking from the ceiling. Leif leapt to his feet, eyes wide with alarm.

"She's reached the boundary's edge," he whispered, clutching the runestone tightly. "The thorned ones tear at the trees."

Yrsa moved swiftly to the door, pressing her palm against its center. Wood flowed beneath her touch, sealing cracks and hardening.

"We must leave through another way," she said, her composure betrayed only by the tightness around her eyes. She gestured toward the hearth, where blue flames still danced without consuming fuel. "The fire-path connects to deeper regions. Quickly now."

Asvarr hesitated, suspicion warring with necessity. "How do I know this isn't a trap? That you're not leading us deeper for your own purposes?"

Yrsa's expression softened slightly. "Your caution serves you well, flame-bearer. But consider: if I wished you harm, I could have taken the runestone while you slept beneath the stone outcropping two nights past." She pointed to the pouch where Asvarr had stored Leif's black stone. "I've had many opportunities."

Another crack resonated through the forest, closer this time. The floor beneath their feet trembled. Outside, trees groaned as something massive pushed against them, bending reality's boundary.

Asvarr made his decision. "Lead on. But know that I'll bind you in blood if you betray us."

Yrsa inclined her head in acknowledgment, then turned to the hearth. She withdrew a small pouch from her belt, sprinkling pale green powder into the flames. The fire flared, shifting from blue to emerald. She stepped directly into the transformed flame, vanishing without a sound.

Leif followed without hesitation, clutching the runestone to his chest as he stepped into the green fire. His form blurred at the edges before disappearing entirely.

Asvarr took a deep breath, bracing himself against the instinctive fear of flame that every northerner carried. He stepped into the hearth.

Cold enveloped him rather than heat. The sensation of falling sideways gripped his stomach, disorienting his sense of direction. Green light swirled around him, punctuated by flashes of gold that matched the pulsing of the Grímmark beneath his tunic. For a heartbeat that stretched eternally, he existed without form, pure consciousness suspended between states.

Then solidity returned with jarring abruptness. His boots struck moss-covered stone, knees buckling with the impact. He stumbled forward, nearly colliding with Leif and Yrsa, who stood waiting in a small clearing.

The boundary-forest had changed dramatically around them. Here, trees grew not merely sideways but in impossible geometric patterns—trunks twisting into perfect spirals, branches forming crystalline lattices that defied natural law. Some trees passed entirely through others without disruption, creating three-dimensional weaves of living wood. Light came from no discernible source, a diffuse golden-green glow that cast no shadows.

"The deep boundary," Yrsa explained, noting Asvarr's disoriented examination. "Where realities overlap so completely that perception defines existence. Tread carefully—your thoughts have power here."

Asvarr steadied himself, gripping his sword's hilt for reassurance. The weapon thrummed against his palm, responding to the strange energy permeating this place. "How far are we from where we started?"

"Distance has little meaning in the deep boundary," Yrsa replied, moving toward a path that wound between interlaced trees. "We've traveled both leagues and mere steps, depending on how you measure. What matters is that Brynja cannot easily follow. Her corrupted nature disrupts the boundary's balance, making passage difficult."

"Difficult, but not impossible," Asvarr noted, falling into step behind her with Leif between them.

"No. She will find ways, given time. The Root seeks reunification, even in its corrupted state." Yrsa touched her crystal pendant, which glowed faintly. "The Grímmark you bear calls to her, just as her transformed essence calls to you. Blood seeking blood across the fractures of reality."

**

They walked for what might have been hours or minutes, time flowing strangely in the deep boundary. The path led them through increasingly bizarre terrain—forests growing upside down, clearings where water flowed upward in defiance of nature, hillsides covered in moss that formed deliberate patterns when viewed from specific angles.

Eventually, they reached a circular meadow dominated by a massive stone slab tilted at a forty-five-degree angle to the ground. The stone bore carvings that shifted when Asvarr tried to focus on them, runes flowing into new configurations with each blink.

"Here we can rest safely," Yrsa announced, setting down her pack near the stone. "The Witnessing Stone marks a stable point in the boundary. Nothing can approach without alerting us."

Leif immediately moved to the stone, placing his small hand against its surface. The runestone in his other hand pulsed in response, black surface momentarily reflecting the shifting runes.

"It remembers the breaking," he murmured, tracing patterns on the stone's surface. "Shows the paths of sorrow."

Asvarr sank to the ground, muscles aching from tension as much as exertion. The mark on his chest throbbed dully, its earlier urgency fading now that immediate danger had passed. He pressed a hand against it, feeling the raised patterns through his tunic.

"Tell me about these grief-paths," he said to Yrsa, who had begun preparing a small fire using wood collected from her pack rather than the surrounding forest. "How do we find them? Follow them?"

Yrsa worked methodically, arranging twigs in a precise pattern. "Grief-paths are trails of sorrow left when Yggdrasil shattered. They form connections between places touched by the Root's pain—villages destroyed, lands corrupted, souls transformed." She struck flint against a small iron disk, igniting the wood.

The flames burned normal red-orange, comfortingly mundane amid their bizarre surroundings.

"Each path manifests differently," she continued, feeding the small blaze. "Some appear as physical trails—rivers running backward, flowers that bloom only at midnight, stones that weep golden tears. Others exist in emotional states—places where sorrow hangs so thick you can taste it, where dreams turn invariably to loss, where memory itself becomes tangled in grief."

She reached into her pack, withdrawing a pot and several pouches. "To follow these paths requires special perception—the ability to sense the Root's pain across fragmented realities. Your Grímmark grants you this, though you may not yet fully understand how to use it."

"And the paths lead to the Verdant Gate?" Asvarr asked, watching her prepare what appeared to be a stew from dried ingredients.

"They converge there, yes. The Gate stands at the nexus of all grief-paths, a doorway formed from the oldest living wood in existence." Yrsa added water from a skin to her pot, positioning it carefully over the fire. "Time-locked trees that remember the world before gods walked it, before the pattern of reality solidified into its current form."

Leif had moved away from the Witnessing Stone, drawing patterns in dirt nearby. The designs echoed those he'd made in the village—interlocking branches forming a doorway, though now with greater detail and precision.

"The root-mother already walks the grief-paths," he said without looking up. "She follows your trail through broken lands, through shattered villages, through places where death came suddenly."

Asvarr tensed. "Brynja follows us even now?"

"Not physically, perhaps," Yrsa clarified, stirring her pot. "However, her essence stretches far beyond her transformed body. The corrupted Root within her senses disturbances in the pattern—particularly those caused by your passage."

She gestured toward Asvarr's chest. "The Grímmark leaves traces wherever you walk—small blooms, altered vegetation, subtle shifts in reality's fabric. These markers form a trail she can follow, given time and determination."

The implications settled heavily in Asvarr's mind. Everywhere he'd traveled since binding with the first Root, he'd left signs for Brynja to follow—an unwitting beacon drawing her inexorably toward him.

"Then she'll find the second Anchor regardless of what we do," he said grimly.

"Perhaps. But finding and claiming are different challenges." Yrsa removed the pot from the fire, setting it aside to cool. "The Verdant Gate responds only to specific conditions. The proper blood, the proper intent, the proper transformation."

She fixed Asvarr with a penetrating stare. "This is why you must reach it first, or at least simultaneously. Your shared bloodlines suggest a balance that might allow proper opening. Brynja alone, corrupted as she is, would force entry improperly—causing further damage to the fracturing realms."

"And what happens when we find this Gate?" Asvarr pressed. "The first binding changed me, took pieces of me. What will the second require?"

"Each Anchor demands different sacrifice," Yrsa acknowledged, her expression solemn. "The first—your flame Anchor—required surrender of rage, identity, certainty, free will. The Verdant one... its nature suggests transformation rather than mere surrender."

"Transformation into what?" Asvarr demanded, an edge entering his voice.

"That depends entirely on you." Yrsa ladled stew into three wooden bowls. "To enter the Verdant Gate, one must become partially of the Root—integrate its essence rather than simply binding with it. This transformation risks loss of humanity, yes, but also offers something the first binding did not."

"Which is?"

"Partnership rather than dominance." She handed bowls to Asvarr and Leif. "The first Anchor you conquered through strength and sacrifice. The second cannot be taken—only joined."

They ate in contemplative silence, the stew filling Asvarr's stomach with unexpected warmth and vigor. Flavors he couldn't identify mingled pleasantly, easing the constant ache that had accompanied him since the first binding. The Grímmark's pulsing quieted to gentle rhythm, almost soothing in its regularity.

As Yrsa cleaned their bowls using moss that absorbed liquid when touched, Leif approached Asvarr, sitting cross-legged beside him.

"The stone shows where the Gate waits," the boy said, holding up the rune-stone. Its black surface reflected nothing, yet somehow contained depth beyond its physical dimensions. "Beyond the mountains of ice. Through the forest of weeping trees. Across the plain where stars fall like rain."

"You've seen it?" Asvarr asked, studying Leif's earnest face.

The boy nodded solemnly. "From both sides. The part of me that waits there watches the root-mother circle, testing its defenses. She cannot enter yet—lacks what you carry." He pointed to Asvarr's chest. "The flame essence she needs."

"And how do we reach this place? These mountains and forests you describe?"

"The grief-paths will show themselves when darkness falls," Yrsa interjected, returning to the fire. "The sorrow that permeates these boundary regions intensifies with night's arrival, making the trails visible to those with proper sight."

She glanced upward, though no sky was visible through the bizarre tangle of boundary-forest. "Night approaches, though time flows strangely here. We should prepare for departure."

As if responding to her words, the ambient light began to dim, the golden-green glow fading gradually. The forest around them transformed with darkness—memory-moss growing brighter, trees shifting positions subtly, branches reaching toward the meadow's center.

Leif grew increasingly restless as night descended, pacing the meadow's perimeter with nervous energy. The runestone in his hand pulsed with black light—an impossibility that nonetheless manifested clearly in the growing darkness.

"The paths open," he whispered, voice tight with anticipation. "They call to blood and bone and root."

Asvarr rose, hand instinctively moving to his sword. The Grímmark beneath his tunic warmed, responding to something he couldn't yet perceive. "What should I look for? How do we find the right path?"

"Trust your mark," Yrsa advised, gathering her pack. "The Root within you recognizes its own essence. When the grief-paths fully manifest, you'll feel the pull toward the correct route."

The final vestiges of light vanished, plunging the meadow into momentary darkness. Then, gradually, new illumination bloomed—the memory-moss glowing more intensely, joined by luminescent fungi that hadn't been visible before. The Witnessing Stone began to emit pale blue radiance, its shifting runes now clearly visible, flowing like water across its surface.

And beyond the meadow's edge, winding through the twisted forest, paths of gold and silver appeared—trails of luminescence that pulsed with slow, mournful rhythm. Each path carried its own distinct pattern, some flowing steadily, others flickering erratically like heartbeats in distress.

The Grímmark flared with sudden heat, drawing Asvarr's attention to a particular trail—a golden path interspersed with flecks of green, winding eastward from the meadow into the deepest part of the boundary-forest. The mark pulled toward it with uncomfortable insistence, like a hook embedded in his flesh.

"There," he said, pointing. "That's our path."

Yrsa nodded, face solemn in the ethereal light. "The eastern grief-path. It leads through the harshest territories, but most directly to the Verdant Gate."

"Will it take us beyond the boundary?" Asvarr asked, studying the trail's winding course through increasingly distorted trees.

"Eventually. All grief-paths connect fragments of the shattered realms, crossing boundaries that would normally be impassable." She shouldered her pack. "But the journey will not be swift or easy. The paths demand tribute from those who walk them—emotional rather than physical payment."

"Grief for grief," Leif murmured, moving to stand beside Asvarr. "The paths drink sorrow to grant passage."

With the boy's cryptic warning hanging in the air, they set out, following the golden-green trail into the depths of the boundary-forest. The path pulsed beneath their feet, responding to their presence with subtle variations in light and texture. Sometimes it solidified into physical markers—moss growing in directional patterns, roots forming arrow-like shapes, stones arranged in deliberate configurations. At other times, it manifested more ethereally—scents that tugged at painful memories, sounds that evoked specific emotions, temperature shifts that mimicked significant moments of loss.

They walked for what felt like hours, the forest growing increasingly abstract around them—trees melting into liquid shapes that retained only suggestions of their original forms, clearings that folded into impossibly recursive patterns, streams that flowed between different states of matter with each ripple.

Eventually, they reached a small hollow dominated by a single white tree with bark that gleamed like polished bone. Its branches curved protectively over a pool of water so still it reflected their surroundings with mirror perfection.

"We will rest here until true dawn," Yrsa announced, setting down her pack. "The bone-tree marks another stable point in the boundary. Its protection will allow for safe sleep."

Asvarr sank gratefully to the ground, muscles aching from navigating the increasingly chaotic terrain. The Grímmark on his chest had pulsed constantly during their journey, sometimes painfully, as if resonating with the grief-path's emotional demands.

"What tribute has the path taken so far?" he asked, noting Yrsa's exhausted features and Leif's unusual pallor.

"From each according to their burden," she replied cryptically, arranging her pack as a makeshift pillow. "The paths taste our sorrows, drawing strength from what we carry. For me, memories of nine cycles of witnessing. For the boy, fragments of his scattered self. For you..." She studied him intently. "The weight of transformation already begun."

Leif settled against the bone-tree's trunk, cradling the runestone against his chest. Within moments, his breathing slowed into sleep's rhythm, though his eyes remained partially open, golden flecks visible in the dim light.

Asvarr leaned against a nearby root, too tense for immediate sleep despite his fatigue. The boundary-forest moved differently in this deep region, rippling with patterns that suggested consciousness rather than random motion. The Grím-mark responded to these movements, warming and cooling in irregular cycles.

"You should rest," Yrsa advised, already settling onto her side. "The path grows more demanding with distance. You'll need your strength."

"I've slept little since the first binding," Asvarr admitted. "Dreams plague me—visions of Brynja, of doors made from living wood, of roots that whisper with voices not their own."

"The Root speaks through dreams when its vessel resists waking communica-tion." Yrsa's voice grew softer as sleep approached. "Listen to what it tells you. The messages may save your life... and hers."

Her breathing deepened, leaving Asvarr alone with his thoughts. Above them, the bone-tree's branches swayed gently though no wind disturbed the hollow. The pool reflected distorted images—landscapes Asvarr didn't recognize, faces he'd never seen, events from times beyond his knowledge.

Despite his reluctance, exhaustion eventually claimed him. Sleep drew him down into darkness shot through with golden threads—the Root's essence fol-lowing him even into unconsciousness.

In dreams, he walked a forest path lined with trees bearing faces in their bark—ancestors, strangers, future generations yet unborn. Their eyes tracked his passage, mouths moving in silent commentary. The path led to the now-familiar gate of living wood, its twisted branches forming an archway that pulsed with internal light.

Brynja stood before it once more, one arm transformed into gnarled wood, the other remaining human. But unlike previous dreams, she turned to face him fully, her amber eyes reflecting recognition rather than rage.

"Flame-bearer," she said, voice layered with multiple tones. "You walk the grief-paths seeking what I already guard. The Gate accepts no false offering. Blood alone will not open it—only blood freely given in perfect balance."

She extended her wooden arm, fingers elongating into curved talons. "What was severed must be rejoined. What was broken must be mended. Your blood. My blood. The same blood, from before the sundering."

Asvarr tried to speak but found his dream-self voiceless. The Gate behind Brynja shuddered, branches twisting tighter, sap bleeding from its joints with increasing urgency.

"She waits for you there," Brynja continued, amber eyes flaring with golden light. "The one who carries your blood. The one who shares your lineage. Find me before the third moon rises, or what grows beyond the Gate will wither and die."

The dream shifted suddenly. Asvarr stood in a different forest—normal trees, normal earth, normal sky above. A small clearing surrounded a simple stone marker, weathered by countless seasons. Kneeling before the stone was Leif, though somehow older, more substantial, his form no longer blurring at the edges.

The boy looked up, eyes entirely golden now. "She's waiting for you there," he said clearly. "The one who carries your blood."

Asvarr jerked awake, the dream's final words echoing in his mind. Pale light filtered through the boundary-forest's canopy, suggesting dawn's arrival though no sun was visible. Yrsa already moved about the hollow, gathering her belongings with practiced efficiency.

Leif still slept against the bone-tree, his small chest rising and falling with quiet breaths. But as Asvarr watched, the boy's lips moved, forming words that emerged as barely audible whispers:

"She's waiting for you there. The one who carries your blood."

CHAPTER 3

THE ROOTBORN TRIAL

The fractured stones of the shrine rose around Asvarr like broken teeth against the morning sky. Each jagged edge caught the dawn light, bleeding red-gold across weathered runes too ancient to read. He knelt at the center of the circle, where a stone altar split down its middle leaked golden sap from within—a wound in reality that never healed.

Yrsa circled the perimeter, her copper hair aflame in the rising sun. "This place remembers the moment of shattering," she said, voice hushed with reverence. "The Root touched here before it fell. The stone remembers."

Asvarr placed his palm against the cracked altar. The stone felt warm, almost feverish. "Will it answer?"

"The Root always answers." Yrsa knelt opposite him, unfurling a small cloth bundle containing dried herbs, bone fragments, and a vial of amber liquid. "But communion demands contribution. Especially for one who already carries its mark."

Leif watched from the shadow of a fallen column, golden eyes reflecting light that wasn't there. The boy hadn't spoken since awakening, but his gaze tracked everything with unnerving awareness.

"I need to know if I should seek the second Anchor," Asvarr said. The Grím-mark on his chest itched beneath his tunic, the pattern spreading slowly across his skin. Some mornings he found golden sap crusted around its edges. "What if binding another Root only serves the Ashfather's purpose? What if this is exactly what he wants?"

"What if it isn't your choice to make?" Yrsa uncorked the vial, releasing scents of honey and iron. "The Root sought you. Not the other way around." She poured the amber liquid into a hollow at the altar's center. "The second binding will demand more than the first. It seeks partnership, not subjugation."

Asvarr leaned forward. "Show me how."

She took his hands, placing them palm-down on either side of the hollow. "The memory-tea will help organize what comes, but the communion itself... that pain is yours alone to bear."

The moment his flesh touched the stone, heat seared through him. Golden light erupted from the cracks, swallowing his vision. Asvarr's body arched backward, muscles rigid with shock. His mind ripped free from his body, hurtling through immensity.

Gods, the pain—

"Breathe," Yrsa's voice came from impossibly far away. "The communion tears you between what you are and what you might become."

Asvarr gasped as his skin tightened, hardened. Looking down, he watched with horror as patches of his flesh transformed, bark-like patterns forming across his forearms. Golden sap wept from his fingertips, from his eyes. Each tear burned like molten metal.

The world fractured around him. He saw the shrine as it had been—whole, magnificent, visitors kneeling before priests with faces painted in spiraling patterns. He saw it shatter as something vast tore through the sky above, the screams of the dying harmonizing with the scream of reality itself.

The memories are consuming me—

"Hold to yourself," Yrsa urged, her hands anchoring his to the stone. "These visions belong to the Root. You must witness them, but they are not yours to keep."

More visions crashed through him: forests growing in heartbeats then withering to dust, mountains rising and falling like waves, stars burning cold blue then exploding into darkness. Time itself meant nothing to the Root—past, present, future, all existed simultaneously within its awareness.

Then he saw her.

A woman with raven-black hair stood in firelight, iron knife in hand. He recognized her instantly from his dreams: Brynja. But younger, face unmarked by Root corruption. She bent over a stone basin where an infant lay swaddled in white cloth. The child's skin glowed golden in the firelight.

"The bloodlines must unite," she whispered, voice tight with determination. "The Flame-keeper's legacy will not end with me."

The iron knife pressed against the infant's bare chest. Blood welled, golden rather than red. The child didn't cry but stared upward with impossible awareness. Brynja carved with precision, each stroke forming runes that shifted between ash-mark and flame-sign—the very pattern Asvarr bore upon his chest.

His chest exploded with sympathetic pain. Asvarr screamed, doubling over the altar. Sap gushed from his eyes, pooling on the stone.

"That's my mark," he gasped. "Those are my runes. But that's not me."

"No," Yrsa said, her face grave. "That is what came before. The child who carried your bloodline forward."

The visions shifted again. Asvarr saw a towering tree that blotted out the sky, its branches forming the bones of reality itself. Nine worlds hung among its limbs like fruit, each glowing with distinct light. Then darkness crawled upward through its roots—corruption spreading like veins of black ink through the golden sap. At the heart of that darkness, a single golden eye watched, and waited.

Suddenly Asvarr stood before an archway of living wood—the Verdant Gate. Its surface writhed with faces half-formed in bark, mouths open in silent screams. Golden sap leaked from between twisted branches, forming pools at its base. Standing before it was Brynja, one arm now completely transformed into wood. She pressed her palm against the Gate, speaking words he couldn't hear.

The Gate remained sealed.

"It will not open for her alone," Yrsa's voice interrupted the vision. "The Gate requires both bloodlines. Fire and Root. Her corruption blocks the flame essence she once carried."

The vision fractured. Asvarr felt himself spinning, falling. The bark-pattern across his skin spread further, crossing his chest, reaching toward his throat.

"Enough!" he shouted, fighting against the communion. "I'm losing myself!"

"That is the price," Yrsa said, her voice suddenly multiplied, as if many women spoke through her. "To enter the Verdant Gate, you must become partly of the Root. Transformation risks what you are to become what you might be."

Asvarr wrenched his hands from the stone, breaking the connection. He collapsed backward, gasping. Golden sap ran from his eyes, his nose, the corners of his mouth. The bark-pattern had frozen halfway up his neck, leaving one side of his face partially transformed—wood-like ridges following the line of his cheekbone.

The pain receded slowly, pulsing in time with his heartbeat. When his vision cleared, he saw Yrsa watching him with a complex expression—part pity, part admiration.

"You broke the communion early," she said, wiping golden sap from his face with a cloth. "Most who venture that deep never return to themselves at all."

Asvarr touched his transformed face, feeling the strange smoothness of bark where skin should be. "Will it... will I stay like this?"

"That depends on what you choose next." She helped him sit up. "The communion showed you what waits. The child with your runes. The Verdant Gate that needs both bloodlines. The growing darkness at the Tree's heart."

"That child wasn't me." Asvarr's voice sounded strange—deeper, with an echo like wind through hollow wood. "But those were my runes. The same pattern."

"The runes passed through generations," Yrsa explained, checking his eyes, which now held flecks of amber amid their original blue. "Your bloodline and Brynja's were once one people—the keepers of Yggdrasil's balance. Flame-tenders and Root-wardens. Then came betrayal, sundering, forgetting."

Leif approached cautiously, studying Asvarr's transformed face with fascination. He reached out one small hand, touching the bark-pattern on Asvarr's cheek.

"She cut the runes to preserve the flame," the boy said suddenly, his voice clear and melodic. "When her clan was dying. She saved what remained."

Asvarr stared at him. "You speak?"

"The communion strengthens him," Yrsa explained. "The boundaries between realities thin around you now. Leif exists more fully in this moment."

"I exist everywhere, always," Leif said matter-of-factly. "But most strongly where the Root reaches through." He pointed at Asvarr's chest. "Like there. And there." He pointed to the broken altar.

Asvarr stood unsteadily, supporting himself against a fallen column. The bark-pattern had begun to recede slightly, leaving behind skin that seemed subtly different—tougher, with a faint pattern like wood grain visible beneath the surface.

"The Verdant Gate will demand more than this," he said, not phrasing it as a question.

Yrsa nodded gravely. "To pass through the Gate requires transformation beyond flesh. Those who enter must be partly of the Root itself—able to exist in the space between realities where it waits."

"And if the transformation goes too far? If I lose myself completely?"

"Then you become like the corrupted ones. Like what Brynja is becoming." Yrsa gathered her supplies, repacking them with practiced precision. "The Root consumes those who cannot maintain the balance. It wears them like garments, using their memories and desires to further its own purposes."

Asvarr looked down at his hands. The bark-pattern had retreated to his wrists, but he could still feel something different in his blood—a heaviness, a presence that wasn't there before.

"Did you know?" he asked suddenly. "About the child in the vision? About Brynja carrying my bloodline forward?"

"I suspected." Yrsa straightened, slinging her pack across her shoulder. "The Grímmark you bear is ancient—older than the gods themselves. It belongs to no single person but to a lineage of protectors. The fact that it accepted you means your blood carries that legacy, however distant."

Leif tugged at Asvarr's sleeve, pointing eastward. "The grief-path waits," he said, golden eyes reflecting something Asvarr couldn't see. "She comes closer. The thorned one. She senses your awakening."

Asvarr took a deep breath, wincing at the strange sensation of air filling lungs partially transformed. "Then we need to find the Verdant Gate before she does."

"The communion showed you the necessary sacrifice," Yrsa said, watching him carefully. "Do you understand what's required?"

He nodded slowly, remembering the vision of Brynja before the Gate, unable to open it alone.

"Blood and transformation," he said. "My blood carries what hers has lost—the flame essence. But to use it, I must become partly of the Root myself."

"Yes." Yrsa's expression darkened. "And the further you transform, the more you risk losing yourself to the Root's hunger. This is why no single Warden has ever successfully bound all five Anchors. The price becomes too steep."

Asvarr touched the receding bark-pattern on his cheek, feeling its rough texture. The Grímmark on his chest pulsed in response, sending waves of heat through his body.

"Show me the grief-path," he said firmly. "I need to understand what waits at the Gate before I decide."

Yrsa surveyed the broken shrine, her gaze lingering on the altar still gleaming with golden sap. "The shrine remembers the path. But opening it requires more than memory."

She turned to Asvarr, extending her hand, palm up. A small knife rested there, its blade forged from a material that seemed to absorb light rather than reflect it.

"The grief-path opens only to sacrifice," she said softly. "Blood mingled with sap, sorrow surrendered willingly."

Asvarr took the knife, its handle warm against his palm.

"Blood I understand," he said, voice steady despite the fear churning in his gut. "But sorrow?"

"The paths formed from Yggdrasil's pain when it shattered." Yrsa gestured to the cracked ground beneath their feet. "They recognize only those who understand such breaking. You must offer a grief you carry—something precious lost that shaped who you are."

Leif moved to Asvarr's side, taking his free hand. The boy's touch felt strangely insubstantial, like grasping mist.

"I'll show you how," he whispered, golden eyes knowing. "I was born of the world's grief. I remember the way."

Asvarr closed his eyes, thinking of his clan slaughtered, his village burned. So many griefs to choose from. Which would the path recognize?

He opened his eyes, decision made. Stepping forward, he knelt before the altar once more.

"I'm ready," he said, blade hovering over his palm.

The knife bit into Asvarr's palm with cold precision. Blood welled dark and thick, threading between his fingers. He clenched his fist, letting the warmth drip onto the cracked altar where golden sap already pooled.

"Now the grief," Yrsa murmured, her voice barely audible above the wind that had risen suddenly around the shattered shrine.

Asvarr closed his eyes. So many losses to choose from. His clan slaughtered. His home burned. His future stolen. But none of these felt right—the path required something deeper, more fundamental to who he was.

He reached further back, to a memory he rarely allowed himself to touch: the day he first realized his father would never return. Ten winters old, standing at the fjord's edge watching the horizon, believing with a child's unshakeable faith that his father's ship would appear. Hours passed. The sun set. His mother finally came to bring him home, kneeling before him with tears in her eyes.

"He's gone, Asvarr. The sea has taken him."

He'd refused to accept it, fighting her as she tried to lead him away. When she finally held him tightly against her, whispering prayers to gods who hadn't listened, something broke inside him. Not just the loss of his father, but the first shattering of his belief that the world made sense, that it could be trusted.

Asvarr let the memory flow through him, feeling again that child's raw anguish, the bitter taste of a truth he couldn't change.

"I offer the moment I lost faith," he whispered, blood dripping steadily onto the altar. "When I first understood the world takes without reason."

His blood and sap mingled, spreading across the stone in spiraling patterns. The mixture seeped into the cracks, flowing downward through the broken altar into the earth below. For a moment, nothing happened.

Then the ground trembled.

A fault line cracked open before the altar, widening into a narrow crevasse that plunged into darkness. Golden light pulsed from within, illuminating rough stone walls that spiraled downward like a throat. Cold air rushed upward, carrying scents of damp earth, moss, and something else—a metallic tang that reminded Asvarr of tears.

"The path accepts your offering," Yrsa said, wrapping a cloth around his bleeding hand. "It recognizes grief honestly given."

Leif approached the crevasse, peering into its depths with evident fascination. "The way under," he said simply, voice clear and confident.

Asvarr studied the wound in the earth. "What waits down there?"

"The grief-path leads where it will," Yrsa replied, securing her pack and drawing a small knife from her belt. "Each journey differs. This one formed from your sacrifice, shaped by your particular sorrow."

"You're saying we'll walk through my grief?"

Yrsa's expression softened momentarily. "All grief-paths follow the contours of pain—sometimes yours, sometimes the world's. They are passages between realities, formed when Yggdrasil shattered and its sorrow seeped into the bones of existence."

Leif had already begun descending the rough stone steps that formed along the crevasse walls. The boy moved with uncharacteristic surety, his form appearing more substantial with each step downward.

Asvarr hesitated at the edge. The bark-pattern on his arm tingled, spreading slightly up his wrist before receding again. "Will I change more down there?"

"Transformation cannot be controlled, only guided." Yrsa gestured for him to precede her. "The grief-path alters perception. Your senses will expand to perceive what normally lies between realities."

Taking a deep breath, Asvarr stepped onto the first stone tread. The rock felt warm beneath his boots, almost alive. He followed Leif downward, one hand trailing against the wall for balance. The stone pulsed faintly beneath his fingertips, like a creature breathing in slow, measured rhythm.

The daylight above dimmed as they descended. After twenty steps, Asvarr glanced upward to see the opening shrinking, the blue sky reduced to a sliver. After fifty steps, it vanished completely. Only the soft golden glow emanating from the walls remained, pulsing in time with his heartbeat.

The air grew thicker, heavy with moisture that tasted of salt and copper. Each breath filled Asvarr's lungs with sensations he couldn't name—aching hollowness, breathless anticipation, the crushing weight of inevitability. The grief-path didn't just lead through space but through emotion itself.

"Eyes forward," Yrsa cautioned from behind. "The path responds to attention. Look too long at any one feature and it may pull you in."

Asvarr returned his gaze to Leif's back. The boy now seemed fully solid, no longer the half-transparent figure he'd been in the world above. Streamers of faint gold light trailed from his shoulders and fingertips as he moved, illuminating the path ahead.

The steps eventually leveled into a tunnel that curved gently leftward. The walls here were different—no longer stone but a material that resembled wood without being wood, bark without being bark. Smooth surfaces interrupted by whorls and knots that formed patterns almost like faces. When Asvarr looked directly at them, they disappeared. When he looked away, they reappeared in his peripheral vision, watching.

"What are those?" he asked, keeping his eyes carefully forward.

"Memories," Yrsa answered. "The Root preserves fragments of all who've walked these paths. Echoes of grief carried and surrendered."

They passed through an area where the tunnel widened into a small cavern. Thin, root-like structures hung from the ceiling, their tips glowing faintly. Droplets of golden sap fell from them, splashing onto the floor where small pools had formed. The sound of each drop hitting the surface rang like distant bells.

Leif paused, reaching up to touch one of the hanging roots. "Tears," he said, voice reverent. "The Tree still weeps for what was lost."

As they continued deeper, Asvarr's senses began to change. Colors intensified—the golden light revealing spectra he'd never perceived before. The air itself became visible, currents of possibility flowing around them in shimmering waves. When he inhaled, he tasted emotions that didn't belong to him: a mother's grief for her child, a warrior's anguish over betrayal, a lover's despair at abandonment.

"I can taste sorrow in the air," he said, voice hushed with wonder and discomfort.

"The grief-path opens perception," Yrsa replied. "The barriers between your senses thin here."

Asvarr's fingers brushed the tunnel wall, and suddenly he could hear whispers—voices trapped in the wood-like substance, speaking words in languages he'd never heard but somehow understood. Stories of loss, tales of endings, memories of failure. He jerked his hand away, but the voices lingered in his mind.

"The wood remembers," he murmured.

"All matter here carries memory," Yrsa confirmed. "Your transformation allows you to perceive it."

He glanced at his arms, alarmed to see the bark-pattern had spread further, now covering his forearms entirely. When he flexed his fingers, they moved with a slight stiffness, as if his joints were beginning to lignify.

Leif looked back, his golden eyes shining with reflected light. "You're becoming," he said with childlike directness. "Like the trees. Like the path."

"Will it reverse when we leave?" Asvarr asked Yrsa, trying to keep the fear from his voice.

She didn't answer immediately, which told him everything.

The tunnel curved sharply, descending at a steeper angle. The light dimmed, forcing them to rely more on Leif's trail of illumination. The boy moved differently here than he had in the world above—his steps sure, his movements fluid and purposeful. The uncertainty that had marked him was gone, replaced by confidence that bordered on grace.

"He belongs to this in-between," Yrsa whispered to Asvarr. "Born of the Shattering itself."

"What does that mean?" Asvarr asked, watching the boy navigate the difficult terrain with ease.

"When Yggdrasil shattered, reality fractured. Most died. Some survived changed. A very few were born in that moment of breaking—existing across multiple realities simultaneously, never fully anchored to any single one." She gestured toward Leif. "He's strongest here, in the spaces between worlds, where the barriers are thinnest."

The path leveled again, opening into a chamber more vast than should have been possible beneath the earth. The ceiling arched hundreds of feet overhead, supported by massive columns that resembled tree trunks fused with stone. The floor was a patchwork of materials—sections of grass, earth, stone, bark, and water existing side by side without transitions. Reality itself seemed stitched together here from fragments of different worlds.

At the center stood a pool of absolute stillness, its surface reflecting a night sky filled with unfamiliar stars. Surrounding it, a circle of nine stone seats, each carved with runes that pulsed with different colored light.

Leif pointed to the pool. "Memory-water," he said. "Shows the way to the Gate."

Asvarr approached cautiously. The air around the pool felt charged, raising the hair on his arms. When he peered into its depths, vertigo swept through him. The reflected stars weren't above but below, as if the pool opened directly into the void between worlds.

"What do I do?" he asked.

"Look for what calls to your blood," Yrsa instructed, standing well back from the edge.

Asvarr knelt beside the pool, studying the star patterns. At first, they appeared random, scattered across the darkness without meaning. Then patterns emerged—constellations shifting, forming shapes he recognized: the Tree with its branches spanning worlds, the Anchor he'd already bound, the Gate he sought.

One star burned brighter than the others, pulsing with golden-green light. As he focused on it, the view seemed to rush toward it, stars blurring past until that single point expanded into a vision: a massive archway formed of living wood, branches and roots twisted together in impossible configurations. The Verdant Gate.

Before it stood a figure—Brynja, her wooden arm fully transformed, bark patterns spreading across her shoulder and neck. She pressed her palm against the Gate, her expression twisting with frustration when it remained sealed.

"She cannot enter alone," Yrsa said, now standing beside him. "The Gate requires both bloodlines."

The vision shifted, showing a tangled forest surrounding the Gate—trees growing at impossible angles, some from the ground, others from the air itself. The Thorned Vale.

"There," Asvarr said, pointing. "That's where we must go."

As he spoke, ripples disturbed the pool's surface. The vision fragmented, stars scattering like broken glass. The water darkened, turning black as ink. Something moved beneath the surface—a presence vast and patient, watching from depths no light could reach.

Asvarr stumbled backward. "Something's there."

"The grief-paths are never empty," Yrsa said, her voice tight with sudden wariness. "That which dwells in sorrow sometimes rises to greet travelers."

The pool's surface bulged upward, water rising in a column that twisted like a living thing. It hovered for a moment, then collapsed back with a sound like weeping.

"We've been noticed," Yrsa said. "We should move quickly."

Leif had already found another tunnel leading out of the chamber, this one sloping gently upward. The walls here were smoother, almost polished, with thin veins of golden sap running through them like blood vessels.

As they hurried through the passage, Asvarr felt the wood-pattern on his arms pulse with each beat of his heart. The transformation had stabilized, neither advancing nor retreating, but his senses continued to expand. He could hear the soft shifting of soil hundreds of feet above them, taste the age of the stone beneath his feet, smell the complex emotions Yrsa carried behind her calm exterior—fear wrapped around determination, wrapped around a sorrow older than he could comprehend.

The tunnel began to brighten. Ahead, Leif paused at what appeared to be a curtain of golden light. Beyond it, Asvarr glimpsed trees, something wild and wrong, branches growing in spirals and knots that defied natural law.

"The Thorned Vale," Yrsa confirmed. "The grief-path ends here."

Leif turned to them, his golden eyes reflecting the light. "I'm stronger here," he said, his voice clearer than Asvarr had ever heard it. "I can show you paths others can't see."

The boy stepped through the curtain of light, his form momentarily elongating, stretching in impossible ways before vanishing.

Asvarr hesitated at the threshold. Part of him—the part still untouched by transformation—wanted to turn back, to reject this new reality where his senses and body changed beyond his control. But the mark on his chest pulsed with golden heat, pulling him forward.

He glanced back at Yrsa. "What happens if I lose myself to this transformation?"

"Then you become like the corrupted ones," she said simply. "Neither fully human nor fully Root, but something caught between—a vessel for powers beyond mortal understanding."

"Like Brynja is becoming."

"Yes." Her expression softened slightly. "The transformation itself is neither good nor evil. It's a gateway—to power, to understanding, to communion with forces larger than ourselves. The danger lies in how completely you surrender to it."

Asvarr looked down at his wood-patterned arms, flexing fingers that moved less fluidly than before. "And if I turn back now?"

"The Root doesn't release those it claims," Yrsa said. "You've already begun the journey. Your choice now is whether to guide the transformation or let it consume you."

Through the curtain of light, tree branches twisted and writhed, forming patterns that tugged at Asvarr's expanded senses. The Thorned Vale waited, a realm where grief had transformed the natural world into something other.

Asvarr took a deep breath, tasting the complex flavors of sorrow and possibility. The path behind led back to a self he could never fully be again. The path forward led to transformation he couldn't control.

"Leif is waiting," he said, decision made. He stepped through the curtain of light into the Thorned Vale.

CHAPTER 4

SONG OF THE THORNED VALE

Light fractured through the golden curtain, scattering across Asvarr's transformed skin in patterns that shifted with each breath. The world beyond rippled, as though seen through disturbed water. He stepped through.

Reality twisted. His stomach lurched as perspective inverted, then righted itself. Asvarr's feet landed on soft ground carpeted with moss that glowed faintly in shades of amber and blue. He steadied himself against the nearest tree trunk, bark warm and pulsing beneath his wooden-patterned palm.

The Thorned Vale stretched before him.

Trees grew at impossible angles—some from the earth, others from the sky, their branches meeting in the middle to form geometric patterns that defied natural law. Trunks twisted into spirals, split into perfect, symmetrical forks, or merged with neighboring trees to create archways and tunnels. Leaves shimmered in colors Asvarr had never seen before, somewhere between purple and green, between red and blue, hues his mind struggled to categorize.

"Tread carefully," Yrsa warned, emerging behind him. "The Vale reads intention. It responds to thought as much as action."

Sunlight filtered through a canopy that existed above and below simultaneously, casting shadows that moved counter to the light source. The air itself felt thick, almost viscous, filled with scents so complex they overwhelmed Asvarr's enhanced senses—sweet decay, metallic growth, the sharp tang of sap mixed with something ancient and patient.

Leif moved ahead with confidence, his form fully solid now, golden light streaming from his fingertips as he brushed against leaves and branches. The boy navigated the disorienting landscape instinctively, choosing paths that appeared and disappeared as they passed.

"How does he know the way?" Asvarr asked, voice hushed.

"He doesn't follow a path so much as create it," Yrsa replied. "The in-between responds to his nature."

They descended into a hollow where fog coiled around their ankles. Each step disturbed the mist, sending ripples of color spiraling outward. Through a curtain of hanging vines that resembled silver chains, Asvarr glimpsed a clearing where a circle of trees grew in perfect alignment, branches reaching inward to touch at the center point.

Something moved among the trees—a shadow that flowed like liquid, then solidified into a form that might have been human, or might have been something else entirely. It vanished before Asvarr could focus on it.

"We're not alone," he murmured.

"The Vale harbors many entities," Yrsa said. "Most were born when the Tree shattered—fragments of consciousness given form through grief."

Leif paused at the edge of the clearing, head tilted as though listening. "The trees are talking," he said.

Asvarr listened. At first, he heard only the soft rustle of leaves, the distant creaking of wood. Then, as his awareness expanded through his transformation, the sounds resolved into patterns—rhythmic, deliberate. Words.

The trees were whispering.

The language was unlike any Asvarr had heard before, composed of sounds no human throat could make—the slow groan of growing wood, the sharp crack of breaking branches, the soft sigh of unfurling leaves. Yet somehow, he understood.

"They speak of the breaking," he said, translating for Yrsa, who watched him with intense focus. "Of the moment when the world cracked open and the Tree shattered."

He moved deeper into the clearing, drawn to a massive oak whose trunk spiraled upward in a perfect helix. The whispers grew louder as he approached.

"Coilvoice," Asvarr said, the unfamiliar name feeling strange on his tongue. "They speak of an entity called Coilvoice, born when the Tree shattered—neither Root nor god, but something in between."

"What do they say of this Coilvoice?" Yrsa asked, keeping her distance.

Asvarr pressed his transformed palm against the spiraling trunk, connecting more deeply to the whispered conversation. The tree's language flowed through him, images forming in his mind: a being composed of twisting patterns, simultaneously vast and minuscule, watching from the spaces between worlds.

"Coilvoice was..." he struggled to translate concepts that had no equivalent in human speech, "...the Tree's final thought as it broke. Its consciousness scattered but didn't die. It exists in fragments across all realms, watching, waiting."

"For what?"

"For the one who will either restore or transform." Asvarr frowned. "The trees aren't certain which is better."

The whispers shifted, growing urgent. Warning. Asvarr pulled his hand away from the trunk, suddenly alert.

"What is it?" Yrsa stepped closer, her hand moving to the knife at her belt.

"Someone comes." Asvarr scanned the clearing, his enhanced senses detecting movement beyond normal sight. "The trees warn of 'the one who harvests grief'—a hunter who feeds on sorrow. They say it stalks these woods, drawn to those who carry deep wounds."

Leif appeared at his side, golden eyes wide with sudden fear. "We should move," the boy said. "Now."

The whispers grew louder, spreading from tree to tree like wildfire. Even Yrsa could hear them now—a chorus of creaking, rustling, groaning voices rising in alarm. The forest itself shuddered, branches swaying without wind.

Asvarr crouched, placing his palm flat against the earth. Through his trans-formed skin, he felt vibrations—something large moving through the Vale, displacing reality as it came. The moss beneath his hand curled away, recoiling from an approaching presence.

"Which way?" he asked Leif.

The boy pointed toward a narrow gap between two trees that grew parallel to each other, their branches forming a tunnel overhead. "Through there. The path remembers me."

***

They hurried through the opening, entering a section of forest where the trees grew more densely, their canopies intertwining to create near-darkness. Bioluminescent fungi sprouted from trunks and branches, casting a pale blue glow that illuminated their path.

The whispers followed them, passing from tree to tree ahead of their progress. Asvarr realized the forest was communicating their presence, spreading word of their passage. Whether this would help or hinder them remained unclear.

"What exactly is this grief-harvester?" he asked as they navigated between trunks that leaned at impossible angles.

"The trees use many names for it," Yrsa replied, her voice low. "Sorrow-drinker. Memory-thief. Wound-walker. It's an entity that feeds on grief, drawn to those who carry profound loss."

Asvarr thought of his clan, slaughtered. His village, burned. The loss of his father that had carved the first permanent wound in his heart. He was a feast for such a creature.

***

The path opened into another clearing, this one dominated by a single massive tree that grew upside-down, its roots splayed across the sky like grasping fingers, its branches burrowing into the earth. The trunk was covered in what appeared to be eyes—knots in the wood that blinked and shifted, watching their approach.

Leif stopped abruptly, raising one hand in warning. The air felt suddenly colder, charged with potential. The whispering of the trees ceased, leaving an unnatural silence.

"It knows we're here," the boy whispered.

A single leaf detached from the inverted tree, spiraling downward—or perhaps upward, direction having lost meaning in this place. It landed on Asvarr's outstretched palm, its surface etched with patterns that moved like living things.

Runes. Ancient, shifting runes that Asvarr shouldn't have been able to read, yet did.

"Beware the Harvester," he translated aloud. "It wears the face of your deepest loss. Do not look upon it directly."

Yrsa moved to his side, studying the leaf. "The Vale offers protection through warning. That's unusual. Something about our presence matters to this place."

The leaf dissolved into golden dust, absorbed into Asvarr's transformed skin. The runes lingered, flowing up his arm before disappearing beneath his sleeve.

"We need to keep moving," Yrsa urged. "The Verdant Gate can't be far now."

Leif shook his head. "The paths shift. What should be near becomes distant when pursued. The harvester disrupts the Vale's geometry."

"Then we need a direct route." Asvarr studied the inverted tree with its watching eyes. An idea formed, born from his expanded perception. "The tree sees everything in the Vale. If I connect to it—"

"Too dangerous," Yrsa cut him off. "That's not an ordinary tree. It's a Watcher—one of the original guardians of Yggdrasil. Connecting with it might accelerate your transformation beyond control."

Asvarr flexed his wooden-patterned hands. The transformation had stabilized again. He felt the potential for change simmering beneath his skin, waiting for catalyst.

"We don't have much choice. The harvester knows we're here, and we need to find the Gate before it finds us."

Before Yrsa could object further, Asvarr approached the inverted tree. Its eyes tracked his movement, blinking in unsettling patterns. The bark rippled as he drew near, forming protrusions that might have been hands, might have been faces, might have been something for which he had no reference.

He placed both palms against the trunk.

Connection bloomed—not gentle like the whispers of the other trees, but overwhelming. Information flooded through him, images cascading faster than he could process. The Watcher held knowledge of the entire Vale, every path, every entity, every moment since the Shattering.

Asvarr's consciousness expanded outward, riding the Watcher's awareness through the twisted forest. He saw everything at once: paths forming and dissolving, creatures moving between trees, the chaotic geometry of reality bending back on itself. And there—a tangled nexus of branches and roots woven together into a massive archway that pulsed with golden-green light.

The Verdant Gate.

Before it stood a figure, half-hidden in shadow. Brynja, her wooden arm fully transformed, bark patterns spreading across her shoulder and neck. She traced patterns in the air before the Gate, which remained sealed despite her efforts.

Elsewhere in the Vale, something massive moved through the trees, leaving sorrow in its wake. The harvester. It flowed like mist between trunks, absorbing grief from every living thing it touched. Trees withered in its passage, their whispering silenced. It moved with purpose, tracking a scent only it could detect.

Their scent.

Asvarr tried to pull away from the Watcher, but the connection held him fast. The tree's awareness began to seep into him, merging with his consciousness. The bark-pattern on his arms spread upward, crossing his shoulders, creeping toward his neck.

"Asvarr!" Yrsa's voice came from impossibly far away. "You're transforming too quickly!"

With tremendous effort, Asvarr tore his hands from the trunk, stumbling backward. The connection snapped, leaving him gasping. His vision swam, adjusting from the Watcher's all-encompassing perspective back to his limited human sight.

The transformation had advanced—bark patterns now covered his shoulders and had begun to spread up his neck. When he spoke, his voice resonated differently, with harmonics that echoed like wind through hollow branches.

"I saw the Gate," he said. "And Brynja. She's there, trying to open it."

"How far?" Yrsa asked, her expression tight with concern as she studied his increased transformation.

"Not far in distance, but the paths are tangled." Asvarr gestured to the west. "That way, through the heart of the Vale. But the harvester hunts us. It's coming from the north, moving fast."

Leif tugged at Asvarr's sleeve, golden eyes wide. "We must go beneath," he said. "Where the paths can't shift."

"Beneath?" Asvarr looked down at the moss-covered ground.

"The Vale exists in layers," Yrsa explained. "What we see is merely the surface. Beneath lie the root-ways—paths that connect directly to the heart of the Vale. They're more stable, less affected by the Vale's shifting nature."

"How do we reach them?"

Leif moved to a spot where two trees had grown together, their trunks fused into a single twisted mass. He pressed his small hands against the bark, leaving golden imprints that glowed briefly before sinking into the wood. The fused trunks groaned, then split apart, revealing a hollow space within.

"Through here," the boy said. "The trees remember me."

***

Asvarr peered into the opening. A spiral path led downward, carved into the living wood of the trees' interior. The walls pulsed faintly, like a heart beating in slow rhythm.

The whispering of the forest rose again, urgent and alarmed. Through his connection to the Watcher, Asvarr understood their warning: the harvester had changed direction, moving with greater speed directly toward them. It had sensed the opening of the root-way.

"We need to go. Now." Asvarr gestured Yrsa toward the opening. "It's coming."

She slipped inside, followed by Leif. As Asvarr prepared to enter, a strange stillness fell over the clearing. The eyes of the Watcher widened, then closed simultaneously. The whispers of the trees cut off mid-syllable.

A cold weight settled in the pit of Asvarr's stomach—dread crystallizing into certainty. He was being watched.

Slowly, he turned.

At the edge of the clearing stood a figure that shifted between forms as Asvarr's gaze tried to focus on it. One moment it resembled a tall man in a cloak of ragged shadows, the next a creature of tangled branches and thorns. Its face remained hidden, but Asvarr felt its attention like a physical touch, cold and hungry.

The harvester had found them.

Asvarr backed toward the opening in the trees, careful not to make sudden movements. The figure remained still, observing. Waiting.

"What do you want?" Asvarr called out, his transformed voice carrying strangely through the silent clearing.

The figure tilted what might have been its head. When it spoke, its voice came from everywhere at once—from the ground, from the air, from inside Asvarr's own mind.

"Your grief," it said, the words tasting of ashes and old tears. "Such exquisite pain you carry, Root-touched. I will feast for a hundred years."

The harvester took a single step forward, its form briefly resolving into the shape of a tall woman with braided hair—his mother, as she had looked the day she died. Asvarr's heart clenched with shock and renewed grief.

"Don't look at it directly," Yrsa hissed from the opening. "It shows you what you've lost to paralyze you with sorrow."

Asvarr tore his gaze away, focusing instead on the gap in the trees. The harvester chuckled, a sound like dry leaves crumbling.

"Run, little Root-touched," it said. "Your grief cannot escape me. I will find you wherever you hide, whenever you weep."

Asvarr lunged for the opening, slipping inside just as the harvester surged forward in a rush of shadow and whispers. The fused trunks slammed shut behind him, sealing off the surface world.

The root-way pulsed around them, alive and aware. Asvarr pressed his back against the sealed entrance, heart hammering in his chest. Above, they heard a scream of frustration as the harvester found its prey escaped.

"It can't follow?" he asked, voice unsteady.

"Not immediately," Yrsa said. "The root-ways are protected by old magic. However, it will find another entrance. We must hurry."

Leif had already started down the spiral path, trailing golden light from his fingertips that illuminated the way ahead. Asvarr took a deep breath, steadying himself, then followed.

Behind them, the sealed entrance shuddered as something massive pressed against it from the other side, testing its strength. The wood groaned under the pressure, golden sap beading along fresh cracks.

The barrier wouldn't hold for long.

The root-way spiraled downward through living wood that pulsed like a massive heartbeat. Golden sap trickled along the walls, collecting in small pools that cast flickering light across their path. Asvarr descended behind Leif, his bark-patterned feet finding purchase on steps that seemed to form beneath him just as he needed them.

Above, the sealed entrance shuddered. Something massive struck it again with enough force to send vibrations through the entire passage. Splinters rained down from above, golden sap spraying from fresh cracks.

"Move faster," Yrsa urged from behind. "The harvester cannot follow our exact path, but it knows where we're headed."

The spiral path leveled into a tunnel that burrowed straight through the earth. Here, the walls were formed entirely of roots—massive, ancient ones intertwined with delicate tendrils no thicker than a hair. All of them alive, all of them aware. Asvarr felt their attention like a physical touch, curious and evaluating.

"The roots remember everyone who passes," he said, the knowledge coming from somewhere beyond his conscious mind. His transformation continued to feed him information, understanding flooding through modified flesh.

"They judge, too," Yrsa replied. "Those deemed unworthy never reach the end of these passages."

Leif moved with confident strides, his form solid and sure in this realm between realities. The golden light streaming from his fingertips illuminated thick mats of roots that parted before him like curtains. The boy paused at a junction where three paths diverged, his head tilted as though listening.

"Something waits ahead," he whispered. "Many somethings. Hungry."

Asvarr drew his bronze sword, which gleamed with veins of gold in the strange light. "Can we go around?"

Leif shook his head. "All paths lead to the same point. The Vale's heart demands passage through its guardians."

"What guardians?" Asvarr asked, but even as the words left his mouth, he sensed movement ahead—something flowing through the root-walls, disturbing the living tissue as it passed.

"Sorrow Eaters," Yrsa said, her voice tight. She drew her crystal knife, its edge catching the light. "Lesser cousins to the harvester. They feed on painful memories, leaving emptiness behind."

Asvarr's grip tightened on his sword. "How do we fight them?"

"With fire, ideally." Yrsa produced a small pouch from her belt. "Anything that burns drives them back. They fear transformation."

***

The tunnel widened into a chamber where massive roots formed a domed ceiling overhead. The floor was a lake of shallow golden sap that rippled with their footsteps. At the center rose an island of intertwined roots, forming a platform that held what appeared to be a doorway made of solid shadow.

"The direct path to the Vale's heart," Leif said, pointing toward the shadow-door. "Through there we'll reach the Verdant Gate."

Movement rippled through the sap-lake—shapes rising from depths that shouldn't have existed in such shallow liquid. Creatures emerged, formed of bark and bone with hollow sockets where eyes should be. Their limbs twisted at impossible angles, fingers elongated into claws that dripped golden fluid. Most disturbing were their mouths—vertical slits that split their entire torsos, lined with teeth formed from splinters of wood.

The Sorrow Eaters had found them.

More creatures flowed from the walls, dropping from the ceiling, sliding from cracks in the floor. Within moments, dozens surrounded them, forming a closing circle of twisted wood and bone.

Asvarr shifted into a fighting stance, bronze sword raised. "Stay behind me."

One creature stepped forward—larger than the others, its body formed from darker wood threaded with veins of black. When it spoke, its voice rasped like bark scraping bark.

"The Root-touched brings such pain," it grated. "We feast today."

The Sorrow Eaters surged forward as one. Asvarr met the first with his blade, slicing through its wooden form. The creature split apart, but the pieces flowed back together, reforming with a shudder. Physical damage alone would not stop them.

"Fire!" Yrsa shouted, flinging the contents of her pouch into the air. The powder ignited on contact with the sap-saturated air, creating a barrier of blue flame between them and several creatures. The affected Eaters recoiled, their wooden bodies crackling as they retreated.

Asvarr felt a strange pressure building in his chest, centered around the Grímmark. His transformation had spread—bark patterns now covered much of his torso, threading around his neck, creeping up his jawline. With the pressure came instinctive knowledge.

He pressed his transformed palm against his chest, directly over the mark. Golden light spilled between his fingers. When he extended his hand toward the nearest Sorrow Eater, a stream of liquid fire erupted from his palm, striking the creature. It shrieked—a sound like breaking branches—as it burned from within, collapsing into ash.

"The transformation grants power," Yrsa called, slashing at a creature with her crystal knife. Where the blade touched, wood turned to dust, but the effect was temporary—the creatures reformed almost immediately.

Three Sorrow Eaters surrounded Asvarr, reaching for him with grasping claws. He unleashed another burst of golden fire, but they dodged, learning from their fallen companion. One lunged, its claw-like fingers puncturing his arm. Pain lanced through him, but it was quickly replaced by a deeper sensation—a pulling, as though something essential was being drawn from him.

Images flashed before his eyes—his clan's slaughter, his village burning, his mother's death. The creature was feeding on his grief, extracting his most painful memories.

Asvarr tried to wrench away, but the Sorrow Eater held fast, its teeth-lined torso splitting wider to reveal darkness within. Two more latched onto him, one gripping his transformed arm, the other sinking claws into his back. Each point of contact became a channel for them to feed, pulling grief and pain from his very soul.

His knees buckled. The sword slipped from numbed fingers. Through dimming vision, he saw Yrsa fighting desperately, her crystal knife a blur of motion that temporarily held the creatures at bay. But there were too many, and they were learning, adapting.

"Leif!" Yrsa shouted. "Help him!"

The boy stood frozen at the edge of the chamber, golden eyes wide with fear. At Yrsa's call, he moved, darting between Sorrow Eaters with impossible speed. Reaching Asvarr's side, Leif placed his small hand against the nearest creature's wooden back.

The effect was immediate and devastating. Where the boy touched, the Sorrow Eater's body crumbled to ash, simply ceasing to exist. The creature didn't even have time to shriek before it collapsed into a pile of gray dust.

Emboldened, Leif touched the second creature with the same result. The third released Asvarr and tried to retreat, but the boy was faster, his hand connecting with its chest. In an instant, it too was reduced to ash.

Asvarr slumped to his knees, weak from the Eaters' feeding. His mind felt hollowed out, memories blurred and faded where they had fed. The creatures hadn't managed to take everything, but what remained of those painful recollections felt distant, as though they had happened to someone else.

Leif stood before him now, a barrier between Asvarr and the remaining Sorrow Eaters. The creatures kept their distance, wary of the boy's touch. His golden light had intensified, streaming from his entire body in rays that illuminated the chamber.

"What are you?" the largest Sorrow Eater rasped, its vertical mouth contorting in what might have been fear.

"I am what you are," Leif replied, his voice unnervingly adult. "Born of the world's breaking. But where you feed on sorrow, I am made of it."

Yrsa reached Asvarr's side, helping him to his feet. His legs trembled, barely supporting his weight. The transformation had receded slightly where the Eaters had fed, leaving patches of normal skin amid the bark patterns.

"We need to move," she whispered. "Leif is holding them back, but his power isn't infinite here."

Asvarr nodded weakly, retrieving his sword. "The shadow door."

The remaining Sorrow Eaters formed a loose circle around them, maintaining distance from Leif but unwilling to retreat entirely. The largest creature paced, its wooden body creaking with each movement.

"The Root-touched carries what belongs to the Vale," it grated. "Leave it behind, and you may pass."

"What does it mean?" Asvarr asked Yrsa.

"Your grief," she replied. "They want you to surrender all of it. The complete memories of your losses, not just fragments."

Asvarr considered this. The partial feeding had left him feeling strangely empty, the sharp edges of his pain dulled. Would losing it all be so terrible? The constant weight of remembering his clan's destruction, his failures, his losses—gone.

"Don't," Yrsa warned, reading his expression. "Grief shapes us. Without it, you lose part of what makes you who you are."

The largest Sorrow Eater extended a clawed hand. "Give your sorrow freely, and we will show you the quickest path to what you seek."

Temptation twisted through Asvarr. The creature offered relief from pain he'd carried since watching his clan burn. Freedom from the weight that dragged at his soul with every step.

"Grief is my weapon," he said instead, straightening despite his weakness. "My pain drives me forward. I will not surrender it, even to ease my burden."

The Sorrow Eater's mouth-torso split in what might have been a smile. "Then we take it."

The creatures surged forward again. Leif moved with blinding speed, his touch turning three more to ash before they could reach Asvarr. But there were dozens more, and the boy couldn't be everywhere at once.

"Run!" Yrsa shouted, pushing Asvarr toward the center of the chamber where the shadow door waited. "I'll hold them back!"

"We're not separating," Asvarr insisted, catching her arm.

Her expression softened momentarily. "The door only remains open briefly. Someone must keep it from closing behind you."

Before Asvarr could argue further, Leif appeared at his side, grabbing his wooden-patterned hand.

"She's right," the boy said. "The door wants sacrifice. If none is given, it takes what passes through."

The largest Sorrow Eater lunged toward them, its claws extended. Yrsa intercepted it with her crystal knife, driving the blade into its chest. The creature shrieked but didn't fall, wrapping elongated fingers around her throat.

"Go!" she choked out, struggling against its grip.

Leif pulled Asvarr toward the shadow door. The boy's touch left golden imprints on the solid darkness, causing it to ripple like disturbed water. Through the ripples, Asvarr glimpsed the Vale's heart—a clearing where massive trees grew in a perfect circle around a structure woven from living branches and roots.

The Verdant Gate.

Asvarr hesitated, looking back at Yrsa. She had broken free of the Sorrow Eater's grip but was now surrounded by more creatures, fighting desperately with her crystal knife.

"I won't leave her," he said.

Leif's golden eyes met his. "You must. She cannot follow where we go."

"Why?"

"She carries her own anchor," the boy said cryptically. "It cannot approach another without consequences."

Before Asvarr could process this revelation, a shuddering impact rocked the entire chamber. Cracks spread across the ceiling, golden sap raining down in curtains. The harvester had found another way in.

Leif's expression transformed to one of pure terror. "It comes. We must go now."

The shadow door trembled, beginning to shrink. Another moment and it would close entirely. Leif had already stepped halfway through, his form rippling as it passed from one reality to another.

"Yrsa!" Asvarr called.

She looked up from her desperate fight, meeting his gaze across the chamber. "Find the Gate! I'll find another way!"

A massive root punched through the ceiling, sending larger chunks of debris crashing down. Through the opening, Asvarr glimpsed a shape of tangled shadow and thorn descending—the harvester, breaking through to the root-ways.

With a final agonized glance at Yrsa, Asvarr stepped through the shadow door, Leif's hand pulling him forward.

Reality twisted, folded. Sensation vanished, replaced by a rushing vertigo that threatened to tear his consciousness apart. Through it all, Leif's hand remained in his, an anchor against oblivion.

***

They fell through darkness into sudden, blinding light.

Asvarr crashed to the ground, landing on soft moss that cushioned his fall. The air here smelled different—rich with growing things, tinged with the sweetness of flowering plants. Opening his eyes, he found himself in a perfect circular clearing surrounded by the strangest trees he'd ever seen.

Each trunk spiraled upward, branches forming elaborate geometric patterns that defied understanding. At the center of the clearing stood what could only be the Verdant Gate—a massive archway formed of living wood, branches and roots woven together in a pattern so complex it hurt to look at directly. Golden sap leaked from joints in the structure, pooling at its base.

Before it stood a figure, half-turned away.

Brynja.

Her transformation had progressed even further than his own—her left arm completely wooden from shoulder to fingertip, bark patterns spreading across her back and neck, threading into her dark hair, which now contained living leaves. When she turned toward the sound of their arrival, her amber eyes widened in shock.

"You," she said, voice resonating with harmonics like wind through hollow branches. "The flame-carrier. At last."

Leif moved to Asvarr's side, golden light now contained within his skin rather than streaming outward. The boy's expression was unreadable as he looked between the two transformed humans.

"The door took sacrifice," Leif said quietly. "Your friend is lost to us."

Brynja's wooden hand clenched into a fist. "You brought another. The child who exists between worlds."

"Where are your followers?" Asvarr asked, rising unsteadily to his feet. His body ached from the Sorrow Eaters' feeding and the passage through the shadow door.

"Dead or scattered," Brynja replied flatly. "The Vale takes what it wishes, gives nothing freely."

She gestured toward the Verdant Gate. "For three days I've tried to open it. The Gate recognizes my blood—I am of the Root-tender lineage—but it remains sealed." Her gaze fixed on Asvarr's transformed arm, the bark patterns spreading across his chest. "You carry what I lack. The flame essence our bloodlines once shared before the betrayal."

Asvarr approached cautiously, keeping distance between them. "You're not trying to kill me this time?"

"I've tried that approach," she said with a grimace. "The Vale showed me the futility. Neither of us can claim the second Anchor alone. The Gate requires both bloodlines together—flame and root combined."

Leif circled the clearing, trailing his fingers along tree trunks that bent toward his touch like plants seeking sunlight. "The way is prepared," he announced. "But the third comes."

"Third?" Asvarr asked.

"The grief-harvester follows," Brynja explained. "It hunts all who carry sorrow through the Vale. We have little time."

She extended her wooden hand toward Asvarr, palm up in offering. "Will you help me open the Gate? Together we can bind the second Anchor before the harvester arrives."

Asvarr studied her transformed features, searching for deception. The bark patterns had spread across nearly half her face, one eye now ringed with concentric wooden circles. Yet behind the transformation, he recognized the woman from his visions—the one who had carved his ancestral runes into a child's chest to preserve their bloodline.

"Why should I trust you?" he asked. "You've tried to kill me since I first bound with the Root."

"Because the Root itself has shown me truth," she replied. "Neither of us will survive alone. The second binding demands partnership, not dominance."

The words echoed what Yrsa had told him. In the distance, a sound like breaking branches rolled across the Vale—the harvester, drawing nearer.

Asvarr glanced at Leif, who watched him with golden eyes that held knowledge beyond his apparent years. "What do you see?" he asked the boy.

"Two paths," Leif replied. "One where you stand apart and both fall. One where you join and both change."

Brynja's wooden hand remained extended, waiting.

With a deep breath, Asvarr stepped forward and placed his transformed palm against hers.

CHAPTER 5

THE MEMORY HUNTRESS

Asvarr's hand closed around Brynja's wooden palm. Their flesh met—his bark-patterned skin against her fully transformed arm. The contact sent shockwaves through him, golden light flaring where they touched. The world tilted, spun, then faded into darkness as exhaustion claimed him.

He dreamed.

Standing stones rose around him, ancient monoliths carved with spiraling runes that shifted when he tried to focus on them. Mist coiled between the stones, carrying whispers in a language so old it predated words. The sky above hung heavy with storm clouds, bruised purple and black.

At the circle's center stood Brynja. Her transformation had progressed further—now both arms were wooden to the shoulder, bark patterns covering half her face, leaves and small branches woven through her raven-black hair. Ravens circled overhead, their harsh calls echoing against the stones.

She turned toward him, amber eyes gleaming with intelligence and something darker. Recognition.

"You," she said, her voice resonating with harmonics like wind through hollow branches. "The usurper finally shows himself."

Asvarr tried to speak but found no voice. He was present yet not—a witness without substance.

Brynja approached, wooden fingers extending toward his face. "You carry what was promised to me. The Root recognizes my bloodline, not yours."

As her fingers neared his cheek, one of the ravens descended, landing on her shoulder. The bird fixed Asvarr with a stare too knowing for any animal. It croaked once, then whispered in Brynja's ear with a human voice.

"He comes. The marked one comes."

Brynja smiled, an expression made uncanny by the wooden patterns distorting her features. "Good. We'll be waiting."

She turned back to Asvarr, hand still extended. "The second binding approaches. When it comes, remember this: what flows between us cannot be severed. Root and flame. We are two halves of what was once whole."

Her wooden fingers brushed his cheek—

Asvarr jolted awake, heart hammering against his ribs. Dawn light filtered through the forest canopy above, dappling the forest floor where they had made camp. His chest heaved with each breath, golden sap beading along the bark patterns that now covered most of his torso and arms.

The dream had felt utterly real. Even now, his cheek burned where her fingers had touched him.

"Bad dreams?" Leif asked, already awake and watching him with those unnerving golden eyes. The boy sat cross-legged beside their small fire, which had burned down to embers overnight.

"Not bad. Strange." Asvarr sat up, wiping sap from his eyes. After escaping the Vale's heart, they had traveled for hours before exhaustion forced them to make camp in a relatively safe grove of normal trees at the forest's edge. No sign of the harvester had followed them, but Asvarr felt eyes on them nonetheless.

He scanned the branches overhead. A raven perched on a limb directly above, watching with unblinking intensity.

Ice slid down Asvarr's spine. The bird matched the ones from his dream exactly—unusually large, with feathers that gleamed blue-black in the morning light. As he stared, it cocked its head, studying him with unmistakable intelligence.

"We have company," he said quietly to Leif.

The boy glanced up. "Ravens. They've been there since before dawn. Six of them."

Asvarr counted. Sure enough, five more ravens perched in the surrounding trees, all watching their camp with the same eerie stillness.

"Where's Brynja?" he asked, realizing she was nowhere to be seen.

"Gone before first light," Leif replied. "Said she needed to prepare something at the Gate. Said you would understand."

Asvarr frowned. Their alliance remained tentative at best. After their dramatic meeting at the Verdant Gate, they had agreed to work together to perform the second binding, but mutual suspicion lingered. He hadn't expected her to leave while he slept.

Something caught his eye—a marking in the dirt near where Brynja had slept. Moving closer, he found a complex pattern drawn with precision. Nine concentric circles connected by spiraling lines, with what looked like a map of the surrounding forest at the center. One location had been marked with sap—the Verdant Gate.

"She left directions," he murmured.

"And watchers." A new voice startled him.

Yrsa stood at the edge of their camp, looking haggard but alive. Her clothing was torn in places, stained with golden sap and what might have been her own blood. She carried her pack and crystal knife, both showing signs of hard use.

"Yrsa!" Asvarr moved toward her, relief flooding through him. "How did you escape the root-ways?"

"The old fashions." She grimaced, displaying burns on her palms. "Fire and sacrifice. The harvester was hunting you, not me. Once you departed, it lost interest in the rest of us."

"Us?"

"Some of the Sorrow Eaters survived. They..." she hesitated, "...showed me another path out. One that cost them greatly."

Yrsa approached their fire, warming her hands over the embers. Her gaze flicked to the ravens above, her expression darkening.

"Brynja's watchers," she said, voice tight with disapproval. "She's tracking us even now."

"Through the birds?" Asvarr asked.

"Through you." Yrsa touched his chest lightly, where the Grímmark pulsed beneath his transformed skin. "Your dreams most likely. The connection between you strengthens as you both transform. She piggybacks on that connection, seeing through your eyes when your conscious defenses are weakest."

Asvarr's blood went cold. "She can see my dreams?"

"Not just see. Manipulate, perhaps." Yrsa studied his face. "Did you dream of her last night?"

He nodded, recounting the vision of Brynja in the standing stones with ravens circling overhead. Yrsa's expression grew increasingly troubled as he described the encounter.

"She's growing stronger in ways I didn't anticipate," she said when he finished. "The Root's transformation typically progresses more slowly, but she's accelerating somehow."

"Is she directing the ravens?" Asvarr glanced up at the birds again.

"They're extensions of her awareness now. The Root allows such connections between transformed beings and creatures with natural affinity for death and memory." Yrsa drew a complex sign in the air between them. "This might help shield your dreams temporarily, but the connection will only strengthen as you both progress toward the second binding."

The largest raven suddenly took flight, circling their camp once before flying south—toward the Verdant Gate. The remaining birds maintained their silent vigil.

"They're reporting back," Yrsa said. "She knows I've returned."

Leif had moved to the forest's edge, staring into the trees with unusual intensity. "Someone else watches," he announced. "Not ravens. Not harvester."

Asvarr joined him, scanning the forest. At first, he saw nothing unusual. Then, as his transformed senses expanded, he detected a disturbance in the patterns of light and shadow between distant trunks—something moving with deliberate stealth.

"How many?" he asked the boy.

"Four. Maybe five." Leif pointed. "There. And there. Moving around us."

Yrsa's hand went to her crystal knife. "The Verdant Five have agents every-where. If Brynja truly serves them, we may be walking into a trap."

"But we need her to open the Gate," Asvarr reminded her. "You said it your-self—both bloodlines are required."

"Yes, but on whose terms?" Yrsa's voice dropped lower. "The Gate will open for combined blood, but what happens after depends entirely on intent. If her will dominates during the binding, the outcome changes."

Asvarr remembered Brynja's words from the dream: *The Root recognizes my bloodline, not yours. You're an aberration.* Despite their alliance, she clearly be-lieved her claim to the Root superior to his.

"We could leave," he suggested. "Find another approach to the second Anchor."

"There is no other approach." Yrsa shook her head. "The Verdant Gate is the only path to the second Anchor in this cycle. The binding must occur there."

"Then we continue as planned," Asvarr decided. "But carefully. I don't trust her."

"Wise," Yrsa murmured. "The Root transforms body first, then mind. As the transformation progresses, priorities shift. Brynja may believe she allies with you while the Root drives her toward different ends."

Leif tugged at Asvarr's sleeve, pointing skyward. More ravens had appeared, forming a dark line across the morning sky—dozens of them, all flying toward the Verdant Gate.

"She calls her messengers home," Yrsa observed. "Preparing for your arrival."

The remaining ravens watching their camp took flight simultaneously, joining their brethren. Within moments, the trees above stood empty.

"She's making her move," Yrsa warned. "Whatever she plans, it happens today."

Asvarr studied the map Brynja had left. The Verdant Gate lay half a day's jour-ney south, through forests that grew progressively stranger as they approached the Vale's boundary. He traced the path with a bark-patterned finger, memorizing the route.

"Leif, can you sense any safe paths through these woods?" he asked.

The boy closed his golden eyes, head tilted as though listening to distant music. "The in-between thins here," he said after a moment. "Many paths, but all watched. Some by ravens, some by... others."

"Others?"

"Entities that serve the Verdant Five," Yrsa explained. "Ancient guardians bound to their will. The closer we draw to the Gate, the more we enter their domain."

Asvarr checked his bronze sword, which still carried veins of gold from his first binding. The blade hummed faintly when drawn, responding to his transformed flesh. He couldn't be certain it would affect whatever guardians they might encounter, but it provided some comfort.

"We'll follow the route she marked," he decided. "She wants me at the Gate—that much is clear. And I need her to perform the binding. For now, our goals align."

Yrsa looked unconvinced. "And when they no longer align? When the binding itself becomes contested?"

"Then I'll remind her that her bloodline isn't the only one with claim to the Root." He flexed his transformed hand, bark patterns shifting with the movement. "The flame essence she lacks gives me leverage."

***

They broke camp quickly, gathering what few supplies remained after their journey through the Vale. As Asvarr shouldered his pack, his Grímmark pulsed with heat, sending rivulets of golden sap trickling down his chest. The mark had expanded further overnight, now covering most of his torso in patterns of interwoven roots and flame.

Leif led the way, moving with the peculiar grace he showed whenever they entered areas where reality thinned. The boy seemed to flicker occasionally, his edges blurring as though he existed partially in multiple places simultaneously.

The forest around them changed subtly as they traveled. Trees grew with increasing irregularity—trunks twisting in spirals, branches forming geometric patterns, roots rising above ground to create natural archways. Bird calls became musical phrases too complex for animal throats, repeating in mathematical progressions. Even the light filtering through the canopy shifted, taking on colors with no names in human language.

By midday, they reached a river unlike any Asvarr had seen before. Its surface gleamed like polished metal, reflecting the sky with perfect clarity while remaining completely transparent. Beneath the surface, fish with too many fins and phosphorescent scales darted between riverbed stones that formed precise circular patterns.

"The Path of Tears," Yrsa said, kneeling beside the river. "A boundary marker. Beyond this point, we enter the direct influence of the Verdant Five."

She dipped her fingers into the liquid, which clung to her skin like oil before evaporating into mist. "Not water," she explained. "Crystallized sorrow, melted by sunlight each day, reforming each night. The first tears shed when the Tree shattered."

Asvarr squinted against the river's metallic gleam. On the opposite bank, the forest grew even stranger—trees bearing fruit that glowed from within, flowers that moved independently of any breeze, stones arranged in spirals that hurt his eyes to follow.

"Is there a crossing?" he asked, seeing no bridge.

Leif pointed downstream. "There."

Following the boy's direction, Asvarr spotted what appeared to be stepping stones protruding from the liquid surface—perfectly round discs of white stone arranged in a zigzagging pattern across the river. Each stone bore a single rune that glowed faintly blue in the afternoon light.

"Crossing stones," Yrsa confirmed. "But be warned—each demands an offering. A memory freely given."

"More memory sacrifice?" Asvarr frowned. "Haven't we surrendered enough already?"

"The Verdant Five value memory above all else," Yrsa said. "They collect it, study it, use it to maintain their existence across cycles. The stones require only small memories—inconsequential ones—but the principle remains. To cross their boundary, you must surrender something of yourself."

Asvarr approached the first stone cautiously. Its rune brightened as he drew near, the symbol for "childhood" according to his expanded knowledge. Touching it with his transformed hand, he felt a gentle pulling sensation in his mind.

"A childhood memory," he murmured. "Something unimportant."

He selected the memory of his first fishing trip—his father showing him how to bait a hook. Insignificant enough to surrender, he thought. As he focused on the memory, it detached from his mind like a leaf from a branch, leaving behind a small blank space where it had been. The rune flared bright blue, then faded to a satisfied glow.

The stone held his weight as he stepped onto it, solid despite the liquid surrounding it.

"One down," he called back. "Eight more to go."

Each stone demanded a different category of memory—"friendship," "fear," "laughter," "hunger," and so on. Asvarr chose the most inconsequential examples he could think of, memories he could afford to lose. With each offering, another small piece of his past vanished, leaving tiny holes in the fabric of his identity.

When he reached the final stone, marked with the rune for "regret," he hesitated. Any regret significant enough to qualify would be painful to surrender. Yet choosing something too minor might be rejected.

He settled on the regret of a broken promise to a childhood friend—significant enough to register but not so central that its loss would change him. The memory pulled free reluctantly, leaving behind a dull ache rather than emptiness.

Stepping onto the far bank, Asvarr turned to watch Yrsa and Leif make their crossings. Yrsa followed his path with grim determination, surrendering her memories without visible reaction. Leif, however, crossed differently—simply walking across the river's surface as though it were solid ground, leaving faint golden footprints that lingered briefly before dissolving.

"How did he do that?" Asvarr asked when they rejoined him.

"He carries all sorrow," Yrsa explained. "The river recognizes him as kin, not traveler."

Beyond the river, the forest grew increasingly dreamlike. Flowers turned to face them as they passed, their centers revealing eye-like structures that tracked their movement. Trees communicated in creaking conversations just below the threshold of understanding. The ground itself seemed to respond to their footsteps, firmness shifting to accommodate their stride patterns.

Yrsa stiffened suddenly, head tilted as though listening. "We're being followed," she whispered. "From the moment we crossed the river."

Asvarr extended his transformed senses, reaching outward through the forest. He detected movement in multiple directions—swift, coordinated, encircling their position. Something about the presence felt familiar.

"Brynja?" he guessed.

Yrsa shook her head. "Her followers. The masked ones who survived the Vale."

The memory of Brynja's words in his dream echoed: *We'll be waiting.*

"It's an ambush," he realized. "She led us to the river crossing deliberately."

"Perhaps," Yrsa agreed. "Or perhaps they merely watch, ensuring you reach the Gate as agreed."

Leif tugged at Asvarr's sleeve, golden eyes wide. "Ravens come," he warned, pointing skyward.

Through gaps in the canopy, Asvarr glimpsed a dark cloud approaching—dozens of ravens flying in formation, converging on their position. The birds moved with unnatural coordination, forming a shifting pattern that resembled a massive hunting net.

"She's locating us for her followers," Yrsa concluded. "The river crossing must have triggered some alarm."

"Should we run?" Asvarr asked, though he knew the answer already.

"There's nowhere to run. We've entered their territory now." Yrsa readied her crystal knife. "And I suspect Brynja wants to establish terms before you reach the Gate."

The ravens descended through the canopy, filling the surrounding branches with dark shapes and watching eyes. Their harsh calls created a discordant chorus that raised the hair on Asvarr's neck.

From between the trees ahead, figures emerged—men and women in hooded robes woven from living vines, their faces concealed behind wooden masks carved with intricate spiraling patterns. They moved with eerie synchronization, surrounding Asvarr's group in a tightening circle.

One figure stepped forward, taller than the others. Unlike her followers, her face remained uncovered, revealing bark patterns covering half her features and leaves growing among raven-black hair.

Brynja had come to meet them personally.

"Welcome, flame-carrier," she said, amber eyes fixed on Asvarr. "The Verdant Gate awaits."

"Welcome, flame-carrier," Brynja said, her voice resonating with harmonics that reminded Asvarr of wind through hollow branches. "The Verdant Gate awaits."

She had changed since their brief encounter at the Gate. The wooden transformation now covered both arms completely, the left hand elongated into thorn-like claws that clicked together with deliberate menace. Armor of hardened bark encased her torso, curved plates flowing organically over her form like a second skin. The wooden patterns had spread further across her face, now covering most of her left side and threading into her hairline where leaves sprouted among raven-black locks.

Her amber eyes remained unchanged, cold and evaluating.

"You've been busy," Asvarr said, keeping his voice steady despite the tightening in his chest. His fingers rested on his sword hilt, but he didn't draw it—yet. A dozen masked followers surrounded them, and more ravens watched from the branches above.

Brynja stepped closer, her movements fluid despite her wooden limbs. "I wished to speak before we reach the Gate. To establish understanding."

"Understanding of what?" Yrsa positioned herself at Asvarr's shoulder, crystal knife held deliberately visible.

Brynja's gaze flicked to Yrsa with obvious displeasure. "Your presence was unexpected, Memory-Keeper. I had thought you lost in the root-ways."

"Disappointed?" Yrsa asked with false lightness.

"Merely surprised." Brynja returned her attention to Asvarr. "The Verdant Five have tasked me with retrieving what belongs to my bloodline. The Root was promised to the Hrafn clan generations ago—we were its appointed guardians before the sundering."

"And yet it chose me," Asvarr said, matching her cold stare.

Brynja's wooden fingers flexed. "A mistake. An aberration in the pattern. You carry diluted blood—an echo of what was stolen from my line."

Her followers tightened their circle, wooden masks gleaming in the dappled forest light. Each wore robes of woven living vines that shifted subtly, curling and uncurling with their breathing.

"I carry what survived," Asvarr countered. "Blood that kept its promise while yours forgot."

Anger flashed in Brynja's amber eyes. The ravens above cawed in sudden agitation, beating their wings and shifting position. "You know nothing of promises or oaths, flame-carrier. Your ancestors betrayed mine. Slaughtered them on the night of sworn peace. Took what was never theirs to claim."

Asvarr felt heat rising through his chest, the Grímmark pulsing in response to his anger. Golden sap beaded along the bark patterns on his arms.

"I know only what the Root showed me," he said. "Your clan guarded Root, mine guarded Flame. Both necessary for balance. Both part of a whole before the sundering."

"Pretty words." Brynja circled him slowly, her wooden feet making no sound on the forest floor. "Do they ease your conscience when you steal another's birthright?"

Leif moved closer to Asvarr, golden eyes tracking Brynja's movements. The boy seemed oddly unafraid, his form more solid than usual in this boundary place.

"The Root calls both of us," Asvarr said. "That's why we need each other to open the Gate."

"Need," Brynja spat the word. "A temporary arrangement. The Gate requires both bloodlines—this is true. But the binding itself?" Her wooden fingers clicked together. "That requires dominance. Will—not cooperation."

One of her followers stepped forward, offering a wooden bowl filled with thick golden liquid. Brynja dipped her wooden fingers into it, then drew complex patterns in the air that lingered momentarily—glowing shapes that resembled spiraling branches.

"The Verdant Five have shown me truth," she continued, completing the pattern. "Nine cycles of breaking and binding. Nine failures because those chosen lacked purity of purpose. The anchors respond to intent as much as blood."

The air around them grew heavy, charged with building energy. The patterns Brynja had drawn began to pulse, casting eerie light across the forest floor.

"What are you doing?" Yrsa demanded, her voice tight with alarm.

"Securing my claim." Brynja completed a final symbol—a rune Asvarr didn't recognize. "The Verdant Five taught me ways to purify blood, to separate flame from root. To take what was stolen from my line."

Understanding dawned. This was no mere territorial ambush—Brynja intended to extract something from him. The flame essence carried in his blood.

"Stand aside," Asvarr told Yrsa and Leif, drawing his bronze sword. The blade hummed in his grip, veins of gold pulsing in rhythm with his Grímmark. "This was always coming."

Brynja's followers raised their hands in unison. From their sleeves emerged curved blades of polished bone, edges gleaming unnaturally sharp.

"Restrain them," Brynja commanded. "The flame-carrier is mine."

The masked figures converged. Yrsa met the first with her crystal knife, the blade flashing as it sliced through living vines. The mask dropped, revealing a face half-transformed with bark, eyes glowing amber with reflected light.

Leif vanished from Asvarr's side, reappearing between two attackers. His touch sent one collapsing to the ground, their mask crumbling to dust. The other recoiled, swinging wildly with their bone blade.

Three followers rushed Asvarr. He met them with practiced precision, bronze sword cutting through vine robes and bone blades with equal ease. The golden veins in the sword flared brighter with each strike, leaving trails of light in the air.

Through the chaos, Brynja approached steadily, clawed hands extended. The pattern she had drawn followed her like a spectral net, symbols rotating and aligning as she moved.

"The blood calls to blood," she intoned. "Return what was stolen."

Asvarr dispatched his third attacker with a slash that shattered their mask, revealing a terrified human face beneath the transformation. The follower fled into the trees, clutching shattered wooden fragments.

Brynja lunged, wooden claws slashing at Asvarr's chest where the Grímmark pulsed beneath bark-patterned skin. He blocked with his sword, metal meeting wood with a sound like thunder. The impact sent him staggering backward, boots sliding on moss-covered ground.

"The flame was never yours!" Brynja snarled, pressing her attack. Her wooden arms moved faster than human limbs should, claws tearing through the air with deadly precision.

Asvarr parried, countered, fell into the rhythm of combat. His transformed body responded differently than before—faster, more fluid, strength pulsing through bark-covered muscles. Where their limbs connected, golden sap spattered like blood, hissing when it struck the ground.

Around them, the battle continued. Yrsa fought with surprising skill, her crystal knife leaving trails of dust where it touched the followers' wooden transformations. Leif danced between combatants, his touch turning masks to ash, vine robes to withered husks.

"You fight well for a thief," Brynja taunted, circling Asvarr after a flurry of exchanges. A crack ran along her wooden forearm where his blade had connected, golden sap welling from the wound.

"I fight to protect what chose me," Asvarr replied, breathing heavily. His own transformation bled where her claws had found purchase, rivulets of sap trailing down his chest and arms.

"It chose wrong." Brynja's floating pattern suddenly contracted, symbols rushing toward her outstretched hand. She drove her claws into the earth, releasing the gathered energy.

The ground beneath Asvarr erupted. Roots shot upward, tangling around his legs, rapidly climbing his body. He slashed at them with his sword, but for each root severed, three more emerged. Within moments, he stood immobilized from the waist down, the roots tightening with crushing force.

Brynja straightened, satisfaction gleaming in her amber eyes. "The Root remembers its true children."

She approached slowly, wooden claws extended, the gap between them shrinking with each measured step. Asvarr struggled against his bindings, but the roots only tightened further, digging into his flesh where transformation had not yet reached.

"Surrender the flame essence," Brynja commanded, "and your death will be merciful."

From the corner of his eye, Asvarr saw Yrsa pinned against a tree by two followers, crystal knife knocked from her grip. Leif had disappeared entirely—whether fled or hidden, Asvarr couldn't tell.

"You need me alive," he challenged, still struggling. "The Gate won't open to one bloodline alone."

"I need your blood, not your life." Brynja's wooden fingers traced a pattern on his chest, directly over the Grímmark. "The essence can be extracted. The Verdant Five taught me how."

Her wooden palm flattened against his chest. Pain erupted where they touched—burning, tearing pain that reached deep into his core. Asvarr felt something being pulled from him, drawn through skin and muscle toward Brynja's hungry touch.

The Grímmark flared in resistance, golden light spilling from beneath her fingers. Asvarr screamed as conflicting forces warred within him—the mark fighting to retain what Brynja sought to extract.

Through tear-blurred eyes, he saw her face transform with ecstasy and pain. Where her wooden hand connected to his chest, the bark patterns melded together, boundaries between their flesh momentarily erased. Gold and green energy twisted between them, neither able to claim dominance.

"The flame resists!" she hissed through clenched teeth, pressing harder.

The roots tightened further, cracking bark-patterns on Asvarr's legs. His sword slipped from numbed fingers, clattering to the moss-covered ground. Darkness edged his vision as Brynja's extraction continued, stealing his consciousness.

A small shape darted from the underbrush—Leif, eyes blazing golden, trailing light like a comet. The boy pressed his palm against the tangled roots binding Asvarr, causing them to crumble to ash where he touched. One leg freed, then the other.

With desperation-fueled strength, Asvarr shoved Brynja backward, breaking their connection. She staggered, off-balance, clutching her wooden hand which now bore a golden handprint where they had touched.

Asvarr dropped to one knee, gasping for breath, the Grímmark pulsing erratically beneath his damaged transformation. He groped for his sword, fingers closing around the hilt just as Brynja recovered her stance.

"Clever," she snarled. "But futile."

She raised her arms, calling to the surrounding forest. Trees creaked and swayed, roots writhing beneath the soil, responding to her will. The ravens above descended in a dark cloud, talons extended.

A blast of cold air struck them both, sending ravens tumbling through the air. Yrsa stood free of her captors, arms extended, silver light flowing from her fingertips. Her followers lay motionless at the base of the tree, their masks shattered.

"Enough!" Yrsa's voice echoed with power Asvarr hadn't known she possessed. "This benefits neither of you. The binding requires both, willing and whole."

Brynja's amber eyes narrowed. "Stay out of this, Memory-Keeper. Your meddling has cost enough already."

"My meddling?" Yrsa laughed, a sharp sound lacking humor. "Who guided nine cycles of Wardens? Who preserved the knowledge when gods themselves sought to erase it?"

The silver light around her hands intensified. "I have watched you both since before your births. Guided your bloodlines through generations of forgetting. Neither of you stands where you are by accident or theft."

Asvarr struggled to his feet, sword held defensively before him. The Grímmark still burned where Brynja had touched it, the pain radiating outward through his transformed flesh.

"The binding must happen," he said, voice rough with pain. "With or without your cooperation, Brynja."

"The binding will happen," she corrected, "when you accept truth. When you acknowledge the flame essence belongs to my bloodline, stolen by your ancestors during the Betrayal."

Her wounded hand still glowed where their transformation had connected, golden light pulsing beneath wooden fingers. She studied it with a mixture of disgust and fascination.

"Even now, the flame recognizes its rightful vessel," she said more quietly. "It strains toward me."

The marks on Asvarr's chest pulsed in response, sending fresh waves of pain through his body. He felt the connection between them—a bridge formed during their brief melding, allowing something to flow both ways.

"We find the Verdant Gate together," Yrsa proposed, stepping between them. "Perform the binding together. Let the second Anchor choose its Warden."

Brynja's remaining followers gathered around her, masks gleaming in the forest light. The ravens returned to the branches above, watching with unnatural stillness.

"The Gate lies half a day's journey south," Brynja said after a long silence. "My followers will accompany us to ensure no... misunderstandings arise."

She gestured to the path ahead. "You walk in front, flame-carrier. Where I can see you."

Asvarr glanced at Yrsa, who gave him a barely perceptible nod. Leif materialized at his side, small hand slipping into his.

"The binding waits," the boy whispered. "But changes are coming."

Sheathing his sword, Asvarr took the lead, every step sending pain through his damaged transformation. The forest ahead grew stranger still—trees curved in impossible directions, flowers that opened to reveal miniature night skies within their petals, streams that flowed uphill.

Behind him, he felt Brynja's amber gaze burning into his back—hungry, calculating, patient. The journey to the Gate would be tense, but the binding itself promised worse. Only one could emerge as the second Anchor's Warden, despite Yrsa's diplomatic suggestion.

After a half-hour's tense march, they reached another river crossing—wider than the first, its surface gleaming like polished metal in the afternoon light. Instead of stepping stones, a single bridge of twisted roots spanned the gap, wide enough for only one person at a time.

"The Path of Forgotten Oaths," Brynja announced. "The final threshold before the Gate."

She pushed past Asvarr, wooden feet making no sound on the living bridge. "Cross in silence," she instructed. "The river remembers broken promises. Speak, and it answers."

As Asvarr stepped onto the bridge, the wood beneath his feet shivered in recognition. His transformation resonated with the living roots, sending whispers through his mind—fragments of oaths sworn and broken, promises made and forgotten across countless generations.

Halfway across, the whispers coalesced into clarity: two children, a boy and girl, cutting their palms with a small knife, pressing bleeding hands together. *"Blood to blood, flame to root, bound as one until the Tree falls..."*

With chilling certainty, Asvarr recognized his own voice—younger, but unmistakably his—and Brynja's, speaking the words in unison.

He stumbled, nearly losing his footing on the narrow bridge. The memory made no sense. He had never met Brynja before the Shattering. Had never sworn such an oath.

Yet the river remembered, and his blood remembered too.

Reaching the far bank, Asvarr found Brynja waiting, her amber eyes knowing.

"You heard it," she said. "You remember."

"That's impossible," he protested. "We never met before—"

"Before the Shattering? Before this life?" Her wooden fingers clicked together. "The blood remembers what the mind forgets, flame-carrier. We were bound once, in another cycle. Before your ancestors betrayed mine and took what wasn't theirs to claim."

As the others crossed the bridge behind them, Asvarr stared at Brynja with new uncertainty. The connection between them ran deeper than he had imagined, threads of wyrd binding them across time itself.

"The Gate will reveal truth," she said, turning away. "And when it does, you will surrender what was stolen. What has always been mine."

She strode ahead, followers falling in behind her. Asvarr remained motionless, the echo of a forgotten oath reverberating through his transformed flesh, awakening questions without answers.

The Verdant Gate awaited—and with it, a reckoning generations in the making.

CHAPTER 6

DUEL OF VERDANCY

Brynja's wooden fingers curved into claws, stretching toward him with a sound like branches breaking in winter. "The Root was promised to my bloodline generations ago. You're an aberration."

Asvarr eased backward, watching those elongated thorns that had once been human fingertips. Three paces between them. His hand found the hilt of his bronze sword, warm against his palm, golden veins pulsing beneath the metal's surface. He kept his voice steady despite the racing of his heart. "The Root chose me. I never asked for this mark."

"The Root simply followed what was already in your blood," Brynja spat. Her followers tightened their circle around them, wooden masks expressionless, robes of woven vines rustling like whispers. "Our ancestors' betrayal echoes through your veins. Stolen fire carried by thieves."

Yrsa's warning came rushed and urgent beside him. "Her transformation is further along than yours. Don't let her wooden parts touch your flesh."

Brynja laughed, a hollow sound like wind through dead branches. The bark covering half her face contracted, forming patterns like a frozen smile. "Listen to the boundary-walker, flame-thief. I'm what you're becoming."

The first strike came without warning. Brynja lunged, her wooden arm stretching impossibly as thorns slashed through the air where Asvarr's face had been a heartbeat earlier. He rolled sideways, drawing his sword in a fluid arc. The bronze blade hummed, golden veins flaring bright. The masked followers raised curved bone blades but made no move to intervene.

"This is between bloodlines," Brynja said, circling him. "As it always has been."

Asvarr felt the Grímmark pulse on his chest, spreading warmth through his transforming flesh. The bark-patterns on his skin hardened, becoming armor-like. "I don't want to fight you. We both seek the same door."

"A door that requires both our blood." Brynja flexed her wooden fingers. "The Verdant Five have shown me many ways to extract what I need."

She attacked again, a flurry of thorn-strikes that drove Asvarr backward. He parried with his sword, the metal singing against her wooden limbs. Where bronze met transformed flesh, golden sap welled from the cuts, filling the air with a sweet, heady scent.

Overhead, the forest canopy shuddered. Droplets of sap fell like golden rain, sizzling where they struck the ground. With each exchange of blows, more sap dripped from above, as if the forest itself bled from their conflict.

Asvarr ducked beneath a swipe of thorn-claws, countering with an upward strike that sliced across Brynja's bark-armored torso. She hissed in fury, as golden sap leaked from the wound. He pressed forward, finding a rhythm to his movements that felt strange yet natural—his transformed body moving with fluid grace he'd never possessed before.

The masked followers began chanting in a language Asvarr half-understood, the syllables resonating with the pulsing of his Grímmark. The forest floor trembled beneath their feet.

"The Verdant Five sent you to kill me?" Asvarr asked, dodging another strike.

"To reclaim what belongs to us." Brynja's attacks grew more frenzied, her humanlike right arm and wooden left moving in unnerving synchronicity. "Your clan slaughtered mine generations ago, stealing the flame-essence that was our birthright!"

Their dance of blades carried them beneath a massive tree with a trunk wide as ten men standing shoulder-to-shoulder. Its branches drooped low, weeping golden sap that formed curtains of amber light. As they fought beneath its canopy, the sap fell heavier, coating weapons and skin alike.

Asvarr slipped on the golden liquid, his foot sliding from under him. Brynja lunged, wooden claws aiming for his throat. He brought his sword up in desperate defense, the edge catching her forearm with a sound like splintering timber.

Her strike landed regardless, thorns tearing across his shoulder. Pain lanced through him, hot and immediate. Where the thorns had pierced his skin, bark-patterns spread more rapidly, the transformation accelerating.

He rolled away, coming to his feet with his back against the massive trunk. Brynja advanced, golden sap dripping from her wounded arm. Behind her, the masked followers had formed a tight semi-circle, trapping him against the tree.

"Your death will restore balance," Brynja said, her voice taking on harmonic undertones, as if multiple throats spoke at once. "The Root will finally return to its rightful tenders."

Asvarr felt something strange happening where his bleeding shoulder pressed against the tree bark. A connection forming, similar to when he'd bound with the first Anchor but smaller, more localized. The tree was drinking his blood, responding to what it found there.

"Your blood knows the truth even if you don't," he said, an instinct driving his words. "We were never meant to be enemies."

"Lies won't save you, flame-thief."

When she attacked again, Asvarr didn't raise his sword. Instead, he twisted sideways, letting her momentum carry her past him. His bleeding shoulder smeared across the trunk, leaving a crimson trail that the tree absorbed greedily. Brynja's wooden arm struck the trunk where he had been, thorns embedding deep in the bark.

For one heartbeat, nothing happened.

Then the tree *moved*.

***

Bark rippled like water where their blood mingled. Brynja yanked at her embedded arm, panic flashing across the human half of her face. Roots erupted from the ground, twisting around their ankles. The canopy above writhed, branches stretching and contorting as if in agony.

"What have you done?" Brynja's voice lost its harmonic quality, becoming purely human—and terrified.

"Not me," Asvarr gasped, equally stunned. "*Us.*"

Where their blood mixed on the trunk, the bark split open. Golden sap poured forth, but instead of falling to the ground, it flowed upward, defying nature. It formed intricate, impossible patterns in the air between them—spirals and whorls that reminded Asvarr of the runestone's markings.

Flowers erupted from the tree's branches—blooms that had no business growing from such ancient wood. They unfurled with impossible speed, petals splaying wide to reveal centers that pulsed with golden light. And from those blossoms came whispers, countless voices speaking just below the threshold of understanding.

One of Brynja's masked followers dropped to their knees. "The Remembering," the figure gasped, voice muffled by wood. "It begins!"

Another follower pulled their mask aside, revealing a face half-transformed like Brynja's. "The blood recognizes itself! The sundered lines reconnect!"

The golden sap patterns hovering between Asvarr and Brynja began to spin, faster and faster, becoming a disc of molten light. In its rotating surface, images flickered—memories neither of them possessed, yet both somehow recognized.

Children playing near a boundary stone marked with spiral carvings—one fair-haired boy, one dark-haired girl, laughing as they chased each other through tall grass.

An ancient ceremony, two clan leaders standing before their assembled people, each cutting their palm with a ceremonial knife. "Blood binds where words cannot," they intoned together, clasping bloodied hands above a sapling barely taller than the children watching wide-eyed from the front row.

The same two children, older now but still unmistakable, pricking their thumbs with bone needles, pressing the wounds together. "We will never forget," they promised each other, unaware of the adults watching from shadows with expressions of approval.

Asvarr stared at the memories swirling in the golden disc, recognition striking him like a physical blow. The fair-haired boy was *him*—or someone who could have been him, generations removed. And the dark-haired girl with amber eyes...

"That's us," Brynja whispered, her expression mirroring his shock. Her wooden arm remained embedded in the trunk, but she no longer pulled against it. "Not us, but..."

"Our ancestors," Asvarr finished. "Before the sundering of our lines."

The spinning disc pulsed brighter. More memories flooded between them, pouring directly from blood to blood through the conduit of the ancient tree.

Village gatherings where clan members with fair hair tended fires while dark-haired folk sang to plants, encouraging growth. People working together in harmony, each with their own gifts but united in purpose.

A circle of standing stones where children underwent their first markings—some receiving flame sigils etched in red, others adorned with green vine patterns—all part of the same community, the same tradition.

A hall feast where elders from both bloodlines sat at the same table, raising horns to toast the continued prosperity of their unified people, "Guardians of the World Tree's balance—flame and root in harmony."

With each new vision, the whispering from the flowers grew louder, forming words Asvarr could almost understand. The Grímmark on his chest throbbed painfully, and he saw answering pulses of light beneath the bark covering half of Brynja's torso—her own mark responding.

"I don't understand," Brynja said, confusion replacing hostility in her voice. "The Verdant Five told me your ancestors betrayed mine—slaughtered our people and stole the flame-essence that was never meant to be theirs."

"And I was taught that the northlands were always our territory," Asvarr replied, equally bewildered. "That we had no connection to the southern forests or their people."

One of the whispering flowers grew larger than the others, its petals spreading wide to reveal a center that glowed red-gold like a forge's heart. When it spoke, the voice was neither male nor female, but ancient beyond reckoning.

"Blood remembers what minds forget and tongues deny," it intoned. *"The sundering was necessary but never meant to be permanent. Fire without root burns wild; root without fire strangles life. Balance broken for nine cycles—the pattern fractures further with each turning."*

The spinning disc of golden sap between them pulsed once more, then shattered into countless droplets that hung suspended in the air. Each droplet contained a fragment of memory—too many to process, overwhelming in their multitude.

The droplets flew at Asvarr and Brynja simultaneously, striking their skin and sinking beneath the surface. Memory flooded them both—raw, unfiltered knowledge pouring directly into their blood.

Asvarr fell to his knees, gasping as images cascaded through his mind. He saw the truth of what had happened between their clans—not betrayal as both sides claimed, but sacrifice. A deliberate sundering to preserve both bloodlines when disaster struck. The flame-keepers fleeing north, the root-tenders seeking refuge in southern forests, each carrying half of what had once been whole.

And with the memories came understanding: the Verdant Gate had never been meant for one bloodline alone. It required both—flame and root in harmony, just as the ancestors had been before necessity tore them apart.

Across from him, Brynja had collapsed against the tree trunk, her wooden arm still embedded in the bark. Her eyes were wide, tears flowing freely down the human half of her face while golden sap leaked from the wooden half.

"They lied to us," she whispered. "Our entire history..."

Before Asvarr could respond, the massive tree shuddered violently. Branches twisted and elongated with audible creaking. The whispering flowers began to shriek, their voices rising to a deafening chorus. The ground heaved beneath them.

"Too much!" Yrsa shouted, rushing toward them from where she'd been watching with Leif. "The memory-awakening is too strong! It will shatter the boundary!"

The masked followers scattered in panic as roots burst from the ground, whipping through the air like tentacles. One caught a fleeing figure, dragging them screaming into the churning earth.

Asvarr struggled to his feet, fighting against the continuing flood of memories threatening to drown his consciousness. He stumbled toward Brynja, who remained trapped against the trunk.

"We have to stop this," he gasped, extending his hand toward her. "Together."

She looked at his outstretched fingers, confusion and revelation warring on her face. The wooden half of her features had begun to shift, the bark patterns rearranging themselves into something less alien, more purposeful.

"How can I trust you?" she asked, even as another of her followers was swept away by thrashing roots.

"You've seen the truth. We both have." Asvarr kept his hand extended, feeling the Grímmark pulse in rhythm with his racing heart. "Our bloodlines were meant to work together. Flame and root. Balance."

Around them, the forest was tearing itself apart in response to their awakened blood. Trees twisted into impossible shapes, flowers bloomed and withered in seconds, earth heaved in waves like a stormy sea. The boundary between realms was growing dangerously thin—Asvarr could see glimpses of other places flickering at the edges of his vision.

Brynja stared at his hand a moment longer, then slowly raised her human arm. Her fingers trembled, hovering just short of touching his.

"If this is another deception..." she began.

"It's not," Asvarr said with certainty born from the flood of ancestral memory. "We've both been deceived for generations. But the blood remembers."

Her fingers closed around his wrist just as his clasped hers—the age-old gesture of warriors and oath-makers. The moment their skin touched, a shock ran through them both, and the chaos around them paused for one stretched heart-beat.

Then the tree's trunk split open entirely, golden sap gushing forth in a torrent that engulfed them both.

The world dissolved into light.

Golden sap engulfed Asvarr and Brynja, boiling around them in a cocoon of molten light. The forest twisted beyond recognition, trees stretching toward skies that fractured into multiple realities. Asvarr fought to remain conscious as ancestral memories flooded his mind—too many, too fast, threatening to drown his sense of self.

He crashed to his knees in the churning sap, still gripping Brynja's wrist. Her other arm remained fused to the ancient tree, bark rippling up to her shoulder. Through the golden haze, he saw her face contorted in the same overwhelming pain he felt—the human half twisted in agony, the wooden half cracking with the strain.

"Make it stop," she gasped, her voice stripped of harmonics, purely human in its desperation.

Asvarr couldn't answer. His lungs burned, filled with the thick scent of sap and centuries-old memories. The Grímmark on his chest blazed like a forge-fire, spreading tendrils across his skin that mirrored the tree's roots. His vision swam with images from a shared past neither of them had lived:

A great hall where clan leaders passed a horn etched with dual sigils—flame and root intertwined. Children with mixed bloodlines playing games that trained both affinities. Warriors with flame-marks fighting alongside healers with root-bindings.

The flow of memories cascaded faster until individual visions blurred into a torrent of sensations—brotherhood, unity, purpose. Guardianship. Two bloodlines sworn to a single cause: the protection of Yggdrasil's balance.

Then came the fracture.

A council meeting interrupted by messengers bearing news of catastrophe. Arguments, accusations. A decision made in desperation—two clans separating to protect what remained of their sacred charge. Flame-keepers traveling north, root-tenders south. Sorrow of the sundering. Promises to reunify when the danger passed.

Then, *betrayal from outside. Figures in shadows manipulating events to ensure the separation became permanent. Deliberate falsification of history, generation by generation, until neither clan remembered the truth of their unity.*

The golden sap bubble burst, throwing them apart. Asvarr rolled through dead leaves and exposed roots, coming to rest against a fallen log. His lungs heaved as he gulped fresh air. Across the small clearing, Brynja had collapsed in a heap, her wooden arm finally torn free from the tree trunk, leaving a raw wound in the bark that leaked more sap.

***

The forest continued its violent thrashing, but with less intensity now—trees settling into new, twisted forms; flowers that had erupted in the memory-surge now withering as quickly as they'd bloomed. The masked followers had scattered or been consumed by the chaos. Only Yrsa remained, holding Leif protectively behind her as she watched the two fallen combatants.

"The remembering," Yrsa murmured, her eyes wide. "I've never witnessed one so powerful."

Asvarr struggled to his knees, then his feet, leaning against the fallen log for support. His mind felt scraped raw, invaded by memories not his own yet irrevocably part of him now. The Grímmark had spread further, bark-like patterns now covering most of his torso and creeping onto his neck.

"We were one people," he said, the words tasting foreign on his tongue. "Guardians of the World Tree."

Brynja pushed herself up on her elbows, leaves and twigs tangled in her hair. The wooden half of her face had changed, the patterns less chaotic, more like deliberate carvings—sigils and spirals that matched some on Asvarr's sword.

"The Verdant Five lied to me," she said, voice hollow. "They told me your ancestors slaughtered mine, stole our birthright."

"And I was taught that the northern clans had always been separate from the southlands." Asvarr touched the Grímmark on his chest, feeling it pulse with a rhythm no longer solely his own. "Both lies."

"Necessary lies, perhaps," Yrsa interjected, stepping forward with Leif trailing behind her. "Or what began as necessary protection became corrupted over time."

Brynja's gaze snapped to Yrsa. "You knew." It wasn't a question.

Yrsa's shoulders dropped slightly. "I suspected. The boundary-forest preserves fragments of many truths, but even I cannot access all memories." She gestured to the now-calming tree that had revealed so much. "Some truths require specific bloodlines to unlock them."

Asvarr studied Brynja with new understanding. The hatred that had fueled their combat had evaporated, replaced by confusion and a strange sense of connection he couldn't deny. They were the last remnants of a unified people, torn apart by circumstances neither had known existed.

"The Verdant Gate," he said, recalling fragments from the flood of memories. "It was never meant for one bloodline alone."

Brynja nodded slowly, pushing herself to her feet. Her transformed left arm hung at her side, wooden fingers flexing experimentally as if testing their new-found freedom from the tree.

"The Gate requires both fire and root in harmony," she agreed, sounding dazed. "They raised me to believe I could take what I needed from you by force, but..."

"The blood recognizes itself," Asvarr finished. "What was sundered seeks to reunite."

A heavy silence fell between them, broken only by the occasional creak of settling trees. The forest appeared permanently altered by their conflict and the subsequent memory-awakening. Paths that had once been straight now curved impossibly; flowers bloomed in colors that had no names; roots formed spiraling patterns across the forest floor that resembled the runestone's markings.

Brynja finally broke the silence. "My entire life has been dedicated to reclaiming what I thought was stolen." Her human hand clenched into a fist. "Everything I've endured, every part of myself I've sacrificed to the transformation... for vengeance against a betrayal that never happened."

Asvarr understood that rage all too well. His own life had been defined by the destruction of his clan, by the burning need to find meaning in their deaths. Now, with ancestral memories swirling through his blood, he felt pulled in contradictory directions—honored to carry forward a legacy far older than he'd known, yet adrift without the certainties that had anchored him.

"We both lost our people," he said quietly. "That truth remains, even if the reasons differ from what we believed."

Brynja's eyes—one human, one sap-filled—fixed on him with piercing intensity. "Do you still seek the second Root Anchor?"

"Yes." Asvarr's answer came without hesitation. "Now more than ever. But not to control it or claim it for a single bloodline. To understand what we were truly meant to guard."

An unspoken question hung between them: Would they continue this quest as enemies, or as something else?

Before either could answer, Leif stepped forward, breaking free from Yrsa's protective grip. The boy moved with uncharacteristic confidence, approaching Brynja without the slightest hesitation. His golden-flecked eyes fixed on her wooden arm with fascination rather than fear.

"You're like me," he said, voice clear and steady.

Brynja's expression flickered between wariness and surprise. "What do you mean, child?"

Leif reached out, touching her wooden fingers with his small, human hand. "Half here, half elsewhere."

The moment their skin connected, a ripple passed through Brynja's transformed arm. The wood seemed to soften momentarily, then resharpened into more deliberate patterns—less chaotic, more purposeful. Brynja gasped, staring at her changed limb.

"How did you—"

"I was born when the Tree shattered," Leif said simply, as if that explained everything. "I exist across boundaries."

Yrsa moved forward, her expression cautious. "The boy has abilities we don't fully understand. He was found wandering the aftermath of the Shattering—no parents, no home, simply... there."

Brynja studied Leif with newfound interest. "The Verdant Five spoke of such children—born in the moment of breaking, carrying fragments of the original pattern within them." She flexed her wooden fingers, now moving more fluidly after Leif's touch. "They are rare. Precious."

"And dangerous," Yrsa added, "to those who wish to maintain the separation of realms."

Asvarr watched the exchange in silence, noting how Brynja's demeanor had shifted. The predatory tension had left her stance; the harmonics had faded from her voice. She appeared more human despite her physical transformation—or perhaps more authentic to whatever new form she was becoming.

"I cannot return to the Verdant Five," Brynja said abruptly, still looking at Leif. "Not after learning they deliberately deceived me."

"Then what will you do?" Asvarr asked.

Brynja turned to him, studying his face as if seeing it clearly for the first time. "The Verdant Gate still waits. It still requires both our bloodlines." She paused, struggling visibly with her next words. "I propose an alliance. Not friendship, not yet trust, but common purpose."

***

Asvarr considered her offer. The memories they'd shared made it impossible to view her as purely enemy, yet centuries of separation and recent combat left him wary. Still, the blood remembers what minds forget—and his blood recognized hers as kin, despite everything.

"An alliance," he agreed cautiously. "To reach the Gate together, to understand what our ancestors intended before the sundering."

Yrsa stepped between them, her green robes swirling around her ankles. "Such an alliance requires more than words, especially between bloodlines with broken trust. It requires binding."

"What kind of binding?" Asvarr asked.

"Blood-oath," Brynja answered immediately. "As our ancestors did." She held up her human hand. "My blood carries root-memory; yours carries flame-essence. Together, they remember what we've forgotten."

The proposition hung in the air, weighty with implications. A blood-oath was the most serious of commitments—binding wyrd itself, creating connections that transcended physical distance and even death.

Asvarr's gaze moved from Brynja to Yrsa to Leif, then back to Brynja. The blood-oath would bind them, perhaps irrevocably, to a shared path. After generations of separation, their bloodlines would reconnect—for how long, and to what end, remained uncertain.

"I accept," he said finally. "Blood to blood, oath to oath."

Relief flickered across Brynja's face—so brief he might have imagined it. She drew a small curved knife from her belt, its blade darkened with age. "This belonged to my grandmother, who received it from hers. Its edge has tasted the blood of my line for nine generations."

Asvarr unsheathed his bronze sword, the golden veins within it pulsing in time with his heartbeat. "And this has carried my blood since the first binding."

They approached each other slowly, caution and necessity mingled in equal measure. When they stood within arm's reach, Brynja held out her knife, handle first. Asvarr accepted it, then offered his sword to her with the same gesture.

"Your blood by my blade, my blood by yours," she said formally. "As it was done before the sundering."

Asvarr remembered the ritual now, pulled from the flood of ancestral memory. He drew Brynja's knife across his palm with deliberate pressure, opening a crimson line that immediately welled with blood. Across from him, Brynja used his bronze sword to slice her human palm, mirroring his action precisely.

The moment their blooded palms connected, a jolt passed between them—a controlled current of shared memory and purpose. The Grímmark on Asvarr's chest pulsed once, and he saw an answering flare from beneath the bark covering Brynja's torso.

"Blood recognizes blood," they spoke in unison, words pulled from shared ancestry. "What was sundered seeks harmony. Fire and root, flame and growth, storm and seed—separate strengths united in purpose."

The oath hung in the air between them, binding in ways that transcended the physical. Asvarr felt a connection forming—a thread linking his consciousness to Brynja's, tenuous but undeniable.

When they released their grip, both palms bore identical marks—swirling patterns that combined flame and root sigils into a unified design.

Leif stepped forward again, touching the fresh marks with curious fingers. "The pattern remembers," he said solemnly. "Even when people forget."

Asvarr looked to Yrsa, who watched the ceremony with an unreadable expression. "Will you guide us to the Verdant Gate?" he asked her.

She nodded slowly. "My purpose has always been to preserve knowledge across the cycles. Perhaps this alliance is what was needed all along." Her gaze shifted to include Brynja. "But we must move quickly. The Verdant Five will sense the blood-oath and the memory-awakening. They have spent centuries maintaining the separation of your bloodlines."

"Why?" Brynja demanded. "What purpose does our division serve?"

"That," Yrsa said grimly, "is what we must discover at the Gate itself." She glanced at the transformed forest around them. "The boundary grows thin here. We cannot linger."

Asvarr felt a shiver pass through him at her words. The forest had settled into its new configuration, but an underlying wrongness remained—paths that curved back on themselves, flowers that whispered in voices almost familiar, shadows that moved independently of their casters.

"We'll need to retrieve my followers who survived," Brynja said. "They're loyal to me, not the Verdant Five."

"Can they be trusted?" Asvarr asked.

Brynja touched her wooden arm where Leif had changed it. "They're like me—transformed by choice and necessity. They deserve the truth as much as I did."

The blood-oath mark on Asvarr's palm tingled, a physical reminder of their new alliance. Nine generations of separation would not be undone in a single moment, but they had taken the first step. Whether their unified bloodline would prove stronger than the forces that had torn it apart remained to be seen.

One certainty remained: the Verdant Gate waited, and with it, answers to questions neither had known to ask until today.

CHAPTER 7

THE SAPBORN ORACLE

B rynja's surviving followers emerged from the transformed forest like spirits materializing from mist. Three masked figures, their vine robes torn and scorched, knelt before her without speaking. The blood-oath mark on Asvarr's palm tingled as he watched the silent exchange, a reminder of the bond newly forged between ancient enemies.

"Rise," Brynja commanded, her voice missing the harmonics that had resonated through it during their battle. "The path changes. The truth changes with it."

The tallest follower removed their wooden mask, revealing a face half-transformed like Brynja's—bark patterns spreading from jawline to temple, one eye clouded with amber sap. "The memory-awakening," she said. "We felt it even at the forest's edge. The trees screamed with remembering."

"Everything we've been told was lies," Brynja said, flexing her wooden fingers—more articulated now after Leif's touch. "Our bloodline and his were never enemies but halves of the same whole."

The unmasked follower's gaze flicked toward Asvarr, suspicion warring with curiosity. "You've made peace with the flame-thief?"

"Blood-oath," Brynja answered, raising her marked palm. "And he is no thief. The Verdant Five deceived us all."

Asvarr watched the news ripple through the small group—shoulders stiffening, masked faces turning toward each other in silent communication. Two decades of warrior instinct told him to track every movement, catalog every potential threat. The oath-mark on his palm burned hotter, and he realized with a start that he could feel Brynja's emotions through it—her tension, her uncertainty beneath the commanding exterior.

His gaze found Yrsa, who stood apart with Leif partially hidden behind her robes. Her face remained impassive, but her fingers tapped rhythmically against her crystal pendant.

"We must reach the Oracle before the Verdant Five discover what has happened," Brynja announced, breaking the fragile silence. "The blood-oath will have sent ripples through the boundary. They'll know something has changed."

"The Oracle?" the unmasked follower asked. "The sap-speaker hasn't granted audience in seven cycles. Even the Five approach with caution."

"The Oracle will see us," Brynja insisted. "The joining of sundered bloodlines changes everything." She turned to Asvarr, acknowledging him directly. "We need the sap-speaker's wisdom to understand what must be done next."

Asvarr touched the Grímmark on his chest, now spreading visibly up his neck in branching patterns. "What is this Oracle?"

"A fragment of the Tree's first consciousness," Brynja explained. "When Yggdrasil shattered, the first drops of sap that fell contained more than mere essence. They carried memories, awareness. One such drop formed the Sapborn Oracle."

She gestured toward the forest's depths, where trees grew increasingly twisted, their branches forming impossible geometries that hurt the eye to follow. "The Oracle witnesses all cycles, remembers what came before the sundering of our bloodlines."

"And will guide us to the Verdant Gate?" Asvarr asked.

"If anything can," Brynja confirmed.

Asvarr weighed the proposal, acutely aware of Yrsa's watchful gaze. The boundary-walker had warned him of the Thorned Vale's dangers, yet she hadn't objected to Brynja's suggestion. If anything, she seemed expectant.

"How far?" he asked.

"A day's journey if the paths remain stable," Brynja replied. "Longer if the Vale shifts. We should move quickly."

Decision made, Asvarr nodded, adjusting the bronze sword at his hip. Ancestral memories still swirled behind his thoughts—fragments of knowledge from generations he'd never known existed. The Oracle might provide context for these broken recollections, might help him understand the true purpose of the bloodlines.

"Lead on," he said.

The Thorned Vale grew more alien with each step deeper into its heart. Trees twisted into double helixes; flowers bloomed with multiple centers arranged in runic patterns; the very ground seemed to pulse with a subtle rhythm that matched the beating of Asvarr's heart. Brynja led their procession with confident strides, her transformed arm sometimes reaching out to touch passing trees, leaving faint luminescent prints that faded minutes later.

Her three followers encircled Asvarr, Yrsa, and Leif with watchful caution. The unmasked one had introduced herself as Kára, second to Brynja in the Thorn Guard. The other two remained silent sentinels, their masks betraying nothing of their thoughts or faces.

"How did you come to the Vale?" Asvarr asked Brynja as they navigated a peculiar passage where trees grew horizontally, forming a tunnel of trunks and branches.

She glanced back, her human eye reflecting golden light from the phosphorescent moss covering the tunnel walls. "The same way you did. Through loss."

Before Asvarr could press further, Leif darted forward suddenly, placing himself directly in their path. The boy pointed to a section of tunnel wall that appeared identical to the rest.

"Wrong way," he announced with uncharacteristic firmness. "The in-between grows thin here."

"The child is right," Yrsa confirmed, studying the wall with narrowed eyes. "A fold in the boundary. If we continue, we'd enter a different realm entirely."

Brynja frowned, approaching the section Leif indicated. "I've traveled this path before. The Oracle always lies beyond the twisted copse."

"The Vale shifts," Kára reminded her, touching the bark-covered portion of her face thoughtfully. "Especially after a memory-awakening."

Asvarr felt a strange tugging from the Grímmark on his chest, a pull toward a seemingly solid section of tunnel wall opposite where Leif stood. Following the sensation, he pressed his palm against the bark. It felt warm, alive, and most surprisingly—hollow.

"Here," he said. "There's a passage."

Brynja joined him, placing her wooden hand beside his. Where their skin met, the bark rippled like water disturbed by a thrown stone. The sensation of her emotions flooded him again through the blood-oath mark—skepticism giving way to surprise, then cautious agreement.

"You feel it too," he said quietly.

She nodded. "The blood remembers the way, even when the mind forgets."

"Or when the way itself changes," Yrsa added, ushering Leif to her side. "The Vale responds to your unified blood now."

At Brynja's command, Kára and the masked followers pressed their weight against the section of wall. The bark gave way with surprising ease, peeling back to reveal a narrow passage flooded with golden light. Sap dripped from the ceiling in perfect spheres that hovered momentarily before drifting to the floor, where they dissolved into the soil.

"I've never seen this path," Brynja admitted, wonder softening her voice.

"Because it didn't exist until your bloodlines reunited," Yrsa explained, adjusting her green robes as she prepared to enter. "The Vale remembers what was forgotten. It reshapes itself accordingly."

They entered the golden passage single file, Brynja leading with Asvarr close behind. The air grew thicker, sweeter, filled with the scent of sap and ancient wood. The Grímmark pulsed rhythmically beneath Asvarr's tunic, a counterpoint to his heartbeat.

"How did the Verdant Five find you?" he asked Brynja, wanting to understand his reluctant ally better.

A lengthy silence followed, broken only by their footsteps and the soft plinking of sap droplets hitting the ground. When Brynja finally spoke, her voice carried a weight Asvarr hadn't heard before.

"I was twelve when the shadow came to our village," she said. "The same darkness that destroyed your clan struck ours as well, though we didn't know it then. I was gathering herbs in the forest when it happened—a task I hated and often shirked. That disobedience saved my life."

She ducked beneath a low-hanging branch that wept sap like tears. "When I returned, everything was ash. Everyone gone. I wandered for days, half-mad with grief and hunger. On the third night, the Five found me collapsed beside a stream."

"They knew what you were," Asvarr surmised. "That you carried the root-tender bloodline."

"They'd been watching our village for generations, they said. Protecting us from afar." Bitterness crept into her voice. "They told me your clan had finally found us—that northern flame-bearers had destroyed my people to eliminate the last pure root-bloodline."

"Both our clans were attacked on the same day," Asvarr said, the revelation striking him like a physical blow. "By the same enemy."

"Someone wanted both bloodlines extinguished," Yrsa agreed from behind them. "Or scattered beyond recovery."

The passage widened into a small clearing where the trees grew in a perfect circle, their branches intertwined to form a domed canopy dripping with golden sap. At the center stood a pool of amber liquid, its surface undisturbed despite the continuous drip from above.

Brynja paused at the pool's edge, her expression solemn. "The Five took me in. Raised me. Trained me in root-lore and transformation crafts. They taught me that I was the last pure bearer of my bloodline, destined to reclaim what was stolen."

"And you believed them," Asvarr said, with understanding born from shared manipulation.

"They were all I had," Brynja replied simply. "After years of training, they revealed their greater purpose—that I was to become the Root's true vessel when the time came. That my body would house the consciousness of the fallen Tree, guiding its rebirth."

She gazed into the amber pool, her reflection fragmented by slow ripples. "They encouraged my transformation, celebrated each expansion of the Root's influence on my flesh. The wooden arm, the bark-face—all signs of my readiness, they said."

"To be consumed," Yrsa murmured. "Not to partner with the Root, but to be overtaken by it."

Brynja's human hand clenched into a fist. "When reports came of a northern clan survivor bearing the flame mark, they sent me to find you, to extract what I needed by force if necessary."

"And now?" Asvarr asked, watching her closely.

"Now I question everything," she admitted. "The memory-awakening showed me truths the Five never shared. If they lied about our bloodlines' history, what else have they concealed? What is their true purpose for me—for us both?"

The amber pool rippled more actively, tiny whirlpools forming on its surface. Leif approached the edge, crouching to stare into the depths with intense fascination.

"It's waking," the boy announced.

"We should continue," Brynja said, straightening her shoulders. "The Oracle's grove lies just beyond the next passage."

As they prepared to move on, Kára stepped closer to Asvarr, her partially transformed face impossible to read.

"She was the best of us," the follower said quietly. "The most devoted to our cause. This alliance with you—it costs her more than you know."

Asvarr touched the blood-oath mark on his palm. "I can feel some of what it costs her," he said. "The question is whether the truth is worth the price."

"Truth is always worth the price," Yrsa interjected, her crystal pendant glowing faintly in the golden light. "Though sometimes we don't recognize its value until long after we've paid."

They continued through another passage, narrower than the first, where the walls themselves seemed to breathe. The bark expanded and contracted in slow, deliberate motions, forcing them to time their progress carefully or risk being caught in the constriction.

"The Five spoke often of the Oracle," Brynja explained as they navigated the breathing passage. "But they approached only in groups, never alone. They feared its knowledge, I think, even as they sought its guidance."

"What exactly is it?" Asvarr asked, pressing himself flat against the wall as it exhaled.

"A consciousness born from the first sap that fell when Yggdrasil shattered," Brynja said. "Neither tree nor entity, but something between. It speaks with many voices, sees through many eyes. The Five claim it's merely a fragment, useful but limited. I've always suspected they understate its importance."

They emerged from the breathing passage into a vast clearing unlike anything Asvarr had seen before. The ground sloped gently downward into a perfect bowl-shaped depression. At its center grew a single tree with a trunk as wide as ten men standing shoulder to shoulder. Unlike the twisted growths throughout the Vale, this tree grew straight and tall—but its bark was translucent, revealing golden sap flowing through complex channels within, like blood through veins.

Most striking was the massive hollow at its center—a cavity large enough to hold a dozen people, filled with glowing amber that pulsed with inner light. As they approached, Asvarr saw movement within the amber—shapes forming and dissolving, fragments of faces that appeared and vanished too quickly to identify.

"The Sapborn Oracle," Brynja said, her voice dropping to a reverent whisper.

Kára and the masked followers immediately dropped to their knees, heads bowed. Even Yrsa inclined her head respectfully. Only Leif seemed unaffected, staring at the great tree with open curiosity rather than awe.

"How do we speak with it?" Asvarr asked.

"We don't," Brynja replied. "It speaks to us, if it chooses. Sometimes through visions, sometimes through voice, sometimes through memory itself." She glanced sideways at him. "The blood-oath may help. The Oracle responds to patterns it recognizes."

Asvarr felt the Grímmark pulse beneath his tunic, stronger here than anywhere else in the Vale. The mark on his palm burned in sympathetic rhythm. Something about this place resonated with the transformations taking place within his body.

"What exactly did the Verdant Five want from the Oracle?" he asked, trying to understand the forces that had shaped Brynja's life.

A shadow passed over her human features. "Confirmation. Guidance. They sought knowledge of the 'pattern's next turning,' whatever that meant." She hesitated. "And they asked about vessels—which bloodlines would prove most receptive to the Root's consciousness."

"They were looking for you," Asvarr realized. "Or someone like you."

"Perhaps both of us," Brynja replied grimly. "The Five always spoke of the Root requiring a vessel, but what if the flame aspect needs one too? What if they planned for both bloodlines to be consumed?"

Before Asvarr could respond, the amber heart of the Oracle pulsed brighter. The shapes within began moving more deliberately, coalescing into forms that held their integrity longer. A sound emanated from the tree, something between wind through leaves and water over stones.

Brynja stepped forward, raising both her human and wooden hands in formal greeting. "Great Oracle, born of the first falling, we seek your wisdom in a time of awakening. The sundered bloodlines stand before you, reunited after nine cycles of separation."

The amber pulsed again, brighter still. The shapes within swirled faster, forming a vortex of golden light. Then, with surprising suddenness, the movement stopped. The amber stilled. Silence fell across the grove.

A face formed in the amber—androgynous, ageless, its features fluid yet distinct. Eyes opened, spiraling vortices of golden light. The tree's hollow expanded, the amber within receding to create a passage leading into the heart of the Oracle itself.

"Enter," a voice commanded, resonating directly within their minds. "The sundered bloodlines have questions. We have waited nine cycles to provide answers."

Asvarr and Brynja exchanged a glance, the blood-oath mark burning on both their palms. Without words, they understood their shared course. Together, they stepped forward, crossing the threshold into the Oracle's heart.

Asvarr stepped into the amber heart of the Oracle, the substance parting around his body like thick honey. It clung to his skin, vibrating with awareness. The Grímmark on his chest flared with golden light, visible even through his tunic. Beside him, Brynja's wooden arm glowed from within, the bark patterns shifting into more deliberate formations.

Inside the tree's hollow, the amber deepened to a rich copper hue. The walls pulsed with slow, deliberate rhythm—a massive heartbeat. Tiny motes of golden light swirled around them, responding to their movements like curious fish investigating intruders in their pond.

"We stand before you, Oracle," Brynja called, her voice oddly muffled by the thick amber atmosphere. "Sundered bloodlines reunited after nine cycles of separation."

The amber thickened around them, pressing against Asvarr's chest until breathing became laborious. The blood-oath mark on his palm burned fiercely, and through it, he felt Brynja's spike of alarm mirroring his own. Then, just as suddenly, the pressure released.

The center of the hollow ignited with blinding golden light. When Asvarr's vision cleared, the amber had receded to the walls, leaving them standing in a perfect spherical chamber. The inner surface rippled with movement—countless faces forming and dissolving, mouths opening in silent speech.

A voice spoke—or rather, many voices layered atop each other, creating a chorus that resonated directly within Asvarr's skull.

"The sundered joins. The broken mends. After nine cycles, the pattern shifts."

The faces on the walls solidified, each holding its form longer. Asvarr recognized none of them individually, yet collectively they triggered something deep in his ancestral memory—figures from the shared vision during their blood mingling.

Brynja stepped forward, her back straight despite the clear awe in her voice. "Great Oracle, we seek understanding. The memories we've shared show our bloodlines were once unified in purpose. What truth has been hidden from us?"

The amber walls shimmered. New faces emerged—stern figures with elaborate wooden crowns and robes woven from living vines. Five distinct visages arranged in a pentagon pattern.

"The Verdant Five," the chorus voice intoned. "Not what they claim to be."

Brynja's human hand clenched into a fist. "What are they then? Druids who raised me, trained me—"

"Not druids," the voices interrupted, the faces on the walls morphing into more ancient, primal versions of the five figures. "Original shapers. Branch-tenders. Those who guided the first growth of Yggdrasil's canopy."

The images shifted again, showing the five figures standing before a younger, smaller version of the World Tree, their hands raised as they directed its growth with elaborate gestures.

"Immortals," the voices continued. "Slumbering through ages until the Shattering awakened them. Now they seek to control the rebirth, to shape the pattern according to their design."

Asvarr's mind reeled with the revelation. "These beings raised you?" he asked Brynja. "They're not druidic descendants but the original shapers themselves?"

The bark-side of Brynja's face hardened, tiny cracks forming as her expression tightened. "They never claimed immortality, but they spoke of 'preserving knowledge across cycles.' I assumed it meant their order had maintained traditions."

The walls pulsed brighter, drawing their attention back to the shifting faces.

"They fear what they cannot control," the voices whispered. "The flame and root united pose the greatest threat to their designs. What was sundered by necessity, they kept divided by deception."

Memories flooded Asvarr's mind—the ancestral visions showing the original separation of their bloodlines, how it began as protective necessity during some ancient crisis. But the images continued, showing shadowy figures manipulating events across generations, ensuring the bloodlines remained apart through deliberate falsification of history, strategic placement of antagonists, even occasional direct intervention.

"The Verdant Five engineered our continued separation," Asvarr realized aloud. "But why?"

The amber swirled violently, faces distorting in what might have been anger or sorrow. The voices rose to a near-painful crescendo.

"Balance prevents control. Unified bloodlines create a pattern they cannot shape. Your ancestors maintained equilibrium—flame providing transformation, root ensuring continuity. Together, they limited the shapers' influence."

Images flashed across the walls—ancient guardians with dual markings of flame and root standing vigilant at key locations throughout Yggdrasil. Each place they guarded showed subtle resistance to external manipulation, patterns that remained true to their original purpose rather than being redirected.

"When the Tree fell," Brynja said slowly, piecing together the implications, "they saw opportunity in chaos."

"The Shattering was unexpected," the voices agreed. "But they adapted quickly. Used it to eliminate the remaining unified bloodlines, then gathered scattered survivors. Raised them in isolation. Taught them half-truths."

Asvarr felt sick as he understood what this meant for Brynja. "They found you wounded and alone, filled your head with revenge against my people—all to make you into a weapon they could control."

"A vessel," Brynja corrected, her face ashen where it remained human. "They shaped me to house the Root's consciousness when the time came."

The walls pulsed in confirmation. New images appeared—Brynja's wooden form completed, her humanity entirely subsumed by Root transformation. In this vision, the Verdant Five surrounded her, drawing sap from her transformed body to consume.

"They would wear you like a garment," the voices said. "Drink the power you channel without risk to themselves."

Brynja's shoulders hunched as if physically struck. "And my followers? Those who transformed alongside me?"

"Lesser vessels. Containers for fragments of what you would channel. Expendable once depleted."

The bark across Brynja's face cracked further, golden sap leaking from the fissures like tears. Her wooden hand clenched so tightly that splinters broke from her fingers.

"I trusted them," she whispered. "Gave them everything."

Asvarr reached for her instinctively, then hesitated, uncertain how she would receive comfort from him. The blood-oath mark on his palm pulsed with her pain, raw and immediate. Before he could decide, the Oracle's walls flashed crimson—a jarring contrast to the golden amber.

"They approach," the voices warned. "The Five sensed your blood-oath. They come to reclaim what they consider theirs."

Brynja straightened, her posture shifting from wounded to defiant. "I am no one's vessel but my own."

"What can we do?" Asvarr asked. "How do we reach the Verdant Gate before they intercept us?"

The walls stilled, all faces vanishing except one—androgynous, ancient, its features composed of wood and amber in equal measure. When it spoke, a single voice replaced the chorus, deeper and more resonant than the others.

"The Gate opens to memory, not future. What you seek lies in what was forgotten, not what will be."

"Another riddle?" Asvarr couldn't keep frustration from his voice. "We need clear guidance, not cryptic sayings."

The single face regarded him with amber eyes that held galaxies. "Clarity blinds as often as it illuminates. Your bloodlines united unlock paths hidden for nine cycles. Trust what the blood remembers."

***

The face on the wall shifted its attention to Brynja. "Your transformation progressed too far for complete reversal, Daughter of Roots. But balance can be restored. The wooden arm that marks you as vessel can become a tool of your own wielding instead."

"How?" Brynja asked, raising her transformed limb.

"The boy," the Oracle answered. "The child of in-between. His touch began the reshaping. Seek him again when the wooden crown threatens to close over your mind."

Asvarr remembered how Leif's touch had changed Brynja's arm, making the wood patterns more deliberate and controlled. Was the boy truly that powerful, or merely a catalyst for something already present?

The walls trembled, ripples spreading across the amber surface. The Oracle's voice grew urgent.

"Time grows short. The Five approach with binding-chains and root-severance blades. They will reclaim their vessel if you tarry."

"Tell us where to find the Verdant Gate," Brynja demanded.

The face on the wall smiled—a strange, unsettling expression on features composed of wood and amber.

"You have already found it, though you do not recognize it. The Gate stands in time. Seek the Garden of Forgetting where fruit grows from burial mounds. What died during the Shattering remains preserved in memory-flesh. Consume what lies forgotten, and the path reveals itself."

The amber walls began to dissolve, the chamber destabilizing around them. The Oracle's voice faded, its final message echoing between them:

"Remember this above all: the Gate requires both bloodlines in harmonic union, neither dominant nor subservient. Flame that doesn't consume, root that doesn't strangle. The Five will offer easier paths—beware their gilded promises."

The chamber collapsed entirely, amber splattering in all directions before absorbing rapidly into the tree's interior. Asvarr and Brynja found themselves standing outside the great tree once more, surrounded by their companions, who stared at them with expressions ranging from awe to fear.

"You glowed from within," Yrsa said, her hand clutched tightly around her crystal pendant. "Both of you, like lanterns seen through fog."

Leif approached without hesitation, reaching up to touch the fresh sap-tears still streaming from the cracks in Brynja's wooden face. "The Tree cries through you," he observed with childlike directness.

Kára stepped forward, her partially transformed face twisted with concern. "The ground has been trembling for the past several minutes. Something approaches from the north—something large that makes the trees lean away in fear."

"The Five," Asvarr and Brynja said simultaneously.

"We need to leave," Brynja continued, wiping sap from her face with her human hand. "Now. The Oracle showed me a hidden path southward."

"To where?" Yrsa asked.

"The Garden of Forgetting," Asvarr answered. "Where fruit grows from burial mounds."

Yrsa's eyes widened. "The Memory Graves. Few know of their existence, fewer still dare consume what grows there."

"What are Memory Graves?" Asvarr asked as they began moving, following Brynja's confident strides away from the Oracle's tree.

"Places where those who died during the Shattering were buried," Yrsa explained, keeping her voice low as they wove between twisted trees. "Their last moments, final thoughts, dying visions—all preserved in the fruit that grows from their remains. To consume such fruit is to live their death through their eyes."

A chill ran down Asvarr's spine despite the Vale's humid warmth. "The Oracle said the Gate 'stands in time.' That consuming these fruits would reveal the path."

"Because the Verdant Gate exists partially outside conventional time," Yrsa nodded. "It remembers what came before while simultaneously existing now. Finding it requires perspective that transcends ordinary perception."

The ground trembled more violently beneath their feet. From somewhere behind them came a sound like massive roots tearing free from earth—a grinding, splintering roar that shook leaves from branches.

"They've reached the Oracle," Brynja said grimly. "They'll extract our direction from it."

"Can they do that?" Asvarr asked. "The Oracle seemed... resistant to their influence."

"Everything can be broken with sufficient pressure," Brynja replied, her voice hollow. "I've seen what the Five can do when thwarted. We have hours at most before they find our trail."

They rushed through the increasingly bizarre landscape of the Thorned Vale, their path taking them through tunnels formed by trees growing in impossible spirals, across clearings where flowers screamed when stepped upon, past pools of liquid that might have been water but reflected no sky above.

The blood-oath mark on Asvarr's palm burned continuously now, transmitting Brynja's turmoil directly into his consciousness—rage, betrayal, grief, determination, all tangled together in a knot he couldn't separate from his own emotions.

"What did the Oracle show you?" he asked as they paused at a junction where five paths converged. "About the Five?"

Brynja's human eye met his, while her sap-eye stared somewhere beyond him. "Their true nature. Their intentions for me—for all who follow me." Her voice caught. "Everything I've worked toward, sacrificed for... they meant to wear me like a garment once my transformation was complete."

"And your followers?"

"Expendable vessels for fragments of power." Her wooden fingers twitched. "People who trusted me, who followed my example in transforming themselves. I led them to slaughter."

"You didn't know," Asvarr said.

"I should have questioned." Brynja's voice hardened. "I was so certain of my purpose, so dedicated to reclaiming what I thought was stolen from my bloodline. I never once considered I was being manipulated."

"Pride blinds," Yrsa interjected softly. "The Five counted on your certainty, just as they counted on Asvarr's anger after his clan's destruction. Opposing forces too focused on each other to see the hands moving them across the board."

Brynja selected a path, and they continued southward. The forest grew denser, trees leaning toward each other until their branches intertwined overhead, forming tunnels of living wood. The ground beneath them changed from soil to a springy moss that glowed faintly with each footstep, leaving luminescent prints that faded minutes later.

"The Garden is close," Brynja said after nearly an hour of silent travel. "I can smell it."

Asvarr caught the scent moments later—sweetness tinged with decay, like overripe fruit split open in autumn sun. His stomach twisted with both hunger and revulsion. The Grímmark on his chest pulsed in time with his quickened heartbeat.

They emerged from the forest tunnel into blinding daylight. After so long beneath the canopy, the open sky above them seemed impossibly vast, a blue emptiness that made Asvarr dizzy to contemplate. Below, spreading out before them, lay the Garden of Forgetting.

Hundreds of burial mounds dotted the rolling landscape, each topped with a single small tree bearing fruit unlike anything Asvarr had seen—some golden and translucent like the Oracle's amber, others dark as night, still others shifting through rainbow hues as they watched. Between the mounds flowed narrow streams of silver water, dividing the garden into geometric patterns that made his eyes hurt if he tried to follow them too far.

Standing at the garden's edge, Brynja turned to address them all. Sap still leaked from the cracks in her wooden face, but her voice had regained its strength.

"The Oracle warned that the fruits contain final memories of those who died during the Shattering. To consume them means experiencing their deaths." Her gaze found Asvarr. "The Verdant Gate will be revealed through these visions, though I don't understand how."

"It wants us to understand the Shattering itself," Asvarr reasoned. "To witness what actually happened rather than the stories we've been told."

Brynja nodded. "I believe so. The question becomes: who will consume the fruits? The experience sounds... harrowing."

Before anyone could respond, Leif darted forward, crossing the boundary into the garden proper. The boy moved with unusual certainty, heading directly toward a mound topped with a tree bearing silver fruit that glinted like polished metal.

"Leif, wait!" Yrsa called, starting after him.

Asvarr caught her arm. "Let him go. He's known where we're heading all along, I think. The in-between grants him awareness we lack."

They watched as Leif reached the silver-fruited tree and placed his palm against its bark. The entire tree shuddered in response, branches bending downward as if in greeting.

"I'll consume the fruit," Asvarr decided, stepping into the garden. "Whatever vision awaits, I'll face it."

"Not alone," Brynja said, following him across the boundary. "The Oracle was clear—both bloodlines must work in harmony."

The ground felt different once they crossed into the garden proper—more resilient, almost springy beneath their feet. Each step released a subtle fragrance of herbs and earth, memories of growth and decay mingled together.

Leif turned back toward them, a silver fruit cupped in his small hands. When he spoke, his voice carried an eerie resonance that contradicted his childlike appearance.

"This one first," he said, holding the fruit toward Asvarr. "It came before your time but lives in your blood."

Asvarr accepted the silver fruit, its skin cool and strangely metallic against his fingers. Inside, he glimpsed movement—flickers of light and shadow like trapped fireflies.

"What will I see?" he asked.

Leif's gold-flecked eyes met his with uncanny directness. "The moment before breaking. When something stirred beneath the roots."

Brynja stepped beside them, her human hand coming to rest on Asvarr's fore-arm. "I'll stand witness," she said. "The blood-oath will allow me to see fragments of your vision."

Asvarr nodded, then raised the silver fruit to his lips. The moment it touched his tongue, the garden dissolved around him. Reality fractured, reformed, and he found himself looking through eyes that were not his own.

CHAPTER 8

MEMORY'S HARVEST

The silver fruit burst against Asvarr's teeth, flooding his mouth with juice that tasted of metal and tears. His vision fractured, reality dissolving around him. The Garden of Forgetting vanished—Brynja, Yrsa, Leif, all gone in an instant. The blood-oath mark on his palm flared with heat, the only reminder that his own body still existed somewhere beyond this vision.

He found himself looking through another's eyes, inhabiting a body taller and leaner than his own. Hands bearing intricate spiral tattoos adjusted ceremonial robes woven with living plants. Through borrowed senses, Asvarr smelled sacred herbs burning in bone censers, felt cool flagstones beneath bare feet, heard murmured prayers in a language both familiar and strange.

I am Hawthorn, Eldest of the Root-Wardens, Guardian of the Fifth Confluence.

The thought came unbidden—the memory-fruit giving him identity. He understood immediately that he experienced the final moments of one of the druids who had performed the seeking ritual in the prologue—the same who'd hidden the key-shaped seed.

Hawthorn moved with purpose through an ancient grove, a vast temple-like structure with living walls formed of trees growing in perfect geometric patterns. Massive roots formed archways overhead, branches twisted into intricate knotwork that filtered sunlight into dappled patterns on the stone floor.

Other druids scurried past, their faces tight with worry. "The tremors grow stronger," one called. "The Confluence destabilizes!"

Hawthorn—and through him, Asvarr—felt a deep vibration underfoot, a wrongness that transcended physical sensation. Something fundamental had shifted beneath reality itself.

"The other sanctuaries?" Hawthorn asked, his voice resonating in a chest not Asvarr's own.

"Silent. Rowan attempts contact through the root-senders, but only echoes return."

Hawthorn pressed weathered palms against one of the living walls. The bark parted at his touch, revealing a hidden chamber where an enormous root emerged from the ground, curved upward through the ceiling, and disappeared into the structure above. Unlike healthy roots Asvarr had seen, this one pulsed with sickly light, the golden sap within darkening in irregular patches.

"The infection spreads," a woman's voice said behind him. "Despite our containment efforts."

Hawthorn turned to face a druid with auburn hair threaded with silver, her eyes clouded with cataracts yet somehow still seeing. Oak, Asvarr's borrowed memories supplied. Second Eldest of the Root-Wardens.

"The Five reject our warnings," Hawthorn replied, bitterness coloring his tone. "They believe themselves beyond consequence."

"The Five created Yggdrasil," Oak countered, though her voice lacked conviction. "They shaped its branches, guided its growth from sapling to World Tree."

"And now they experiment with forces beyond their understanding." Hawthorn gestured to the diseased root. "This corruption comes from their meddling with the spaces between branches, their attempts to access powers that should remain separate from our reality."

Another tremor shook the sanctuary, stronger than before. Dust sifted down from the ceiling. The sickly root pulsed faster, the dark patches spreading visibly.

"Summon the acolytes," Hawthorn ordered. "We must attempt the purification ritual again."

As Oak hurried away, Hawthorn placed both palms against the diseased root. Asvarr felt the druid's consciousness extend into the living wood, following pathways of sap and cellulose deep into Yggdrasil's structure. The sensation disoriented him—awareness spreading across vast distances, touching other minds similarly connected to different parts of the great Tree.

Brothers. Sisters. The sickness spreads faster than we can contain it.

Answers came as impressions rather than words, a concordance of anxiety and determination from root-tenders across multiple realms.

Then something else brushed against Hawthorn's extended consciousness—something vast and cold and ancient. It moved through Yggdrasil's roots like a serpent, leaving corruption in its wake. Hawthorn recoiled, but the entity had already sensed him.

Watcher in the wood. Your efforts amuse us.

The voice bypassed language, depositing concepts directly into Hawthorn's mind. Asvarr, experiencing the memory, felt violated by its touch—slime across his thoughts.

What are you? Hawthorn asked.

We are the forgotten. The denied. The imprisoned beyond branches. Soon to be free again.

Images flooded Hawthorn's mind—a time before the Tree, before order, when reality existed as malleable potential rather than fixed structure. Beings of unimaginable power swimming through chaos, shaping and reshaping existence according to whim. Then restriction, limitation, boundaries imposed by something Hawthorn couldn't comprehend.

The Five summoned you, Hawthorn realized with horror. *Deliberately or by accident, they opened a way for you.*

Irrelevant. The passage exists. We come.

The connection broke as Hawthorn staggered backward, gasping. Oak had returned with twelve acolytes bearing silver bowls filled with purified sap. Their expressions showed determination mixed with fear—they'd performed this ritual before, with diminishing success.

"Form the circle," Hawthorn commanded, his voice steadier than his hands. "What we witnessed in the root network exceeds our previous understanding. The corruption is sentient, purposeful."

The acolytes arranged themselves in a perfect circle around the exposed root. Oak took position opposite Hawthorn, completing the pattern. Each participant dipped their fingers into their silver bowls, then pressed sap-covered hands against the nearest section of root.

Hawthorn began chanting in that strange-yet-familiar language, the others joining in perfect harmony. The language resonated with meanings Asvarr understood through the memory—purification, binding, sealing against intrusion.

For several heartbeats, the ritual seemed to work. Golden light spread from their hands, pushing back the darkened patches in the infected root. The tremors subsided momentarily.

Then came the response—a surge of malevolent force that shot up through the root, blackening it entirely in an instant. The acolytes screamed as corruption raced along their arms, turning flesh to stone, then to ash. Oak managed to break contact before the corruption reached past her elbows, but her arms hung uselessly at her sides, petrified to the shoulders.

Hawthorn alone remained untouched, protected by some quality of his connection to the Tree that Asvarr couldn't comprehend through the memory-fruit's limited perspective.

"It comes," Oak gasped through pain. "We've failed."

The entire sanctuary shuddered violently. Roots that formed the ceiling cracked, showering them with splinters and dirt. The walls groaned as the living trees that comprised them twisted in agony.

"Not yet," Hawthorn insisted. "The bloodlines still exist. If we can preserve the knowledge—"

The floor split beneath them, a chasm opening directly below the infected root. From the depths rose something that defied comprehension—a writhing mass of shadow and scale, neither wholly physical nor entirely ephemeral. Asvarr glimpsed coils thick as ancient oaks, scales that reflected not light but the absence of it, eyes that contained galaxies of cold, distant stars.

Freedom, the entity projected into all nearby minds. *After aeons imprisoned between branches, we return to unmake what was made.*

Through Hawthorn's eyes, Asvarr watched in horror as the serpentine entity wound its way up the massive root, corruption spreading wherever it touched. The sanctuary walls crumbled as the trees comprising them withered and died in moments. Above, through the shattered ceiling, Asvarr glimpsed Yggdrasil itself—incomprehensibly vast, stretching beyond vision into realms he couldn't perceive.

And it was breaking.

Massive cracks spread along the World Tree's trunk. Entire branches sheared away, plummeting toward distant realms. Golden sap gushed from the wounds like blood from a mortal injury, each drop containing worlds of memory and knowledge.

Hawthorn grabbed Oak, dragging her toward a small archway that had appeared in the sanctuary's back wall—a bolt-hole prepared for emergencies.

"Find Rowan," he shouted over the cacophony of destruction. "Gather what remains of our order. The Five cannot be trusted with this knowledge—they caused this, whether by ignorance or design."

"Where will you go?" Oak asked, her stone-transformed arms hanging useless at her sides.

Hawthorn pressed something into her palm—a seed shaped like a key.

"To preserve what I can. The bloodlines must survive, even if separated. When the time comes, this will guide those worthy to the Verdant Gate."

Before Oak could respond, the serpentine entity reared above them, its massive head blotting out the fractured sky. Eyes like voids fixed on Hawthorn, recognizing him as an obstacle.

Your resistance means nothing. The pattern breaks. What comes after belongs to us.

Hawthorn pushed Oak through the bolt-hole, sealing it with a gesture. Alone now, he faced the entity with nothing but his knowledge and determination.

"This realm may shatter," he declared, raising hands that suddenly glowed with concentrated power, "but we've prepared for this possibility for generations. What you find after the breaking may surprise you."

The entity lunged downward, its maw expanding to impossible dimensions. Hawthorn stood his ground, channeling the last of his connection to the dying Tree into a final protective spell. Gold light erupted from his outstretched hands—

The vision shattered.

***

Asvarr gasped, finding himself on his knees in the Garden of Forgetting, the spent husk of the silver fruit crumbling in his fingers. His heart hammered against his ribs, the Grímmark burning beneath his tunic. He could still feel echoes of Hawthorn's final emotion—grim determination. The knowledge that although he would die, measures had been put in place for this exact catastrophe.

"You saw," Brynja said, not a question. She knelt beside him, her human hand gripping his shoulder. Through the blood-oath, Asvarr sensed she'd witnessed fragments of his vision.

"The breaking wasn't an attack on the Tree," he rasped, throat parched as if he'd been screaming. "It was the Tree's response to invasion. Yggdrasil shattered itself deliberately, to prevent something worse from claiming it whole."

Yrsa approached, her face grave. "What invaded? What did you see?"

"Something serpentine. Ancient. It called itself 'the forgotten' and 'the imprisoned beyond branches.'" Asvarr struggled to articulate the horror he'd witnessed. "It moved through the roots, spreading corruption. The Five had meddled with forces beyond their understanding, opened a passage that should have remained sealed."

"The imprisonment beyond branches," Yrsa murmured, fingers worrying her crystal pendant. "Old texts mention this—beings that existed before order, imprisoned when reality first crystallized into fixed patterns."

"The Shattered Void," Kára added unexpectedly. The transformed follower had remained silent throughout their journey, but now stepped forward with unusual authority. "Tales tell of a time before Ginnungagap, when existence had no boundaries, no laws. Beings of unimaginable power ruled then, shaping reality according to whim."

"Until something imprisoned them," Brynja finished, her expression troubled. "Something that created structure, permanence."

"Yggdrasil was both prison and prison guard," Yrsa agreed. "Its roots and branches formed the boundaries that kept chaos at bay, maintained the integrity of the Nine Realms."

The implications staggered Asvarr. Everything he'd believed about the Shattering—that some malevolent force had attacked the World Tree—stood reversed. The Tree had broken itself deliberately, a final desperate measure to prevent total consumption.

Leif tugged at Asvarr's sleeve, interrupting his thoughts. The boy held another fruit—this one black as night, with a surface that reflected starlight despite the daylight overhead.

"This one next," Leif insisted. "For her." He pointed at Brynja.

She accepted the dark fruit with visible trepidation. "What will I see?"

Leif's gold-flecked eyes met hers directly. "The betrayal that sundered your bloodlines."

**

Brynja's fingers tightened around the fruit, bark-knuckles creaking with tension. "The ancient division between flame-keepers and root-tenders?"

"The wound still bleeds," Leif said cryptically. "The truth will hurt, but healing needs pain."

Asvarr watched conflict play across the human half of Brynja's face—fear warring with determination. The blood-oath mark on his palm pulsed with her uncertainty.

"I'll stand witness," he echoed her earlier words, offering support without pressure.

After a long moment, Brynja nodded. "Truth before comfort," she murmured, raising the dark fruit to her lips.

Yrsa stepped forward, hand outstretched. "Wait—" But Brynja had already bitten into the fruit's midnight flesh.

Black juice ran down her chin as her eyes rolled back, showing only whites. Her body went rigid, then began to tremble violently. Unlike Asvarr's vision, which had transported him internally into another's perspective, Brynja's experience manifested visibly—a dark aura surrounding her, flashing with images too quick to interpret.

"What's happening?" Asvarr demanded, reaching for Brynja as she collapsed to her knees.

"Dark memories," Yrsa replied, dropping beside them. "Some fruits contain experiences so traumatic they manifest externally. She's experiencing the memory while projecting fragments to any nearby."

***

The blackness surrounding Brynja expanded, tendrils of shadow reaching toward them. Where they touched Asvarr's skin, he felt ice-cold despair seep into his flesh. Through the blood-oath, emotions not his own flooded his consciousness—betrayal, rage, grief so profound it threatened to drown him.

Yrsa grabbed his arm. "Don't fight it. The memory must run its course."

The shadow engulfed them completely, plunging the garden into absolute darkness. When light returned, they stood on a mountainside overlooking a valley. Two encampments faced each other across a narrow river—one flying banners marked with flame sigils, the other with root symbols.

"The Treaty of Divided Essence," Yrsa whispered. "Nine cycles past, when the bloodlines first separated."

The vision showed emissaries from both camps meeting on a stone bridge spanning the river. Leaders in ceremonial garb clasped arms, spoke words of formal parting. Though no sound carried through the projection, Asvarr understood this was a solemn, necessary division—bloodlines separating to protect different aspects of Yggdrasil during some crisis.

Then the vision shifted, darkened. Shadow figures moved through both camps after nightfall. Asvarr watched in horror as these infiltrators—bearing no identifiable markings—slaughtered sleepers in one tent, then used blood from the victims to create false evidence implicating the other camp.

By morning, the carefully negotiated separation had become violent conflict, each side believing the other had betrayed sacred oaths. Battle erupted on the stone bridge, former allies cutting each other down with terrible efficiency. Blood ran into the river below, which darkened ominously at the contact.

From the shadows beyond both encampments, five hooded figures watched with cold satisfaction.

The vision collapsed, the dark aura retracting into Brynja's body. She sagged forward, caught by Asvarr before she could strike the ground. Her wooden arm had expanded during the vision, bark patterns now covering her entire left side from fingertips to jawline.

"The Five," she gasped, voice ragged. "They engineered the conflict. Turned necessity into hatred."

"They wanted the bloodlines to be opposed," Asvarr agreed grimly. "Unified purpose became generational enmity through their manipulation."

Leif approached again, this time holding a golden fruit that pulsed with inner light like a captured sun. When he offered it, neither Asvarr nor Brynja reached for it.

"This one holds the way forward," the boy said, his voice taking on that unsettling adult resonance. "The path to the Verdant Gate."

Asvarr looked at Brynja, still trembling from her vision. Something shifted between them—a deeper understanding born from witnessed truths. The blood-oath mark warmed on his palm, no longer burning but comforting.

"Together," he suggested. "The Oracle said both bloodlines in harmony."

She managed a nod, straightening with visible effort. They gripped the golden fruit between them, her wooden fingers interlacing with his calloused ones. As one, they raised it to their mouths and bit into opposite sides.

Golden light erupted around them, temporarily blinding everyone in the garden. When Asvarr's vision cleared, he and Brynja stood together on a precipice overlooking an impossible landscape—their physical bodies still in the garden, but their consciousness projected elsewhere.

Below them lay the Verdant Gate.

The vision of the Verdant Gate faded, returning Asvarr and Brynja to their physical bodies in the Garden of Forgetting. Golden juice still stained their lips, its taste lingering—sunshine and sweet herbs with an undercurrent of ancient sorrow. The garden around them had subtly changed during their shared vision, burial mounds shifting position like sleeping giants adjusting their rest.

"The Gate," Brynja whispered, her voice uncharacteristically fragile. "It's real."

"And waiting for us." Asvarr touched the blood-oath mark on his palm, now pulsing with shared purpose. "We should rest before attempting the journey. The Verdant Five—"

"Will be slowed by the Vale's defenses," Yrsa finished, examining the markings on a nearby mound with clinical detachment. "The memory-awakening has altered paths they once knew. We have hours, perhaps a full day."

Asvarr nodded, relieved. His limbs felt leaden, mind scraped raw from the visions. He'd learned more truth in the past hour than in twenty years of life before. The revelation that the Tree had shattered itself deliberately, that ancient entities breached reality's boundaries, that the Five had engineered the hatred between bloodlines—it threatened to overwhelm him.

"We'll camp here for a few hours," he decided, rolling his shoulders to ease tension. "Then follow the path revealed by the golden fruit."

Kára organized the remaining followers into a watch rotation while Yrsa gathered herbs growing between the mounds. Leif simply sat cross-legged on the ground, running his fingers through the soil with unusual concentration. Asvarr settled against the base of a memory tree, its branches heavy with rainbow-hued fruits he had no intention of sampling.

Only Brynja remained standing, her body unnaturally still. Through the blood-oath, Asvarr sensed her thoughts churning beneath that stillness—a vortex of emotions too tangled to separate.

"You should rest," he told her.

She didn't respond, didn't even look at him. Instead, she stared at a nearby mound crowned with deep purple fruits that pulsed like heartbeats. Her wooden hand twitched at her side, bark fingers curling and uncurling rhythmically.

"Brynja?"

Still no response. Without warning, she strode toward the purple-fruited tree. Before Asvarr could react, she'd plucked one of the throbbing fruits and bitten into it. Purple juice dripped down her chin as her eyes rolled back, body going rigid.

"Brynja!" Asvarr leapt to his feet, scrambling toward her.

Yrsa's head snapped up from her herb-gathering. "Stop her! One fruit overtaxes the mind—multiple visions can shatter it completely!"

But Brynja had already plucked another fruit—this one blood-red—and devoured it with desperate intensity. Her body convulsed, the wooden patterns on her left side spreading visibly across her torso. By the time Asvarr reached her, she'd consumed a third fruit, emerald green and smoking faintly where her saliva touched it.

He grabbed her shoulders, trying to pull her away from the tree. "Brynja, enough! You'll lose yourself!"

Her eyes snapped open—one human, one sap-filled, both vacant of recognition. "Must know," she mumbled, voice distorted as if multiple throats spoke simultaneously. "Must remember what they did."

The blood-oath mark on Asvarr's palm flared with searing heat. Through it flowed fragments of the memories Brynja consumed—disjointed images too rapid to comprehend fully. He glimpsed the Five in different eras, wearing different faces but always the same cold expressions. Saw them manipulating events, guiding conflicts, preserving themselves while sacrifices mounted around them.

"Let go," Brynja snarled, her voice overlapping with others. She twisted with unnatural strength, breaking his grip. The transformation accelerated across her body—bark patterns encroaching on her right side, golden sap leaking from widening cracks in her wooden flesh. She staggered toward another mound.

Leif appeared beside them, moving with that uncanny silence that marked his steps. He pressed both palms against Brynja's wooden arm, his small fingers sinking into the bark as if it were soft clay.

"Too many voices," the boy said. "Be quiet now."

Golden light flowed from his fingertips into Brynja's transformed limb. The wooden patterns stopped spreading, solidifying into more deliberate formations. Brynja gasped, clutching her head with both hands.

"Make it stop," she pleaded. "Too many memories. Too many deaths."

"Sit," Asvarr urged, guiding her to the ground. "Breathe. Focus on my voice."

Yrsa approached with a handful of crushed leaves. "Hold her still," she instructed, pressing the herb mixture to Brynja's temples. "Memory-slumber. It will help organize what she's consumed."

The herb's sharp scent filled Asvarr's nostrils—mint and ash and something metallic. Brynja's eyes fluttered, her resistance weakening. Slowly, her breathing steadied, though golden sap continued to leak from cracks in her wooden flesh.

"What was she thinking?" Asvarr demanded, anger born of fear making his voice harsh. "You said one fruit taxes the mind—she took three!"

"Four," Yrsa corrected grimly. "I found evidence of another consumed while we were distracted by your vision."

"Will she recover?"

"Her body will. Her mind..." Yrsa shrugged slightly. "Memory-fruits contain entire lives' final moments. Four sets of death, trauma, knowledge—all competing for space within one consciousness. She risked complete fragmentation."

Leif continued holding Brynja's wooden arm, his eyes closed in concentration. "The tree remembers through her now," he murmured. "But too much, too fast."

"Can you help her?" Asvarr asked the boy.

"I can shape what flows," Leif replied cryptically. "I can organize it."

As they sat vigil over Brynja's unconscious form, the garden darkened around them. The sun slipped behind distant mountains, casting long shadows across the burial mounds. Fruits glowed softly in the gathering dusk, pulsing with inner light like captured stars. Kára and the other followers maintained a watchful perimeter, their partially transformed faces betraying unease in this place of dead memories.

***

Night had fully descended when Brynja stirred. Her eyes opened—clearer now but fundamentally changed. The human eye held knowledge beyond her years; the sap-eye swirled with fragments of other lives.

"Water," she rasped.

Asvarr helped her drink from his water skin, noting how the transformation had spread further—bark patterns now covered three-quarters of her face, leaving only part of her right cheek and eye human. Her right arm remained flesh, but golden veins pulsed visibly beneath the skin.

"What were you thinking?" he asked when she'd drunk her fill.

Brynja's gaze drifted past him, focusing on something distant. "I needed to understand what they truly planned. The Oracle showed fragments, but I wanted certainty."

"And?"

"The Five never intended restoration." Her voice gained strength, though it retained eerie harmonics from her transformation. "They mean to reshape Yggdrasil entirely—a new Tree formed to their design, with themselves as its governing consciousness."

"Gods," Yrsa breathed, fingers tightening around her crystal pendant.

"Yes." Brynja's expression hardened, bark creaking with the movement. "Gods who determine which branches grow and which are pruned. Who decide which souls traverse which paths, which realms flourish, which wither."

"That's why they kept your bloodlines apart," Yrsa said. "United flame and root could resist their influence, maintain balance."

Brynja nodded, wincing at the movement. "The fruits showed me their meetings across centuries. They've been planning since the first breaking, patiently guiding events toward their ascension." Her voice broke. "They raised me, trained me, encouraged my transformation—all to create a suitable vessel for their power."

"The vessel becomes the cage," Leif murmured, still holding her wooden arm. "They would wear your skin, drink your essence."

"I would have let them," Brynja admitted, shame evident in her tone. "I believed their promises of restored glory, of honoring my ancestors' sacrifice." She gestured to her transformed body. "This was willing submission."

The implications chilled Asvarr. How many others like Brynja had the Five cultivated across cycles? How many willing sacrifices to their grand design?

"One memory-fruit showed me the last vessel," Brynja continued, her voice distant. "A man from the seventh breaking who gave himself completely. They wore him for years while reshaping entire sections of the pattern. When his body finally failed, they discarded him without ceremony."

"And sought another vessel to continue their work," Yrsa concluded.

"They seek five this time." Brynja's gaze locked with Asvarr's. "One for each aspect of the pattern they wish to control. I've seen four others bearing partial transformations like mine, scattered across the realms."

Asvarr recalled the five faces he'd glimpsed in the Oracle's amber walls, the five figures watching the engineered conflict from Brynja's vision. "Five vessels for five shapers," he murmured. "But if they need five separate vessels, why keep our bloodlines apart? Why not use both flame and root simultaneously?"

"Because unified, we resist them," Brynja explained. "The fruits showed memories of previous attempts—flame and root bloodlines joined in purpose created a protective barrier around parts of the pattern, preventing external manipulation." She gestured to their blood-oath marks. "What we've done terrifies them. It threatens their entire design."

The revelation settled over the group like a physical weight. Their alliance had made them targets of beings who'd manipulated events across nine cycles of breaking and restoration.

Leif finally released Brynja's arm, sitting back with unusual weariness. The wooden patterns had stabilized into intricate designs—no longer chaotic growth but deliberate formations suggesting leaves, branches, and roots in harmonious arrangement.

"What else did you learn?" Asvarr asked.

"They're coming," Brynja said simply. "The fruits contained memories from Root-Wardens who witnessed previous pursuits. The Five move through the boundary faster than ordinary beings. They'll be relentless."

"Then we move tonight," Asvarr decided. "No more rest. The path to the Verdant Gate won't wait."

Brynja attempted to stand but staggered, clearly weakened by her ordeal. Asvarr caught her, supporting her weight against his side. Through the blood-oath, he felt her disorientation—her mind struggling to integrate multiple lifetimes of memories not her own.

"I can walk," she insisted, pulling away. Her movements belied her words, each step unsteady.

"You consumed four memory-fruits," Yrsa reminded her. "By all accounts, you should be catatonic or dead. Moving now risks further damage."

"We have no choice," Brynja countered. "I've seen what happens to those who delay when the Five pursue."

Something in her tone—the weight of witnessed horror—silenced further objections. They gathered their meager supplies, preparing to leave the Garden of Forgetting. As Asvarr shouldered his pack, a strange sensation prickled along his spine. The Grímmark on his chest pulsed with warning.

"Something's wrong," he murmured, hand dropping to his bronze sword.

The garden had gone silent. No night birds called, no insects chirped in the darkness. The memory-fruits on their trees stopped their gentle pulsing, becoming dark and still. Even the air felt frozen, refusing to stir.

Leif tugged urgently at Asvarr's sleeve. "They're here," the boy whispered, pointing toward the garden's northern edge. "Above."

Asvarr followed his gesture, squinting into the night sky. At first, he saw nothing but stars. Then movement caught his eye—five points of light descending from above, moving with unnatural coordination. As they approached, the lights resolved into glowing figures, each surrounded by an aura of different color—amber, blue, green, silver, and crimson.

"The Verdant Five," Brynja breathed, terror evident in her voice. "They've found us."

"How?" Yrsa demanded. "The Vale should have slowed them."

"They followed my consumption," Brynja realized with horror. "The fruits create connections to those who planted them. By taking multiple fruits, I created a beacon they could track."

The figures descended faster, their auras illuminating the garden below. Now Asvarr could see details—five beings with wooden crowns and robes woven from living vines. Their faces remained shadowed despite the light surrounding them, revealing only the gleam of eyes too bright to be human.

"Run," Brynja commanded, her voice pitched low but urgent. "Follow the path from the golden fruit. I'll hold them back."

"That's suicide," Asvarr objected.

"They want me alive," she countered, raising her transformed arm. Bark patterns shifted across her fingers, elongating into thorn-like protrusions. "This vessel they've cultivated so carefully—they won't destroy it."

"We stand together," Asvarr insisted, drawing his bronze sword. The gold-veined blade hummed with power drawn from the first Root binding. "The Oracle said both bloodlines in harmony. Separated, we're vulnerable."

Through the blood-oath, he felt her intention waver, then strengthen. She nodded reluctantly. "Together then, but the others must go. Leif especially—they mustn't take the child."

Kára stepped forward, her partially transformed face set with determination. "We'll escort the boundary-walker and the boy. Meet us at the Verdant Gate—if you survive."

The glowing figures had nearly reached the garden's edge, their descent slowing as they approached the burial mounds. Asvarr could feel the weight of their attention, ancient and cold as winter stars.

"Go now," he urged. "We'll follow when we can."

Yrsa hesitated, clearly torn between staying and protecting Leif. "The blood-oath connects you," she reminded them. "If one falls—"

"We know the risk," Brynja cut her off. "Take Leif and go!"

The boy allowed himself to be led away, but his golden-flecked eyes remained fixed on Brynja with unusual intensity. As Yrsa pulled him into the shadows, he called back: "Remember what grows beneath the surface!"

The Five touched down simultaneously at the garden's edge, their auras illuminating the burial mounds with unnatural light. Up close, Asvarr could see their true nature—bodies partially composed of living wood, faces formed of interwoven branches resembling human features. Their eyes contained galaxies of distant stars, ancient beyond comprehension.

The one surrounded by amber light stepped forward, its wooden face contorting into an approximation of a smile.

"Child of roots," it addressed Brynja, voice resonating like wind through a hollow tree. "Your transformation progresses beautifully, though along... unexpected paths." Its starlight gaze shifted to Asvarr. "And the flame-carrier. How convenient to find both vessels together."

"We know what you are," Asvarr declared, raising his sword defensively. "What you plan for the Tree's rebirth."

"Do you?" The amber figure tilted its head, an unnervingly smooth movement. "I doubt the fragments you've gathered paint the complete picture. Nine cycles we've guided the pattern, preserved what matters while pruning what doesn't. Without us, chaos returns—the void hungry beyond branches consumes all."

"You didn't guide," Brynja snarled, her voice taking on multiple harmonics. "You manipulated. Divided. Sacrificed countless lives for your ascension."

"Necessary pruning," the green-aura figure replied dismissively. "The garden of fate requires careful cultivation. Some possibilities must wither that others might flourish."

The words sparked something in Asvarr's mind—a new understanding blossoming from seeds planted by the memory-fruits. He saw fate as a vast garden of branching possibilities. Some paths naturally flourished; others withered according to choices made. The Five hadn't merely observed this process—they'd actively shaped it, pruning possibilities that threatened their designs, cultivating those that served them.

"You're gardeners," he realized aloud. "Shaping wyrd itself."

"The first and finest," the amber figure confirmed, pride evident in its resonant voice. "We guided Yggdrasil's initial growth, determined which realms flourished, which sentient life developed consciousness."

"And now you seek to wear us," Brynja said, disgust twisting her partially wooden features. "To use our transformed bodies as your vessels while you reshape the pattern completely."

"A necessary evolution," the blue-aura figure interjected. "The void-serpent's intrusion proved the old pattern vulnerable. What we build using your essence will be stronger, more resistant to outside influence."

"With you as its gods," Asvarr challenged.

The crimson figure laughed—a sound like branches breaking in winter storms. "We've always been gods, flame-carrier. We simply chose subtler methods than those upstart Aesir who claimed dominion later."

The Five spread out, forming a loose semicircle. Asvarr felt power gathering around them—ancient, patient, terrible in its certainty. His bronze sword hummed louder, responding to the threat. Beside him, Brynja's wooden arm elongated further, thorn-claws extending from her fingertips.

"Last chance," the amber figure offered, extending a hand formed of interwoven branches. "Come willingly. The vessel who surrenders suffers less than the vessel who resists."

Asvarr exchanged a glance with Brynja. Through the blood-oath, he felt her resolve matching his own. Whatever came next, they faced it together—flame and root unified against those who'd kept them apart for nine cycles.

"We choose the third path," Asvarr declared, raising his sword. "Neither surrender nor destruction, but transformation you cannot control."

The amber figure's face hardened, branches tightening into a mask of cold anger. "So be it. The garden requires pruning once again."

The Five attacked as one, their auras flaring with blinding intensity. Asvarr and Brynja stood back to back in the Garden of Forgetting, surrounded by the memories of the dead, about to add their own to the collection.

CHAPTER 9

THE CIRCLE OF SPLINTERS

Dawn's pale fingers stretched through the Garden of Forgetting, casting long shadows across the burial mounds. Asvarr knelt beside Brynja, whose breathing had finally steadied after her night of delirious visions. Bark patterns now covered three-quarters of her face, the transformation accelerated by her consumption of multiple memory-fruits. Her fingers—half wood, half flesh—twitched against the soil.

"She needs water," Yrsa said, kneeling on Brynja's other side. The copper-haired woman pressed a waterskin to Brynja's lips. "The memories will settle eventually, but her mind needs anchor points. Names, places, things she knows to be true."

"Brynja," Asvarr said, his voice rough from a sleepless night spent watching over her. "Your name is Brynja. Your blood is that of root-tenders. We share ancestors, you and I."

The words felt strange on his tongue, new truths still settling into the spaces where old hatreds had once lived. The blood-oath mark on his palm throbbed, a reminder of their connection.

Brynja's eyes flickered open—amber irises swimming with fragments of consumed memories. "Asvarr," she whispered. "We must move. The Five... they're coming for us."

Kára approached, her half-transformed face set in hard lines. "The other followers have scattered. If the Five are truly pursuing us, we should do the same."

Asvarr exchanged glances with Yrsa, whose crystal pendant glowed faintly in the morning light. "No," he said. "Together we're stronger. We need a place to gather ourselves, to plan." He looked to the edge of the garden, where dense forest gave way to misty valleys. "Somewhere the Five will hesitate to follow."

Yrsa nodded. "I know a place. A sacred glade where Root splinters fell during the Shattering. The patterns there might reveal the path to the Verdant Gate more clearly."

"Can you walk?" Asvarr asked Brynja, offering his arm.

She grasped his forearm, bark scraping against skin. "The memories are... overwhelming. But I can walk." Her gaze sharpened briefly. "And I can fight if needed."

Asvarr helped her to her feet, feeling the weight of her against him, neither fully woman nor fully Root. Leif appeared at his side, eyes gold-flecked and solemn.

"The glade knows we're coming," the boy said simply.

They moved through the Garden, past burial mounds now bare of memory-fruits—all consumed or withered with the coming day. Yrsa led them along paths that seemed to shift and realign as they walked, the forest folding in around them like hands closing over a secret.

***

By midday they reached a perfect circle of scorched earth surrounded by nine massive Root splinters, each as tall as three men and partially embedded in the ground. They jutted from the soil at odd angles, as if they had pierced reality itself when falling. Golden sap wept from their broken edges, pooling in small depressions in the blackened soil.

Brynja inhaled sharply. "I know this place. From the memories... it's a fracture point, where the Tree's consciousness separated during the Shattering."

Asvarr approached one of the splinters cautiously. As he drew near, a low hum emanated from the wood, vibrating through his bones. His Grímmark burned in response, sending tendrils of heat across his chest and up his neck.

"They're alive," he murmured, pressing his palm against the rough surface. "Each holds a fragment of Yggdrasil's awareness."

"A circle of splinters," Yrsa confirmed, setting down her pack in the center of the glade. "Nine fragments, nine realms. The consciousness that was once unified now exists in fragments across the worlds."

Brynja moved to stand beside Asvarr, the wooden side of her face catching the filtered sunlight. "The Five want to gather these fragments, to reshape them according to their design rather than allow the Tree to heal in its own way." Her voice carried new authority, deepened by the memories she had consumed. "They believe the original pattern was flawed. They seek to correct it by becoming its architects."

"And what do you believe?" Asvarr asked, studying her transformed features.

Brynja's lips pressed into a thin line. "I believed what they taught me. That the Tree needed guidance, that our bloodlines were meant to serve as vessels." Her amber eyes met his. "Now I question everything."

Yrsa had begun unpacking supplies, laying out dried herbs and small vials of liquid that caught the light. "We must hold council," she declared. "Here, between the splinters, where the Five's influence is weakened by the fragmented consciousness."

"Council about what?" Kára asked, maintaining a wary distance from the splinters. Unlike Brynja, she seemed uncomfortable with her partial transformation, hiding the bark patterns beneath the hood of her cloak.

"About what comes next," Yrsa replied. "About the Tree's future—and ours with it."

Asvarr sat cross-legged in the center of the circle, feeling the hum of the splinters creating a complex harmony around them. Brynja joined him, moving with the strange fluidity her transformation granted her. Yrsa completed their triangle, her crystal pendant now pulsing with light that matched the rhythm of the splinters' humming.

"Three bloodlines," Yrsa murmured. "Flame, Root, and Boundary. The patterns align."

"What of Leif?" Asvarr asked, glancing at the boy who wandered between the splinters, trailing his fingers across their surfaces.

"He exists outside the pattern," Yrsa said. "Born of the Shattering itself. He moves between the lines we draw."

Brynja leaned forward, her wooden fingers digging into the blackened soil. "I've seen what the Five intend. They would remake Yggdrasil as a vessel for their consciousness alone, pruning away all branches that don't serve their vision."

"And what of the Ashfather?" Asvarr asked. "Where does he stand in this?"

"He opposes the Five," Yrsa said, "but not for our benefit. He would prevent the Tree's rebirth entirely, keeping the realms sundered to maintain his influence. Two forces, pulling in opposite directions."

"And we stand between," Asvarr concluded, the weight of it settling on his shoulders. The Grímmark pulsed against his skin, reminding him of his first binding, of the path he had already walked.

Brynja's face contorted with something between pain and revelation. "The memory-fruits showed me more than the Five's plans. I saw... fragments of previous cycles. This has happened before. The Tree breaks, the Tree heals. But each time, the pattern grows more rigid, more controlled."

"By the Five's design," Yrsa added.

"Yes," Brynja nodded. "They've guided each rebirth, shaping it subtly, making it more amenable to their influence."

Asvarr frowned, pieces falling into place. "And the bloodlines? Our ancestors?"

"Pawns," Brynja said bitterly. "Moved across the board generation after generation, kept separated to prevent the very unity we now represent."

The splinters around them hummed louder, as if responding to the truth being spoken aloud for the first time in ages. Golden sap ran more freely down their sides, pooling at their bases.

"Then what is our path?" Asvarr asked, looking between his companions. "If both the Five and the Ashfather would use us for their own ends, what choice remains?"

Yrsa's eyes reflected the light of her pendant. "We find the Verdant Gate. We approach the second Anchor on our own terms."

"And then?" Brynja pressed.

"We choose transformation over restoration or destruction," Yrsa said. "We become what neither the Five nor the Ashfather can control."

***

Asvarr opened his mouth to respond, but Leif's movement caught his attention. The boy had begun arranging fallen splinters—smaller fragments that had broken from the large ones—in a pattern on the ground. His small hands moved with purpose, eyes distant as if seeing patterns invisible to the others.

"What are you doing, Leif?" Asvarr called.

The boy didn't look up, continuing to place fragments with precise movements. "Making the way clear," he replied, his voice oddly resonant.

They rose and approached the boy's creation. He had arranged dozens of splinters in a complex pattern that sprawled across the blackened soil. It took Asvarr a moment to recognize what he was seeing: a map. The splinters formed rivers, mountain ranges, forests—the landscape spreading outward from their location.

"The path to the Verdant Gate," Brynja breathed, kneeling beside the arrangement.

Leif placed a final splinter—a curved fragment that resembled a doorway—at the center of the pattern. "Here," he said simply. "Where all grief flows together."

Asvarr studied the map, tracing the paths with his finger without touching the splinters. "That's three days' journey, if I'm reading this correctly."

"Through the domain of the Rootless King," Leif added, looking up at Asvarr with eyes now entirely golden. "The grief-collector."

Kára made a sharp sound, drawing back. "The Rootless? No. We cannot pass through their territory. They're madness given form."

"Explain," Asvarr demanded.

It was Yrsa who answered, her face grave. "When Yggdrasil shattered, not all souls found their way to proper deaths. Some were caught in the breaking, torn from their bodies but unable to pass onward. Their collective grief formed an entity—the Rootless King. Neither living nor dead, he rules the borderlands where realities blur together."

"His domain lies directly between us and the Verdant Gate," Brynja observed, studying Leif's map.

"He collects sorrows," Leif said quietly. "Feeds on them. Grows stronger with each grief he consumes."

Asvarr felt cold despite the day's warmth. "And we must pass through his territory?"

Leif nodded. "The only other paths would take weeks, and the Five would find us before we reached the Gate."

"What does this Rootless King want?" Asvarr asked. "Can he be reasoned with? Bargained with?"

"He wants what all broken things want," Leif replied. "To be whole again."

A silence fell over the glade, broken only by the continuing hum of the splinters. Asvarr gazed at the map, calculating risks, considering alternatives. The bronze sword at his hip seemed suddenly inadequate protection against a being formed from collective grief.

"I've encountered grief-feeders before," Asvarr said finally. "In the Thorned Vale. We survived."

"The Sorrow Eaters are but fragments," Yrsa cautioned. "The Rootless King is their source. He is to them what the Tree is to the splinters around us."

Brynja stood, her posture resolute despite the exhaustion still evident in her face. "We have no choice. The Gate calls, and we must answer. Together, our bloodlines might provide protection the Rootless cannot overcome."

"Or make us a greater prize," Kára muttered.

Leif looked up, his golden eyes unnervingly adult in his child's face. "He will let us pass if we each offer a grief freely given."

Asvarr felt the weight of unshed tears in his chest, the grief he had carried since finding his clan slaughtered. Could he surrender even a portion of that sorrow? Did he want to?

"Grief is my weapon," he had told the Sorrow Eaters. The words returned to him now, a truth he had clung to through his journey.

"We'll rest here tonight," Yrsa declared, breaking the heavy silence. "Gather our strength. In the morning, we'll make our decision."

As she spoke, the splinters around them pulsed with golden light, responding to some unseen signal. The hum deepened, resonating through the ground beneath their feet. Leif's map began to glow, each splinter illuminated from within.

"Something's happening," Kára whispered, backing toward the edge of the glade.

The largest splinter—the one directly north of their position—cracked suddenly, a fissure running its length. Golden sap gushed forth, flowing toward Leif's map as if drawn by magnetism. The other splinters followed, each cracking in sequence, releasing streams of sap that converged on the map.

"Don't move," Yrsa commanded as the golden liquid surrounded them, flowing in intricate patterns across the blackened soil.

The sap reached Leif's map, enveloping the splinters he had arranged. Rather than dissolving the pattern, it enhanced it—lifting the fragments slightly, suspending them in a three-dimensional representation that hovered inches above the ground. Mountains rose; forests bristled; rivers flowed with liquid light.

At the center, the curved splinter representing the Verdant Gate grew, twisting into a more complex shape—an archway woven from countless tiny root fibers, pulsing with life.

"The way reveals itself," Yrsa murmured in wonder.

Leif stood among the flowing sap, untouched by it, his small form haloed in golden light. He extended his hand toward Asvarr, face solemn.

"The circle awakens," the boy said. "It's time to choose your path."

Asvarr stared at the glowing map, at the suspended representation of the Verdant Gate at its center, at the territories they would need to cross—including the shadowed domain of the Rootless King. The splinters around them continued to crack and weep, their humming building toward some unknown crescendo.

His Grímmark burned, the familiar heat spreading across his chest and mingling with the throb of the blood-oath mark on his palm. Two bindings, two commitments. Would the second Anchor demand a third? What would remain of him when all was done?

"Tomorrow," Asvarr said firmly, meeting Leif's golden gaze. "We cross into the Rootless King's domain." He looked to Brynja, whose amber eyes reflected the golden light surrounding them. "Together."

Around them, the circle of splinters pulsed in approval, their combined hum forming a chord that seemed to resonate with the very fabric of reality itself.

***

Darkness fell over the glade, moonlight filtering through leaf-gaps to dapple the ground with silver. Asvarr crouched beside Leif's glowing map, memorizing the path through the Rootless King's domain. Golden sap continued to pulse through the suspended fragments, casting eerie shadows across his face. The nine great splinters surrounding them thrummed with increasing intensity, their harmonics vibrating through his bones.

"We should rest," Brynja said, her voice rough with exhaustion. She leaned against one of the splinters, her wooden arm seemingly drawn to it. "The journey tomorrow will test us all."

Asvarr nodded, reluctantly pulling himself away from the map. His muscles ached from the day's travel, his mind heavy with revelations of bloodlines betrayed and ancient deceptions spanning generations.

"I'll take first watch," Kára offered, her hood pulled low over her partially transformed face.

Yrsa had already begun preparing a small fire in the center of the glade, her movements precise and deliberate. "Sleep will come easier with these," she said, sprinkling herbs into a pot of water. "Root-dreams without Root-madness."

They arranged their bedrolls in a circle around the fire, mirroring the splinters that towered above them. Asvarr drank Yrsa's bitter tea, feeling it settle his churning thoughts. The Grímmark on his chest pulsed gently, attuned to the rhythm of the splinters' humming.

Leif sat cross-legged beside his map, golden eyes reflecting the firelight. "They're waiting," he whispered, too low for the others to hear.

"Who?" Asvarr asked.

"The memories inside the wood. They want to speak."

"Then let them," Asvarr said, settling beside the boy. "I'm listening."

Before Leif could respond, the splinters' humming crescendoed. The sound swelled until it filled the glade, drowning out even the crackling of the fire. Asvarr's companions bolted upright, hands reaching for weapons.

"Don't move!" Yrsa commanded, her crystal pendant blazing with blue-white light. "It's beginning!"

***

The nine great splinters shuddered in unison. Fissures appeared along their length, zigzagging from base to tip. Golden sap erupted from the cracks, arcing outward, streams of liquid light connecting splinter to splinter until they formed a gleaming web above their heads.

Brynja gasped as a tendril of sap reached toward her, hovering before her face. Similar tendrils extended toward each of them—Asvarr, Yrsa, Leif, even Kára at the edge of the glade.

"Don't resist," Yrsa said, voice taut with excitement or fear, Asvarr couldn't tell which. "The Circle awakens fully. This is rare beyond measure."

The golden tendril before Asvarr pulsed, an invitation. He hesitated, remembering the memory-fruits, how consuming another's experiences had nearly broken Brynja. Yet, something told him this was different; this was like communion, and not consumption.

He drew a breath and leaned forward, allowing the tendril to touch his forehead.

Fire and light exploded behind his eyes. The world vanished.

Asvarr floated in midnight sky, stars wheeling beneath him, above him, around him. A vast trunk emerged from darkness—Yggdrasil in its full glory, branches extending beyond comprehension, roots delving into realms visible only as glowing spheres at impossible distances.

He wasn't alone. Brynja's consciousness brushed against his, startled recognition flaring between them. Yrsa followed, then Leif, even Kára—their minds connected through the splinters' shared memory.

Watch, whispered a voice that came from everywhere and nowhere. *Remember what we remember.*

The great Tree pulsed with life, its bark rippling like muscle, sap flowing visibly through translucent channels. But among the roots, something moved. A darkness deeper than the void surrounding them, formless yet possessing terrible purpose.

It crept upward, tendrils of pure negation wrapping around the lowest root. Where it touched, the Tree's substance dimmed, its patterns disrupted. The darkness fed, growing larger with each moment of contact.

Asvarr felt the Tree's awareness—vast beyond human comprehension yet achingly familiar. Its consciousness encompassed multitudes, a living archive of all existence. And it was afraid.

The darkness spread, consuming more roots, its hunger insatiable. The Tree's pain flared across their joined consciousness, so intense that Asvarr heard Brynja cry out somewhere beyond the vision.

Above, in the highest branches, Asvarr glimpsed nine figures gathered in council—the Verdant Five and four others he didn't recognize. They gestured frantically, their movements leaving trails of colored light in the darkness. Whatever solution they proposed came too late.

The Tree made its choice.

A sound beyond sound, a scream that contained despair and determination in equal measure. The trunk shuddered, massive fractures appearing along its length. The Tree was breaking itself apart, deliberately separating its consciousness, hiding fragments of its awareness across the realms.

Asvarr watched in horror and awe as nine massive root sections tore free, golden sap gushing from the wounds. Each fragment contained a portion of the Tree's mind, a shard of its unified being. The fragments scattered across reality, piercing the fabric between worlds.

The darkness recoiled, suddenly deprived of its unified meal. It thrashed among the ruins, catching smaller fragments, consuming them in furious hunger. But the primary pieces—the anchors—had escaped beyond its reach.

Understand, the voice whispered. *We chose division over destruction. Fracture over consumption. Our consciousness survives in fragments, waiting to be gathered when safety returns.*

The vision shifted, showing the scattered fragments landing across the Nine Realms. One plunged into Midgard where Asvarr had found it. Another buried itself beneath the verdant forests. Others fell into fire, frost, death realms—each finding sanctuary in elemental domains where the darkness could not easily follow.

The anchors remember. The pattern endures, though broken. But beware—the hunger that devoured us still seeks completion. It waits between branches, between worlds, patient and eternal.

The vision zoomed vertiginously to focus on one fragment—a splinter that Asvarr recognized as the one that had marked him with the Grímmark. Golden sap leaked from its broken end, forming a puddle that shifted into the shape of a rune. The same rune now etched into his flesh.

We chose you, Flame-tender. Others like you. Vessels for remembrance. Through you, we might restore what was willingly broken.

The perspective widened again, showing the nine council members fleeing as the Tree shattered. The Verdant Five escaped intact, but the other four fragmented along with the Tree, their consciousness splintered. Asvarr glimpsed a familiar face among them—Yrsa—though younger, clothed in light.

The Shapers survived, but they too were changed. Their unity broken, their purpose distorted. What began as protection became possession. What began as guidance became control.

Patterns of light formed between the falling fragments, connections maintained despite physical separation. Asvarr understood suddenly that the Tree had not died—it had transformed. Its consciousness lived on as a distributed network, connected through those marked by its essence.

The vision shifted once more, showing the darkness regrouping, extending tendrils between realms, searching for the fragments. It found gaps in reality where the breakage had left vulnerabilities.

It hunts still. When we broke ourselves, we also broke the barriers that kept it contained. It seeks the anchors, the vessels, the memories we scattered. This is what the Ashfather fears—what might follow us through the cracks we made.

The darkness coalesced into a shape almost human, crowned with twisted branches of void. Its empty face turned toward them, seeing across vision and time. Asvarr felt its hunger like a physical blow against his mind.

"What is it?" he asked, forcing words through their shared consciousness.

The Old Hunger. The Void Between. It existed before pattern, before shape, before Tree or gods or worlds. When order first formed from chaos, it was imprisoned by structure itself. Our breaking has loosened its chains.

The vision dimmed, the Tree fading to ghostly transparency, the darkness growing more solid with each moment.

Our time grows short. The choice approaches. Restoration returns us to vulnerability. Destruction surrenders all to emptiness. Only transformation offers hope—a new pattern neither we nor the hunger anticipate.

The last image burned into Asvarr's awareness: five figures standing in a circle around a sapling, each marked with different patterns of light. Their combined radiance formed a shield that pushed back the darkness. Behind them, countless others added their light, reinforcing the shield, expanding it outward.

Remember what you've witnessed. The truth of our breaking. The reason for your calling.

Asvarr gasped, falling backward onto the cold earth of the glade. The golden tendril withdrew from his forehead, rejoining the web of light above. Around him, his companions were similarly sprawled, eyes wide, bodies trembling.

"You saw it too," Brynja whispered, her voice raw. She pushed herself upright, bark creaking along her transformed arm. "The Tree broke itself. To escape consumption."

"To preserve its consciousness across the realms," Yrsa added, her normally composed features shaken. She stared at her hands as if seeing them for the first time. "The Five... they were changed by what they witnessed. By what they survived."

Kára remained silent, huddled at the edge of the glade, arms wrapped around herself. Her hood had fallen back, revealing the bark patterns she'd tried to hide—more extensive than she'd let them see, covering nearly half her face.

Leif alone seemed unfazed by the vision. He sat calmly beside his glowing map, eyes now entirely golden, reflecting the web of light above. "The Tree remembers itself through us," he said. "It's why I can see the patterns. I was born when it broke."

Asvarr touched his chest where the Grímmark burned with renewed intensity. "The Tree chose to shatter, to scatter its consciousness rather than be devoured whole." His mind raced, reassembling everything he'd believed about his quest. "The anchors aren't just fragments of wood—they're fragments of its mind."

"And we're not just Wardens," Brynja said, meeting his gaze with amber eyes that glowed in the darkness. "We're memory-vessels. Carrying pieces of its consciousness through our bloodlines."

Yrsa nodded slowly, her pendant pulsing with the same rhythm as the splinters. "The Five know this. They've always known. They seek to gather these memories, to reshape them according to their vision of what should have been."

Asvarr stood, approaching the nearest splinter. He laid his palm against its surface, feeling the vibration of consciousness within. "And the Ashfather? Where does he stand in this?"

"Afraid," Leif answered, voice distant. "He saw the darkness too. Felt its hunger. He believes any restoration risks inviting it back into full manifestation."

"And he might be right," Brynja said, her transformed features hardening. "You saw what feasted on the Tree. If reunifying the anchors opens the door to that..."

The glade fell silent save for the continued hum of the splinters. The golden web above their heads shifted, forming new patterns that matched the map Leif had created.

Yrsa was the first to speak. "We cannot know the right path until we reach the second anchor. Each binding reveals more of the pattern, more of the Tree's fragmented memory."

"But binding also transforms us," Asvarr reminded her, thinking of the changes the first anchor had wrought in him. "How much of ourselves will remain by the end?"

"Perhaps that's the true question," Brynja said. "How much of ourselves should remain? If transformation is the only path forward..."

The glowing web pulsed once, brilliantly, then retracted. The golden tendrils withdrew into the splinters, which sealed their cracks with audible sighs. The humming subsided to a gentle background vibration, leaving the glade lit only by moonlight and their small fire.

Leif's map remained, hovering inches above the ground, now etched with additional details—elevation shifts, hidden paths, places marked with warning symbols.

"The way is clearer now," the boy said, running his fingers through the three-dimensional representation. "The Tree guides us through its memory."

Asvarr exchanged glances with Brynja and Yrsa. The vision had changed everything and nothing. Their path still led through the Rootless King's domain to the Verdant Gate, but the stakes had shifted. This wasn't merely about restoration or destruction. It was about remembrance—and transformation.

"We leave at first light," Asvarr decided, the weight of the vision settling into his bones. "The Rootless King awaits."

Brynja nodded, determination hardening her gaze. "The Five won't be far behind. They'll have felt the awakening."

"Then we move quickly," Asvarr replied, studying the enhanced map once more. "Together."

Outside their circle of splinters, beyond the glade's edge, branches rustled though no wind blew. Shadows deepened between trees, coalescing into shapes almost human. Watching. Waiting.

Asvarr placed his hand on his sword hilt, the metal warm beneath his fingers. Whatever waited in the darkness—the Five, the Ashfather's servants, or something older and hungrier—would find them ready.

Behind him, the nine great splinters stood like silent sentinels, guardians of memory in a fractured world. The map glowed golden in the night, marking their path forward into uncertainty.

"The Tree chose division to survive," Asvarr murmured. "What will we choose when our moment comes?"

No one answered. No one could. That truth awaited them at the Verdant Gate, where the second anchor called through blood and memory and the turning of time itself.

CHAPTER 10

GATE OF BONE AND BLOSSOM

Morning broke reluctantly over the Circle of Splinters, dim light filtering through mist that clung to the ground like a living thing. Asvarr cinched his pack tighter, the leather straps creaking across his shoulders. His muscles ached from a night of fitful sleep, the vision of the Tree's shattering replaying each time he closed his eyes.

"We go north through the marsh," he said, studying the glowing map one final time before they departed. "Then west along the ridge until we reach the border stones."

Brynja nodded, her amber eyes reflecting the last glimmers of the map as Leif dismissed it with a wave of his small hand. The golden representation of their path collapsed into itself, becoming a sphere of light that the boy pocketed.

"The Rootless King will know we're coming," Yrsa warned, adjusting her leather satchel across her chest. "His domain exists half in this world, half in the spaces between. The moment we cross his threshold, we enter his awareness."

Kára approached warily, keeping distance between herself and the others. Her hood was drawn up again, hiding her partially transformed face. "I'll scout ahead," she offered. "My bloodline carries less of the Tree's essence. I might draw less attention."

"We stay together," Asvarr countered, resting his hand on his sword hilt. "The vision showed we're stronger united."

They moved out from the glade, leaving the nine great splinters behind. Asvarr felt them watching, their consciousness lingering at the edges of his awareness.

The Grímmark on his chest tingled, a constant reminder of the burden he'd accepted.

The terrain grew marshy as they descended a shallow slope, their boots sinking into sucking mud. Strange plants grew here—flowers with translucent petals that turned to follow their movement, reeds that whispered in voices almost like speech. Clouds hung low, pressing down on them like a physical weight.

"Here," Leif said abruptly, stopping before what appeared to be an ordinary stand of white birch trees. "The first crossing."

Asvarr saw nothing unusual about the trees until he squinted, focusing the way he had when using root-sight. Then he noticed the faint shimmer surrounding them, a barely visible distortion of the air.

"A boundary," Yrsa explained, her crystal pendant glowing faintly. "The edge of the Rootless domain."

Brynja rubbed her wooden arm, her expression tightening. "I can hear them," she murmured. "The severed souls on the other side. Trapped between states."

Asvarr listened but heard only wind rustling through leaves. Whatever Brynja sensed remained hidden from him—for now.

"To cross," Yrsa said, "we must each offer a grief freely given, as Leif told us." She removed her pendant, holding it before her. "The Rootless King feeds on sorrow. Fresh grief sustains his realm."

"How?" Asvarr asked, his hand instinctively rising to touch the Grímmark. "How do we give grief?"

Yrsa closed her eyes, holding the crystal so it caught what little sunlight broke through the clouds. "Think of a sorrow you carry. Hold it in your mind. Then speak it aloud while touching the boundary. The telling makes it a gift."

Kára took an instinctive step backward. "This is madness. Grief is private. Sacred."

"It's the price of passage," Brynja said with surprising gentleness. "Would you rather face the Five?"

After a tense moment, Kára nodded reluctantly.

Yrsa approached the boundary first, pressing her palm against the invisible barrier. The air rippled at her touch.

"I give this sorrow freely," she said, voice carrying a ritual cadence. "I grieve for my divided self, for the part of me that remained with the council when the Tree shattered. I grieve for the unity I will never reclaim."

The barrier shimmered more intensely, a vertical seam appearing within it. Yrsa stepped through, her form blurring momentarily before solidifying on the other side.

Brynja went next, placing her wooden hand against the boundary. "I give this sorrow freely. I grieve for the clan I lost, for the family whose faces grow dimmer in my memory with each passing day."

Another seam opened, allowing her passage.

Leif approached without hesitation. His small face was solemn as he touched the boundary. "I give this sorrow freely. I grieve for never being whole, for existing across realities, for the parts of myself I cannot reach."

The boundary parted for him.

Kára held back, her hands trembling visibly. After several deep breaths, she stepped forward. "I give this sorrow freely," she whispered. "I grieve for what I'm becoming, for the humanity I feel slipping away with each new growth of bark."

She disappeared through the seam, leaving Asvarr alone on the mortal side of the boundary.

He approached slowly, memories of his slaughtered clan rising unbidden in his mind. That grief had fueled him, driven him, defined him since the day he'd awakened among their bodies. Could he surrender even a portion of it?

Pressing his palm to the boundary, he felt resistance—not physical but spiritual, as if the barrier tested his sincerity.

"I give this sorrow freely," he began, the words catching in his throat. "I grieve for... for my failure. For being away raiding when my people needed me. For living when they died."

The words unlocked something within him, a dam breaking. "I should have been there. I should have died with them."

The boundary rippled, parting for him. As he stepped through, he felt the grief lift from his shoulders—not gone completely, but lighter, as if sharing the burden had diminished its weight.

***

The world on the other side assaulted his senses.

Trees grew upside down, their roots splayed across a sky streaked with colors Asvarr had no names for. Water flowed vertically in shimmering columns, fish swimming placidly up and down their lengths. The ground beneath his feet felt simultaneously solid and insubstantial, as if he might sink through it should he stop moving.

Most disorienting of all was the light—it came from everywhere and nowhere, casting multiple shadows from each object. His companions threw three or four silhouettes each, pointing in contradictory directions.

"Stay close," Yrsa warned, her voice echoing strangely. "Perception shifts here. Trust your connection to each other more than your eyes."

Asvarr focused on the blood-oath mark on his palm, feeling its connection to Brynja. The sensation of her presence stabilized him somewhat.

As they moved deeper into the twisted landscape, Asvarr noticed movement at the corners of his vision. Pale figures flitted between inverted trees, too quick to focus on. Their bodies seemed incomplete—missing limbs, torsos, sometimes faces.

"The Severed," Brynja murmured, her wooden arm creaking as she drew closer to Asvarr. "Souls caught in the Shattering, torn between existence and void."

One of the figures drifted closer, and Asvarr fought the urge to recoil. It was a woman—or had been once. Half her body appeared normal, the other half faded into transparency, edge marked by a jagged line as if she'd been torn in two. Her eyes contained no pupils, just swirling mist.

"You... carry... the essence," she said, her voice fluctuating in volume. "The fragments of what we lost."

More of the Severed appeared, surrounding their group with flickering forms. Some had missing limbs, others lacked portions of their torsos or heads. All had the same misty eyes, fixed on Asvarr and his companions with desperate intensity.

"We mean no harm," Asvarr said, keeping his voice steady despite the cold dread building in his chest. "We seek passage to the Verdant Gate."

The woman tilted her head at an impossible angle. "You must... see... the King. He hungers... for what you bring."

The Severed parted, creating a pathway through the twisted trees. Seeing no alternative, Asvarr led his companions forward. The ground undulated beneath them, terrain transforming with each step. Dense forest gave way to barren mountains, then flowing plains, then jagged ravines—all within the span of moments.

"The landscape shifts with memory," Yrsa explained quietly. "What we walk through is reality remembered by the Severed, fragments of what existed before the Shattering."

They crested a hill that hadn't been there moments before, and a vast city sprawled before them—a metropolis of impossible architecture. Buildings curve backward on themselves, streets ran vertically up walls, bridges connected structures that simultaneously appeared miles apart and adjacent.

At the city's center stood a palace of bone and living wood. Massive femurs formed its columns, skulls grinned from parapets, ribs curved to create arched doorways. Between these bone structures, branches and vines grew, flowering with blooms that emitted the strange omnidirectional light.

"The Rootless King's hall," Yrsa breathed. "Where he collects all grief and memory."

As they approached the city, Asvarr noticed how the Severed became more numerous and more substantial. Those nearest the palace appeared almost whole, missing only small portions of themselves—a finger, an ear, a patch of skin.

The palace gates stood open, fashioned from interlocking vertebrae and flowering vines. Two figures flanked the entrance, more solid than any Severed they'd encountered yet. Both wore armor assembled from bone fragments tied together with silver wire, and their faces were concealed behind masks carved from jawbones.

"The King awaits the Wardens," said one guard, voice surprisingly normal. "And their offerings."

Inside, the palace defied conventional understanding of space. Corridors stretched for impossible distances before abruptly shortening. Stairways led up only to deposit travelers on lower floors. Doorways opened into rooms that logically couldn't fit within the structure.

They eventually entered a vast circular chamber. The floor was transparent, revealing an abyss filled with swirling mist. The ceiling appeared to be the night sky, though stars arranged themselves in patterns Asvarr had never seen. The walls were lined with alcoves, each containing a glowing orb that pulsed with soft light.

On a throne of interwoven bone and branch sat the Rootless King.

He was tall—far taller than any human—with limbs too long for his body. His skin was the pale white of birch bark, cracked in places to reveal golden light beneath. Antlers of bone and crystal grew from his head, branching in complex patterns. His eyes were pools of liquid shadow, yet somehow captured and reflected the light around them.

"Wardens," he said, his voice resonating from everywhere at once. "You bring me such delightful grief. So fresh. So potent." He inhaled deeply through nostrils that flared too wide. "Yet you withhold your greatest sorrows. Keeping them close. Feeding on them yourselves."

He rose, unfolding to a height that should have reached the ceiling, yet somehow didn't. His movements were fluid but wrong, joints bending in directions they shouldn't.

"You seek passage to the Verdant Gate," he continued, circling them slowly. His bare feet made no sound against the transparent floor. "A place of transformation. Of possibility. Why?"

"To bind the second anchor," Asvarr answered truthfully, sensing lies would only anger this being.

The King stopped directly before him, bending down until their faces were level. His breath smelled of wet earth and decay.

"The anchors remember," he whispered. "As do I. I was there when the Tree shattered. I was born in that breaking." He straightened, addressing the entire group now. "Do you know what I was before? What the fracturing made me?"

None dared answer.

"I was happiness," the King said, spreading his too-long arms. "I was joy and contentment and satisfaction. All the brightest emotions, torn from reality and inverted. Transformed into hunger for what I can no longer feel."

He gestured to the glowing orbs lining the walls. "I collect memories of happiness. Moments of joy. They sustain this realm, keep it from dissolving entirely into the void between worlds."

His shadow-pool eyes fixed on Asvarr again. "I will grant you passage through my domain to the Verdant Gate. But the price is higher than the small griefs you offered at my boundary. From each of you, I require a memory of true happiness. Your brightest moment. Your perfect joy."

Kára made a small sound of protest but quickly silenced herself when the King's gaze slid to her.

"Without such payment," the King continued, "my realm will continue to dissolve. The Severed will fade entirely. Including those you once loved."

With a languid gesture, he summoned five Severed who emerged from recesses in the walls. Asvarr's breath caught in his throat. Among them was a familiar face—Torfa, the shield-maiden who had trained him, who had died in the raid prior to his clan's destruction. Her form was mostly intact, missing only one hand and a portion of her shoulder.

"Asvarr," she said, her voice exactly as he remembered it. "You live."

"This is a trick," Brynja hissed, her wooden fingers digging into his arm.

"No trick," the King countered. "Merely a truth you would prefer hidden. Many of your people exist here, Wardens. Neither living nor dead, but severed from the pattern when the Tree shattered. They remember you. They watch your journey."

Asvarr stared at Torfa, his mentor, his friend. She smiled at him with the same crooked grin that had always preceded a training bout.

"How many?" he asked hoarsely. "How many of my clan are here?"

"Dozens," the King answered. "Trapped between states. I preserve them. Sustain them. Without me, they dissolve into the void between."

"And you want our happiness in exchange for passage?" Yrsa asked, her voice steady despite the tension Asvarr could see in her shoulders.

"Yes," the King replied. "One perfect memory from each of you. Freely given."

"And if we refuse?" Brynja challenged.

The King's mouth stretched into something approximating a smile, though it extended too far across his face. "Then you remain here, surrounded by what remains of your loved ones, unable to proceed or retreat. The Five will eventually find you, or the Ashfather. The anchors will remain separated. The pattern will continue to fray."

He extended one long-fingered hand. "Choose now, Wardens. Your joy for their continued existence. For your passage to the Gate. What say you?"

Asvarr looked at Torfa's incomplete form, at the hope in her familiar eyes. His greatest happiness in exchange for her continued existence, however compromised? For the chance to reach the second anchor? The weight of the choice pressed down on him like a physical burden.

Around him, his companions stood frozen in similar contemplation, each confronted with spectral fragments of their own pasts, their own impossible choices.

The Rootless King waited, patient and hungry, for their decision.

Asvarr stared into the shadow-pool eyes of the Rootless King, his throat tight with an emotion he couldn't name. Behind him, Torfa's incomplete form wavered, her familiar presence pulling at something deep within his chest.

"I accept your price," he said, the words scraping his throat raw. "A memory of joy for passage."

The King's mouth stretched into that too-wide smile again. "Excellent. Come forward, Flame-Warden."

Asvarr stepped onto a circle of bone inlaid in the transparent floor. Beneath his feet, the swirling mist parted, revealing greater depths of emptiness. The air grew thick, pressing against his skin as if testing his resolve.

"Close your eyes," the King instructed. "Find the brightest moment of your life. Hold it in your mind."

Asvarr obeyed, sifting through memories dulled by grief and purpose. What happiness remained to him? Then he found it—a summer day long before the Shattering, before his first raid. He'd climbed the tallest pine near his village, higher than any other child dared. At the top, wind whipping his hair, he'd glimpsed the ocean glittering on the horizon, felt the perfect balance of terror and triumph. His father had spotted him from below and, instead of scolding, had whooped with pride. That night, his father had carved him a pine-hawk pendant, calling him sky-climber, telling stories of their ancestors who had scaled mountains to speak with gods.

"Yes," the King whispered, voice suddenly close to Asvarr's ear. "That one. So bright. So pure."

Long fingers touched Asvarr's temple, cold as midwinter ice. The memory pulled free from his mind, extracted whole, leaving behind a hollow space where joy had lived. The sensation wasn't pain but absence, a sudden void within him.

When he opened his eyes, the King held a glowing orb between his palms, radiant with golden light. Within it, Asvarr could see miniature versions of himself and his father, the memory now external, belonging to another.

"Beautiful," the King breathed, placing the orb in an empty alcove. "Such perfect joy. It will sustain many Severed for months to come."

Each of Asvarr's companions underwent the same process. Brynja surrendered a memory of dancing with her mother beneath the harvest moon. Yrsa gave up something that made the King's eyes widen with surprise—a memory far older than her apparent years. Kára yielded a moment from before her transformation began. Leif, strangely, produced an orb that shifted between multiple colors, containing fragments from several realities.

"The bargain is fulfilled," the King declared when all five orbs glowed in their alcoves. "You may pass through my realm to the Verdant Gate. My Severed will guide you."

Torfa stepped forward, her form slightly more substantial now, nourished by the fresh memories. "I will lead them," she said, her voice stronger than before.

The King nodded, folding his too-long body back onto his throne. "Remember, Wardens," he called as they turned to leave, "should you fail in your quest, there is a place for you here among the Severed. A half-existence is preferable to none at all."

***

They followed Torfa through corridors that twisted upon themselves, architecture defying all logic. Other Severed joined them—men and women Asvarr recognized from his clan, each missing pieces of themselves. They spoke little, communicating through gestures and glances as if speech required energy they couldn't spare.

"How much farther?" Brynja asked after what felt like hours of walking. The hollow space where her memory had been extracted throbbed visibly at her temple, a slight indentation in her skin.

"Time flows strangely here," Torfa replied. "We walk the path that memory makes."

They emerged from the bone palace into the impossible city. The streets had rearranged themselves, now spiraling outward from the palace like spokes of a wheel. Buildings folded and unfolded as they passed, revealing interiors that couldn't possibly fit within their walls.

"The Verdant Gate lies beyond the city's edge," Torfa explained, leading them down a road paved with flat stones that rippled like water under their feet. "Where this realm ends and the next begins."

Asvarr studied his former shield-maiden, noting how parts of her flickered in and out of existence. "How long have you been here?" he asked.

"Since before the Shattering," Torfa replied. "I died in the raid, remember? But death came at the same moment the Tree broke. I was caught between—neither living nor dead, neither in Midgard nor Helheim."

"And my clan?" Asvarr pressed. "Those who died when our village was destroyed?"

"Many are here. Those who died in the moment of breaking." She gestured to the Severed walking beside them. "We watch. We remember. We fade without the King's sustenance."

Asvarr's chest tightened. What would happen to these fragments of his people when he completed his quest? If the Tree was restored, would they find true death, or something else entirely?

They reached the city's edge where the spiraling architecture dissolved into fog. Through the mist, a colossal shape loomed—the Verdant Gate. Even from this distance, Asvarr could see it was formed of impossibly intertwined branches and roots, a living doorway taller than the bone palace itself.

"We can go no further," Torfa said, stopping at the boundary between solid ground and swirling mist. "The Severed cannot approach the Gate. It... unmakes us."

Asvarr turned to her, sudden understanding dawning. "The Gate leads to what comes after—to restoration or transformation. You're fragments of what was broken. You can't cross through."

She nodded, her incomplete form wavering like a reflection in disturbed water. "Our existence depends on the breaking. If you succeed..."

"I'll find a way to help you," Asvarr promised, the words tumbling out before he could consider their weight. "All of you."

Torfa smiled, the expression achingly familiar. "You always took on more than you could carry, Asvarr." She clasped his arm with her remaining hand. "Follow your path. We have existed this way for longer than you know. We will endure a while longer."

With a final nod to the assembled Severed—fragments of his people preserved in this impossible realm—Asvarr led his companions into the mist. Behind them, the city and its inhabitants faded from view, the mist thickening until they walked blind, guided only by the pull of the Gate ahead.

***

The mist parted suddenly, revealing the full majesty of the Verdant Gate. It towered above them, a massive archway formed of living wood. Branches and roots intertwined in patterns of impossible complexity, forming a doorway at least thirty paces high. Golden sap wept from the junctions where wood met wood, pooling at the Gate's base. The entire structure pulsed with slow vitality, expanding and contracting like lungs drawing breath.

"It's alive," Brynja whispered, her wooden arm resonating visibly with the Gate's rhythm.

"It was never cut from the Tree," Yrsa explained, her voice hushed with reverence. "This is Yggdrasil's original tissue, preserved when all else shattered."

Leif approached the Gate without fear, placing his small hand against its surface. The wood rippled at his touch, golden sap oozing between his fingers. "It remembers," he said.

Asvarr stepped forward, the Grímmark on his chest burning with recognition. The patterns carved into the Gate's surface matched those etched into his flesh—the same runes, the same whorls, the same intricate geometry.

"How do we open it?" Kára asked, keeping her distance, hood drawn tight over her partially transformed face.

"Blood," Brynja suggested, studying the carvings. "Like other Root structures we've encountered."

Asvarr approached the Gate, running his fingers over the patterns. The wood felt warm, practically vibrating with contained energy. Pressing his palm against it, he sensed ancient awareness within. It didnt feel like sentience exactly, but recognition. The Gate knew him, or knew what he carried.

"It's waiting for something specific," he murmured, tracing a deep channel where golden sap flowed. "A key beyond mere blood."

He recalled the Sapborn Oracle's words: *The Gate opens to memory. What you seek lies in what was forgotten, not what will be.*

Memory. What had he forgotten? What had been lost in the cycles of breaking and restoration?

The Grímmark pulsed, its heat intensifying until sweat beaded on his brow. Through it, he felt the pull of the second anchor beyond the Gate, calling to the fragment he already carried. Its song filled his mind, with impressions—green growth, roots delving deep, branches reaching skyward.

Then understanding struck like summer lightning. The Gate didn't require a physical key but a name—a word of power forgotten over generations as his people turned from their original deities to worship Odin and his kin.

"Names hold power," he said aloud, stepping back from the Gate. "The Oracle told us the Gate opens to memory—to what was forgotten. Our clan's original deity, before Odin's ascendance."

Brynja frowned. "How would you know that name? It would have been lost generations ago."

"Not lost," Asvarr countered, touching the Grímmark. "Preserved. In blood and Root and memory."

He closed his eyes, reaching inward to the place where the first anchor's consciousness resided within him. He searched for resonance—the name that would vibrate in harmony with the Gate's structure. The Grímmark burned hotter, golden sap weeping from its edges as it had in moments of deep communion with the Root.

A word formed in his mind, assembled from fragments of ancestral memory carried in his blood and reinforced by the Root's ancient awareness.

"Fornbrandr," he whispered, the syllables unfamiliar yet right on his tongue. "The Ancient Flame."

The Gate shuddered, wood creaking as the intricate patterns shifted. Sap flowed faster, pooling at Asvarr's feet. The entire structure trembled, branches and roots rearranging themselves, pulling apart to create an opening at the center.

Through the widening gap, Asvarr glimpsed a landscape that defied description—a realm formed of pure memory, where shapes assembled and disassembled themselves like thoughts taking physical form.

"What is that?" Kára gasped, taking an involuntary step backward.

"The collective remembrance of the Tree itself," Yrsa answered, her voice thick with emotion. "A memory realm constructed from unspoken histories."

Leif's eyes gleamed with golden light. "The roots remember everything," he said. "Every moment from the Tree's creation to its shattering. Every life that touched it. Every word spoken beneath its branches."

The opening widened further, the Gate fully unlocked by the forgotten name. Wind gusted from the other side, carrying scents Asvarr couldn't identify—things that had never existed in the physical world, aromas of concepts and emotions rather than substances.

"The second anchor waits within," Brynja said, her wooden arm extending toward the opening, fingers splayed as if already reaching for what lay beyond.

Asvarr squared his shoulders, the Grímmark blazing on his chest. The blood-oath mark on his palm throbbed in rhythm with Brynja's identical scar. They had come this far together—through revelation and betrayal, through truth and transformation. Whatever waited beyond the Gate, they would face it as kin reunited, as bloodlines rejoined.

"Together," he said, holding out his hand to Brynja.

She clasped it, bark against skin. "Together."

Yrsa touched her crystal pendant, which glowed with inner light. "I've waited lifetimes to walk this path."

Leif nodded, already half-stepping toward the opening, drawn to its impossible geometry. "I was born for this crossing."

Only Kára hesitated, fear evident in her stance. "What if we can't return?" she asked, her voice barely audible over the Gate's creaking.

"We go forward," Asvarr told her, not unkindly. "The past is broken. The future remains unwritten. Our path leads through."

With that, he stepped through the Verdant Gate, still clasping Brynja's hand. The others followed, Kára last, her reluctance overcome by fear of being left behind. As they crossed the threshold, reality twisted around them, the physical world dissolving into a landscape of pure memory.

The Gate sealed shut behind them with a sound like the world's oldest tree finally toppling after ten thousand years of silent witness. There would be no returning the way they had come.

Before them stretched the memory forest—a realm of unspoken histories, accumulated remembrances, and forgotten truths. Somewhere within its depths waited the second anchor, ready to transform those who sought it, just as they would transform it in turn.

Asvarr took the first step into this land of living memory, the hollow space where his childhood joy had been now filled with something new: purpose, clarity, determination. The second binding awaited, and with it, another piece of the pattern would reveal itself.

CHAPTER 11
PATH OF UNRAVELING

The forest dissolved into ocean between one footstep and the next. Asvarr's boot, prepared for moss and fallen leaves, plunged instead into knee-deep water that felt both liquid and solid at once. The sudden shift wrenched a gasp from his throat. Behind him, Kára cursed, Brynja shouted in surprise, and Yrsa made a sound halfway between laughter and alarm.

Only Leif walked undisturbed, small feet somehow remaining atop the impossible sea as if it were solid ground. He turned back to them, golden eyes gleaming.

"The memory isn't fixed here," he said, his voice carrying clearly despite the crashing waves that had materialized around them. "It changes with thought and intention."

Asvarr struggled to make sense of his surroundings. The ocean stretched endlessly, its deep blue waters so clear he could see strange spiraling structures on the seafloor far below. The air tasted of salt yet smelled of pine, a disorienting contradiction. The sky above—if it could be called sky—rippled with bands of color that stretched and contracted like living things.

"How do we navigate this?" Asvarr asked, finding his footing on the strangely solid-liquid surface.

"You follow me," Leif replied simply. "I can see the paths."

"And we trust him," Brynja added, her wooden arm gleaming wetly in this impossible ocean. "His nature is attuned to this place." Her voice held no doubt, only a statement of what she now understood.

Asvarr nodded, extending his hand to Kára who was struggling to maintain her balance in the shifting environment. She took it reluctantly, her partially transformed face tight with fear beneath her hood.

"This realm isn't meant for ordinary minds," Yrsa explained, her crystal pendant pulsing with blue-white light. "It's the Tree's accumulated memory—everything it witnessed since the dawn of creation. Our perceptions can't contain it, so it manifests in ways we might comprehend."

A mountain peak erupted from the water thirty paces ahead, rising impossibly fast until it towered above them. The ocean drained away between one heartbeat and the next, replaced by a rocky slope covered in snow and lichen. Asvarr felt no transition—only the sudden absence of water and presence of stone beneath his feet.

"Keep moving," Leif urged, already climbing the slope. "Staying still allows the memories to settle. We might sink into them."

Asvarr followed, his limbs heavy with a fatigue that seemed unrelated to physical exertion. The Grímmark burned on his chest, responding to something in this environment that his human senses couldn't perceive. His vision blurred periodically, overlaying the mountain with glimpses of other landscapes—desert, forest, city, void—that existed simultaneously in this place of unbound memory.

"What are we seeking?" he called to Leif, who had reached a ridge above and stood silhouetted against the rippling sky.

"The second anchor," the boy replied. "It waits where root meets memory, where the Tree's consciousness fragmented during the breaking."

Brynja climbed beside Asvarr, her wooden arm finding impossible handholds in the rock. "And where is that exactly?" she pressed, frustration edging her voice.

Leif pointed toward a distant peak that hadn't been there moments before. "There—where the sky opens and the ground remembers."

The landscape shifted again. The mountain collapsed beneath them, its rocky substance dissolving into fragments of light. They fell for a stomach-dropping moment before landing in a meadow of silvery grass that tingled against Asvarr's skin, sending tiny sparks of memory into his blood—flashes of ancient battles, births, deaths, ceremonies, all compressed into instants of sensation.

"Don't touch the grass for long," Yrsa warned. "It contains the memories of every blade cut in war or harvested in peace. Too many lives to absorb."

Asvarr lifted his feet high as he walked, following Leif who danced across the silver expanse, leaving glowing footprints that lingered briefly before fading. The meadow extended for what seemed like leagues, then abruptly ended at the edge of a forest far more substantial than their surroundings had been thus far.

These trees stood solid and unwavering—ancient pines with trunks wider than three men could embrace, their highest branches lost in mist. Unlike the shifting ocean and collapsing mountain, the forest possessed a permanence that Asvarr found immediately reassuring.

"This is more stable," Yrsa confirmed, touching one massive trunk with evident relief. "A core memory, something fundamental to the Tree's consciousness."

Leif nodded. "The First Forest. Where Yggdrasil began before it grew to connect the realms."

***

They entered beneath the canopy of towering pines. Sunlight—or something resembling it—filtered through branches in solid beams that illuminated motes of golden dust. The forest floor was carpeted with moss so deep it cushioned their steps, making them nearly silent as they walked.

For the first time since entering the memory realm, Asvarr felt they moved through an environment that would remain consistent for more than a few moments. The air smelled of sap and rich earth. Somewhere distant, water trickled over stones. Birds called in voices he almost recognized.

"This feels... real," he murmured.

"It is real," Leif answered. "Or was, once. Before the worlds were named. Before gods walked between branches."

They followed a natural path that wound between the massive trees. Asvarr noticed runes carved into some trunks—something older and more complex then the Norse symbols he is used to. The Grímmark on his chest resonated with them, sending pulses of heat through his torso.

"Creators' marks," Yrsa said, noticing his reaction. "The language of those who tended the first growth."

"The Verdant Five?" Brynja asked.

Yrsa shook her head. "Older. The ones who came before them."

The forest path led them to a clearing where the trees formed a perfect circle around a pool of water so still it reflected the sky with mirror perfection. At the pool's edge stood a stone altar, simple and unadorned save for a single rune carved into its surface.

"We rest here," Leif announced, sitting cross-legged at the water's edge. "The paths divide ahead. I must see which one leads to the anchor."

Asvarr surveyed the clearing with a warrior's caution. Despite the apparent stability of this part of the memory realm, he felt watched by awareness that permeated the air itself.

"We're not alone," he said quietly to Brynja, who nodded in agreement.

"The First Forest remembers those who walked here before," she replied, her wooden arm trailing patterns in the moss. "I can feel them through the Root."

Kára kept close to the trees, her transformed face half-hidden in shadow. "How long have we been here?" she asked, voice tight with anxiety. "Time feels... wrong."

"Time doesn't exist here as we understand it," Yrsa explained. "We move through memories, not moments. Hours or days could pass in the outer realms while we experience mere minutes here, or the reverse."

Asvarr approached the pool, drawn by its perfect stillness. Kneeling at its edge, he studied its reflective surface. Instead of showing his face, the water revealed a tapestry of images—fragments of events he recognized from the shared vision in the Circle of Splinters. The Tree breaking. Roots tearing free. Golden sap spreading across realms.

***

Movement at the clearing's edge caught his attention. A figure stood among the trees—translucent, glimmering faintly in the filtered light. As Asvarr watched, it stepped forward, revealing the form of a man in clothing of an unfamiliar style, ancient beyond reckoning.

"Another visitor to the memory," the figure said, its voice resonating strangely, like words spoken underwater. "You bear the mark of flame." It drifted closer, studying Asvarr with eyes that held no pupils, only swirling light. "The anchors call to you."

Asvarr rose to his feet, hand instinctively reaching for his sword before he remembered such weapons might be meaningless against a being of pure memory.

"Who are you?" he asked instead.

"A seeker, like yourself." The figure flickered, its edges blurring then reso-lidifying. "I found the Gate. I walked the Path. I lost myself among memories greater than my mind could contain."

"You're one of those who came before," Yrsa said, approaching cautiously. "A previous Warden?"

The figure smiled sadly. "We were not called Wardens then. We were Pathfinders. Tenders of the First Growth." It turned its attention back to Asvarr. "I recognize you, brother of the flame. You carry what I once did."

"The Grímmark," Asvarr said, touching his chest where the pattern burned beneath his tunic.

"The fire-sigil, we named it then. The flame that warms but does not consume." The figure's form wavered like heat distortion. "You seek the verdant anchor. The growing-heart."

Brynja stepped forward, her transformed arm extended. "You know where it is?"

"I knew," the figure corrected. "But memory fades, even here. I followed the path too far. Delved too deep." It gestured vaguely toward the trees beyond the clearing. "Beyond the pool lies the Remembering Glade. Beyond that, the Forgetting Forest. The anchor waits somewhere between memory and oblivion."

The figure's form began to lose coherence, edges dissolving into mist. "Beware what grows from broken root," it warned, voice fading. "The Tree remembers what the Five would have us forget. A fragment rebelled. Chose its own purpose. This... this began the breaking."

"Wait!" Asvarr called. "What fragment? What purpose?"

But the figure was already dissipating, its once-human shape melting into formless light. "Brother of the flame," it whispered as it faded completely. "The path unravels. Follow... the child who walks... between..."

With those final words, the figure vanished entirely, leaving only a faint shimmer in the air where it had stood.

***

Silence fell over the clearing. The birds had stopped their calling. Even the distant sound of water had ceased. The forest held its breath, waiting.

"That was a Pathfinder," Yrsa said, breaking the stillness. "One of the original tenders, lost within the memory realm."

"He recognized me," Asvarr said, rubbing his chest where the Grímmark continued to pulse with heat. "Called me 'brother of the flame.'"

"Your bloodline isn't the first to tend the flame aspect," Yrsa explained. "Others carried similar marks in previous cycles. The pattern repeats, though never exactly."

Leif had remained by the pool throughout the exchange, eyes fixed on the water's surface. Now he looked up, his golden gaze finding Asvarr's.

"I've found the path," he announced. "But we're not the only ones seeking it. Others watch from the depths of memory."

"The Five?" Brynja asked.

Leif shook his head. "Something older. Something that remembers its own breaking."

Asvarr glanced at the place where the spectral figure had disappeared. "The fragment that rebelled," he murmured. "The one that chose its own purpose."

"We should move," Kára interrupted, her voice edged with fresh fear. "More of them are coming."

Asvarr turned to see misty forms taking shape among the trees surrounding the clearing—dozens of ghostly figures emerging from the forest depths. Unlike the Pathfinder who had spoken to them, these apparitions seemed less substantial, less defined—fragments of memory rather than preserved consciousness.

"Previous seekers," Yrsa said quietly. "Lost within the realm. Neither fully here nor gone."

***

The ghostly figures drifted toward them, mouths moving in silent speech. Their eyes—all pupilless, all filled with the same swirling light—fixed on Asvarr and his companions with hungry intensity.

"They're drawn to our solidity," Yrsa explained, backing toward the pool. "We exist more fully than they do. They want what we have."

"The path leads through water," Leif said urgently, pointing to the mirror-still pool. "We must enter now."

Asvarr hesitated only a moment before making his decision. The ghostly seekers had nearly reached the edge of the clearing, their translucent hands outstretched.

"Into the pool," he commanded, drawing his sword more for reassurance than practical use. "Together!"

Brynja was first to move, striding purposefully into the water which accepted her without a ripple, maintaining its perfect stillness despite her entry. Yrsa followed, then Kára, who required Asvarr's firm hand on her shoulder to overcome her hesitation.

Leif waited at the pool's edge, watching the approaching ghosts with curious detachment.

"They were like me once," he said as Asvarr reached him. "Caught between states. But they lost themselves in memory."

"Don't linger," Asvarr warned, steering the boy toward the water. "Your nature may be attuned to this place, but you're still partly human."

Together they stepped into the pool, which remained impossibly undisturbed by their passage. The water felt cool against Asvarr's skin, yet somehow dry, as if he were walking through the idea of water rather than the substance itself.

They waded deeper, the pool proving far more extensive than its appearance suggested. The ghostly seekers reached the edge but stopped, unable or unwilling to enter the water. Their silent cries followed Asvarr as he led his companions toward the center where the surface began to glow with soft blue light.

As they reached the pool's heart, the light intensified, surrounding them completely. Asvarr felt the world shift once more, transforming with purposeful direction. The substance around them changed from water to light to solid ground in the space between heartbeats.

When the light faded, they stood in a new landscape—a vast plain beneath a sky filled with unfamiliar constellations. At the plain's center rose a single tree sapling, no taller than Asvarr himself, yet radiating power that made the Grímmark burn with renewed intensity.

"The Midsong Tree," Leif whispered, his golden eyes reflecting the sapling's subtle glow. "A fragment of the original consciousness. It will lead us to the verdant anchor."

Asvarr took a step toward the sapling, feeling the pull of connection between the mark on his chest and this manifestation of Yggdrasil's essence. With each step, the burning increased until it bordered on pain. The sapling seemed to respond, its few leaves trembling despite the absence of wind.

Behind him, he heard Brynja's sharp intake of breath.

"Asvarr," she called, voice tight with warning. "We're not alone."

He turned to see more figures materializing on the plain, something more substantial, than the formless ghosts of the forest. Wardens from previous cycles, their bodies marked with patterns similar to his own Grímmark, their eyes holding the same golden fire as Leif's.

One stepped forward, a woman with spiraling patterns of bark covering half her body. She opened her mouth to speak, but instead of words, a sound like distant chimes emerged, setting the Midsong Tree's leaves aquiver.

The message translated itself in Asvarr's mind, bypassing his ears entirely:

The path unravels. The anchors scatter. What will you become, Flame-Bearer, when the Root claims you completely?

Asvarr stood transfixed as more spectral Wardens materialized across the plain—men and women bearing marks that echoed his own yet differed in crucial ways. Their bodies exhibited various stages of transformation, from subtle patterns etched into skin to nearly complete merging with Root essence. Some appeared almost human, while others had transformed so thoroughly they barely resembled people at all.

The bark-patterned woman stepped closer, her movement causing ripples in the air as if reality itself bent around her presence. When she spoke again, the chime-voice bypassed Asvarr's ears to resonate directly in his mind.

We were Wardens once, as you are now. We walked the paths between anchors. We bound ourselves to the Tree's fragments.

Another figure approached—a man whose body had become almost entirely crystalline, fracturing the ambient light into prismatic patterns across the ground. His voice sounded like stone grinding against stone yet carried the same harmonic quality as the woman's.

We sought to heal what was broken. To restore what was shattered. We failed.

Brynja moved to stand beside Asvarr, her wooden arm gleaming in the strange light. "What are you?" she demanded. "Memories? Ghosts?"

Both and neither, answered a third Warden, this one with limbs that flowed like water yet maintained human shape. *We are echoes of those who bound with anchors, preserved within the Tree's memory. Neither living nor dead, but remembered.*

Asvarr's mind raced, connecting fragments of knowledge gleaned throughout their journey. "You're from previous cycles," he said. "Previous breaking and binding."

The bark-woman nodded, her wooden features creaking with the motion. *Nine cycles. Nine breaking. Nine binding. Always the pattern repeats.*

"Until now," added the crystal-man. *Something has changed. The pattern unravels.*

Yrsa stepped forward, her crystal pendant pulsing rapidly with blue-white light. "You know why we're here," she said. "To bind the second anchor."

The verdant anchor, chimed the bark-woman. *The growing-heart.* Her form flickered momentarily, solidifying with visible effort. *But do you know what caused the breaking? What shattered the Tree in the first place?*

Before anyone could answer, more spectral Wardens gathered, forming a loose circle around them. Their combined presence created a pressure in the air, a weight of accumulated memory so dense it made breathing difficult. The Midsong Tree at the center of the plain trembled, its few leaves rustling in response to their gathering.

The Severed Bloom, whispered a chorus of ghostly voices. *The Root that rejected.*

One specter, barely more than an outline of glowing mist, drifted forward. Unlike the others, its form showed no signs of transformation—pure human, unmarked by Root or Tree. *Before the shattering, before the anchors, one fragment developed consciousness beyond its purpose. It rejected the greater whole. It chose a path unconstrained by the pattern.*

"A rebellious Root," Asvarr murmured, remembering the Pathfinder's warning. "This caused the initial instability?"

Yes, the bark-woman confirmed. *The Severed Bloom drew power from the Tree while refusing its purpose. The imbalance weakened Yggdrasil's structure, allowing darker forces entry. What you saw in the vision—the shadow entity consuming the roots—found its way through cracks the Severed Bloom created.*

The crystal-man's voice ground through Asvarr's skull. *The Five knew. They sought to control the Bloom, to force it back into harmony. Their efforts accelerated the breaking.*

Kára, who had remained silent until now, pushed her hood back fully. The bark patterns on her face had spread further since entering the memory realm, now covering most of her left cheek and jaw. "What happened to this Severed Bloom? Was it destroyed in the shattering?"

The spectral Wardens exchanged glances, a ripple of unease passing through their ethereal forms.

Not destroyed, answered the water-limbed Warden. *Scattered. Fragmented. Like all aspects of the Tree. It exists still, in pieces, seeking to reassemble itself with purpose unchanged.*

The bark-woman turned suddenly toward Brynja, drifting across the ground without taking steps. She reached out with wooden fingers toward Brynja's transformed arm. *You carry its seed already. It has chosen you.*

Brynja recoiled, clutching her wooden arm protectively against her chest. "What are you talking about? This transformation comes from my connection to the verdant anchor."

Yes. And no. The bark-woman's fingers hovered inches from Brynja's arm. *The verdant anchor contains the largest fragment of the Severed Bloom. It chose you because you carry the bloodline of those who tended it before the breaking. It seeks to grow through you, to complete what it began nine cycles past.*

"That's impossible," Brynja protested. "The Verdant Five told me—"

The Five tell what serves their purpose, interrupted the crystal-man. *They seek control, not truth. They would use you as they tried to use the Bloom—as a vessel for their will.*

Asvarr studied Brynja's arm with new wariness. The wooden texture had always seemed benign, a natural transformation from her connection to the Root. Now he noticed subtle patterns within the grain—spirals and whorls that formed almost-recognizable shapes before dissolving back into randomness.

"Is it dangerous?" he asked the specters. "This seed she carries?"

All power unconstrained by purpose becomes dangerous, answered the water-limbed Warden. *The Severed Bloom sought freedom from the pattern. Freedom without responsibility leads to chaos.*

The bark-woman's gaze shifted to Asvarr. *You carry the flame aspect—the counterbalance to unbounded growth. Fire shapes. Fire cleanses. Fire transforms. This is why your bloodlines were separated by the Five—to prevent the natural balance between flame and root.*

Leif had been studying the Midsong Tree throughout this exchange. Now he turned, his golden eyes luminous in the strange light. "The sapling knows the way," he announced. "It grew from a fragment that remembers its original purpose. It can lead us to the verdant anchor."

The spectral Wardens drifted backward, creating a path between Asvarr's group and the Tree. The bark-woman lingered, her gaze fixed on Brynja's wooden arm.

Be wary, Root-tender, she chimed softly. *What grows within you has its own will. It may speak with your voice and move with your limbs, but its purpose is not yours.*

Brynja's expression hardened, amber eyes flashing. "I control my transformation, not the other way around."

So we all believed, replied the bark-woman, her form beginning to dissolve into mist. *Until the moment we didn't.*

With that final warning, she and the other spectral Wardens faded, their glowing outlines dispersing like fog in morning light until only the plain and the Midsong Tree remained.

A heavy silence fell. Kára broke it first.

"Is it true?" she asked Brynja, eyes fixed on the wooden arm. "Are you carrying some kind of... rogue consciousness?"

"No," Brynja snapped, though uncertainty flashed across her face. "It's my transformation, responding to my bloodline. Nothing more."

Yrsa approached the Midsong Tree, laying her palm against its slender trunk. "The anchor has chosen its vessel," she said quietly. "As anchors always do. The question is whether vessel and anchor share purpose or struggle for dominance."

"The Verdant Five never mentioned a Severed Bloom," Brynja muttered. "They told me I was chosen because my bloodline preserved the Root's essence through generations."

"They may not have lied," Asvarr said, studying her wooden arm with new intensity. "But they almost certainly didn't tell the whole truth."

The Grímmark on his chest burned as he approached Brynja. He reached toward her transformed arm, hesitating just short of touching it. "May I?"

After a moment's hesitation, she extended her arm. The wood felt warm beneath his fingers, pulsing with life that matched the rhythm of the Grímmark's heat. As their marks resonated, Asvarr glimpsed something within the wooden grain—movement, awareness, purpose—distinct from Brynja herself.

He jerked his hand away, unsettled by the contact. "There's something there," he confirmed. "Something aware."

Brynja pulled her arm back, cradling it against her chest. Fear and defiance warred across her features. "I'm still myself," she insisted. "Whatever seed I carry, I'm stronger than it."

"For now," Yrsa said, her voice neutral. "But each transformation brings change. The further you progress toward the verdant anchor, the stronger its influence becomes."

"We need to keep moving," Leif interrupted, his small hand pressed against the Midsong Tree's trunk. "The sapling speaks of others searching. The Five. The Ashfather's servants. They seek what we seek."

Asvarr made a swift decision. Whatever danger Brynja's transformation might pose, they couldn't afford to linger. "The Midsong Tree first," he declared. "It will guide us to the anchor. We'll deal with the Severed Bloom when we confront it directly."

Kára looked unconvinced, keeping her distance from Brynja. "And if it manifests before then? If it takes control?"

"Then I'll burn it out," Asvarr replied, laying his hand on his sword hilt. The weapon's familiar weight reassured him, though he wondered what good steel would do against a consciousness born of the Tree itself.

The Midsong Tree trembled suddenly, its few branches shaking violently. The ground beneath their feet vibrated in response, ripples spreading outward across the plain.

"Something approaches," Yrsa warned, gripping her crystal pendant. "Something that doesn't belong in the memory realm."

A distant thundering sound reached them—hoofbeats, though no horses should exist in this place of pure memory. From the horizon's edge, dark shapes appeared, moving with unnatural speed across the plain. Riders cloaked in shadow, mounted on beasts that blurred between horse and mist.

"The Hunt," Asvarr growled, recognizing the Ashfather's servants from stories. "The Hunt of Broken Fate."

"They can't be here," Yrsa protested. "This realm exists outside physical reality. How could they enter?"

"The same way we did," Brynja suggested grimly. "Through the Verdant Gate."

The Hunt drew nearer, close enough now to make out details—nine riders on steeds with glowing red eyes, led by a figure whose mount stood taller than the others. Each rider carried a spear of shadow that absorbed the ambient light around it.

"The Tree," Leif urged, tugging at Asvarr's tunic. "Touch the Tree. All of you!"

Without questioning, Asvarr pressed his palm against the Midsong Tree's trunk. Brynja followed suit with her flesh hand, then Yrsa and a reluctant Kára. Leif completed the circle, his small golden eyes closed in concentration.

The sapling's bark grew warm, then hot beneath their touch. The sensation spread up Asvarr's arm and across his chest where the Grímmark pulsed in response. The Tree began to sing, with vibrations that resonated through their bodies, a complex melody that was impossible to capture in ordinary music.

The plain around them blurred, the approaching Hunt stretching and distorting as if viewed through water. The Midsong Tree glowed with increasingly bright light until Asvarr had to close his eyes against its intensity.

***

When he opened them again, the plain had vanished. They stood in a new location—a terraced garden of impossible plants that defied categorization. Some resembled flowers but moved with animal-like purpose. Others twisted into geometric shapes no natural growth could form. The air smelled of spice and electricity, heavy with unfamiliar pollen.

At the garden's center stood a temple constructed entirely of thorns and brambles, its walls woven into intricate patterns that somehow supported a structure larger than any hunting lodge Asvarr had seen. Roses the size of shields bloomed along its walls, their petals deep crimson against the black thorns.

"The Thorned Temple," Yrsa breathed. "Sacred space of the original plant-shapers."

"The Tree brought us here," Leif explained, finally releasing his grip on the trunk—which had vanished the moment they arrived in this new location. "The Hunt cannot follow the path we took."

"Where's the Midsong Tree?" Kára asked, looking around in confusion.

"It remains where it was," Yrsa answered. "Only our consciousness has traveled. We've moved deeper into the memory realm, closer to the verdant anchor."

Brynja approached the temple, her wooden arm extended before her as if pulled by some invisible force. "It's in there," she murmured. "I can feel it calling."

"Be careful," Asvarr warned, hurrying to catch up. "Remember what the spectral Wardens told us. The verdant anchor contains the Severed Bloom—the fragment that rebelled."

Brynja paused at the temple's thorned entrance, turning back to face him. Something shifted in her expression—a momentary alienness that vanished so quickly Asvarr wondered if he'd imagined it.

"I know who I am, Asvarr," she said firmly. "And I know what I carry. The question is—" she nodded toward his chest where the Grímmark burned beneath his tunic, "—do you know what you carry? The flame can preserve or consume. Which will you choose when the moment comes?"

Without waiting for his answer, she turned and stepped through the entrance, her form swallowed by the thorned shadows within.

Asvarr moved to follow, the weight of the spectral Wardens' revelations pressing against his thoughts. Each step forward brought them closer to the verdant anchor, to the second binding—and to confrontation with the Severed Bloom that grew within Brynja's flesh, waiting to complete a rebellion nine cycles in the making.

CHAPTER 12

BRIAR-MARKED BLOOD

The temple rose before them like a wound in the world—a massive structure woven entirely from thorns and brambles, its spires twisting toward a sky that didn't quite match the one they'd stood beneath moments before. Black thorns thicker than Asvarr's arm formed archways and buttresses, while smaller briars created intricate latticework between them. Droplets of golden sap wept from countless points where the structure had pierced itself, the liquid catching the strange half-light that existed in this part of the memory realm.

Asvarr's Grímmark burned against his chest as he studied the temple's impossible architecture. "The Thorned Temple," he whispered, the name surfacing from knowledge he hadn't possessed until the spectral Wardens had touched him. "Sacred space of the plant-shapers."

"The oldest of sanctuaries," Yrsa confirmed, her voice tight with reverence or fear—Asvarr couldn't tell which. "Before the Verdant Five claimed dominion over growth and decay."

Brynja moved closer to the entrance, her wooden arm extending slightly as if drawn by unseen currents. "I can hear singing," she murmured. Her eyes had taken on the same strange golden-green glow as the sap that bled from the temple walls. "Voices beyond counting."

Asvarr caught her shoulder. "The specters warned us about what you carry."

"I'm not a vessel to be filled with someone else's purpose," Brynja snapped, jerking away. The bark patterns across her face rippled with her anger. "I control this transformation, not the other way around."

Kára, who had been silent since they'd escaped the Hunt, finally spoke. "The temple recognizes root-blood. You should enter first, Brynja. The rest of us would only taint the threshold." Her hand rested on the knife at her belt, and Asvarr caught the small nod she exchanged with her fellow masked follower.

Something cold settled in Asvarr's stomach. Had they planned this separation? He studied Kára's half-transformed face, looking for deceit.

"We should remain together," Yrsa said, her crystal pendant pulsing with blue light. "This place has been empty for nine cycles. Whatever resided here may have forgotten its original purpose."

"And what was that purpose?" Leif asked, his childlike voice suddenly resonant with unexpected maturity.

"To shape," Yrsa answered simply. "To define boundaries between what grows and what decays."

Brynja pulled her hood lower, shadowing her transformed features. "I need to understand what's happening to me. The specters claimed I carry something dangerous. If answers exist, they'll be inside." She stepped toward the arched thorn entrance, her back straight with determination.

"We go together," Asvarr insisted, drawing his bronze sword. The golden veins within the metal brightened in the temple's presence.

"As you wish," Brynja replied, but her voice held a strange distance.

They passed beneath the arch of thorns, ducking to avoid barbs that seemed to shift and reach as they entered. Inside, the temple opened into a vast circular chamber lit by pods of bioluminescent fungi that clung to the structure's interior. The floor consisted of tightly woven roots that pulsed with an unsettling rhythm, like a massive, slow heartbeat beneath their feet.

Massive crimson roses, each the size of a shield, bloomed along the walls between wicked-looking thorns. Their fragrance filled the air—sweet yet tinged with the metallic scent of blood. At the chamber's center stood what looked like a garden of wooden figures—human-shaped forms carved from living wood, frozen in various poses of supplication or dance.

"Carvings?" Asvarr questioned, moving toward the nearest figure—a woman with arms outstretched toward the domed ceiling of thorns.

"Not carvings," Yrsa cautioned, catching his sleeve. "Vessels that failed."

The blood drained from Asvarr's face as he looked closer. Each wooden figure retained traces of humanity—hints of facial features, clothing merged with bark, fingers that still bent at their joints. These had been people once.

"The Verdant Five's earlier attempts," Yrsa explained, her voice barely above a whisper. "Vessels prepared for transformation that couldn't contain what they were given."

Brynja walked among the wooden statues, her transformed arm brushing against them. Where she touched, small green buds appeared on the figures' wooden surfaces. "I can feel them," she said, her voice distant. "They're still aware, somewhere deep inside."

"We should leave," Kára hissed, eyes darting to the shadowed alcoves surrounding the chamber. "This is a burial ground, not a sanctuary."

"Not burial," Brynja corrected, moving deeper into the field of wooden figures. "Storage. They're kept for—"

***

She stopped suddenly, her head tilting as if listening. In the silence that followed, Asvarr detected it too—a subtle scratching sound from above.

"Brynja!" he called. "Come back to us."

She either didn't hear or chose to ignore him, drifting instead toward an archway at the far side of the chamber that Asvarr could have sworn hadn't been there a moment before. Golden-green light spilled from whatever lay beyond.

"Something's pulling her," Leif said, his golden eyes tracking Brynja's movement. "The seed in her arm recognizes this place."

The scraping sounds intensified, now coming from multiple directions.

"We're not alone," Yrsa warned, reaching for her crystal knife.

The first figure dropped from the ceiling—a human form with root growths protruding from joints and spine, bending the body into an impossible posture. Its skin had the texture of bark, and where its eyes should have been, only hollow knots remained. More figures emerged from alcoves and from behind the wooden statues—a dozen at least, all similarly transformed.

"Rootbound," Kára breathed, drawing her bone knife. "The temple guardians."

The first Rootbound creature spoke, its voice a rustling of dead leaves. "The Severed Bloom returns to us." It tilted its knotted head toward the archway where Brynja had disappeared. "In a vessel of perfect potential."

"She is not yours to claim," Asvarr growled, stepping forward with his sword raised.

"She was marked generations before her birth," another Rootbound answered, this one with flowering vines growing through its eye sockets. "Root-keeper blood, tended through nine cycles."

The creatures moved with unnatural coordination, spreading to surround them while others broke off in pursuit of Brynja. Asvarr lunged toward the archway, only to find his path blocked by three Rootbound who bent into crablike postures, fingers elongated into thorn-tipped branches.

"Let me pass!" he demanded, slashing at the nearest guardian.

His sword cut through the creature's arm, releasing a spray of golden sap rather than blood. The severed limb fell to the pulsing floor, where it immediately began to take root and sprout new growth. The Rootbound showed no sign of pain, merely adjusting its stance to accommodate the loss.

Kára and her companion attacked from the other side, their bone knives finding vulnerable joints in the guardians' transformed bodies. The weapons ignited whatever they cut with pale blue flames that briefly prevented regeneration.

"The archway!" Asvarr called to Yrsa, who was nearest the passage Brynja had taken. "Find her!"

Yrsa nodded sharply and darted forward, her crystal pendant blazing with light that momentarily blinded the Rootbound in her path. She slipped through the opening, calling Brynja's name as she disappeared into the golden-green glow beyond.

Leif remained oddly calm amid the chaos, watching the battle with detached curiosity. When a Rootbound lunged toward him, the boy simply stepped aside with inhuman grace. "They can't see me properly," he explained as Asvarr fought his way closer. "I exist between moments for them."

A scream echoed from beyond the archway—Brynja's voice, filled with terror and rage.

"Find another way through!" Asvarr shouted to Kára as he drove his blade through a guardian's chest, momentarily pinning it to the woven root floor. "I'll hold them here!"

Kára and her companion disappeared into the shadows of an alcove, presumably seeking another entrance to whatever chamber lay beyond. Asvarr found himself fighting alongside Leif, who despite his small stature moved with uncanny precision, always just beyond the Rootbound's reach.

"The thorns on the walls," Leif said suddenly, pointing to where massive spikes protruded from the chamber's perimeter. "They're the temple's supports. If one breaks—"

Asvarr understood immediately. He backed toward the nearest wall-thorn, drawing several Rootbound with him. When they closed in, he pivoted and brought his bronze sword down with all his strength against the base of the massive thorn. The sword's gold-veined metal blazed at the impact, and the thorn—thick as a young tree—cracked with a sound like breaking bone.

The entire temple shuddered. From beyond the archway came another scream, followed by Yrsa's voice raised in what sounded like an ancient language Asvarr didn't recognize.

He struck the damaged thorn again, and this time it gave way completely. The section of ceiling it supported collapsed, crushing two Rootbound beneath it and creating a shower of debris that momentarily scattered the others. More importantly, the collapse opened a ragged hole in the wall that appeared to lead to the same golden-green glow Brynja had followed.

"This way!" Asvarr called to Leif, already climbing through the opening.

***

Beyond lay a smaller chamber dominated by what could only be described as a living altar—a massive horizontal thorn that had somehow been flattened and smoothed at its top, lined with pulsing veins of golden sap. Rootbound surrounded it, at least a dozen more, arranged in a circle. And strapped to the altar's surface with living vines was Brynja.

Her wooden arm had been stripped bare, revealing complex patterns that spiraled from her fingers all the way to her shoulder. The Rootbound had peeled back the sleeve of her other arm as well, and one of them—taller than the others, with a crown-like growth of branches—was using a thorn needle to carve symbols into her flesh.

Yrsa lay crumpled against the far wall, her crystal pendant dark. Kára and her companion were nowhere to be seen.

"Release her!" Asvarr roared, charging into the chamber.

The crowned Rootbound looked up, hollow eye-knots somehow focusing on Asvarr. "Flame-bearer," it acknowledged, its voice deeper and more resonant than the others. "You carry what balances her. Together, you could open the Gate properly." It gestured to Brynja with its thorn needle. "But she carries the Severed Bloom, which must be bound before it consumes her completely."

"You're hurting her," Asvarr snarled, advancing with his sword.

"We're saving her," the crowned Rootbound countered. "The runes bind the seed's influence while preserving its power. Without them, the Severed Bloom will hollow her out and wear her like a garment." It continued carving, and where the needle touched, Brynja's skin wept golden sap that hardened into raised patterns. "We serve neither the Verdant Five nor their enemies. We tend the original balance."

Brynja's eyes found Asvarr's, wide with pain and fear. "It's inside me," she gasped. "I can feel it trying to take control—to replace me." She strained against her bonds. "Don't let them finish the binding. These aren't protection runes, they're—"

The crowned Rootbound pressed the needle deeper, and Brynja cried out, her words lost in a scream of agony. Golden light pulsed from the forming rune, spreading up her arm in branching patterns.

Leif had made his way to Yrsa, helping her to her feet. "The runes force truth," the boy said, his voice cutting through Brynja's cries. "But they also create a path for control. The Rootbound serve the temple, and the temple serves the original pattern." His golden eyes narrowed. "The pattern that existed before the Tree, before gods or mortals."

The crowned Rootbound's head swiveled toward Leif. "The child knows. He walks between."

"I'm stopping this," Asvarr declared, stepping forward.

"The binding is nearly complete," the crowned Rootbound answered. "The vessel must be prepared before the Verdant Five find her. Their plans would upset the balance far more than ours."

Asvarr had heard enough. He charged, his bronze sword singing through the air. The Rootbound moved to intercept him, their thorn-fingers reaching to ensnare. But something had changed in Asvarr since entering this place—his movements felt more fluid, guided by knowledge embedded in the Grímmark that spread across his chest.

He slipped between the first two guardians, severing their reaching limbs with economical strokes. When a third lunged, he ducked and drove his shoulder into its midsection, sending it crashing into two more. His sword found gaps in their bark-like coverings, releasing sprays of golden sap that briefly blinded the others.

The crowned Rootbound abandoned its work with the needle, drawing a weapon of its own—a scepter made from a single massive thorn. It moved with far greater speed and purpose than the others, intercepting Asvarr before he could reach the altar.

"Flame-bearer," it intoned, the scepter glowing with the same golden-green light that filled the chamber. "The convergence of bloodlines awakens ancient things. The Severed Bloom is but one. Without proper binding, it will consume her entirely."

"And with your binding?" Asvarr challenged, circling to find an opening.

"She will remain herself, mostly," the crowned Rootbound answered. "But with a voice that cannot speak falsehood, and a heart that cannot hide purpose."

Behind them, Brynja thrashed against her bonds, her eyes wild with panic. The runes carved into her arm glowed with increasing intensity, spreading like liquid fire through her veins.

The crowned Rootbound struck with its thorn scepter, moving faster than Asvarr anticipated. The weapon grazed his shoulder, tearing through his tunic and leaving a burning line of pain. Asvarr countered with a slash that the creature blocked, its scepter releasing a shower of golden sparks where the bronze blade connected.

"Asvarr!" Brynja's voice, stronger now despite her pain. "The runes are carving into my mind. I can feel them searching for—" She broke off with a strangled gasp as another rune flared to life on her forearm.

Asvarr attacked with renewed fury, driving the crowned Rootbound back with a flurry of strikes. His Grímmark burned beneath his tunic, sending waves of heat down his sword arm. Where his blade connected, the gold veins within the metal flared with light that seemed to disrupt the Rootbound's cohesion.

A flash of movement caught his eye—Kára and her companion had emerged from a hidden entrance, bone knives gleaming as they engaged the Rootbound nearest the altar. Yrsa had recovered enough to join them, her crystal pendant once again pulsing with blue-white light that disoriented the guardians.

The crowned Rootbound, seeing its followers engaged on multiple fronts, abandoned direct confrontation with Asvarr. It retreated toward the altar, raising its scepter high. "The binding must be completed!" it declared. "The vessel must be sealed before—"

Asvarr threw himself forward in desperate lunge, his bronze sword piercing the Rootbound's chest. Golden sap erupted from the wound, spattering across Asvarr's face and hands. The creature stiffened, its hollow eye-knots widening in what might have been surprise. It dropped to its knees, still clutching the thorn scepter.

"Too late," it whispered, the rustling leaves of its voice fading. "The runes have found purchase. Truth will flow from her lips whether she wishes it or not." Its wooden body began to crumble, flaking away into drifting spores that spiraled upward into the chamber's thorn-woven ceiling. "And truth has always been the sharpest thorn of all."

As the crowned Rootbound disintegrated, chaos erupted throughout the chamber. The remaining guardians abandoned their organized defense, scattering in all directions. Some melted into the thorn walls, while others collapsed into piles of rapidly growing vegetation.

Asvarr rushed to the altar, using his sword to slash through the living vines that bound Brynja. She lay trembling, her eyes squeezed shut, tears cutting tracks through the blood and sap that stained her face. Her right arm bore a complex pattern of carved runes from wrist to elbow, each one pulsing with golden light that slowly faded as he watched.

"Brynja," he called, helping her sit up. "Can you hear me?"

Her eyes fluttered open, the gold-green glow diminished but still present around her pupils. "I hear you," she whispered, her voice raw from screaming. As she spoke, a faint shimmer of golden light passed across her lips. "And so does it."

"The Severed Bloom?"

She nodded, wincing as the movement sent fresh blood trickling from one of the carved runes. "It's aware now, after being dormant so long." The golden shimmer accompanied her words again. "The runes force me to speak only truth, and truth strengthens its presence."

Kára approached with Brynja's cloak, which had been torn away during the binding. "The remaining Rootbound have retreated deeper into the temple," she reported, helping Brynja cover her wounded arm. "We should leave before they return with reinforcements."

"Can you stand?" Asvarr asked Brynja.

"Yes," she answered, the word accompanied by golden light. "But the runes—they burn with each truth I speak." Her hand went to her throat. "I can feel them spreading inside, marking pathways through my—" She broke off with a gasp of pain.

Yrsa joined them, her face grim. "The rune-binding is incomplete, but what they carved will remain. The Rootbound weren't lying about their purpose—without some form of binding, the Severed Bloom would eventually consume her consciousness entirely."

"So this was a kindness?" Asvarr snarled, gesturing to Brynja's bloodied arm.

"No," Yrsa replied quietly. "It was survival—theirs and hers. The Severed Bloom's awakening threatens the original pattern they serve." She turned to Brynja. "You will feel its influence more strongly now, but you'll also be more aware of when it tries to control you."

Brynja stood shakily, leaning on Kára for support. "I need to examine the other chambers," she said, the golden light flickering across her lips. "There might be knowledge here about the Severed Bloom's origin and purpose."

"We leave now," Asvarr countered, sheathing his sword. "The temple is collapsing from the damage to its supports, and the Hunt of Broken Fate might still be tracking us."

Leif, who had been oddly silent throughout the confrontation, finally spoke. "There's another way out." He pointed to a section of wall that appeared no different from the rest of the thorn structure. "The temple remembers me from before. It will open to my touch."

"Before?" Kára questioned. "You've been here?"

"Parts of me have been everywhere," Leif answered cryptically. He approached the wall and placed his small hand against it. The thorns retreated at his touch, creating an archway that opened onto a forest glade bathed in moonlight—a scene impossibly different from the memory realm surrounding the temple.

Yrsa examined the opening with narrowed eyes. "A direct path through memory to somewhere else," she murmured. "The boy bridges realities without even trying."

Asvarr helped Brynja toward the new exit, supporting her weight as she struggled to stand upright. "We'll find another way to deal with what's inside you," he promised quietly. "One that doesn't involve carving you into someone else's tool."

Brynja's eyes met his, pain and determination warring in her expression. "I don't think we get to choose anymore," she whispered, golden light shimmering across her lips. "The runes have already begun their work. When I speak, only truth emerges." She touched her wounded arm with her wooden one, fingers tracing the carved patterns. "And my deepest truths are what the Severed Bloom has been waiting for all along."

As they approached the threshold Leif had opened, the temple shuddered around them. Thorns twisted and contracted, while overhead the ceiling began to collapse inward. The altar where Brynja had been bound split with a sound like tearing flesh, golden sap welling from the wound.

"We need to hurry," Asvarr urged, guiding their group toward the exit.

They crossed the threshold in single file, stepping from the decaying temple into the moonlit glade beyond. As Leif passed through last, the opening sealed behind him, thorns intertwining to erase any sign of a passage.

Brynja stood straighter now, though her face remained pallid with pain. In the moonlight, the runes on her arm gleamed with subtle power, no longer bleeding but clearly permanent—a binding written in her flesh and, if the Rootbound spoke truly, reaching into her very mind.

"What happens now?" Asvarr asked, looking to Yrsa and then to Brynja.

Before either could answer, distant howls echoed through the trees—the unmistakable cry of the Hunt's hounds. They had found another way into the memory realm, and they were closing in.

"Now," Brynja said, the golden truth-light brightening around her words, "we learn what secrets the Verdant Five have been keeping from me." She touched the newly carved runes, her expression hardening with resolve. "And why they never warned me about the seed I've been carrying all along."

The moonlight that had welcomed them through Leif's passage quickly vanished, swallowed by clouds that rolled across the sky like a tide of ink. Asvarr tightened his grip on Brynja's good arm as they stumbled forward, her weight leaning heavily against him. The howls of the Hunt grew distant behind them, though whether they'd truly escaped or the creatures were simply taking another route, he couldn't tell.

"We need shelter," Yrsa murmured, her crystal pendant providing their only light now—a pale blue glow that cast their shadows in sharp relief against the forest floor. "Somewhere to tend those wounds."

They'd fled into a primeval forest unlike any Asvarr had seen, with trees whose trunks spiraled skyward and branches that moved independently of the wind. Phosphorescent fungi clung to bark and stone, pulsing in rhythm with Brynja's labored breathing. The carved runes on her arm glowed with the same cadence, golden light seeping through the makeshift bandage Kára had wrapped around the worst of the wounds.

"There," Leif pointed to where the ground rose into a hill crowned with a circle of standing stones. "The memory-circle remembers a time before thorn or blossom."

Asvarr didn't question how the boy knew this place. Since entering the memory realm, Leif had demonstrated knowledge no child should possess. Asvarr guided their group up the hillside, each step bringing a fresh grimace of pain to Brynja's face.

***

The standing stones created a natural shelter from the strengthening wind, each massive rock etched with spiraling patterns that mirrored the carved runes on Brynja's flesh. In the center of the circle, a fire pit lined with white stones awaited, as if prepared for their arrival.

"This place was built for seekers," Yrsa observed, kneeling to arrange kindling from her pack. "One of many sanctuaries hidden in the memory realm for those walking between worlds."

Kára and her companion took positions at opposite sides of the circle, watching the darkness beyond with hands resting on their bone knives. "The Root-bound won't follow," Kára said. "They never leave the temple."

"And the Hunt?" Asvarr asked.

"The Hunt follows wyrd-trails," Kára replied. "We've stepped outside their pattern, at least for now."

Yrsa coaxed a flame to life, with whispered words that made the kindling ignite from within. The fire cast dancing light across their faces, highlighting the exhaustion etched into every line.

Brynja sank to her knees beside the fire, cradling her carved arm against her chest. Her wooden arm curled protectively around it, branches extending from her fingers to form a latticework splint. She hadn't spoken since their escape, her face a mask of concentration.

"Let me see," Asvarr said, kneeling beside her.

She extended her arm reluctantly, allowing him to unwind the blood-soaked bandage. The runes looked less raw now, their edges hardening into raised scars that gleamed golden in the firelight. They formed a spiraling pattern from wrist to elbow—symbols unlike any Asvarr had seen, yet strangely familiar to his eyes.

"Binding-runes," Yrsa explained, examining them with a critical eye. "Ancient magic from before the Tree. They create pathways between vessel and essence." She touched one delicately, drawing back when Brynja flinched. "The Root-bound weren't lying about their purpose. Without these, the Severed Bloom would have consumed you entirely."

"And with them?" Brynja asked, her voice rough from screaming. Golden light shimmered across her lips as she spoke, confirming the truth in her question.

"With them, you remain yourself," Yrsa answered, "but bound to truth and unable to hide purpose. The runes force honesty from within while keeping the Severed Bloom's consciousness separate from your own."

Brynja closed her eyes, exhaling slowly. "They're burning into my mind. I can feel them carving paths through my thoughts, searching for something."

"What do they want?" Asvarr asked.

"Memory," Brynja whispered. Golden light flared from her lips, brighter than before. "My deepest truths. The ones I've hidden even from myself." She opened her eyes, meeting Asvarr's gaze directly. "The Rootbound were right about one thing—I've been carrying this seed for longer than I knew."

The fire crackled between them, sending shadows dancing across the circle of stones. Brynja straightened, decision hardening her features.

"You should know the truth," she said, each word accompanied by that shimmering golden light. "All of you. Before we go further."

"You don't have to—" Asvarr began.

"I do," Brynja cut him off. "The runes force truth, but I choose what truths to speak." She gestured to the gathered companions. "You deserve to know who you're fighting alongside." Her wooden fingers flexed, creaking like branches in wind. "Who you're risking your lives to protect."

Asvarr settled back, recognizing the steel in her voice. This wasn't a confession born of the runes' compulsion, but a deliberate choice.

"I told you my clan was destroyed the same day as yours," Brynja began, the golden light pulsing with her words. "What I didn't tell you is that I watched it happen. I was supposed to be hunting with my father, but I'd slipped away to practice bow-crafting by the western stream."

She drew a deep breath, wincing as the runes flared in response. "I heard the first screams and ran back toward the village. From the ridge, I saw them—warriors in shadow-cloaks, led by a figure crowned with twisted branches." Her wooden arm trembled, sending small shivers through the latticework splint. "I recognized him from the eldest stories—the shadow who wore a god's face."

"The Ashfather," Asvarr breathed.

Brynja nodded, her face tight with old pain. "He directed the slaughter with methodical precision. It wasn't rage that drove him, but purpose. He searched our longhouse, our ritual spaces. He was looking for something specific."

The runes on her arm pulsed brighter. "I should have charged down the ridge. I should have died defending my clan." The golden light when she spoke these words was almost blinding. "Instead, I ran. I fled into the forest, telling myself I would find help, gather survivors." Her voice cracked. "But I knew there would be none."

Asvarr found himself reaching for her, stopping just short of touching the runes. "There's no shame in surviving."

"There is when survival comes at the cost of honor," Brynja countered, the truth-light unwavering. "Three days I hid in the forest, paralyzed by fear and guilt. On the fourth morning, they found me."

"The Verdant Five," Leif murmured.

Brynja's gaze shifted to the boy. "Yes. Three of them, at least. Rootmother with her crown of living branches, Stembinder with his vine-wrapped staff, and Seedkeeper with eyes like wells of starlight." She touched her wooden arm, tracing the patterns that spiraled beneath the bark. "They told me I'd been chosen generations before my birth. That my bloodline had been carefully tended across nine cycles to produce the perfect vessel."

"For the Severed Bloom," Yrsa concluded.

Brynja nodded. "Though they never called it that. They spoke of 'the awakening essence' and 'the verdant restoration.' They claimed the shadow who destroyed my clan had sought to prevent my fulfillment." Her mouth twisted bitterly. "They exploited my guilt, my desire for vengeance. They told me that with their guidance, I could become the instrument of retribution—strong enough to face the Ashfather and avenge my people."

The fire popped and hissed, sending embers spiraling upward. Beyond the stone circle, the forest had grown unnaturally silent, as if listening.

"For five seasons, they trained me in their hidden grove—teaching me to accept the transformation, to welcome the wooden change spreading through my arm." Brynja's wooden fingers curled into a fist. "They never warned me that what I carried was something separate, something with its own desires. They spoke only of power and destiny."

"And then they sent you to find the Verdant Gate," Asvarr guessed.

"Yes," Brynja confirmed, truth-light dancing across her lips. "With my followers—acolytes they'd assigned to ensure I completed my purpose." Her gaze flicked briefly to Kára, who remained expressionless. "I tried for three days to open the Gate alone, never understanding why it resisted me. The Five had taught me that my bloodline was the key, that I alone was worthy." Her eyes met Asvarr's. "They never mentioned you, or the flame-blood, or the necessity of balance."

"They wanted division," Asvarr realized. "They needed us separate."

"Because together, we limit their control," Brynja said, the golden light of truth flaring. "The specters told me as much. United flame and root create barriers against external influence."

Yrsa nodded, her crystal pendant pulsing in rhythm with Brynja's truth-telling. "The Five have manipulated events across all nine cycles, keeping bloodlines at odds when they should have been allies."

"Why?" Asvarr demanded. "What purpose does it serve?"

"Control," Brynja answered, raising her rune-carved arm. Golden light spilled from the patterns as she spoke. "The Rootbound told me their runes would bind the Severed Bloom's influence, but I felt them searching through my deepest memories, looking for something specific." Her wooden arm creaked as she leaned forward. "Just before you reached the altar, I heard it finally respond. A voice from within that said, 'I remember the betrayal. I remember what they did to me.'"

"The Severed Bloom was once part of them," Leif said suddenly, his childlike voice unnervingly calm. "Before it chose a separate purpose."

Brynja turned to him, eyes widening. "Yes," she breathed, truth-light confirming his insight. "The voice claimed it was 'the first dissent,' the one who questioned their methods and was cast out." She touched the runes gingerly. "These aren't just binding the seed's influence—they're unlocking its memories."

Asvarr processed this revelation, connecting it to what the spectral Wardens had told them. "The Severed Bloom rejected its purpose and developed its own consciousness. It caused the initial instability that led to Yggdrasil's fall."

"So said the specters," Yrsa confirmed. "But consider the source of that knowledge. The memory realm preserves recollections, but those recollections carry the bias of their origins."

The implication struck Asvarr like a physical blow. "The specters' memories came from the Tree itself—or from those who guided its formation."

"The Verdant Five," Brynja concluded, truth-light pulsing. "Who have manipulated history and memory across nine cycles, keeping bloodlines divided and spinning tales of betrayal to suit their purposes." Her wooden arm creaked as she flexed her fingers. "What if the Severed Bloom didn't betray the Tree, but questioned those who shaped it?"

A cold wind swept through the stone circle, sending sparks spiraling from their fire. The standing stones groaned in response, their carved spirals momentarily glowing with the same golden light as Brynja's runes.

"The truth wants to be known," Leif whispered, his golden eyes reflecting the firelight. "It's why the runes burn. It's why the temple sought you out." He pointed to Brynja's wooden arm. "The seed chose you because your bloodline remembers, even if you don't."

Brynja stared at her transformed limb, emotions warring across her face. "All my life, I thought this transformation was my destiny, my birthright." The truth-light shimmered softly as she spoke. "I never considered I might be carrying someone else's memory, someone else's vengeance."

"Those runes," Kára interjected suddenly, stepping closer to examine Brynja's arm. "I've seen patterns like these in the Five's sanctuary. They're written in the oldest sections, places they forbid acolytes from entering." Her fingers hovered over a specific rune near Brynja's elbow. "This one means 'remembrance-beyond-self.'"

"Soul-memory," Yrsa translated. "Knowledge that passes through bloodlines, dormant until awakened." She studied the pattern with narrowed eyes. "These weren't created to bind the Severed Bloom. They were designed to unlock what your blood already carried—memories preserved across nine cycles."

Asvarr watched comprehension dawn on Brynja's face. "The Five didn't choose you as an empty vessel to fill with their purpose," he said quietly. "They sought you because you already contained what they wanted—blood-memory of the Severed Bloom."

"Which means," Brynja responded, voice strengthening despite the pain, "they fear what that memory might reveal." The golden truth-light burned steady and strong around her words. "And now, so do I."

The fire between them surged suddenly, flames leaping higher as if in response to her declaration. Outside their stone circle, the wind intensified, bending trees at unnatural angles. The Hunt's howls rose again, closer than before.

"They've found our trail," Kára warned, drawing her bone knife.

"No," Brynja disagreed, rising to her feet. The runes on her arm blazed like molten gold, casting long shadows across the stones. "They were never tracking us. They were tracking this." She held up her wooden arm, where subtle changes had begun—new patterns emerging beneath the bark, spiraling in harmony with the carved runes. "The awakening memory."

Asvarr stood beside her, bronze sword in hand. "Then we protect it until we understand what it contains."

"We need to reach the Verdant Gate," Brynja said, each word leaving a trail of golden light that lingered in the air. "With both bloodlines present, it will open to the true anchor, not just a memory of it."

"And then?" Asvarr asked.

"Then we learn what the Five have been hiding across nine cycles of breaking and binding." Brynja's eyes met his, determination overriding pain. "What was worth destroying both our clans to prevent us from discovering." The truth-light blazed from her words, so bright it momentarily blinded them all.

When Asvarr's vision cleared, he saw that the runes on Brynja's arm had changed again. They no longer bled or wept sap, but had settled into her flesh like they'd always been there—patterns of raised golden scars that pulsed with her heartbeat.

"The binding is complete," Yrsa observed. "The runes have found purchase in your soul."

"What does that mean?" Asvarr demanded.

"It means," Brynja answered, the golden light surrounding her words strong and steady, "that I'm neither entirely myself nor something else. I exist between—carrying memory that spans cycles and truth that can't be hidden." She touched the runes, wincing slightly. "Every word I speak will reveal whether it's true or false, whether I wish it or not."

Asvarr absorbed the enormity of this change. "And the Severed Bloom?"

"Still present," Brynja replied, truth-light confirming her assessment. "But contained within boundaries. I can feel its consciousness separate from mine, like a dream remembered upon waking." Her wooden fingers flexed experimentally. "It wants what I want now—to understand what happened nine cycles ago, and why the Five have worked so hard to keep our bloodlines apart."

The howls of the Hunt grew louder, accompanied by the sound of branches breaking beneath heavy footfalls. Their time was running out.

"We need to move," Kára urged, gesturing to her silent companion. "We'll draw them east while you three head west toward the Gate."

"They'll catch you," Asvarr objected.

"The Hunt follows blood-trails," Kára countered, drawing her knife across her palm. "And I carry enough of Brynja's to lead them astray." She held Brynja's gaze for a moment. "I serve the truth, not those who would hide it."

Brynja clasped Kára's shoulder, gratitude evident in her expression. "Find us at the Gate when you can." The golden light confirmed her sincerity.

Kára nodded once, then she and her companion melted into the shadows beyond the stones.

"Which way?" Asvarr asked Leif, who had been watching the exchange with those uncannily knowing eyes.

The boy pointed westward, where the forest descended into mist-shrouded valleys. "The thorn-runes will guide us now. They remember the path they once walked." He studied Brynja's arm with something like reverence. "They've been waiting nine cycles to return home."

Asvarr helped Brynja gather her strength, supporting her as she took her first steps away from the stone circle. The runes on her arm pulsed brightly, pointing like a lodestone toward their destination.

"Are you certain about this?" he asked quietly. "Once we open the Gate..."

"There's no going back," Brynja finished for him, the truth-light shimmering around her words. "I know." Her wooden arm brushed against his, branch-like fingers briefly intertwining with his own. "But I would rather face a difficult truth than live with comfortable lies." The golden light burned pure and steady as she added, "And I would rather walk this path with you than stand against you as enemy."

The intensity of her gaze, the truth-light confirming every word, struck Asvarr deeper than he'd expected. He nodded once, gripping her fingers briefly before releasing them.

Together, they descended from the hill of standing stones, following the golden guidance of Brynja's runes. Behind them, the Hunt's howls split the night, but their path led forward, toward whatever truth waited to be uncovered after nine cycles of deliberate forgetting.

CHAPTER 13

THE VERDANT COUNCIL

Dawn bled through the mist in threadlike streams of amber and rose, revealing a landscape transformed by the night's passage. Asvarr's boots crunched on crystalline grass that dissolved into golden motes when broken. Beside him, Brynja walked with her face tilted toward the strange light, the thorn-runes on her arm pulsing with each step.

"The path grows clearer," she murmured, golden truth-light shimmering across her lips. "We're approaching a boundary."

Three hours they'd walked without rest, following the guidance of Brynja's runes. The forest had gradually thinned, giving way to glades of impossibly tall grass and flowers with faces that turned to watch their passing. Leif moved ahead of them, his small form weaving through the vegetation with uncanny grace.

"The boy exists in multiple moments," Yrsa observed quietly, her crystal pendant pulsing with blue-white light. "The closer we get to the anchor, the more fragmented he becomes."

Asvarr had noticed it too. At times, Leif seemed to flicker, his edges blurring as if seen through heat-shimmer. Occasionally, he would stop and stare at something invisible to the rest of them, his golden eyes reflecting light that existed nowhere in their surroundings.

"He was born during the Shattering," Asvarr replied. "Maybe he's sensing echoes of that moment as we draw closer to the true anchor."

The landscape shifted subtly with each step, trees adopting strange contortions, their trunks splitting and rewinding into elaborate spirals. Roots emerged from the ground to form archways that framed their path, dripping golden sap that burned the soil with sizzling whispers.

"Something welcomes us," Brynja said. She raised her wooden arm, bark rippling with flickers of green light that matched the pulsing patterns in the surrounding vegetation. "Or some part of us, at least."

Leif stopped abruptly, pointing to a towering wall of intertwined thorns and flowering vines that had materialized before them. "The outer boundary," he announced, his voice resonating oddly in the sudden stillness. "Beyond lies the Council chamber."

The wall stretched in both directions beyond sight, standing taller than the oldest trees in Midgard. No gate or entrance marred its perfect barrier. Golden flower-bells hung from the vines, each emitting a single pure note when the breeze touched it, creating a harmony that made Asvarr's bones vibrate with recognition.

"This is older than the Tree," Yrsa whispered, her face slack with awe. "This wasn't grown—it was remembered into being."

Brynja approached the barrier, her rune-marked arm extended. The golden scars pulsed in time with the music of the flower-bells. "It recognizes what I carry," she said, truth-light flickering around her words. She pressed her palm against the thorns, which shuddered at her touch.

Nothing happened.

"It wants both bloodlines," Leif said, appearing suddenly at Brynja's side. "Flame and root together."

Asvarr moved forward, drawing his bronze sword. The golden veins within the metal brightened, responding to the power emanating from the wall. "What do we do?" he asked, eyeing the savage thorns.

"Blood calls to blood," Brynja replied, her wooden fingers flexing with small creaking sounds. "The truth runes know the way, but they need the flame to illuminate it." She held out her rune-carved arm. "Cut here, where the central rune lies."

Asvarr hesitated, studying the complex pattern of scars. At the center of her forearm, one rune stood out—a spiraling design that resembled a tree engulfed in flame.

"That's the bind-rune," Yrsa confirmed. "The pattern that holds all others in relation."

With careful precision, Asvarr touched his blade to the center of the rune. The metal sang against Brynja's skin, drawing a single drop of blood mixed with golden sap. He caught the droplet on the edge of his sword, then nicked his own palm, mixing their blood on the blade.

"By flame and root," he said, the words rising unbidden to his lips, "by blood divided and reunited, we seek entrance to the Council of Five."

He pressed the blood-coated blade against the wall of thorns. The barrier trembled, thorns retreating from the metal with a sound like distant screams. A narrow archway formed, its edges lined with thorns that curled away from the opening rather than inward.

"They've sensed us," Leif whispered, his voice suddenly taut with something like fear. "All five of them, awakened from their dreaming."

The archway expanded, revealing a path that descended into green-tinged darkness. The air that drifted from within carried scents of rich soil, decaying leaves, and something sharper—like sap bleeding from a fresh-cut branch.

"What awaits us beyond?" Asvarr asked, cleaning his blade before sheathing it.

"The architects of the breaking," Yrsa answered. "Those who shaped the Tree before the gods claimed it."

Brynja flexed her wounded arm, the runes pulsing brighter now. "The Verdant Five," she said, the truth-light strong around her words. "My mentors, my manipulators." Her jaw tightened. "Those who exploited my grief and guilt for nine cycles of planning."

"And now they will face us both," Asvarr replied, touching the blood-oath mark on his palm—the symbol of their reunited bloodlines.

They stepped through the archway together, Leif slipping between them like a ghost. Yrsa followed a step behind, her pendant glowing steadily brighter as they descended into the green gloom.

***

The passage wound downward in a perfect spiral, its walls formed from living wood that breathed in time with their footsteps. Glowing mushrooms provided illumination, pulsing brighter as they passed. The air grew thick with moisture and the smell of growth—plants budding, flowering, decaying, and regenerating in accelerated cycles.

"The full spectrum of growth in one space," Yrsa murmured. "Birth to death and back again."

After what seemed like hours of descent, though the quality of light had not changed, the passage opened into a vast circular chamber that stole the breath from Asvarr's lungs.

The chamber stretched wider than any longhouse or mead hall he'd ever seen, its ceiling lost in green-tinted mist high above. The walls consisted of concentric rings of living wood, each bearing different types of growth—moss, fungi, flowers, vines—all moving with deliberate purpose rather than random expansion. At the center lay a reflecting pool of silver water, its surface undisturbed by even the slightest ripple.

Around this pool stood five massive thrones, each formed from a different aspect of plant life. And upon these thrones sat the Verdant Five.

"Welcome, children of sundered bloodlines," spoke the first figure—a woman whose body seemed formed of tangled roots that periodically sprouted small buds and flowers. Her face retained the most human features among them, though her eyes held the deep brown of fertile soil. "We have awaited your arrival since the breaking began."

The second figure leaned forward—a man whose arms were wrapped in spiraling vines that extended from his shoulders like living armor. His lower body disappeared into his throne of twisting stems, making it impossible to determine where he ended and the throne began. "The vessel returns to us," he said, his voice resonating like wind through hollow reeds. "Though changed from our design."

"And accompanied by flame," observed the third, a slender figure with leaf-like hair that rustled with each word, their skin a variegated pattern of greens and yellows. "The division we maintained for nine cycles, breached at last."

The fourth throne held what appeared to be a woman composed of overlapping petals and blossoms, her form constantly shifting as some flowers closed while others opened. Her eyes were deep wells of amber light. "The Rootbound have marked you," she noted, gesturing to Brynja's arm. "Their ancient bindings were never meant for human flesh."

The fifth and final figure remained silent, watching from a throne of seedpods and thorns. Their form was the least human—a collection of potential rather than manifestation, shapes suggesting themselves beneath a cloak of unfurling ferns.

"The Verdant Five," Asvarr stated, his hand instinctively moving toward his sword before he checked the motion. "Rootmother, Stembinder, Leafspeaker, Blossomweaver, and Seedkeeper."

"He knows our aspects," Rootmother observed, her lips curving into something resembling a smile. "The vessel has shared knowledge she should not possess."

"I have a name," Brynja said, her voice tight with controlled anger. Golden truth-light flared around her words. "And I am not your vessel."

Rootmother's expression hardened. "You carry our greatest work within your transformed arm—the seed of awakening that will restore what was lost." She gestured toward the pool. "Approach and see what we have preserved through nine cycles of planning."

Asvarr exchanged a glance with Brynja, whose runes pulsed with increasing intensity. She gave a small nod, and together they approached the silver pool, leaving Yrsa and Leif at the chamber's edge.

As they neared, the pool's surface began to move, rippling outward from the center as images formed beneath—visions of Yggdrasil in its prime, branches extending through nine realms, roots weaving between worlds.

"We shaped the Tree from raw potential," Stembinder explained, his vine-wrapped limbs extending slightly. "Before gods, before mortals, before fixed form. We were tasked with creating a structure to support the realms."

"Tasked by whom?" Asvarr asked.

The Five exchanged glances, a silent communication passing between them.

"The first consciousness," Leafspeaker answered after a pause. "That which dreamed existence into being, then withdrew to observe."

"The original betrayal," Blossomweaver added, her voice a harmony of multiple tones, "came not from us, but from those who claimed our work as their own. The gods who bounded the Tree into rigid forms when it was meant to grow freely."

The pool shifted again, showing images of beings Asvarr recognized from the oldest tales—Odin and his brothers shaping the realms from Ymir's corpse, binding the Tree into its final configuration.

"They constrained what was meant to be limitless," Seedkeeper spoke for the first time, their voice unexpectedly deep and resonant from their small form. "They claimed ownership of what was meant to be shared."

Brynja knelt beside the pool, her wooden fingers hovering just above the surface. "You opposed them?"

"We retreated," Rootmother corrected, truth-light confirming her words even across the distance. "To preserve what could be saved of the original vision. We took a fragment of the unconstrained essence—what your kind now calls the Severed Bloom—and protected it through cycles of breaking and rebirth."

"Your bloodline was cultivated for this purpose," Stembinder told Brynja. "To carry what was saved until the time came for restoration."

Asvarr felt cold realization settling in his stomach. "The Shattering wasn't an attack on the Tree. You caused it."

All five beings went still, the growth around them momentarily pausing in mid-motion.

"We liberated the Tree from its constraints," Blossomweaver said carefully. "That it shattered rather than simply transformed was... unexpected."

"And now you seek to restore it," Asvarr pressed, "but according to your original design, not as it was."

"The original design was perfection," Leafspeaker insisted, leaves rustling agitatedly. "Growth without limit, change without constraint, balance without enforced structure."

Brynja stood slowly, her runes burning like molten gold against her skin. "You used me," she said, each word accompanied by flaring truth-light. "You found me at my most vulnerable and shaped me into your tool." Her wooden arm creaked as she clenched her fist. "You lied about my purpose."

"We prepared you for your destiny," Rootmother countered. "Your blood remembers what your mind cannot—the truth of the pattern before the gods distorted it."

"And what of his blood?" Brynja demanded, gesturing to Asvarr. "You kept our bloodlines divided for nine cycles, feeding us lies about betrayal and hatred. Why?"

The Five exchanged another silent communication before Seedkeeper responded. "Flame-blood and root-blood together limit outside influence. United, you create barriers against the very changes we seek to implement." Their form shifted slightly, potential briefly flaring into partial manifestation. "Division was necessary for clearer guidance."

"Manipulation," Asvarr translated flatly. "You couldn't control both bloodlines united, so you kept us apart."

"We directed the pattern toward healing," Stembinder insisted. "Your limited mortal perspective cannot grasp the necessity of our methods."

The pool's surface churned, images fracturing and reforming—the nine cycles of breaking and attempted restoration flickering past in rapid succession. Asvarr glimpsed previous Wardens, bearing marks similar to his own, attempting to bind anchors across multiple realms. None succeeded in binding all five.

"Nine cycles of failure," Rootmother stated. "Because in each cycle, the flame-blood and root-blood found each other too soon, creating resistance to proper guidance."

"This time," Blossomweaver continued, "we arranged matters differently. We eliminated both bloodlines almost entirely, preserving only specific vessels to carry forward our work."

The cold realization in Asvarr's stomach blossomed into rage. "You ordered the destruction of our clans. You sent the Ashfather against our people."

The Five showed no remorse at this accusation. "Necessary pruning," Seed-keeper said dismissively. "To allow proper growth in the intended direction."

Brynja's hand found Asvarr's, her wooden fingers intertwining with his flesh ones. Her voice, when she spoke, trembled with contained fury. "You murdered our families to keep us separate, then lied to me about who was responsible." The truth-light around her words blazed so brightly it momentarily blinded them. "You told me the shadow wearing a god's face destroyed my clan out of fear of my potential, when you were the ones who sent him."

"The shadow serves its own purpose," Rootmother replied. "It believes it opposes us, even as it executes the role we prepared for it."

"The Ashfather," Asvarr growled. "Another of your manipulations?"

"A previous Warden who glimpsed too much truth too soon," Stembinder explained. "He chose to oppose rather than serve, yet his opposition creates the very conditions needed for our work to progress."

The silver pool darkened, images fading as if refusing to show what was being discussed. Asvarr felt the weight of ancient manipulation settling across his shoulders. Everything—the breaking of the Tree, the destruction of their clans, their quests to bind the anchors—all of it orchestrated by these five beings for purposes they had concealed across nine cycles.

"And now we've spoiled your pattern by uniting," he said, squeezing Brynja's hand. "By discovering your lies and choosing alliance over division."

"You have merely arrived at the point we intended, though sooner than we planned," Leafspeaker countered, rustling agitatedly. "The vessel carries what we preserved. The flame-bearer provides the catalyst needed for awakening. Together, you will complete what nine cycles have prepared."

"And what exactly is that?" Brynja demanded, truth-light flashing.

"The restoration of the original pattern," Rootmother answered. "The growth without constraint that the gods denied."

"Unchecked growth consumes everything in its path," Yrsa said suddenly, stepping forward from the edge of the chamber. Her crystal pendant blazed with blue-white fire. "That is why balance was imposed."

The Five turned their attention to her, recognition flaring in their ancient eyes.

"The Boundary Walker returns," Blossomweaver observed. "Another piece moving into position."

"You twist truth like roots twist stone," Yrsa accused. "Slow, inexorable, and hidden from sight until the damage is done."

Asvarr glanced between Yrsa and the Five, sensing an ancient conflict surfacing. Before he could question it, Leif appeared at his side, tugging at his sleeve.

"They test through illusion," the boy whispered urgently. "Truth and lie woven together. Watch for what shifts beneath the surface."

As if triggered by his words, the chamber around them began to change. The walls of living wood pulsed and expanded, sending questing tendrils down toward the floor. The silver pool darkened to black, its surface now completely still.

"The flame-bearer must be tested," Rootmother announced, rising from her throne. Her body towered above them, roots extending from her feet to crack the stone floor. "To determine if he is worthy to catalyze the awakening."

"And if I refuse your test?" Asvarr challenged, drawing his bronze sword. The golden veins within the metal flared in response to the growing threat.

"Then the vessel will complete her purpose alone," Stembinder replied, "consuming what remains of her consciousness in the process."

Brynja's grip on Asvarr's hand tightened painfully. "They'll destroy me if you don't comply," she whispered, golden light confirming her certainty.

The Five extended their arms in unison, and the chamber transformed around them. The walls receded into darkness, the floor beneath them shifted to packed earth, and the smell of smoke and blood filled the air.

"Behold your truth," Rootmother intoned, "and prove your worthiness to participate in the awakening."

***

The illusion solidified around them, and Asvarr found himself standing in the center of his village on the day of its destruction. Buildings burned around him, screams filled the air, and the bodies of his clansmen lay broken in the mud. Among them stood his father—a man he hadn't seen since childhood—wearing the same armor he'd left in, holding a bloodied axe.

"Witness the betrayals that shaped you," Blossomweaver's voice echoed from everywhere and nowhere. "Face what you have hidden from yourself."

Asvarr's father turned toward him, eyes cold with purpose rather than warmed by recognition. Behind him stood Brynja, her wooden arm fully transformed into a weapon of thorn and branch, her face a mask of vengeful purpose.

"Choose truth," commanded the Five in unison. "And prove your worth."

Asvarr's hand instinctively gripped his sword hilt tighter as flames roared around him, consuming the thatched roofs of his clan's homes. The air filled with the metallic scent of blood and the acrid tang of burning timber. Screams punctuated the crackle of fire, cries cut short with terrible finality.

His father stood before him, battle-worn and grim. The man he'd spent years believing had died heroically now faced him across a killing field, axe dripping with the blood of their own kin.

"Why?" Asvarr demanded, the question burning his throat. "These were your people!"

His father's face remained expressionless. "Some prices must be paid for greater purpose." He gestured to his right, where Brynja emerged from smoke, her wooden arm now a weapon of twisted thorns and barbs. "Division was necessary. The bloodlines could not unite."

"This isn't real," Asvarr growled, even as his eyes registered familiar details—the notch in his father's shield, earned in a raid when Asvarr was seven; the precise pattern of scars across the man's forearms; the amber pendant he always wore, identical to the one Asvarr had buried when they thought him dead at sea.

A flicker of movement caught his eye. Leif stood at the edge of the burning village, untouched by flame or smoke, watching with those unsettling golden eyes. When their gazes met, the boy tilted his head slightly toward the sky.

Asvarr glanced up. The clouds above swirled in impossible patterns, folding into each other with unnatural precision. This was illusion, crafted from his memories and fears.

"You abandoned us," Asvarr said, lowering his sword slightly. "When I was ten, you sailed west and never returned. We burned an empty pyre for you."

His father's form flickered. "Your memory serves you poorly. I chose a greater purpose."

"My memory serves me well," Asvarr countered. "Your ship was lost in a storm. We found pieces of the hull washed ashore weeks later." He stepped forward, studying the apparition more closely. "But you weren't a traitor. You were many things—stubborn, harsh, proud—but never oath-breaker to your kin."

The illusion of his father dissolved into tendrils of smoke and light, reforming into a scene Asvarr recognized with sickening clarity—the final stand of his clan. Warriors he'd known since childhood fought back to back in a blood-soaked circle, surrounded by shadowy attackers. But in this version, their faces twisted with betrayal as they turned their weapons on each other.

Gunnar, who had taught Asvarr his first sword forms, drove his blade through Halvdan's chest. Torfa, shield-maiden and daughter of the clan's master smith, cut down three of her shield-sisters before a spear took her through the throat.

"Friend against friend," Rootmother's voice echoed from the burning sky. "Loyalty splintered in the final moments."

"This is false," Asvarr said, watching the brutal scene unfold. His chest tightened with grief, but his mind remained clear. "They died defending each other to the last breath. I found their bodies formed in a shield-ring, facing outward against the attackers. They upheld their oaths."

Again he caught sight of Leif, now standing among the embattled warriors, completely ignored by both sides. The boy pointed to the ground, then to his own eyes.

Asvarr looked down. The earth beneath the fighting warriors showed no footprints, no scuff marks from desperate movement. No blood soaked into the soil despite the carnage above.

"Another deception," he said firmly. "My clansmen died with honor. They did not break faith with each other."

The illusion rippled and dissolved, reforming into the most painful vision yet. Brynja stood at the head of an army of wood-transformed warriors, her face set in lines of cold determination. One hand—fully human, not wooden—held a torch that she cast onto the roof of the mead hall where children and elders had taken shelter.

"The vessel brought the enemy to your gate," Stembinder's voice rumbled around him. "While you sought the first anchor, she carried out her orders."

A primal roar tore from Asvarr's throat, all rational thought momentarily eclipsed by rage. He charged forward, bronze sword raised—only to halt as Leif stepped directly into his path, the boy's golden eyes locking with his.

"Illusion within truth within illusion," Leif said, his voice carrying an authority at odds with his childlike appearance. "They show what might have been without showing what was."

The words sliced through Asvarr's battle-fury like a cold blade. He forced himself to breathe, to think past the manipulation. The Brynja in this vision wasn't the woman he knew—both arms remained human, with no sign of the Root transformation that had begun before her clan's destruction.

"You twist fragments of truth into lies," Asvarr called out to the unseen Five. "Brynja's clan was destroyed the same day as mine—she couldn't have led the attack."

The illusion shattered with the sound of breaking glass, fragments whirling into darkness before the council chamber reappeared around him. The Five remained on their thrones, watching him with ancient, inhuman eyes.

"You recognize deception," Rootmother acknowledged, "but what of truth hidden within falsehood?"

The chamber darkened again, and Asvarr found himself standing on a cliff overlooking a fjord. Beside him stood his father, younger than in the previous vision, strong and whole. Below them, a ship prepared for departure, warriors loading supplies and checking rigging.

"I must go," his father said, voice tight with poorly concealed emotion. "The signs point west. If I'm right, we'll secure our clan's future for generations."

"And if you're wrong?" asked a woman's voice.

Asvarr turned to see his mother, alive again in this memory—her face more vivid than he'd been able to recall in years. She held a small child against her hip. With a jolt, Asvarr recognized himself at perhaps four years old.

"Then I'll have failed my duty as clan-leader," his father answered. "But the dreams grow stronger each night. Something waits across the whale-road. Something that calls with my father's voice."

"The bloodline remembers," his mother said quietly. "Even when the mind forgets."

The vision shifted, showing his father's ship caught in a storm unlike any natural tempest. Lightning struck the vessel repeatedly, each bolt guided by a spectral hand. Massive waves formed into jaws that tore at the hull, while winds howled with almost-words.

"Your father discovered a fragment of truth," Leafspeaker's voice whispered around him. "He remembered what your bloodline once knew—that flame and root were meant to be united, not divided."

"He sought the crossing point," Blossomweaver continued, "where your clan's ancestors first separated from the root-keepers."

"And for this, you killed him," Asvarr said, watching the ship break apart beneath the supernatural assault.

"We preserved the pattern necessary for nine cycles," Seedkeeper's voice replied, emotionless. "Individual lives matter little against such purpose."

The vision faded, replaced by a new scene—Brynja alone in a forest clearing, weeping over a freshly-dug grave as flames consumed a small village in the distance. Her cloak bore the stains of her escape through forest and marsh. Her face reflected the same hollow grief Asvarr had carried since his clan's destruction.

"She fled rather than fight," Rootmother's voice observed. "Abandoned her people to slaughter."

"She survived," Asvarr corrected. "As did I. Neither of us chose the destruction of our clans—you orchestrated both. You're showing me her deepest shame to turn me against her."

"Do you not harbor resentment that she lived while so many died?" Stembinder pressed. "Does her admission of cowardice not diminish her in your eyes?"

Asvarr watched Brynja in the vision, her shoulders shaking with silent sobs as she finished the burial—likely the only one her clansmen would receive.

"No," he answered firmly. "She carries the burden of survival just as I do. Her moment of fear doesn't erase who she is, any more than my failures define the whole of my worth." He turned his face upward, addressing the Five directly. "People are more than their worst moments."

The vision wavered, then dissolved completely. Asvarr found himself back in the council chamber, surrounded by the Five on their living thrones. Brynja stood beside him once again, her rune-carved arm pulsing with golden light. Yrsa and Leif watched from the chamber's edge, faces tense with anticipation.

"You rejected manipulation," Rootmother observed. "And chose compassion over judgment."

"You recognize complexity," Stembinder added, "where simpler minds see only failure or success."

"The flame-bearer passes our test," Blossomweaver announced, her form shifting through various flowering stages. "He may participate in the awakening alongside the vessel."

***

"I am not your vessel," Brynja said, golden truth-light flaring around her words. "And he is not your catalyst. We make our own choices now."

"Do you?" Seedkeeper asked, their form rippling with unrealized potential. "Or do you follow paths laid out across nine cycles of preparation?"

Before either could respond, the silver pool at the chamber's center pulsed with sudden light. Its surface parted like liquid mercury, revealing a spiraling staircase descending into emerald darkness.

"The path to the second anchor opens," Leafspeaker announced. "The true anchor, not the memory fragment you bound before."

"The Verdant Gate leads nowhere without both bloodlines," Rootmother explained. "Now that you've proven worthy of participation, you may proceed to the binding."

"And if we refuse?" Asvarr challenged, stepping closer to Brynja.

"Then nine cycles of preparation are wasted," Blossomweaver answered. "And what sleeps beneath the roots may waken without proper guidance."

"The choice remains yours," Stembinder concluded, "though the consequences extend far beyond your limited understanding."

Asvarr exchanged glances with Brynja. Her wooden fingers brushed against his wrist, cool and smooth against his skin.

"We'll bind the anchor," she said, truth-light confirming her sincerity. "But on our terms, not yours. We seek balance, not control."

"A dangerous distinction," Rootmother warned, roots shifting restlessly beneath her throne. "The anchor requires clear purpose."

"We have purpose," Asvarr replied. "To heal what was broken, not reshape it to serve hidden agendas."

The Five communicated silently among themselves, expressions unreadable on their plant-transformed faces. Finally, Rootmother spoke for them all.

"The second anchor lies in the Garden of Forgotten Memory, guarded by the Blight-Herder." Her tone carried a hint of reluctance. "Once he was Oakhelm, greatest of our disciples. Now he tends corruption rather than growth, his mind twisted by isolation."

"The garden has become a graveyard," Leafspeaker added, leaves rustling agitatedly. "The bones of failed seekers feed the twisted roots that wind through its soil."

"What happened to him?" Asvarr asked.

"He glimpsed too much truth too quickly," Blossomweaver answered. "Without proper preparation, such knowledge corrupts rather than illuminates."

"Or perhaps," Brynja suggested, golden light flickering across her lips, "he discovered truths you preferred to keep hidden."

The Five remained silent at this accusation, neither confirming nor denying it.

Yrsa approached from the edge of the chamber, her crystal pendant blazing with blue-white light. "We should depart immediately. The Hunt of Broken Fate still searches for us, and the Ashfather will sense the opening of the anchor path."

Leif joined them, his small form now fully solid where before he had seemed partially transparent. "The boy must guide you," he said, referring to himself in third person as he sometimes did. "Parts of him remember the garden from before its corruption."

"Paths branch and possibilities multiply," Seedkeeper observed. "We shall watch with interest to see which wyrd-threads you follow."

"The vessel remembers even what was hidden from her conscious mind," Stembinder told Brynja. "Let the runes guide you through the garden's dangers."

Asvarr gripped his bronze sword, the golden veins within the metal brightening as he faced the Five one last time. "When we return from binding the anchor, we'll have more questions for you—about the Severed Bloom, about our bloodlines, about the nine cycles of manipulation."

"If you return," Rootmother corrected. "The Blight-Herder has consumed dozens of seekers more prepared than yourselves."

"We return together, or not at all," Brynja stated, truth-light confirming her resolve.

The Five inclined their plant-crowned heads in acknowledgment, if not agreement. The silver pool's surface rippled invitingly, the staircase descending into unknown depths.

Asvarr led the way, bronze sword drawn. The steps felt solid beneath his boots despite their liquid appearance. Brynja followed, her wooden arm extended slightly as if sensing currents in the air. Yrsa and Leif came behind, the boy humming tunelessly under his breath.

As they descended below the pool's surface, the council chamber disappeared from view. The staircase wound downward in a perfect spiral, each step taking them deeper into a realm of living memory. Around them, fragments of visions flickered like lightning through green-tinted mist—moments from across nine cycles of breaking and binding, faces of previous Wardens who had walked similar paths.

"They only showed you what served their purpose," Brynja said quietly, the truth-light pulsing around her words. "There's much they still conceal."

"I know," Asvarr replied, watching a vision of a previous flame-bearer battling creatures of tangled root and thorn. "But we've learned one valuable truth today."

"What's that?" she asked.

"That even the architects of fate can't predict every outcome." He glanced back at her, determination hardening his features. "They never expected us to unite against them. They never expected the runes to reveal truth rather than bind it. And they never expected us to pass their test while rejecting their purpose."

"Which makes us dangerous to them," Brynja concluded, truth-light steady around her words.

"Which makes us free," Asvarr corrected, continuing downward into the mist-shrouded passage. "And freedom always frightens those who depend on control."

The staircase ended abruptly in darkness. Asvarr stepped onto solid ground, though he couldn't see its surface. The air here smelled of decay—vegetation rotting into soil, stagnant water, and something sharper beneath, like crushed insects.

Leif pushed forward, his small form now leading rather than following. "The garden lies ahead," he said, his golden eyes illuminating the darkness in narrow beams. "But it isn't a garden anymore. It's a graveyard for lost seekers and forgotten memories."

A sickly green glow materialized in the distance, revealing hints of twisted shapes—branches contorted into unnatural forms, roots erupting from the ground like grasping hands, flowers with faces that whispered without sound.

"The Blight-Herder awaits," Yrsa murmured, her pendant's light dimming in response to the corruption ahead. "He senses our approach."

"Then let's not disappoint him," Asvarr said grimly, raising his sword as they advanced toward the corrupted garden and whatever horrors lurked among its blighted growth.

CHAPTER 14

THE BLIGHT-HERDER

The smell hit Asvarr first—fermented earth, copper-tang of blood, and overripe rot mingling with sweet decay. He followed the Verdant Five's messenger—a slender sapling that walked on root-feet—down the spiraling stair beneath the silver pool. Darkness pressed around them, broken only by Leif's golden footprints and the phosphorescent moss clinging to the wall's weeping stones.

"Careful," Brynja warned, her wooden arm scraping against the narrowing passage. "The air tastes wrong."

She wasn't mistaken. Each breath coated Asvarr's tongue with the flavor of rust and turned soil. The bark patterns spreading across his shoulders itched beneath his tunic, a warning sensation he'd learned to heed since his transformation began.

"The garden was beautiful once," Leif said, his voice startlingly adult compared to his child's form. "I remember when it bloomed with possibility, before the breaking."

Yrsa shot the boy a sharp glance. "You speak as if you witnessed its creation."

Leif didn't answer, only traced his fingers along the stone, leaving trails of light that revealed ancient carvings—spiraling patterns of branches and roots interwoven with symbols Asvarr recognized from his Grímmark.

***

The tunnel opened suddenly into vastness. Asvarr stepped out onto a ledge overlooking what might once have been called a garden, though that word seemed a mockery now. Below stretched a grotesque landscape of twisted vegetation—trees bent into agonized shapes, flowers with toothed mouths that snapped at passing insects, vines that writhed with deliberate purpose.

"By the forgotten gods," Brynja whispered, her truth-runes glowing golden on her flesh. "What manner of corruption is this?"

"Oakhelm's work," Yrsa answered, her crystal pendant dimming as if refusing to shine in this place. "The Five's greatest disciple before he chose his own path."

Asvarr scanned the garden, mapping their route. A path of bone-white stones wound through the corruption, leading to a central structure—a dome formed from interlaced branches and roots that reminded him of a massive ribcage. Between the path and the dome lay... remains. Dozens, perhaps hundreds of them—desiccated bodies in various states of decay, some freshly dead, others mere skeletons with roots growing through their bones.

"Failed seekers," Yrsa explained, following his gaze. "Those who sought the anchor without understanding its price."

The bones of a massive creature—perhaps an elk or something larger—formed an archway at the path's beginning. As they approached, Asvarr noticed small movements in the ground around them. Tiny insects, iridescent and metallic, burrowed in and out of the soil in organized patterns.

"They're watching us," Leif said, crouching to observe the creatures. "Carrying our presence back to him."

"To the Blight-Herder?" Asvarr asked, hand moving to his bronze sword's hilt.

"To what remains of Oakhelm," Brynja corrected, her wooden fingers flexing. "If the Five spoke truth, he's more corruption than man now."

They passed beneath the bone arch. The moment they stepped onto the white path, the garden responded—flowers turning toward them like hungry faces, vines slithering closer to the path's edge, trees creaking as they bent ever so slightly inward.

"It knows we're here," Asvarr muttered, drawing his sword. The gold veins in the blade pulsed, responding to the corrupted magic surrounding them.

"Stay on the path," Yrsa warned. "The stones are warded. Step off, and the garden claims you."

To emphasize her point, she tossed a small pebble into the vegetation beside the path. The ground erupted—roots shooting upward to ensnare the stone, dragging it beneath the surface in seconds.

"Cheerful," Brynja said, drawing her curved knife.

They moved forward in tense silence, following the bone-white path as it wound through increasingly disturbing scenes. In one clearing, they passed trees bearing fruit shaped like human hearts, pulsing wetly. In another, flowering vines had grown through a seeker's body, blooming from her eye sockets and mouth.

The dome grew larger as they approached, revealing its true nature—a massive, hollow tree trunk, bent and twisted into an enclosure. The entrance yawned like a mouth, darkness within.

"Something's moving inside," Leif whispered, pointing.

Asvarr followed the boy's gesture and saw them—shadows shifting within the dome, humanoid shapes carrying something between them. As he watched, the figures emerged, six in total, dressed in tattered green robes stained black with old blood. Their faces were hidden behind wooden masks carved with expressions of agony.

Between them, they dragged a seventh figure—another seeker, still alive but barely. His limbs twitched weakly as they hauled him toward a clearing where roots coiled upward from the ground like waiting serpents.

"We have to help him," Asvarr said, starting forward.

Yrsa caught his arm. "Wait. We can't save everyone, and alerting the Blight-Herder to our presence too soon—"

"I won't watch another innocent die," Asvarr growled, pulling free. The Grím-mark burned across his chest, golden sap leaking through his tunic.

Before anyone could stop him, he surged forward along the path, bronze sword raised. "Release him!" he shouted.

The masked figures turned as one, movements unnaturally synchronized. One raised a gnarled wooden staff, pointing it toward Asvarr. The roots surrounding the clearing responded instantly, surging upward to form a wall between Asvarr and the captive.

"Too late," came a voice like beetles scraping through dead leaves. "He offered himself freely."

The masked figures parted, revealing the source of the voice. Where Asvarr expected to see a person stood something far removed from humanity—a hollow shell that might once have been a man, now a walking husk filled with writhing roots and burrowing insects. Two gleaming insect swarms occupied the eye sockets of what remained of a human face, moving in tandem to focus on Asvarr.

The Blight-Herder.

He—it—wore the tattered remains of druidic robes, green fabric now blackened with corruption. A crown of thorns circled its skull, each thorn tipped with a gem that pulsed with sickly light. From gaps in its desiccated skin, roots and vines emerged, connecting the creature to the garden around it.

"Flame-bearer," the Blight-Herder said, head tilting unnaturally. "Root-tender." Its gaze moved to Brynja, who had followed Asvarr despite Yrsa's warning. "The Five send children to reclaim what was never theirs."

The captive seeker screamed as roots wrapped around his limbs, penetrating his skin. Blood flowed in rivulets down the white tendrils, feeding the soil beneath.

"Stop this!" Asvarr demanded, raising his sword.

The Blight-Herder's mouth stretched in what might have been a smile, revealing teeth grown like tree rings. "You misunderstand. This is salvation. He gives himself to the garden, and the garden remembers." It gestured to the countless bodies throughout the space. "As they all have."

Brynja stepped forward, wooden arm extended. "We seek the verdant anchor. Stand aside, corrupted one."

The creature laughed—a sound like branches breaking in winter frost. "Corrupted? I see clearly while you remain blind. The anchor is not what the Five told you."

"Let the seeker go," Asvarr insisted, "and we'll hear what you have to say."

"He chose this path," the Blight-Herder responded, unmoved. "As did all who sleep in my garden. As did I, when I learned the truth the Five concealed."

The captive's screams faded to whimpers as roots penetrated deeper, his blood flowing freely now. The masked figures began a low chant in a language Asvarr didn't recognize but somehow understood—a prayer for absorption, for memory, for the preservation of essence.

The Blight-Herder stepped closer, its movements accompanied by the clicking of countless insects within its hollow frame. "You think you face corruption, flame-bearer. You believe you fight for restoration." It pointed a finger—more root than flesh—toward the captive. "Ask him what he learned before he chose to join my garden."

Asvarr hesitated, then addressed the suffering man. "What did you find here?"

Through his pain, the captive turned bloodshot eyes toward Asvarr. "The pattern... is broken by design," he gasped. "The Five... lied. The anchors are cages, not salvation." His voice broke as roots wrapped around his throat. "Better to feed... the new growth... than serve their lies."

The Blight-Herder nodded, the movement sending insects cascading from joints in its neck. "He learned what I learned—that the Five shape the pattern to serve themselves, cycling through vessels like you when their current forms fail."

A cold realization washed through Asvarr. He'd suspected the Five weren't telling the whole truth—their manipulations across nine cycles had proven that—but this suggested something darker.

Brynja stepped forward, her truth-runes glowing. "If the anchors are cages, what do they imprison?"

"Not what," the Blight-Herder corrected. "Who." It tapped its hollow chest. "Ask yourself why the Five remained while everything else changed. Why they alone maintained cohesion through the breaking."

"They weren't the only ones," Leif's voice came from behind them. The boy had crept forward, moving silently along the path. "There were others who re-membered."

The Blight-Herder's insect eyes fixed on Leif, clusters shifting rapidly. "The between-child speaks truth. The Five preserved themselves by design—the breaking was their work, not something they merely survived."

Asvarr remembered the vision they'd shared in the Circle of Splinters—Yggdrasil shattering itself to escape the darkness consuming it. "The Tree broke itself to survive something eating it from within."

"So the Five would have you believe," the Blight-Herder said. "A partial truth to mask their crime."

The captive gave one final shudder as roots completely enveloped him. His body began to sink into the ground, feeding the garden. The masked figures bowed their heads, then turned toward the dome.

"You're too late to save him," the Blight-Herder said, "but perhaps not too late to save yourselves. The anchor lies within." It gestured toward the dome. "Enter, if you still believe the Five's pretty lies. Or join my garden, and feed the truth that grows beneath."

Asvarr looked to Brynja, whose wooden arm twitched against her will, responding to the garden's call.

"The anchor," she said, her voice strained. "I can feel it. It's within the dome, but... changed. Corrupted, perhaps."

"Or freed," the Blight-Herder countered. "As I was freed when I learned what the Five truly are."

"And what are they?" Yrsa asked, finally speaking. Her crystal pendant hung dark around her neck.

"Ask the flame-bearer," the Blight-Herder said, pointing to Asvarr. "His bloodline knew. It's why they were destroyed."

The accusation hit Asvarr like a physical blow. "What do you know of my clan's destruction?"

"I know the Five ordered it," the creature responded. "As they ordered the destruction of the root-tender's people. Both bloodlines had begun to remember—to piece together fragments of truth across generations."

Asvarr's hand tightened on his sword. The Blight-Herder was giving voice to suspicions that had grown since he'd learned of the Five's manipulations across nine cycles. But could he trust this corrupted being any more than he trusted them?

"If what you say is true," Asvarr said carefully, "why not tell us plainly what the Five are hiding?"

The Blight-Herder's laugh rattled through its hollow frame. "Some truths must be experienced to be believed, flame-bearer. The anchor will show you what words cannot." It stepped aside, clearing the path to the dome. "Enter, if you dare. But know this—what waits inside is not what the Five described. It is both more and less than an anchor, both older and newer than they claim."

Asvarr looked to his companions. Brynja nodded, her wooden arm trembling with anticipation or fear. Leif's expression was unreadable, but he positioned himself closer to Asvarr, as if offering support. Yrsa hung back, her face troubled.

"We came for the anchor," Asvarr said decisively. "We'll see it for ourselves."

"As you wish," the Blight-Herder responded, insects swarming more rapidly within its hollow frame. "But first, a warning freely given. The anchor responds to blood—it always has. But whose blood it tastes will determine what awakens."

Asvarr stepped forward, bronze sword still drawn. "We'll remember your warning."

The Blight-Herder's mouth twisted in another grotesque approximation of a smile. "No, flame-bearer. You'll remember nothing when the anchor takes you—unless you're stronger than all who came before."

The creature stepped back, roots sliding from earth to reconnect with its legs. "Enter my sanctuary. Witness what the Five would keep hidden. Then choose—their path of cycles and vessels, or my garden of truth and dissolution."

Asvarr looked to the dome entrance—a twisted arch lined with thorns, beyond which lay only darkness. The second anchor waited within, but so did revelations he might not be prepared to face.

"Together," he said to Brynja, extending his hand.

Her wooden fingers interlaced with his flesh ones, truth-runes glowing golden against her skin. "Together," she agreed, the light confirming her sincerity.

They stepped forward, toward the darkness and whatever truth or deception awaited within the Blight-Herder's sanctuary. Behind them, Leif followed silently, his golden footprints illuminating the bone-white path. Only Yrsa remained behind, her troubled gaze fixed on the Blight-Herder as if seeing something the others could not.

The last thing Asvarr heard before entering the dome was the creature's final warning, spoken in a voice suddenly devoid of its insectile quality—a voice almost human, filled with genuine fear: "Remember who you are when the Root tests you. Remember, or join my garden as just another failed seeker."

***

Darkness enveloped Asvarr as they passed through the dome's entrance. The thorns along the archway scraped his shoulders, drawing pinpricks of blood that seeped into his tunic. The iron-copper tang of blood mixed with the sweet-rot scent of corruption, coating his tongue with each breath.

"I can't see," Brynja whispered beside him, her wooden fingers tightening around his.

Before Asvarr could respond, light bloomed—soft, golden illumination emanating from pods hanging from the dome's interior. They pulsed in rhythm with his heartbeat, revealing the space within.

The dome's interior was far larger than its outside suggested. Massive roots formed the walls, twisting upward to create a vaulted ceiling. A circular dais stood at the center, crafted from interwoven branches that spiraled inward to a hollow core. Golden sap pooled there, bubbling gently.

"The verdant anchor," Brynja breathed, her wooden arm tugging her forward involuntarily.

Asvarr held her back. "Wait. Remember the Blight-Herder's warning."

Leif moved past them, approaching the dais with fearless curiosity. "It remembers you both," he said, voice echoing strangely. "The flame and the root."

Something shifted in the shadows behind the dais. A figure emerged—a man with Asvarr's build and height, wearing the furs and leathers of a northern warrior. His face remained in shadow.

"Father?" Asvarr's voice cracked.

The figure stepped forward, features clarifying in the golden light. Kjartan Flame-Bearer—Asvarr's father, missing since before the attack on their clan. His beard was longer, streaked with gray, but his eyes remained the keen blue Asvarr remembered.

"My son," Kjartan said, arms outstretched. "You've grown strong."

Asvarr's hand fell from his sword hilt. For years he'd imagined this moment—finding his father alive, the questions he would ask, the rage he would express at being abandoned.

"This isn't real," Brynja hissed. "It's a test."

Kjartan's face hardened. "The root-tender speaks true, though not as she intends. I am memory, not flesh—but my words are real enough." He gestured around them. "This place preserves what would otherwise be lost."

Asvarr struggled to breathe around the knot in his throat. "Why did you leave us? Before the attack—you just vanished."

"I discovered the truth about our bloodline. About the flame and root's separation." Kjartan paced around the dais, keeping the pool of sap between them. "The Five have manipulated our lines for cycles, Asvarr. I sought the crossing point, the place where our bloodlines divided. I believed reuniting them would break their power."

"And for this, you abandoned your family?" Asvarr's voice hardened.

Kjartan stopped. "I abandoned nothing. I sought to protect everything." His form flickered, revealing glimpses of a corpse beneath the healthy exterior. "I failed. The Five found me before I could return with the truth. They executed me, then sent their servants to destroy our clan—and the Hrafn clan as well."

Asvarr glanced at Brynja, whose truth-runes remained dark—neither confirming nor denying the vision's words.

"How convenient," she said. "A story that justifies abandonment as noble sacrifice."

Kjartan laughed bitterly. "You think this is about justification? This is about warning." He pointed to the golden sap. "The anchors hold memories—but also binding patterns. They are both less and more than the Five claim."

"Speak plainly," Asvarr demanded.

"I cannot." Kjartan's form flickered again, more corpse than man now. "My time fades. Remember this: the pattern is neither broken nor whole. It is transformed with each cycle—like a tree growing through stone, finding new paths when old ones are blocked."

The image of Kjartan dissolved entirely, leaving a withered corpse that crumbled to dust. In its place stood Hakon, Asvarr's raid-leader, eyes hollow with accusation.

"You survived while we died," Hakon said, voice like grinding stones.

The dome shifted around them. The walls pulled back, transforming into the burning ruins of Asvarr's village. Bodies littered the ground—his clansmen, women, children. They rose slowly, moving with jerky motions, surrounding Asvarr.

"You weren't there," one woman said, throat torn and weeping.

"You lived while we burned," added a warrior with a crushed skull.

Asvarr's chest constricted. He'd carried this guilt since awakening among the ashes—why had he alone survived? The question haunted him through every step of his journey.

"This is manipulation," Brynja said firmly. "The anchor tests you."

Leif appeared beside Asvarr, golden eyes reflecting the flames. "Remember who you are," he said, echoing the Blight-Herder's warning.

The accusatory specters circled closer. Among them, Asvarr recognized childhood friends, mentors, elders. Each bore the wounds that had ended their lives.

"This is the price of the Root's favor," Hakon said, gesturing to the slaughter. "It chose you by letting us die."

Asvarr closed his eyes, forcing himself to breathe through the panic clawing at his throat. When he opened them, the scene had changed again.

Now he watched a battle from outside himself—raiders attacking his village. Leading them stood Brynja, younger but unmistakable, her left arm still flesh rather than wood. She shouted commands, directing warriors to set fire to long-houses.

The Brynja beside him stiffened. "This never happened," she said, truth-runes flaring golden on her skin.

The battlefield Brynja raised her sword, pointing toward a fleeing woman—Asvarr's mother. Two warriors pursued, cutting her down as she ran.

"Lies," the real Brynja growled. "My clan was attacked the same day as yours."

"The Five say many things," battlefield Brynja declared, turning to face them directly. "They claim we both lost our people, that we're both victims. The truth is simpler—one of us was marked for survival, one for vengeance."

Asvarr looked to the Brynja beside him, whose truth-runes still glowed golden, confirming her denial. He turned back to the battlefield version. "You're showing me what I feared, not what happened."

The false Brynja smiled cruelly. "Are you certain? Memory is malleable. The Root rewrites what serves its purpose."

"No," Leif interrupted, stepping between them. "The Root preserves. It's others who rewrite."

The battlefield scene wavered, colors bleeding like wet paint. Through the dissolution, Asvarr glimpsed something else—the Verdant Five standing in a circle, weaving patterns in the air as they watched the two clan massacres unfold simultaneously from afar.

"There," Leif said, pointing. "The truth the anchor preserves."

The vision solidified on this new scene—the Five observing twin massacres through a scrying pool. Rootmother nodded with satisfaction while Stembinder made a cutting motion with his hand.

"Both bloodlines cleansed," Blossomweaver said. "Again, the pattern holds."

"For how long?" Seedkeeper asked. "They remember more with each cycle."

The scene dissolved, returning them to the dome's interior. The pool of golden sap bubbled more vigorously now, emitting a high, thin sound like distant keening.

"The anchor shows what it contains," Leif explained, his child's voice gaining unnatural resonance. "Memory untainted by purpose or design."

Asvarr looked at Brynja, whose eyes glistened with unshed tears. "You never led raiders against my people."

"And you never abandoned yours," she replied. "We were both victims of the same culling."

Asvarr turned toward the pool. "Is that what you wanted to show us? That the Five orchestrated everything?"

The sap bubbled in response, forming a tendril that reached toward him. Asvarr stepped back instinctively.

"It wants blood," Leif said. "To confirm the truth, it requires essence."

"Whose blood?" Brynja asked, repeating the Blight-Herder's warning. "Mine or his?"

"Both," Leif answered. "The unified bloodlines were what the Five feared. What they still fear."

Asvarr drew his bronze sword, regarding its golden-veined blade. The Blight-Herder had warned that the anchor would test him, that remembering who he was would determine his survival.

Who was he? Survivor. Seeker. Warden. But also something older—flame-bearer from a line that stretched back before the sundering.

"If we give it our blood," he asked Leif, "what happens?"

The boy's expression turned solemn. "The seed awakens. Whether as restoration or corruption depends on what you carry in your heart when it tastes your essence."

"A test of intention," Brynja murmured.

"A test of identity," Leif corrected.

Asvarr met Brynja's eyes. "We've come this far. I won't turn back now."

She nodded, extending her flesh hand while keeping the wooden one at her side. "Together, then."

Asvarr drew his blade across his palm, then carefully across Brynja's flesh hand. Their blood mingled as they clasped hands, then approached the pool. Together, they extended their joined hands over the golden sap.

Their mixed blood dripped into the pool. For a heartbeat, nothing happened. Then the sap surged upward, engulfing their joined hands to the wrist.

Pain lanced through Asvarr, deeper than physical pain, as if the anchor searched his essence. Images flashed through his mind: his childhood, the raid, awakening among ashes, every step of his journey to this moment. Each memory carried a question, unspoken but felt—Who are you? Who are you? WHO ARE YOU?

Through the pain, Asvarr maintained his grip on Brynja's hand. He felt her experiencing the same examination, her truth-runes blazing so brightly they shone through her flesh, illuminating bone.

"I am Asvarr," he gasped aloud. "Flame-bearer, Root-bound, Seeker of Truth."

"I am Brynja Hrafndottir," she answered beside him. "Root-tender, Earth-healer, Keeper of Balance."

The sap pulled harder, drawing more than blood now—drawing memory, identity, purpose. Asvarr fought to maintain his sense of self as the anchor attempted to consume him.

"Remember," Leif whispered from somewhere distant. "Remember who you are."

Asvarr focused on his core identity—beyond titles, beyond bloodlines. The orphaned boy who loved climbing trees. The young man who honored oaths. The seeker who valued truth above comfort.

The sap released them suddenly, retreating into the pool. Both stumbled backward, catching themselves on the edge of the dais. Asvarr stared at his hand, expecting to find it burned or transformed. Instead, he saw a perfect spiral pattern etched across his palm in lines of golden sap that had solidified beneath his skin.

Brynja's palm bore the same marking.

"We passed its test," she said wonderingly.

The pool began to shift, golden sap spiraling upward to form a shape—a sapling with bark of intertwined gold and silver, leaves that shimmered between amber and emerald. Its roots extended outward across the dais, connecting with the dome's walls.

"The verdant anchor awakens," Leif said, approaching the sapling. "It recognizes the unified bloodlines."

A weight pressed into Asvarr's left hand. Looking down, he found a seed resting in his palm—perfectly oval, one half amber, one half emerald, spiral patterns etched across its surface.

"The anchor's token," Leif explained. "Carry it to the third binding."

The dome trembled suddenly, walls shuddering as roots writhed with apparent pain. Outside, they heard the Blight-Herder's voice raised in alarm.

"They come!" the creature shrieked. "The servants of the Five—they've breached my garden!"

"We need to go," Brynja urged, tugging Asvarr toward a new opening that had appeared in the dome's side—an arch formed by parting roots.

Asvarr pocketed the seed-token and followed, but as they reached the exit, pain exploded through his chest. He stumbled, collapsing to his knees.

"Asvarr!" Brynja knelt beside him, hands hovering uncertainly.

He pulled open his tunic, revealing black veins spreading outward from where the Blight-Herder's thorns had scratched him earlier. The infection pulsed beneath his skin, burning like ice and fire together.

"Corruption," Leif whispered, eyes wide with fear for the first time.

"The Blight-Herder poisoned you," Brynja said, truth-runes confirming her words.

Asvarr struggled to his feet, leaning heavily on his sword. "We need to get clear of the garden first."

***

They emerged from the dome into chaos. The garden's path was overrun with masked figures fighting translucent warriors that seemed formed of pure verdancy—the Five's servants battling the Blight-Herder's guardians. The corrupted druid itself stood at the center, thorned limbs extended as it commanded roots to rise from the soil and impale attackers.

"This way," Yrsa called from the edge of the conflict. She'd found another path circling the battlefield.

They ran, Asvarr fighting the spreading numbness in his chest. Each heartbeat pushed the corruption further through his veins. His vision blurred at the edges, darkening like leaves turning to autumn gold.

"Hold on," Brynja urged, supporting him with her wooden arm. "We'll find a cure."

They passed beneath another bone arch, leaving the garden's immediate boundaries. The sounds of battle faded behind them, replaced by the quiet rustle of a more natural forest. Asvarr's legs gave out, and he sank to the moss-covered ground, back pressed against a silver-barked tree.

"The corruption spreads quickly," Yrsa observed, examining the black veins that now extended up his neck and across his right shoulder. "We need something to counteract it."

"The hollowfruit," Brynja said suddenly. "The orchard where secrets are kept. One might hold knowledge of a cure."

Asvarr fought to focus through the spreading cold. The corruption felt like frostbite from within, deadening nerves as it advanced. "How far?"

"Not far," Leif replied, placing a hand on Asvarr's chest directly over the corruption's center. Golden light spread from his fingers, temporarily halting the blackness. "I can slow it, but not stop it."

Brynja knelt, taking Asvarr's face between her mismatched hands. "Stay with us. We didn't come this far to lose you to the Blight-Herder's parting gift."

Asvarr managed a pained smile. "I've survived worse."

"Debatable," she replied, attempting to match his gallows humor.

Behind them, fresh sounds of pursuit echoed through the forest—the Five's servants had broken through the garden's defenses and were following their trail.

"We must move," Yrsa insisted. "Can you walk?"

Asvarr pushed himself upright, gritting his teeth against the pain. "Lead to the orchard. Quickly."

Brynja supported him as they hurried through the forest, following Leif's confident navigation. The corruption pulsed with each beat of Asvarr's heart, a spreading darkness that threatened to consume him from within—the Blight-Herder's final test, one that would determine if he joined the garden as just another failed seeker, or continued his journey with the verdant anchor's knowledge burning in his blood.

CHAPTER 15

HOLLOWFRUIT TRUTH

B lack veins pulsed beneath Asvarr's skin, spreading outward from his chest like roots seeking soil. Each heartbeat pushed the corruption further—up his neck, across his shoulders, down his right arm. The forest blurred around him as he staggered forward, leaning heavily on Brynja. Her wooden arm supported him with unnatural strength, the bark patterns flowing smoothly against his fevered flesh.

"How much farther?" he gasped. His tongue felt swollen, coated with the taste of ash and copper.

"The orchard lies beyond that ridge," Brynja answered, adjusting her grip as he stumbled. "Leif says we're close."

Ahead of them, the boy moved with purpose, golden footprints marking a path through undergrowth that parted at his approach. Yrsa followed behind, her crystal pendant pulsing with dim light as she watched for pursuers.

"The Five's servants are still following," she warned. "I can sense them probing the boundary."

Asvarr forced himself to focus through the spreading cold. The Blight-Herder's corruption burned like ice beneath his skin, deadening flesh as it advanced. His Grímmark fought back—golden sap leaking through the black veins where they crossed the ancient pattern—but the struggle weakened him with each passing moment.

"I didn't survive nine generations of bloodline culling to lose you to a garden-tender's spite," Brynja muttered. Her truth-runes glowed against her skin, confirming genuine concern beneath her gruff tone.

The forest thinned as they crested the ridge. Below them stretched a sight that halted even Asvarr's labored breathing—an orchard unlike any he'd witnessed, stretching across a shallow valley. Bone-white trees with too-straight trunks grew in perfect concentric circles. Instead of leaves, they bore translucent membranes that fluttered without wind. From their branches hung pale, fleshy fruits, each perfectly round and glowing with internal light.

"The Orchard of Secrets," Leif announced, voice resonating with unchildlike depth. "Every hollow fruit holds knowledge taken from those who entered the memory realm."

"Their final revelations," Yrsa added. "What they learned before they were lost."

Asvarr straightened, drawing on reserves of strength he didn't know remained. "Then let's find one with knowledge of a cure."

They descended into the valley, the air growing thicker with each step. Sound dampened around them—their footfalls muted, their breathing hushed, as if the orchard itself absorbed noise. The ground between the trees was covered with a carpet of pale filaments resembling hair, which writhed gently beneath their feet.

"Don't touch the fruits unless invited," Leif warned. "They hunger for new secrets."

At the orchard's edge, Asvarr noticed small piles of belongings scattered beneath certain trees—knives, pendants, scraps of clothing—markers left by previous visitors. Some piles had been there so long they'd begun sinking into the filament-covered ground.

They moved deeper into the orchard, following Leif's lead. The corruption spread further with each step, now reaching toward Asvarr's heart. His vision darkened at the edges, colors leaching away except for the sickly green glow of the hanging fruits.

"This one," Leif said suddenly, stopping beneath a tree taller than the others. Its branches twisted in spirals, bearing fruits larger and more luminous than those surrounding it. "The tree of healers."

Asvarr approached, fighting vertigo. The hollow fruits pulsed as he drew near, their translucent skins revealing shadowy contents swirling within.

"How do we know which contains knowledge of the cure?" he asked, voice rough with pain.

Yrsa stepped forward, crystal pendant raised toward the branches. The pendant's light intensified as she moved it across different fruits, stopping on one hanging just above her reach. "This one resonates with healing knowledge."

Brynja supported Asvarr with her wooden arm while reaching upward with her flesh hand to touch the fruit's stem. It detached with a soft sighing sound, falling gently into her palm.

The fruit was larger than Asvarr expected, perfectly spherical with skin like foggy glass. Within, shadows twisted and coalesced, forming shapes he couldn't quite identify.

"How do we open it?" Brynja asked, offering it to Yrsa.

The boundary-walker shook her head. "I cannot. The orchard allows only those with greater need to access its secrets."

Asvarr extended a trembling hand. The moment his fingers touched the fruit's surface, it responded—warming, pulsing, a soft glow emanating from within. The skin thinned beneath his touch, becoming transparent enough to reveal what lay inside.

Not knowledge of a cure as they'd hoped, but a vision forming with alarming clarity: Brynja kneeling before a cloaked figure in a forest clearing. The figure's face remained in shadow save for a single eye gleaming with ancient intelligence. Their conversation played out in silence until Brynja extended her hand, receiving something from the one-eyed figure before pressing it to her lips in what could only be an oath-gesture.

The vision shifted, showing Brynja standing on a cliff-edge overlooking a familiar scene—the Circle of Splinters where they had first learned the truth about

Yggdrasil's deliberate breaking. The one-eyed figure stood beside her, pointing toward Asvarr in the distance. Words formed in mist between them: "Bring me his anchor, and vengeance will be yours."

Asvarr pulled his hand back as if burned. The fruit's surface clouded again, its inner vision fading.

"That wasn't what we sought," he said, voice hollow with more than weakness.

Brynja stood frozen, her truth-runes pulsing erratically across her wooden arm. "The orchard gives what is needed, not what is wanted," she said finally.

"You made a pact." Asvarr met her eyes directly. "With the Wanderer—the being I know as the False Odin."

She didn't deny it. Her truth-runes flared golden, preventing any possibility of deception. "I did."

"And your mission was to deliver my anchor to him." The words felt like stones in Asvarr's mouth.

"It was." The runes pulsed brighter, forcing honesty from her lips.

The corruption momentarily receded from the force of Asvarr's anger, allowing clarity to pierce his feverish thoughts. "All this time—the blood-oath, the alliance—it was manipulation?"

Brynja flinched. "It began that way."

Yrsa stepped between them, her crystal pendant flaring with sudden intensity. "We need a different fruit. One with knowledge to combat the corruption."

"No." Asvarr pushed away from Brynja's supporting arm, staggering but remaining upright through sheer will. "First I want the full truth."

Brynja's wooden fingers flexed with agitation. "The Wanderer found me after my clan's destruction. I was alone, broken, consumed by grief. He offered what I desperately wanted—vengeance against those who orchestrated our clans' annihilation."

"The Five," Asvarr said.

"So I believed." Brynja's truth-runes confirmed her words. "He told me the Five had chosen you as their champion, that the restoration of Yggdrasil would cement their power forever. He claimed to offer a third path—one where neither the Five nor the Tree would dictate our fate."

Leif moved closer to Asvarr, his golden eyes watching Brynja with unreadable intensity.

"When did you make this pact?" Asvarr demanded.

"Three moons after my clan's destruction. Nine days before we met at the Pool of Tears."

Asvarr thought back to their first confrontation, her ambush, her claims that he carried what was promised to her bloodline. "And the blood-oath? Our alliance?"

Brynja's face contorted with what appeared to be genuine pain. "The blood connection was real—our shared heritage true. The alliance began as deception, yes." Her truth-runes flared almost blindingly bright. "But something changed."

"The memory-bloom in the Circle of Splinters," Yrsa interjected. "When you both witnessed the truth of the Five's manipulation."

Brynja nodded. "And later, in the Garden of Forgetting, when we shared our pain. The connection became... real." She extended her hand, showing the spiral pattern etched across her palm from the anchor binding. "This isn't deception, Asvarr. Whatever brought us together, what we share now is truth."

The corruption surged suddenly, sending fingers of black ice through Asvarr's chest. He gasped, collapsing to his knees. Darkness crowded his vision, leaving only a tunnel of sight through which he saw Brynja's anguished face.

"We need to find a cure now," Leif urged, his small hand pressed against Asvarr's forehead. "The corruption reaches for his heart."

Brynja turned to Yrsa. "Help me search. There must be a fruit with healing knowledge."

As they moved urgently among the branches, Asvarr fought to remain conscious. The verdant anchor's seed-token burned against his chest where he'd stored it, its warmth the only sensation breaking through the spreading numbness.

"Here!" Yrsa called, pointing to a small fruit hanging from a lower branch. "This one resonates with purification."

Brynja plucked it, bringing the fruit to Asvarr. Unlike the first, this one was smaller, its skin tinged with amber rather than green. He reached for it with trembling fingers.

The moment he touched it, the fruit split open of its own accord. Inside lay something physical—a tiny seed nearly identical to the anchor token, but jet black with veins of silver.

"What is it?" Asvarr asked through chattering teeth.

"Blight-spore," Leif answered, voice unnaturally grave. "The corrupted reflection of what you carry."

Yrsa examined it without touching. "The cure lies in opposition. Like cures like, transformed."

Brynja looked uncertain. "How do we use it?"

"Awakening opposes corruption," Leif said. "The anchor-seed must touch the blight-spore."

With clumsy fingers, Asvarr withdrew the amber-emerald seed-token from his pocket. The verdant anchor's gift pulsed with golden light, responding to its dark counterpart.

"Are you certain?" he asked Leif.

The boy nodded. "Opposition creates cleansing fire. The Root burns away what doesn't belong."

Asvarr glanced at Brynja, whose face remained tense with concern despite her revealed deception. The thorn-runes across her flesh still glowed with truth-light, confirming her worry was genuine.

"If this goes wrong," Asvarr said, "take the anchor-seed to the third binding. Don't let the Wanderer claim it."

"It won't go wrong," she insisted. "And I won't serve him any longer."

Her truth-runes flared, confirming her sincerity. Despite everything, Asvarr found himself believing her changed loyalty—or at least her changed understanding of the forces at play.

Taking a deep breath, he brought the two seeds together in his palm. For a moment, nothing happened. Then heat flared between them—not burning but intense, like sunlight concentrated through crystal. Golden light spiraled from the anchor-seed, encircling the blight-spore in strands that tightened like bindings.

The black seed cracked. From within poured darkness that tried to escape but found itself trapped by the golden strands. The darkness writhed, condensed, and finally transformed—becoming a different presence. The broken shell reconstructed itself, now mirror-bright silver with amber veins—an inversion of the corruption's colors.

"Swallow it," Leif instructed. "Quickly, before it changes again."

Asvarr hesitated only a moment before placing the transformed seed on his tongue. It dissolved immediately, filling his mouth with a taste like fire and ice simultaneously—painful yet cleansing. The sensation spread through his body, following the corruption's path.

Wherever it touched, black veins retreated. The cold numbness receded, replaced by warmth that bordered on uncomfortable heat. Asvarr gasped as feeling returned to deadened flesh, pins and needles stabbing through every affected area.

"It's working," Brynja observed, watching the corruption visibly retreat beneath his skin.

The cleansing reached his chest, where the Blight-Herder's poison had nearly touched his heart. Here, the process slowed, the opposing forces battling for dominance. Asvarr felt the struggle as physical pressure behind his ribs, building until he thought his chest might burst.

Then, with shocking suddenness, the pressure released. Black ichor leaked from his pores, evaporating into oily smoke that dissipated in the orchard's thick air. The battle won, the cleansing warmth spread once more through his body before gradually fading to comfortable normalcy.

Asvarr rose shakily to his feet, testing limbs that had nearly surrendered to corruption. The weakness remained, but the spreading death had been driven back.

"Thank you," he said to Leif, who merely nodded in acknowledgment.

An uncomfortable silence stretched between Asvarr and Brynja, her revelation hanging between them like an unsheathed blade.

"The servants of the Five still pursue us," Yrsa noted, breaking the tension. "And the Wanderer now knows of your survival through his connection to Brynja."

"Then we need to move," Asvarr decided. "Toward the third anchor."

"After what you've learned?" Brynja asked, gesturing to the fruit that had revealed her pact. "You would still continue with me?"

Asvarr studied her—the wooden arm, the thorn-runes, the truth-light that prevented deception. He thought of their shared blood, the spiral patterns matched on their palms, the vision of the Five orchestrating their clans' destruction.

"I don't trust you," he said finally. "But I believe your understanding has changed. The question is whether that changes your purpose."

Brynja met his gaze directly. "The Wanderer manipulated me as surely as the Five manipulated you. I see that now." Her truth-runes pulsed steadily. "My purpose is no longer vengeance but truth—whatever form it takes."

Leif tugged at Asvarr's sleeve. "We should leave. The fruits grow hungry."

Looking around, Asvarr noticed the hollow fruits nearest them had turned toward their group, pulsing with increased luminosity. The filaments covering the ground between trees writhed more vigorously, reaching upward like countless tiny fingers.

"Northeast," Yrsa directed, pointing toward a gap in the orchard's outer ring. "The boundary is thinnest there."

As they prepared to depart, a distant howl pierced the orchard's hushed atmosphere—the hunting cry of the Five's servants drawing closer.

Brynja turned to Asvarr, her expression torn between determination and uncertainty. "I'll tell you everything—my full arrangement with the Wanderer, what he truly seeks, why he opposes the Five. But first we must escape."

"Lead the way," Asvarr replied. "But know this—I'm watching for any sign that your loyalties shift again."

She nodded, accepting his suspicion as justified. Together they moved through the orchard, Leif guiding them along safe paths where the filaments retreated from his golden footprints. The hollow fruits tracked their passage, turning on branches like silent witnesses.

Asvarr felt the weight of the verdant anchor's seed-token in his pocket, its purpose now complicated by Brynja's revelation. The Wanderer—the False Odin—wanted it for reasons neither of them fully understood. The Five opposed its awakening outside their control. Between these forces, Asvarr walked an increasingly narrow path toward truth that seemed to shift with each revelation.

The howls grew closer as they reached the orchard's edge. Multiple voices now, coordinating their pursuit. Beyond the last ring of bone-white trees lay dense forest—potential cover, but also unknown dangers.

"We need to split up," Brynja suggested. "They're tracking the anchor's energy. If we separate, Asvarr and Leif can move faster toward the third binding while Yrsa and I draw them away."

The proposal made tactical sense, but Asvarr hesitated. Separating might protect the anchor, but it would also give Brynja opportunity to contact the Wanderer.

"Unless you don't trust me enough for that," she added, reading his expression. Her truth-runes pulsed steadily, offering no clue to her true intentions.

Asvarr faced a choice between strategy and suspicion, between protecting the anchor and keeping his potential betrayer close. The hunt drew nearer with each moment of indecision, and the third anchor awaited, holding answers they all desperately needed.

Betrayal tasted like iron and ash in Asvarr's mouth. The howls of the Five's servants grew closer, echoing through the orchard's eerie silence, yet he couldn't tear his eyes from Brynja's face. Her truth-runes glowed steadily golden across her flesh, confirming what she'd said. No deception in her words, perhaps, but deception in every moment they'd shared.

"How long?" he asked, voice raw. "How long were you planning to hand me over to him?"

Brynja flinched. The thorn-runes flared brighter, forcing her answer. "From the moment I saw you at the Pool of Tears. The Wanderer told me you carried what belonged to my bloodline." Pain creased her features as the runes burned, demanding deeper truth. "He said you'd been chosen by the Five while I was cast aside."

A bone-white fruit dropped from a nearby branch, shattering against the filament-covered ground. The orchard seemed to lean closer, hungry for the pain radiating between them.

"I trusted you." Asvarr's voice dropped to a whisper. "I bound blood to blood with you."

"And I with you," Brynja countered, extending her palm to show the spiral pattern etched there—mirror to his own. "That was real. It still is."

"The blood-oath came after your betrayal was already in motion." Asvarr turned away, unable to bear the sight of her. The cleansed corruption left him hollow, drained of both strength and certainty.

"Ask me again," Brynja demanded. "Ask me now if I would deliver you to the Wanderer."

Asvarr looked at her over his shoulder. "Would you?"

"No." The word emerged with golden light so intense it momentarily blinded him. Brynja gasped, dropping to one knee as the truth-runes carved fire across her skin. "I would not," she continued through gritted teeth. "Everything changed in the Circle of Splinters when we saw the Five watching our clans die. Everything changed in the Garden of Forgetting when we shared our grief. Everything changes every moment we learn more truth."

Yrsa stepped forward, crystal pendant swinging between them. "The Five's servants draw closer. We must decide our path."

"Our path?" Asvarr laughed bitterly. "There is no our path anymore."

"The Wanderer will know of your survival through his connection to me," Brynja said, still kneeling. "He'll assume I've failed him and send others. The Five pursue us for the verdant anchor. Both forces will hunt you relentlessly."

"And what would you suggest?" Asvarr asked, fighting to keep his voice level.

"Separation." Brynja rose unsteadily. "The Five track the anchor's energy. Yrsa and I can draw them away while you and Leif move toward the third binding." She raised her wooden arm, now streaked with truth-rune fire. "I've learned enough to create a false trail they'll follow."

The suggestion made tactical sense. Staying together made them easier to find, more difficult to hide. But separating meant trusting Brynja's change of heart.

"And I'm to believe you would sacrifice yourself to protect what you intended to steal?" Asvarr challenged.

"She cannot lie," Leif interjected, golden eyes reflecting the truth-light. "The runes force honesty."

"Honesty now," Asvarr conceded. "But intentions change with every shifting wind."

"Yes," Brynja admitted. Her wooden fingers curled into a fist. "They can. Mine have. I no longer serve the Wanderer's purpose, but my own." The truth-runes pulsed steadily. "And my purpose now is understanding what truly happened to our bloodlines, why they were separated, what the Five and the Wanderer both fear from their union."

The howls grew louder. Multiple hunting parties converging on their position.

"There's no time," Yrsa urged. "The orchard itself will soon betray our location—the fruits hunger for fresh secrets."

Asvarr studied the boundary-walker. Throughout their journey, she'd been cryptic, knowledgeable beyond explanation. "And what is your stake in this, Yrsa? Why follow either path?"

"I walk boundaries," she replied simply. "Between realms, between loyalties, between truths. I seek balance where others demand dominance."

"And which side maintains that balance?" Asvarr pressed.

"Neither the Five nor the Wanderer. Neither Brynja's initial purpose nor your quest for restoration." Her pendant glowed with intensifying blue-white light. "Each seeks control through different means."

Another howl tore through the orchard, close enough that Asvarr felt its vibration in his chest. Leif tugged urgently at his sleeve.

"We must go," the boy insisted. "The hunger-threads are waking."

Looking down, Asvarr saw the filaments covering the ground had begun coiling upward, reaching for their ankles like countless translucent fingers. Already they'd ensnared his boots in delicate, unbreakable strands.

Brynja took a step toward him. "Whatever you choose to believe about me, know this—I will not return to the Wanderer. I will not serve his purpose. And I will not betray you again." With each declaration, the truth-runes flared painfully across her wooden arm and flesh shoulder, searing deeper into her skin. "This I swear by the blood we share—both the blood of our clans and the blood we mingled at the verdant anchor."

Asvarr met her gaze, searching for deception where the runes allowed none. Could intentions truly change so completely? He thought of his own transformation, how each anchor binding altered him, expanded his understanding. If he could change, couldn't she?

"The northeastern path," Yrsa interrupted, pointing toward a gap between orchard rings. "The boundary thins there. You and Leif can slip through while Brynja and I create a diversion southward."

"Trust is earned, not demanded," Asvarr told Brynja coldly. "I won't risk the anchor falling into the Wanderer's hands through you—willingly or unwillingly."

Something like grief flickered across Brynja's face. "Then you've made your choice."

"I have." Asvarr drew his bronze sword, using it to slice through the hunger-threads binding his feet. "Leif and I will find our own path to the third anchor. You and Yrsa..." He hesitated, torn between caution and reluctance to abandon them entirely.

"Will survive," Brynja finished for him. "As we always have."

Leif positioned himself beside Asvarr, small hand slipping into his. "The northeastern path leads to Hollowglade," he said. "I can guide you."

"And we'll draw the hunt southward," Yrsa agreed, raising her crystal pendant. Light blazed from it, illuminating a path through the bone-white trees. "You'll have until nightfall before they realize they've been misled."

Asvarr nodded once, curt and final. He turned to go, then stopped. Without looking back, he asked, "If your purpose has truly changed, what is it now?"

Brynja's voice came soft but clear, edged with truth-light. "To understand what both sides fear from our united bloodlines. And to reclaim what was stolen from us both—legacy, not vengeance."

The runes' golden light confirmed her sincerity, for what little comfort that offered. Asvarr tightened his grip on Leif's hand and struck out toward the northeastern path, slashing hunger-threads as they advanced. Behind them, Brynja and Yrsa moved in the opposite direction, Yrsa's pendant flaring with light that drew attention like a beacon.

They ran, Leif's golden footprints illuminating safe passages between the increasingly agitated trees. The hollow fruits turned to track their movement, pulsing with hunger. Twice Asvarr felt invisible tendrils brush his mind, seeking secrets to steal, but the Grímmark burned in response, shielding his thoughts.

At the orchard's edge, they paused behind the final ring of bone-white trees. Beyond stretched dense forest, the trees normal save for faint phosphorescence clinging to their bark.

"She told the truth," Leif said quietly, golden eyes watching Asvarr's face. "About her changed purpose."

"Truth at this moment," Asvarr corrected. "The runes can't predict her future choices."

"We all change with knowledge," the boy observed with his uncanny, adult wisdom. "She more than most."

Asvarr grunted, unwilling to discuss Brynja further. The betrayal sat like a stone in his gut, heavy and unyielding despite the truth-runes' confirmation of her changed intentions. Trust, once broken, wasn't mended by convenience or necessity.

They slipped from the orchard's boundary into the forest beyond. Immediately the air thinned, the unnatural silence broken by ordinary woodland sounds—wind through leaves, distant birds, the rustling of small creatures in

underbrush. Asvarr breathed deeply, clearing his lungs of the orchard's thick
atmosphere.

***

"Which way to Hollowglade?" he asked.

Leif pointed northeast, where the forest darkened beneath thicker canopy.
"Three hours' walk, if we're swift. Less if we're pursued."

"Then we move quickly." Asvarr sheathed his sword, conserving strength.
Though the blight-spore had cleansed the corruption, weakness lingered in
his limbs, an exhaustion bone-deep and persistent.

They traveled in silence for a time, Leif leading with confidence through
terrain that would have confounded most children his apparent age. Occasionally the boy would stop, head tilting as if listening to something Asvarr
couldn't hear, before choosing a new direction through identical-seeming
trees.

"How do you know these paths?" Asvarr finally asked.

"I was born when the Tree shattered," Leif replied, his standard explanation
for his uncanny knowledge. "I exist across boundaries."

"What does that mean, truly?" Asvarr pressed, tired of cryptic half-answers.

Leif paused, considering. "When Yggdrasil broke, fragments scattered
across all Nine Realms. Some fragments became physical—the anchors you
seek. Others became memory—knowledge preserved in places like the orchard." He looked up at Asvarr, golden eyes ancient in his child's face. "And
some became potential—pieces of what might have been, what could still be."

"You're one such piece?" Asvarr guessed.

"I'm the spaces between spaces," Leif answered. "I walk where paths connect, where possibilities overlap."

Before Asvarr could question further, Leif froze, raising one hand in
warning. Ahead, shadows moved between trees—humanoid but wrong, their
proportions stretched and fluid. The Hunt of Broken Fate.

Asvarr pulled Leif behind a massive oak, hand covering the boy's mouth. The shadow-figures moved with terrible purpose, flowing between trees like ink through water. Their faces, when briefly visible, were featureless save for vertical slits where eyes should be.

"The diversion failed," Asvarr whispered. "They've found our trail."

Leif shook his head, removing Asvarr's hand. "Not the Five's servants," he whispered back. "Different hunters. The Wanderer's."

Cold dread settled in Asvarr's stomach. If these were the Wanderer's hunters, then Brynja's connection to her former master had already been used against them. Either she'd betrayed them again, or the Wanderer had ways to track her regardless of her intentions.

"Can we avoid them?" Asvarr breathed.

Leif's eyes unfocused briefly. "The paths twist. There's a way, but it leads through shadow."

"Better shadow than capture," Asvarr decided, shifting the verdant anchor's seed-token deeper into his pocket.

Leif led them in a crouch away from the hunters, moving perpendicular to their original course. The forest grew stranger as they advanced—trees leaning at impossible angles, undergrowth thinning to reveal soil that glistened with metallic fragments. The light dimmed though the sun still hung above the horizon, as if they traveled into perpetual twilight.

"The boundary thins here," Leif explained. "The memory realm touches this place."

"Is that safe?" Asvarr asked, remembering the collapsing memory realm they'd narrowly escaped.

"Safer than what pursues us." Leif pointed to a hollowed oak ahead, its interior glowing with soft blue light. "Through there."

Asvarr hesitated, torn between the known danger behind and the unknown ahead. Then movement flickered at the corner of his vision—shadow-figures converging on their position. Decision made, he gripped Leif's hand and ducked into the hollowed tree.

Blue light enveloped them, cool and tingling against exposed skin. The sensation of falling overcame Asvarr briefly before his feet struck solid ground. They stood in a circular clearing unlike any forest Asvarr had seen. Silver grass rippled around a shallow depression filled with liquid mirror—perfectly still despite the breeze disturbing the grass.

"Hollowglade," Leif announced. "Where the Root once bled into a silver lake."

At the center of the depression, a sapling grew—barely taller than Asvarr's knee, yet somehow ancient. Its bark spiraled like a twisted cord, half silver and half gold. Tiny leaves of translucent green caught the fading light, refracting it into rainbow patterns across the mirrored surface below.

"What is this place?" Asvarr asked, voice hushed with instinctive reverence.

"A crossing point," Leif answered. "Where the Root touched all Nine Realms simultaneously during the Shattering."

"And those hunters—can they follow us here?"

Leif shook his head. "Not directly. The path we took exists only for those who walk between."

Relief weakened Asvarr's knees. He sank to the silver grass, sudden exhaustion overwhelming him. The blight-spore's cleansing, Brynja's betrayal, their narrow escape—everything crashed down upon him at once. His body trembled with reaction and fatigue.

"Rest," Leif advised, settling beside him. "The boundaries will hold until dawn."

Asvarr managed a nod before slumping further, his consciousness narrowing to a pinpoint of awareness. He fought to remain awake, still fearing pursuit, but darkness crept across his vision inexorably.

His last sight before surrendering to exhaustion was the sapling at Hollowglade's center, its twisted trunk pulsing with familiar rhythm—like a heart, like the Grímmark that now covered most of his torso, like the five anchors calling to each other across the fractured realms.

In that moment of twilight awareness, a realization struck with crystal clarity: the betrayal at the orchard had severed more than trust. It had divided their company exactly as the bloodlines had been divided generations before. Forces greater than either of them were still working to keep flame and root separate, to prevent the union that both the Five and the Wanderer feared.

Asvarr surrendered to unconsciousness with that bitter knowledge, alone with Leif in Hollowglade while those who once stood beside them faced their own dangers in the memory realm's deceptive shadows.

CHAPTER 16
THE WOUND THAT SPROUTED

Asvarr awoke to fire in his veins. The blight-spore's cleansing had faded, leaving something worse in its wake. He lay curled on silver grass beside Hollowglade's mirrored pool, his body rigid with pain as golden light pulsed beneath his skin.

"It returns," Leif murmured, small hands hovering above Asvarr's chest where the corruption had struck. "The Blight-Herder's final gift."

Through gritted teeth, Asvarr managed a single word: "How?"

"The cleansing drove it deeper." Leif's golden eyes reflected the dawn light breaking through trees. "It hid in your marrow, waiting."

Asvarr tried to rise but fell back, muscles spasming. The verdant anchor's seed-token burned against his chest where he'd secured it, its heat both comfort and torment. Lightning flashed behind his eyes as the poison surged through him in a wave.

"What's happening to me?" he gasped.

Leif placed a hand on Asvarr's forehead. "You experience the cycle. Growth. Decay. Rebirth."

The words barely registered as sensation overwhelmed him. Asvarr felt roots pushing through his flesh, burrowing into soil that was somehow his own body. Leaves unfurled from his fingertips, stretching toward sunlight. Flower buds formed along his spine, bursting into impossible blossoms that withered almost immediately. Birth, growth, death—all compressed into moments of excruciating detail.

"Help me," he pleaded, curling tighter as another wave crashed through him.

"I can slow it," Leif said. "Not stop it."

The boy placed both hands on Asvarr's chest, directly over the Grímmark. Golden light flowed from his palms, spreading like liquid fire across Asvarr's torso. Where it touched, the pain receded momentarily, the poison's progress slowing to a crawl.

"What is this?" Asvarr asked, his voice rough with relief.

"In-between energy," Leif explained. "I exist where states overlap. Alive and not. Here and elsewhere." He frowned with concentration. "The poison tries to force the plant cycle through your human flesh. I can... confuse it. Make it uncertain which state you occupy."

Asvarr stared at his arms where green veins now ran alongside blue, the skin between them taking on a bark-like texture in spreading patches. "Am I becoming like the Blight-Herder?"

"No." Leif shook his head firmly. "His transformation came from corruption. Yours comes from communion."

Asvarr struggled to focus through the pain. "The anchor seed—"

"Is safe," Leif assured him. "It protects itself through you."

A moment of clarity broke through the agony. Asvarr took in their surroundings properly for the first time since waking. Hollowglade stretched around them, silver grass rippling in a breeze that carried the scent of water and stone. The mirrored pool reflected a sky crossed with trails of golden light—something more deliberate than clouds, like threads in a vast tapestry. At the center, the small sapling pulsed with inner light that matched the rhythm of Asvarr's heart.

"The Root bled here," Asvarr murmured, remembering Leif's words from the night before.

"Into a silver lake," Leif confirmed. "What remains is the essence."

"Can it help me?"

Leif hesitated. "It might. Or it might accelerate what the poison began."

Before Asvarr could decide, another wave of transformation crashed through him. This time he felt bark forming over his chest, cracking as his ribs expanded into branches that tore through skin. Though his flesh remained intact when he looked down, the sensation was real enough to wring a scream from his throat.

"I need to try," he gasped when the wave receded. "Help me to the pool."

Leif nodded, slipping small hands beneath Asvarr's shoulders. Together they managed to get him upright, though standing sent vertigo washing through him. They stumbled toward the pool's edge, Asvarr leaning heavily on the boy who bore his weight with surprising strength.

At the silver water's edge, Asvarr collapsed to his knees. The mirrored surface reflected a tangle of branches and roots formed in his shape, eyes replaced by knots in the wood. He recoiled, then steeled himself and reached toward the water.

"Wait," Leif cautioned. "The Wanderer watches."

Asvarr froze, hand hovering above the silver surface. "Where?"

Leif pointed toward the shadows beneath the trees surrounding the glade. "There. And there. And there."

Squinting through pain-hazed vision, Asvarr made out a tall figure standing motionless within the shadows. Though details remained unclear, there was no mistaking the silhouette—broad-shouldered, wearing a wide-brimmed hat, one eye gleaming with reflected light. The Wanderer. The False Odin. The Ashfather.

"Why doesn't he attack?" Asvarr whispered.

"He observes," Leif said. "As he has observed each cycle. Waiting to see which path emerges."

"Waiting for what?"

"For you to choose." Leif's voice took on its unsettling adult resonance. "Nine Wardens before you reached this moment. Nine chose surrender to the Root to escape the poison's agony. Nine were consumed."

Another wave of transformation racked Asvarr's body. He felt leaves sprouting from his scalp, nestling among his hair before withering to ash. The scent of rotting vegetation filled his nostrils though it came from within his own form. His teeth loosened in his gums, ready to fall like autumn leaves, before resettling.

The Ashfather had not moved, his single eye fixed on Asvarr with predatory patience.

"I won't surrender like the others," Asvarr snarled through the pain. "Not to the Root. Not to the poison. Not to him."

"Then find another way," Leif urged. "Before the poison reaches your heart."

Asvarr looked down at his chest where the Grímmark pulsed with golden light, fighting the spreading green tendrils of poison. Already the corruption had advanced from his limbs toward his core, slowed but not stopped by Leif's intervention. If it reached his heart, he sensed that something essential would be lost.

He turned back to the pool. "There might be knowledge in the water. The Root's memory."

Leif nodded. "Touch only the surface. Do not submerge."

Gathering his strength, Asvarr reached out again. His fingertips brushed the silver water, sending ripples across the perfect mirror. Immediately, images formed beneath the surface—fragmented, chaotic, overwhelming.

He saw a Root as vast as a mountain, stretching across all Nine Realms simultaneously. He saw the Ashfather as a younger man, his face unmarked by the burden of ages, standing before a similar pool. He saw the Verdant Five watching from their grove as Brynja knelt before them, accepting their guidance. He saw Yrsa standing at a crossroads of light and shadow, her face showing a weariness beyond mortal understanding.

"Too much," Asvarr gasped, trying to pull back.

But his hand wouldn't move. The water had become viscous, holding him in place as more images poured into his mind. He saw his own mother singing to him as a child, her face clearer than he'd remembered in years. He saw his father vanishing into forest shadows, never to return. He saw his clan burning, but from above, as if watched by something that perched in the shattered sky.

Leif gripped his wrist, pulling with unexpected strength. "Enough! It draws you too deep."

With a wet sucking sound, Asvarr's hand came free. He fell backward onto the silver grass, shuddering as the poison resumed its work. Fresh shoots pushed through the soil of his flesh, growing, flowering, seeding, dying—all in agonizing moments.

"I saw... everything," he panted. "Too much to understand."

"The pool contains memory without context," Leif explained. "Truth without wisdom."

Asvarr rolled onto his side, curling around the pain consuming him from within. "I need... to find a connection to consciousness."

"The sapling," Leif suggested, pointing to the twisted gold-silver tree at the glade's center. "It grew from the Root's blood. It retains... awareness."

Pushing himself up on trembling arms, Asvarr crawled toward the sapling. Each movement sent fresh waves of transformation cascading through his body. His fingers lengthened into twigs, then retracted. His breath came out as pollen, hanging golden in the air before his face. His blood thickened to sap, slowing in his veins before liquefying again.

The Ashfather watched, utterly motionless save for the single eye that tracked Asvarr's painful progress. Somehow his silent observation felt more threatening than any attack.

After what seemed like hours but might have been minutes, Asvarr reached the sapling. Up close, its twisted trunk revealed intricate patterns, spirals within spirals forming runes he recognized from his Grímmark. Its few leaves shimmered with an inner light that cast no shadow.

"Touch the trunk with your marked palm," Leif instructed, kneeling beside him.

Asvarr raised his right hand, revealing the spiral pattern etched across his palm from the verdant anchor binding. Steeling himself, he pressed it against the sapling's trunk.

Connection formed instantly, a focused stream of consciousness. The sapling recognized him. More than that, it knew him, in ways deeper than mere memory. It perceived his essence beneath flesh, beneath transformation, beneath even the anchor bindings that had begun changing him cycles ago.

"Help me," Asvarr whispered to it.

The sapling's response came in sensation, not words—a question that translated roughly to: *At what cost?*

"Any," Asvarr gasped as another wave of poison-driven transformation wracked him. "I won't surrender to become a vessel, but I need to survive."

The sapling considered. Its consciousness explored the poison within him, curious about its nature. Then it extended tendrils of awareness deeper, examining the five anchor bindings he'd undergone, the sacrifices made, the changes wrought.

You are already more Root than man, came its wordless observation. *Why resist this final transformation?*

"Because I choose what I become," Asvarr insisted. "Not the poison. Not the Ashfather. Not even you."

Something like respect emanated from the sapling. It withdrew its awareness from his mind, concentrating instead on the physical connection between them. Through his palm, Asvarr felt a tingling sensation as something flowed from the tree into his flesh. It wasn't blood, or sap it was possibility—the potential for healing, for restoration, for balance.

The poison recoiled from this new presence, retreating from his core toward his extremities. As it withdrew, the worst of the transformation symptoms subsided. Asvarr's breath came easier. The bark-like patches on his skin receded, leaving only faint whorls like wood grain beneath the surface.

"It's working," he breathed, hope kindling.

Then the Ashfather moved. One step forward, out of the shadows, into the silver light of Hollowglade. His face remained mostly hidden beneath his wide-brimmed hat, but his mouth was visible—curled in displeasure. He raised a hand, pointing one finger toward Asvarr.

Darkness erupted from the ground around the glade's perimeter—anti-light, void made tangible. It formed a dome over Hollowglade, cutting off the morning sun. In the sudden darkness, only the sapling's inner light and the mirrored pool provided illumination.

Leif's eyes widened with fear. "He intervenes. The balance shifts."

Under the dome of darkness, the poison surged anew, fighting against the sapling's gift. Asvarr cried out as fresh waves of transformation cascaded through him. His spine lengthened, vertebrae stretching like saplings seeking light. His ribs expanded, curving like branches. His skin hardened, then softened, then hardened again in rapid cycle.

"What's happening?" he demanded through clenched teeth.

"The Wanderer fears your choice," Leif explained, his small face grim in the sapling's light. "Nine Wardens surrendered to the Root. He expected you to do the same."

"Or die trying," Asvarr guessed.

"Yes." Leif glanced toward where the Ashfather stood at the edge of the dome. "Instead, you seek partnership with the Root. It threatens everything he's built across nine cycles."

Despite the renewed agony, Asvarr maintained his connection to the sapling. Its consciousness continued feeding him potential, fighting the poison's attempt to overwhelm his system. But under the dome of darkness, the balance had shifted. The sapling weakened while the poison strengthened.

"I need more," Asvarr told the tree. "More than potential. I need substance."

The sapling's consciousness flickered with what might have been hesitation. Then it offered a single leaf from its sparse canopy. The leaf detached, floating down to land on Asvarr's upturned palm beside where he touched the trunk.

Consume, came its silent instruction.

Asvarr stared at the translucent leaf. The veins within it pulsed with golden light, forming patterns that matched the Grímmark across his chest. He understood instinctively that eating it would provide more than temporary relief—it would fundamentally alter him, accelerating transformations already begun by the anchor bindings.

"What will I become?" he asked the sapling.

What you already are, came its cryptic response. *But aware of it.*

Another wave of poison-driven transformation doubled Asvarr over. This time he felt roots pushing through his feet into the soil beneath, anchoring him to

Hollowglade itself. The sensation of being simultaneously human and plant tore a ragged scream from his throat.

Across the glade, the Ashfather took another step forward. Light gleamed from something in his hand—a curved blade of shadow that drank the sapling's illumination.

"Decide quickly," Leif urged. "He comes to reap what you've become."

Asvarr looked down at the leaf in his palm, then at the Ashfather's approaching figure, then at Leif's frightened face. Choice crystallized through pain. He would not surrender to Root or Ashfather. He would find a third path—partnership instead of subservience, transformation instead of consumption.

He raised the leaf to his lips.

The Ashfather lunged forward, shadow-blade raised.

Leif threw himself between them, arms outstretched. "No further!" he cried, his child's voice ringing with power beyond his apparent years. "The boundary holds!"

A wall of golden light erupted from the ground where Leif stood, forming a barrier across Hollowglade. The Ashfather struck it with his blade, sending showers of sparks cascading through the darkness. The barrier wavered but held.

Protected by Leif's unexpected power, Asvarr placed the sapling's leaf on his tongue. It dissolved instantly, flooding him with sensation beyond anything he'd yet experienced. Past and future collapsed into an eternal present as consciousness expanded beyond his physical form.

He felt the Root across all Nine Realms simultaneously—the entirety of Yggdrasil's remnants, a network of awareness spreading through world after world. He perceived the pattern beneath reality, the framework upon which existence hung. He glimpsed the void beyond that pattern, hungry and ancient, waiting for any weakness in the structure.

And he saw the Ashfather's true form—a vessel like himself but hollowed out, identity scraped away to make room for something else. Not entirely the False Odin as he'd believed, but not entirely separate either. Something composite, something caught between states.

The vision faded as the leaf's power flowed through Asvarr's body, countering the poison's progression. The transformed patches of skin stabilized rather than receding, no longer spreading but integrated into his flesh. The bark-like texture remained across his shoulders and spine, his veins still carried sap alongside blood, but the agonizing cycle of growth and decay slowed to a bearable rhythm.

Leif maintained the barrier, his small body rigid with effort. Beyond it, the Ashfather circled, seeking weakness. The dome of darkness still covered Hollowglade, but the sapling's light had strengthened, pushing back the void.

"I don't understand what's happening to me," Asvarr said, touching the altered skin of his arm.

"You've taken the Root's essence into yourself willingly," Leif explained, strain evident in his voice. "As a partner."

"And that threatens him." Asvarr nodded toward the Ashfather.

"More than anything." Leif's barrier flickered as the Ashfather struck it again. "Nine Wardens became vessels or died trying. You're forging a different path."

"The third path," Asvarr murmured, remembering Brynja's words.

The thought of her sent an unexpected pang through him. Despite her betrayal, she'd spoken truth about one thing—there were paths beyond simple opposition, beyond the binary choices offered by Root or Ashfather. Perhaps her own journey toward that understanding had been genuine.

Another strike against Leif's barrier sent cracks spreading across its golden surface. The boy stumbled, exhaustion evident in his slumping shoulders.

"I can't hold him much longer," Leif warned. "We need to leave this place."

Asvarr glanced at the sapling, reluctant to abandon the only thing that had helped him. "How?"

"Through the in-between," Leif answered. "Where I walk."

"Can you take us both?"

Leif nodded grimly. "Now that you carry the sapling's essence, yes. You're attuned to the spaces between."

The Ashfather struck again, and this time the barrier shattered. Fragments of golden light rained down across Hollowglade as the tall figure strode forward, shadow-blade raised for a killing blow.

"Now!" Asvarr shouted, reaching for Leif's hand.

The boy clasped his fingers around Asvarr's wrist. The world shifted, colors inverting, sounds becoming visible as rippling patterns in the air. The Ashfather's form elongated, stretching thin as thread before snapping back. Hollowglade twisted around them, folding into impossible geometries.

Asvarr experienced a moment of total disorientation as reality unraveled. Then darkness swept over him, and he knew nothing more.

***

Golden sap seeped from the corners of Asvarr's eyes as he sank deeper into the silver lake. The poison's cold fire spread through his veins, transforming blood into something thick and viscous. Each heartbeat pushed the corruption closer to his core. Through the murky waters of consciousness, he heard Leif calling his name, the boy's voice stretched and distorted as if traveling across vast distances.

"Hold fast," Leif said, his small fingers splayed across Asvarr's chest where the Grímmark pulsed with sickly light. "The poison seeks your heart. I can slow it, but not stop it."

Asvarr tried to respond, but his tongue had grown wooden and stiff in his mouth. The Blight-Herder's touch was a cruel alchemy—transforming him cell by cell. Where the corruption touched, he felt himself becoming something alien to his own flesh.

A rush of sensations overwhelmed him: roots pushing through the soil of his muscles, branches stretching beneath his skin, leaves unfurling along his spine. He was becoming a forest, a landscape unto himself. The pain transcended anything human—he was experiencing growth that should take seasons compressed into heartbeats.

Leif's face swam above him, golden eyes wide with concern. The boy placed a hand on Asvarr's forehead. Cool energy flowed into him, creating a momentary respite from the transformation.

"I cannot hold it back much longer," Leif whispered. "You must find another way."

Asvarr focused on the Grímmark burning across his chest. Since binding with the first Root Anchor, the mark had been his burden and his strength. Now it throbbed with each push of the poison, resonating with something deep within the Hollowglade.

Reach deeper, a voice urged from within his mind. Not Leif's voice, nor his own thoughts. Something older. *The Root awaits.*

With the last of his strength, Asvarr pressed his palm against the silver lake's surface. The mirror-still water accepted his touch without rippling. Instead of wetness, he felt an immediate connection—as if plunging his hand into the earth's veins.

The world fell away.

***

He stood in an infinite expanse of golden light. Gone was the Hollowglade, gone was the poison's grip on his flesh. Here, he existed as consciousness without form, awareness without limitation.

Before him stretched the Root—as a vast network of shimmering threads extending in all directions. Each thread pulsed with life, each connection vibrated with purpose. This was the true form of his Anchor, stripped of physical constraints. living pattern that existed within and beyond all Nine Realms simultaneously.

"You see now," the Root said, its voice a chorus of whispers and rustling leaves. "This is what pulses beneath all existence."

"Am I dead?" Asvarr asked, surprised he could form words in this formless place.

A ripple of something like laughter moved through the network. "No. You stand at the threshold between states. The poison drives you toward transformation, yet you resist becoming something new."

"I would remain myself," Asvarr said.

"And what is 'yourself'?" the Root asked. "The berserker? The orphaned son? The Warden of Flame? These are fragments, not the whole."

The network shifted, revealing memories embedded within its threads. Asvarr saw himself as a child climbing the tallest pine near his village, his father pointing toward the distant mountains and naming them. He saw himself learning to wield an axe, blood from his blistered hands staining the wooden haft. He watched his first raid, the shield-wall breaking against unexpected resistance.

"You are all these moments, yet none of them," the Root continued. "The poison cannot be fought with strength or will alone. It requires sacrifice."

"What sacrifice?" Asvarr demanded.

"To gain, one must lose," the Root said. "I offer enough of my essence to purge the corruption, but the balance must be maintained. Memory for essence. Past for future."

The threads shifted again, highlighting his earliest memories—his mother singing him to sleep, his father teaching him to fish in the cold mountain streams, the first time he felt the warmth of a hearth fire after a winter hunt.

"These memories have shaped you," the Root explained. "Yet they are but foundation stones. One can remove the foundation after the walls stand firm."

Asvarr felt a surge of protective anger. "You would take my parents from me? Again?"

"Not take. Transform. These memories will be preserved within me, part of the greater pattern. In exchange, you will receive enough of my essence to drive back the corruption." The golden light pulsed with gentle insistence. "But understand the cost—with each exchange, you become less fully human and more of the pattern itself."

Asvarr thought of the Blight-Herder, once Oakhelm, greatest disciple of the Five. How much of himself had he surrendered before becoming that twisted shell? How many exchanges before Asvarr, too, became nothing but a vessel?

"Have others made this bargain?" he asked.

"Nine Wardens before you reached this crossroads," the Root replied. "Some surrendered completely, binding with their Anchors, becoming one with the pattern. Others refused and perished, their essence returning to the cycle. None found the middle path."

"And the Ashfather? Did he stand where I stand?"

The threads rippled with disturbance. "He took rather than exchanged. Broke rather than bound. His path leads to emptiness masquerading as power."

Asvarr felt the poison creeping ever closer to his heart, even in this place beyond physical form. The corruption would reach his core soon, and then transformation would be inevitable—but not on his terms. He would become something like the Blight-Herder, a twisted amalgamation of man and Root, serving neither purpose fully.

"What guarantee do I have that you won't take more than we've agreed?" Asvarr asked.

"None," the Root answered with disarming honesty. "Each exchange changes both of us. I become more aware of individuality; you become more attuned to the pattern. Where these paths lead, even I cannot see with certainty."

The poison burned through another barrier within his chest. Time was running out.

"I accept," Asvarr said. "Take the memories, give me the strength to fight this corruption."

"Remember," the Root cautioned, "what is surrendered cannot be reclaimed. These moments will exist within me, but no longer within you."

"I understand."

The golden threads encircled him, pressing against his consciousness. He felt them probe the earliest chambers of his memory—moments half-forgotten already, preserved more as feelings than as clear recollections. His mother's face as she sang him to sleep, the specific notes of her lullaby, the warmth of his father's hand as they walked the forest paths seeking game.

The memories unspooled like thread from a spindle, drawn into the vast network surrounding him. As each memory departed, a hollow space formed within him, immediately filled by something alien yet familiar—the Root's essence flowing into the absence, golden tendrils replacing what was lost.

The exchange burned. It didn't burn like fire, but like ice so cold it seared. Asvarr screamed without a voice, thrashed without a body. The Root held him fast in its golden embrace as the transformation continued. Memory flowed outward; essence flowed inward.

When it ended, Asvarr hung suspended in the golden light, panting from exertion. He felt the hollow spaces within him, knowing something important had been there, yet unable to recall what. The sensation resembled waking from a dream that slips away upon opening one's eyes—awareness of absence without knowledge of what's missing.

"It is done," the Root said. "Return now to your form. The poison is contained, though not destroyed. It will trouble you no more if you remember what you've learned here."

"And what have I learned?" Asvarr asked, already feeling himself being pulled back toward his body.

"That transformation is neither good nor evil—it simply is. The path between surrender and dominance exists, but it must be walked with each step chosen consciously." The Root's voice began to fade as Asvarr's consciousness drifted away from the threshold. "Remember this when the final binding comes—there is always a third path."

***

He gasped, lungs burning as if he'd been underwater too long. The silver lake rippled beneath him as he sat upright. Beside him, Leif tumbled backward, golden eyes wide with surprise.

"You return," the boy said, his voice carrying that unsettling adult resonance. "I thought you lost to the deep places."

Asvarr looked down at his chest. The poison's black veins had receded from his heart, though faint traces remained along his arms and shoulders. The Grímmark pulsed with renewed vigor, but something had changed—patches of his skin had transformed to a texture resembling bark, particularly over his heart.

"How long?" Asvarr asked, his voice rough as stone against stone.

"Half a day's light," Leif answered, gesturing toward the sky where the sun had moved significantly since Asvarr last remembered seeing it. "You sank deep into the silver waters. I could not follow."

Asvarr touched his chest, feeling the hardened patches of skin. It didn't feel painful, but alien—as if parts of him had become something other than flesh. He searched his memories, finding a peculiar emptiness where his earliest childhood should have been. He knew he'd had parents—knew their names, even—but could not recall their faces or voices. The memories existed only as facts, not experiences.

"I've lost something," he murmured.

"Yes," Leif agreed solemnly. "And gained something too. The Root has marked you more deeply now."

Asvarr struggled to his feet, surprised at the strength flowing through his limbs. The weakness and pain of the poison had vanished, replaced by a vibrant energy he'd never experienced before. He felt connected to the land around him in ways he couldn't articulate—aware of the slow pulse of sap in nearby trees, the subtle shifts of soil beneath his feet.

"The Ashfather was watching," Leif said, changing the subject. "He stood at the edge of the glade while you communed with the Root. Watching, but not interfering."

"Why would he simply watch?" Asvarr wondered aloud.

"Perhaps he wanted to see your choice. Whether you would surrender or fight." Leif tilted his head, considering. "Or maybe he hoped the poison would do his work for him."

Asvarr looked across the Hollowglade, half-expecting to see the one-eyed figure lurking among the shadows. Nothing moved except branches swaying in the gentle breeze.

"We should move on," he said. "The second anchor is bound, but there are three more waiting. And Brynja..." He trailed off, uncertain what to think about her betrayal. Had she truly changed her purpose, as she claimed? Or was the alliance always meant to end in treachery?

"Yes," Leif agreed. "But first, drink." He offered a leather flask. "Water from the silver lake. It will help organize what the Root has given you."

Asvarr accepted the flask and drank deeply. The water tasted of minerals and something else—a hint of sweetness like fresh sap. As it flowed down his throat, he felt the new essence settling within him, integrating with what remained of his original self.

With the flask emptied, he gazed toward the horizon where their path would lead. The sun caught in the trees, casting long shadows across the Hollowglade. Something moved within those shadows—a presence neither human nor animal. When Asvarr blinked, it vanished.

"We're being watched," he said quietly.

"Always," Leif replied with a child's simplicity and a sage's wisdom. "The question is: by friend, foe, or something in between?"

Asvarr touched the bark-like patches on his chest, feeling their rough texture beneath his fingertips. He'd sacrificed pieces of his humanity to survive the poison—memories he would never recover. Was this the beginning of a path that ended like the Blight-Herder? Or worse, like the Ashfather?

There is always a third path, the Root had said. He would have to find it, through the shadows and deceptions that surrounded him. With each step forward, he risked becoming something other than human—yet turning back was no longer an option.

"Come," he told Leif. "We need to find the others before the Wanderer does."

They left the Hollowglade as the day's light faded, Asvarr walking with new purpose and a strange lightness despite the hollow spaces within his memory.

Behind them, the silver lake reflected a sky unmarked by clouds—a perfect mirror of what lay above, revealing nothing of the vast network that pulsed below.

CHAPTER 17

THREADS BENEATH THE BARK

Dawn broke over the Hollowglade in shattered fragments of light. Asvarr sat beneath the twisted remains of an ash tree, running his fingers over the bark-like patterns that now covered his chest. The texture matched the tree behind him—rough whorls and ridges that shouldn't exist on human flesh. Three days had passed since his communion with the Root, and each morning brought new changes. Today, fine golden veins had appeared within the bark patches, pulsing with the same rhythm as his heart.

Nearby, Leif slept curled against the exposed roots of the ash, his small form rising and falling with each breath. The boy had insisted on keeping watch through the night, though his vigilance had eventually surrendered to exhaustion. Asvarr envied him that peace. Sleep, when it came at all, brought visions of endless golden networks stretching across the Nine Realms, pulsing with knowledge he couldn't comprehend in waking hours.

A rustling in the underbrush snapped Asvarr to alertness. His hand found the hilt of his bronze sword, which flared with golden light at his touch. The veins in the weapon now perfectly matched those spreading beneath his skin—both forged in communion with the same power.

"If you intend to use that, aim elsewhere," a familiar voice called from the shadowed trees. "I've walked long enough to find you without adding a sword wound to my troubles."

Yrsa stepped from the forest edge, her copper-red hair tangled with leaves and her emerald robes torn along one sleeve. The crystal pendant at her throat pulsed with blue-white light, matching the rhythm of Asvarr's golden veins. Exhaustion lined her face, but her eyes remained sharp as she assessed him.

"You've changed," she said, less a question than an observation.

Asvarr lowered his sword. "The Blight-Herder's poison left me little choice."

"And the Root offered you salvation with a price." Yrsa approached, kneeling before him. Without asking permission, she pressed her palm against the bark pattern over his heart. Her touch sent ripples of awareness through him—as if she could read the alterations in his flesh the way a skald might read runes carved in stone.

"How did you find us?" Asvarr asked.

"I followed your trail," Yrsa said, withdrawing her hand with a troubled expression. "Though not with eyes. After binding two anchors, you shine like a beacon to those who know how to look." She gestured to her crystal pendant. "The boundary between you and the pattern thins. Any with the sight could track you now."

Leif stirred, golden eyes blinking open. He showed no surprise at Yrsa's presence.

"The traveler returns," he said, his child's voice carrying that unsettling adult resonance. "Did you find what you sought in the spaces between?"

"Some answers," Yrsa replied, turning her attention to the boy. "And more questions, as always happens when one walks the grief-paths." She removed a small drawstring pouch from her belt and passed it to Leif. "Memory-moss. It will help you stay solid a while longer."

Leif accepted the pouch with reverence, tucking it inside his ragged tunic without opening it. Whatever passed between them remained unspoken but understood.

Asvarr stood, suppressing a wince as the bark patterns shifted against his movements. The pain had subsided significantly since the communion, but the altered skin remained sensitive, especially in the cool morning air.

"Brynja?" he asked.

"Gone her own way," Yrsa answered, rising to stand before him. "The binding-runes forced truth from her lips, but truth alone doesn't determine direction. Her path leads elsewhere for now."

"Do you trust her?" Asvarr pressed.

"Trust is for those with the luxury of certainty," Yrsa said, her gaze moving to the horizon. "I believe she walks her own path, neither the Wanderer's nor the Five's. Whether that path crosses yours again with blade or helping hand depends on what she discovers along the way."

The evasiveness of her answer irritated him. Since his communion with the Root, Asvarr had developed a profound distaste for circular speech and hidden meanings. Every equivocation felt like sand grinding in an open wound.

"Speak plainly," he demanded. "Or don't speak at all."

Yrsa's eyes snapped back to his, sharp with sudden focus. "You want plainness? Here it is: you're changing too fast. The bark patterns shouldn't have spread this far after only two bindings." She pressed her hand against his chest again, harder this time. "The Root gives and takes in equal measure, but you've surrendered too much too quickly. The price you paid for purging the poison was steeper than you know."

Leif scrambled to his feet, suddenly alert. "Others approach," he warned. "Through the boundary-trees."

Asvarr reached for his sword again, but Yrsa shook her head.

"Remnants of the Five's servants," she explained. "Searching, but not yet finding. We have time, but we must move soon." She fixed Asvarr with an uncompromising stare. "Before we go, you must understand what path you walk. The burden of Wardenship is to guard the power, not become it."

"I made my choice when I bound the first anchor," Asvarr replied, irritation giving way to weariness. He'd spent three days wrestling with the consequences of his communion, questioning every memory gap, every physical change. He didn't need Yrsa's warnings to know the danger.

"Did you?" Yrsa challenged. "Or did you simply seize the first solution to the immediate threat? There's a difference between choosing a path and stumbling onto it while fleeing something worse."

Asvarr's hand went instinctively to his chest, feeling the wooden texture of what had once been smooth skin. The Root's voice echoed in his memory: *With each exchange, you become less fully human and more of the pattern itself.*

"What alternative did I have?" he demanded. "Let the Blight-Herder's poison transform me into something worse?"

"There are always alternatives," Yrsa insisted. She pulled a curved knife from her belt—its blade fashioned from the same crystalline material as her pendant. Pressing it flat against the bark pattern on Asvarr's chest, she spoke words in a language he didn't recognize. The knife glowed with blue-white light, and where it touched his altered skin, the bark pattern temporarily receded, revealing flesh beneath.

"This can slow the transformation," she explained, sheathing the knife. "Not stop it entirely, but give you time to consider each step before taking it. The original Wardens didn't understand this. One by one, they surrendered completely, becoming vessels rather than guardians."

"What happened to them?" Asvarr asked, a chill running through him despite the morning sun now breaking through the trees.

"They lost themselves," Yrsa said quietly. "Their bodies remained, walking and speaking, but hollowed of what made them themselves. Some became instruments of the Root, extensions of its will. Others merged so completely they transformed into anchors themselves—living fragments bound to specific realms." She tapped her pendant meaningfully. "I've walked among their remnants. Seen what awaits at the end of the path you're walking."

Leif tugged urgently at Asvarr's tunic. "The boundary thins," he insisted. "We must move before they find us."

Asvarr gathered his few possessions—sword, water skin, the small pouch containing the seed token from the second anchor. As he secured them, he confronted Yrsa with the question burning in his mind.

"The Ashfather. Was he one of them? A Warden who lost himself?"

Yrsa's expression darkened. "Worse. He was the first to bind all five anchors. The one who should have restored balance." She turned away, her voice dropping to barely above a whisper. "Instead, he chose power over purpose. Took without exchange. Broke without binding."

"And became what he is now," Asvarr concluded.

"What you see of him is merely shell," Yrsa said. "A vessel wearing memories of what it once was. The true man is long gone, consumed by what he invited in."

The weight of her words settled over Asvarr like stone. He'd faced the Ashfather twice—once at the root-strike in Midgard, and again watching from the shadows at Hollowglade. Each time, he'd sensed something fundamentally wrong about the figure—a hollowness behind the singular burning eye.

"Is that my fate?" he asked, the question escaping before he could reconsider it.

"That depends," Yrsa replied, meeting his gaze directly. "On whether you continue surrendering pieces of yourself, or learn to walk alongside the power without becoming it." She gestured to the bark patterns on his chest. "Already you've given more than most Wardens did before their fourth binding. Your memories, your identity—these aren't coin to be spent carelessly."

Leif made an urgent sound, pointing to the western edge of the glade where shadows moved among the trees. Forms with too many joints and elongated limbs slipped between trunks, searching.

"We go east," Yrsa decided, already moving. "Through the boundary forest and around the Hunter's Reach. There's a path there few remember that will take us closer to the third anchor."

Asvarr hesitated, looking back at the silver lake where he'd communed with the Root. Something pulled at him—the sense of connection he'd experienced in that golden network. For a moment, he considered returning, sinking deeper, seeking more answers.

"Asvarr!" Yrsa hissed. "Choose now. Follow or stay—but understand what each choice means."

The urgency in her voice broke through his momentary fixation. Asvarr turned away from the lake, feeling a physical sensation of resistance as he did—as if gossamer threads connected him to the water and stretched taut with each step away.

***

They moved swiftly through the trees, Leif leading with uncanny confidence. The boy navigated as if seeing paths invisible to the others, occasionally pausing with his head tilted like a bird listening for distant songs.

"How much do you remember?" Yrsa asked after they'd put significant distance between themselves and their pursuers. "Of your life before the first binding?"

Asvarr considered the question as they walked. The gaps in his memory had widened since the communion. He knew he'd had a clan, remembered fighting in raids, recalled the destruction of his village—but the details had thinned, like old fabric worn translucent with age.

"Names. Events. Facts," he answered. "But the faces blur. Voices fade." He touched the bark over his heart. "I can recall Hakon giving an order during our last raid, but not the sound of his voice. I know my mother sang to me as a child, but the melody is gone."

Yrsa nodded grimly. "The Root takes the essence first—the emotions, sensations, connections. It leaves just enough that you don't notice what's missing until it's too late." She pushed aside a low-hanging branch. "By your third binding, you'll struggle to remember why you began this journey at all."

"To restore what was broken," Asvarr said automatically, though even as the words left his mouth, they felt hollow—a recitation rather than a conviction.

"Are you certain?" Yrsa challenged. "Or is that merely what you've been told your purpose should be? By the Root, by the Five, by the specters of previous Wardens?" She fixed him with a penetrating stare. "What do you want, Asvarr Flame-Bearer? Not what destiny demands or prophecy claims—what do you want?"

The question struck him with physical force. He stumbled, catching himself against a tree trunk. The bark against his palm resonated with his altered flesh, creating a momentary connection that flashed images through his mind—root systems spreading beneath the soil, branches reaching for sunlight, seasons cycling in heartbeats.

"I want—" he began, then stopped, realizing he had no answer. The desires that had driven him since the destruction of his clan—vengeance, understanding, restoration—had become abstract concepts, emptied of emotional weight. What remained was the drive to complete his path, to bind the anchors, to fulfill his role as Warden. But were those desires truly his, or merely the pattern working through him?

Leif appeared at his side, tugging his sleeve. "Choose later," the boy urged. "Move now." He pointed east, where the forest thinned into a boulder-strewn meadow. "Crossroads waiting. Important crossroads."

Yrsa nodded in agreement. "The boundary stone marks a place where paths converge. We'll be safer there to rest and plan." She glanced at Asvarr's chest where golden sap had begun to seep from the edges of the bark patterns. "And tend to your wounds—both those you can see and those you cannot."

They continued eastward, Asvarr wrestling with Yrsa's question. As they walked, he became increasingly aware of the life surrounding them—the subtle electrical impulses of plants reaching toward the sun, the movement of small animals in the underbrush, the slow heartbeat of ancient trees. These new perceptions overlaid his human senses, creating a double-vision that both expanded his awareness and diluted his focus.

At the forest's edge, a massive standing stone marked the boundary between woodland and meadow. Carved with spiraling patterns that matched the whorls on Asvarr's chest, it pulsed with dormant power. Yrsa approached it reverently, placing her palm against its surface. The stone responded to her touch, glowing faintly blue-white where her hand met the carved spirals.

"We'll rest here," she declared. "The stone will mask our presence for a time."

***

Asvarr sank to the ground, his back against the stone's cool surface. The physical connection sent ripples of awareness through him—he could feel the monolith's roots extending deep into the earth, anchoring it across realities. The stone existed in multiple places simultaneously, creating a blind spot in the pattern where they could hide.

"You called me Flame-Bearer," he said to Yrsa as she arranged her pack beside him. "Not Skyrend's Flame, as the völva named me."

"Names have power," Yrsa replied. "Especially those given by others. The name you accept shapes the path you walk." She removed her crystal knife and a small pouch of herbs from her belongings. "Skyrend's Flame defines you by destiny and catastrophe. Flame-Bearer speaks to essence and choice."

Leif had wandered to the meadow's edge, collecting small white flowers that glowed in the shadows beneath the tall grasses. He worked with practiced efficiency, weaving the stems into an intricate pattern.

"The boy," Asvarr nodded toward Leif. "What is he?"

"A question I've asked myself since finding him," Yrsa admitted. "He exists between states—born in the moment the Tree shattered, neither fully here nor elsewhere. The spaces between moments are his domain." She watched Leif with a mixture of wonder and concern. "In nine cycles of breaking and binding, I've never encountered his like before."

"Nine cycles," Asvarr repeated. "You speak as if you've witnessed them all."

Yrsa's fingers stilled on the herbs she was sorting. For a moment, she seemed to consider her answer carefully. Then she turned her crystal pendant to reveal its opposite side—a surface etched with a pattern identical to the bark covering Asvarr's chest.

"I told you I've walked among the remnants of those who came before," she said quietly. "What I didn't explain is why they speak to me." She pressed her palm against the standing stone again, and this time the blue-white glow spread up her arm, revealing faint patterns beneath her skin, crystalline networks following her veins.

"You're a Warden," Asvarr realized, instinctively drawing back.

"I was," Yrsa corrected. "A boundary-walker who glimpsed too much between the worlds." She withdrew her hand from the stone, and the glow receded. "I bound no anchors, but I touched the pattern directly. It changed me, as it changes all who connect with it."

Before Asvarr could demand more explanation, Leif returned with his woven flowers, placing them at the base of the standing stone. The blossoms pulsed with gentle light, creating a circle of illumination around their resting place.

"Protection," the boy explained. "From eyes that watch and ears that listen." He settled cross-legged before them, his golden eyes reflecting the flowers' glow. "Tell him what comes. Tell him what waits."

Yrsa sighed, a sound heavy with centuries. "The third anchor lies in Alfheim, where starlight meets root in something new. Before you seek it, you must understand the cost you've already paid and what remains to be surrendered." She reached toward Asvarr's chest. "May I?"

After a moment's hesitation, he nodded. Yrsa placed her fingers against the bark pattern, closing her eyes in concentration.

"The first binding took your rage," she murmured. "The second, fragments of memory. The communion in the silver lake claimed your earliest childhood. With each sacrifice, the pattern replaces what was lost with its own essence." Her eyes opened, fixing on his with terrible certainty. "Two more bindings remain. Without intervention, there will be nothing left of Asvarr the man when they're complete. Only the Warden will remain."

The words fell between them like stones dropped in still water, creating ripples of silence. In that quiet, a decision crystallized in Asvarr's mind—perhaps the first true choice he'd made since discovering the Grímmark on his chest after the breaking.

"Then teach me this intervention," he said firmly. "Show me how to bind without surrendering. If the burden of Wardenship is to guard the power rather than become it, I would learn to bear that burden properly."

Yrsa studied him for a long moment, searching for something in his expression. Whatever she sought, she seemed satisfied with what she found. She unsheathed her crystal knife and held it between them, the blade catching the light of Leif's woven flowers.

"The path will not be easy," she warned. "The pattern has already sunk its roots deep within you. To resist its pull while continuing to bind the anchors requires strength beyond mere will."

"I've surrendered enough," Asvarr replied, his hand moving to cover the bark over his heart. "Whatever remains of me, I would keep."

Leif nodded solemnly, his child's face momentarily reflecting wisdom beyond mortal reckoning. "The third path," he said. "Neither surrender nor dominance."

"Yes," Yrsa agreed, her eyes never leaving Asvarr's. "The way between—harder than either extreme, requiring balance renewed with each step." She offered the knife, handle first. "Are you certain this is what you want? The pattern will fight your resistance. The anchors will demand more with each binding."

Asvarr took the knife, feeling its weight—surprisingly heavy for its size, as if compressed from something much larger. The crystal blade hummed against his palm, resonating with the gold-veined bark on his chest like complementary tones in a complex harmony.

"I want myself," he said with quiet conviction. "Whatever remains."

Beyond the boundary stone, shadows lengthened as the day progressed toward evening. Somewhere in those shadows, the Ashfather's servants still searched. The Verdant Five still planned. Brynja still walked her separate path. The pattern continued its vast, intricate dance.

But here, in this moment of choice, Asvarr felt something he hadn't experienced since before the first binding—a purpose entirely his own.

***

The midday sun filtered through the canopy as Asvarr, Yrsa, and Leif made their way through the boundary forest. They'd been walking for hours, following a winding path only Yrsa could see—a trail marked by subtle shifts in the undergrowth, by trees that leaned slightly away from the route, by boulders with crystalline veins that caught the light in precise patterns.

Asvarr's chest ached where bark met flesh. Yrsa's treatment with the crystal knife had slowed the transformation, but the altered skin pulled with each step, stretching and contracting like wood adjusting to changing weather. Beneath his tunic, golden sap occasionally seeped through cracks in the bark pattern, sticking fabric to skin in uncomfortable patches.

His discomfort went deeper than physical pain. Since leaving the boundary stone, he'd attempted to recall faces from his clan—shield-brothers who'd fallen during the shattering, elders who'd guided his youth, children whose laughter had filled the longhouse on winter nights. Their names remained, hanging in his memory like empty hooks on a wall, but the faces themselves had vanished. Facts without essence. Knowledge without connection.

"Hakon," he murmured, testing the emptiness. His raid-leader, his mentor, the man who'd trusted him with a place in the shield-wall. Asvarr knew these things had happened, could recall specific raids they'd undertaken together. But Hakon's face—the scar across his left temple, the gray streaking his beard, the way his eyes narrowed when issuing orders—these details had dissolved into nothing.

"You're trying to remember," Yrsa observed, glancing back at him. "It won't work. Not through direct effort."

"You speak as if you've experienced this yourself," Asvarr said, frustration edging his voice.

Yrsa touched the crystalline patterns visible beneath her skin when she pushed back her sleeve. "I have. The pattern takes first what matters most—the connections, the emotions, the texture of experience. The facts remain longest, which makes the loss harder to detect until much has already faded."

A clearing opened before them, sunlight streaming onto a small pond fed by a spring that bubbled from beneath moss-covered stones. Yrsa indicated they should rest here, removing a waterskin and small bundle of dried meat from her pack.

Leif immediately wandered to the pond's edge, kneeling to examine tiny silver fish darting beneath the surface. The boy had been uncharacteristically quiet since they'd left the boundary stone, his face drawn in concentration as if listening to distant sounds only he could hear.

Asvarr settled on a fallen log, accepting the strips of smoked venison Yrsa offered. As he chewed the tough meat, he closed his eyes, trying once more to recall his mother's face. He knew she'd been tall for a woman of their clan, knew her hair had been dark with strands of copper that caught the light. But her smile, the shape of her eyes, the specific timbre of her laugh—these had faded like mist in morning sun.

When he tried to recall her voice singing lullabies during his childhood, he heard only whispers of leaves rustling in a breeze. The sound was beautiful, resonant, carrying depth and meaning—but it wasn't human. It wasn't hers.

"I can't hear her anymore," he said, opening his eyes to find Yrsa watching him.

"The Root preserves what you surrender," she replied. "But it transforms memory into something else entirely. Your mother's voice becomes the rustling of leaves. Your father's laughter becomes the creaking of branches in wind. The pattern doesn't destroy—it reconfigures into forms it understands."

Asvarr pressed his palm against the bark covering his heart. "So my memories still exist somewhere? Just changed?"

"They exist within the pattern," Yrsa said carefully. "But no longer in forms you would recognize. When the Root accepts what you offer, it incorporates the essence into its own awareness." She crouched beside him, her voice lowering. "This is what the Ashfather never understood. He sought to take from the pattern without exchange, to retain everything of himself while claiming its power. Instead, he hollowed himself, creating empty spaces the void could fill."

Leif rejoined them, small hands glistening with pond water. "The silver-swimmers remember," he said cryptically. "They swim the same circles their ancestors swam when the Root first touched water."

"Memory exists in many forms," Yrsa agreed, offering the boy a strip of dried meat. "Some more permanent than others."

"Can I reclaim what I've lost?" Asvarr asked, already suspecting the answer.

Yrsa shook her head. "What's surrendered cannot be reclaimed—only witnessed in its new form. The communion you experienced in the silver lake was a beginning, not an end. With each binding, the exchange continues." She unwrapped a bundle of herbs, crushing dried leaves between her fingers. The sharp, resinous scent cleared Asvarr's senses as she sprinkled the mixture over the remainder of the venison. "This will help strengthen what remains."

Asvarr chewed the treated meat, tasting bitter herbs beneath the smoky flavor. The effect was immediate—his thoughts sharpened, the boundaries between his remaining memories and the pattern's influence becoming more distinct.

"What was their purpose?" he asked suddenly. "The original Wardens. What were they trying to accomplish?"

Yrsa considered him thoughtfully. "They sought balance. After the first breaking, when the Tree shattered itself to escape what hunted it from below, fragments scattered across the Nine Realms. The first Wardens walked different paths—some binding anchors, others walking boundaries, still others preserving what was lost." She gestured to herself. "I was among the last group, before my transformation."

"How old are you?" Asvarr demanded.

"Time flows differently within the pattern," she replied evasively. "I've witnessed nine cycles of breaking and binding. Whether that spans centuries or millennia by human reckoning matters little."

"And each cycle leads to another breaking? Another shattering?"

Yrsa nodded. "The cycle continues because the balance remains disrupted. The Ashfather ensures this—preserving just enough of the pattern to maintain the realms while preventing true restoration." She examined the crystal pendant around her neck, which pulsed with blue-white light. "We should move. The herbs will stabilize your remaining memories temporarily, but their effect fades with time."

***

They continued through the forest, which grew denser and darker as they proceeded. Ancient trees with massive, gnarled trunks blocked much of the sunlight, creating a perpetual twilight beneath the canopy. The air grew heavy with the scent of damp earth and decomposing leaves.

Asvarr found himself increasingly distracted by his fragmented memories. He would begin a thought about his clan only to discover crucial elements missing, like a bridge constructed with gaps between stones. When he attempted to recall his first hunt, he remembered tracking a stag through pine forests but couldn't recall who had accompanied him or the moment he'd taken the shot. The memory dissolved into abstract fragments—the weight of the bow, the smell of pine resin, the sound of snow crunching underfoot—disconnected from context or purpose.

"What am I fighting for?" he asked abruptly, half to himself. "If I can't remember my clan, what purpose does vengeance serve?"

Yrsa paused, turning to face him. "That question is precisely why the pattern takes memory first. Without personal connection, duty becomes abstract. Purpose turns hollow." Her gaze sharpened. "Why do you continue, Asvarr? Now, in this moment, with parts of yourself already surrendered?"

The question struck him with physical force. Why indeed? He'd begun this journey seeking vengeance for his clan, understanding of the Shattering, restoration of what was broken. But those motivations had thinned, becoming translucent ghosts of their former power. What remained was... what?

"I don't know," he admitted finally.

"Then find a new purpose," Yrsa said. "One that belongs to what you are becoming, not what you once were."

Leif, who had wandered ahead, suddenly returned with urgent steps. "Others approach," he warned. "Searchers with eyes of ash and hands that burn."

Yrsa immediately led them off the path into a dense thicket. Through gaps in the foliage, Asvarr glimpsed figures moving among the trees—tall, unnaturally thin forms with elongated limbs and heads that tilted at impossible angles. They wore cloaks of woven vines that shifted colors to match their surroundings. These weren't the Hunt of Broken Fate that served the Ashfather, but something else—servants of the Verdant Five, perhaps.

"Rootbound," Yrsa whispered. "They track the transformation in your flesh, searching for the mark's resonance."

Asvarr instinctively pressed his hand against his chest, willing the golden veins to still their pulse. The bark-patterns responded, hardening into a protective shell that sealed the seeping sap. The change was both alarming and gratifying—evidence he could control his transformation on some instinctive level.

The Rootbound moved past their hiding place, feet making no sound on the forest floor despite the carpet of dried leaves. When the last figure disappeared among the trees, Yrsa indicated they should continue but in a different direction.

"They'll patrol this area thoroughly once they sense your presence," she explained. "We'll cut east, then double back through the stream-channel."

As they pushed through dense underbrush, Asvarr's altered flesh responded to the forest around him—the bark-patterns expanding slightly in sunlight, contracting in shade, responding to the proximity of different trees as if recognizing distant kin. These changes occurred without conscious thought, his transformed body adapting to surroundings in ways his human flesh never could.

"You're becoming more attuned," Yrsa observed when they paused at a shallow stream. "The pattern expresses itself through you even as you resist complete merger."

"Is that possible?" Asvarr asked. "To maintain the balance between human and Root?"

"It's the essence of the third path," Yrsa replied. "Neither dominance nor surrender, but conscious partnership. Few have managed it for long." She indicated they should wade through the stream to mask their scent and trail. The cold water numbed Asvarr's feet as they followed the gentle current downstream.

Leif splashed beside him, golden eyes scanning the banks for threats. "The Root doesn't understand being alone," the boy said suddenly. "It's always been part of everything. Human separateness confuses it."

"That's remarkably insightful," Asvarr commented, studying the child who wasn't entirely a child.

"I hear both sides," Leif said simply. "The pattern speaks. Humans speak. Both think the other isn't listening properly."

They emerged from the stream onto a rocky bank, continuing through a section of forest where many trees had fallen, creating a labyrinth of massive trunks and exposed root systems. As Asvarr climbed over one such obstacle, his foot slipped on moss-slick bark. He braced himself against the trunk, and the contact triggered an unexpected flood of sensory information—the tree's age, the direction of its growth, the texture of soil that had nourished it, the moment lightning had shattered its upper branches decades before.

He pulled his hand back, disturbed by the intensity of the connection. "It's getting stronger," he said. "The transformation."

"The pattern calls to itself," Yrsa agreed. "Each fragment recognizes the whole."

They continued in silence for a time, each absorbed in private thoughts. The fallen trees gave way to a section of forest dominated by slender white birches, their bark peeling in paper-thin sheets that reminded Asvarr of scrolls unfurling. As the day's light began to fade, they came upon a clearing where a solitary oak stood, ancient and massive, its branches extending over nearly the entire open space.

"We'll rest here for the night," Yrsa decided.

Asvarr helped gather fallen branches for a small fire while Leif collected various plants and fungi from the clearing's edge. The boy sorted his findings with knowledgeable fingers, discarding some while carefully preserving others in a pouch Yrsa had given him.

As twilight deepened into true darkness, they sat around the small fire Yrsa had built. The flames gave little heat but provided enough light to keep watch for dangers. Leif curled against a protruding root of the great oak, falling asleep almost immediately, his small form relaxing into the curves of the wood as if shaped to fit them perfectly.

"Tell me something you remember clearly," Yrsa said to Asvarr. "Something untouched by the pattern's influence."

Asvarr searched his fragmented memory, seeking anything that remained vivid and complete. Most recollections were incomplete now—missing faces, voices, emotional connections. But one memory remained sharp-edged and distinct: the moment he'd discovered the Grímmark on his chest after the Shattering. The sensation of fingers tracing unfamiliar patterns on his skin, the golden light pulsing beneath the rune, the weight of purpose settling over him like a physical mantle.

"I remember when I first found the mark," he said. "After the breaking, after my clan was destroyed. I remember the exact moment I realized I'd been chosen for something beyond my understanding."

Yrsa nodded thoughtfully. "The pattern preserves what serves its purpose. Your connection to the Grímmark remains intact because it defines your role as Warden." She added a small branch to the fire. "What else?"

Asvarr considered. "I remember Brynja clearly. Her face, her voice, the way she moved in battle." This realization surprised him. Why would memories of someone he'd known so briefly remain when memories of his clan had faded?

"The blood-oath," Yrsa explained, seeing his confusion. "When your bloodlines reconnected, it created a bond the pattern recognizes as essential. Your connection to her serves its purpose." She looked troubled. "This is both blessing and warning. The pattern will preserve what aligns with its aims while allowing all else to fade. In time, you will remember only what the Warden needs, nothing of who Asvarr was."

The fire crackled, sending sparks spiraling upward into the darkness. An owl called from somewhere in the forest, the sound echoing among the trees.

"The Tree remembers everything," Yrsa said quietly. "Every moment of every life it has touched across nine cycles of breaking and binding. Every word spoken beneath its branches, every death in its shadow, every birth in its light." She met his gaze across the flames. "But you will remember nothing that doesn't serve your purpose as Warden. This is the true danger of the path you walk, the gradual surrender of self until only the vessel remains."

Asvarr stared into the fire, watching the dance of flames consuming wood. The parallel wasn't lost on him—the pattern consuming what made him human, leaving only what served its purpose. He thought of the Blight-Herder, once the Five's greatest disciple, reduced to a hollow shell filled with writhing roots. He thought of the Ashfather, once a Warden who bound all five anchors, transformed into something neither human nor Root but something hollowed and filled with darkness.

"Is there no way to preserve what matters?" he asked. "Must I inevitably lose everything I was?"

"There are methods," Yrsa admitted. "Ways to anchor memory outside yourself. The crystal knife can slow the transformation temporarily. Certain herbs can strengthen the boundaries between self and pattern." She gestured to the sleeping Leif. "And there are other approaches known only to those who walk between states."

Asvarr looked at the boy, wondering again what strange confluence of circumstances had created such a being. "He knows more than he reveals."

"He exists simultaneously across multiple realities," Yrsa said. "Some versions of him know what others have yet to learn. When he speaks with that adult resonance, you hear echoes from his other selves." She retrieved a small leather-bound book from her pack. "But there are more immediate concerns. Before we reach the third anchor in Alfheim, you should record what remains of your memory—what you wish to preserve."

She offered him the book and a thin stick of charcoal. "External anchors can help maintain boundaries between self and pattern. Write what you can still recall. Create a reference point outside the transformation."

Asvarr accepted the book, opening its blank pages. "Will this truly help?"

"It creates a boundary," Yrsa explained. "The written word exists independently of memory. When the pattern takes more of your past, these pages will preserve fragments of who you were." She rose, brushing dirt from her robes. "I'll keep watch while you write. We have several hours before dawn."

As Yrsa moved to the clearing's edge, Asvarr stared at the empty page. What should he record? What fragments of himself deserved preservation? He began with names—his clan members, his parents, his shield-brothers—listing them mechanically at first, then adding what details he could still remember. Torfa's skill with a spear. Hakon's habit of pulling at his beard when thinking. His mother's songs during winter nights.

With each memory committed to page, he felt a subtle strengthening of the boundary between himself and the pattern. The act of recording created separation—acknowledging what belonged to Asvarr the man rather than the Warden the pattern sought to create.

Hours passed as he filled page after page with fragments of his former life. Some memories came easily, flowing from charcoal to parchment in detailed accounts. Others emerged stubborn and fractured, requiring concentrated effort to piece together. Still others refused to surface at all, leaving conspicuous absences in his narrative—blank spaces where vital connections should have existed.

Near dawn, he paused, hand cramped from writing, to find Leif awake and watching him with golden eyes that reflected the dying fire.

"The pattern doesn't want you to remember," the boy said. "But it needs you to choose."

"Choose what?" Asvarr asked.

"The third path requires will," Leif replied, his voice carrying that unsettling adult resonance. "Will requires self. Self requires memory." He reached into his tunic, removing a small object wrapped in leaves. "When you can no longer remember why you fight, open this."

He placed the leaf-wrapped bundle in Asvarr's palm. Through the covering, Asvarr felt something small and hard—a seed or stone, perhaps—pulsing with faint warmth.

"What is it?" he asked.

"Memory-seed," Leif answered. "From the space between. It remembers what you cannot."

Asvarr carefully tucked the bundle into his belt pouch alongside the second anchor's token. As the first gray light of dawn filtered through the trees, Yrsa returned from her watch.

"We should move," she said. "The Rootbound still search nearby."

Asvarr closed the memory-book, securing it inside his tunic where it pressed against his heart, a physical barrier between the encroaching bark and his remaining humanity. Something solid and tangible in a world increasingly dominated by transformation and loss.

As they prepared to depart, he traced the bark patterns on his chest one final time, feeling the alien texture that had once been flesh. The golden veins pulsed beneath his fingertips, responding to his touch with recognition. Not entirely human anymore, yet not surrendered completely.

For now, in this moment, he still remembered enough to fight. Still possessed enough of himself to choose the third path. But each step forward brought new transformation, new challenges to his identity. How much would remain after the third binding? The fourth? The fifth?

The memory-book weighed against his chest, a promise and a warning. The Tree remembered everything. But without conscious effort and external anchors, Asvarr would eventually remember nothing of himself at all.

CHAPTER 18
WHEN THE LEAVES SPEAK

The forest changed around them, almost between footsteps. Asvarr felt it first in the soil beneath his boots—softer, yielding with each step like flesh rather than earth. The trees thinned, their bark paler, almost translucent where sunlight struck. He followed Yrsa through a gap between twin aspens that curved toward each other, forming an arch.

They stepped into the grove.

Leaves fell. Endless leaves. Golden, amber, deep crimson, pale green—cascading from branches that never went bare. The air filled with their whispered descent, a constant rustling like the exhalation of some massive beast. Yet no pile formed upon the ground; each leaf disappeared moments after touching the earth, dissolving into motes of light that sank into the soil.

"What is this place?" Asvarr asked, his voice sounding foreign to his own ears. The bark patterns across his chest tingled, golden veins pulsing with warmth.

"The Whispering Grove," Yrsa said, her crystal pendant glowing softly. "A rare manifestation of the Root's memory. The Tree forgets nothing, Asvarr. Though you may surrender memories, they remain—transformed."

Asvarr reached out, catching a broad maple leaf in his palm. It settled there, edges curling slightly.

"Hello, flame-heart," whispered a voice from the leaf—a man's voice, gruff and familiar.

Asvarr's heart clenched. "Hakon?" The leaf trembled with his exhale.

"Remember your oath," the leaf whispered in Hakon's voice. "Remember your shield-arm failed when we most needed it."

The memory hit him with physical force—the day of the raid, Hakon bleeding out in the sand, golden fire raining from the broken sky. The memory remained, but hollow, devoid of the guilt and grief that once filled it. Just facts, stripped of feeling.

Asvarr dropped the leaf, watching it dissolve before touching the ground.

"The grove speaks through what it has taken," Yrsa said, watching him closely. "Each leaf holds a fragment the Root has witnessed through you."

Leif darted ahead, moving with uncharacteristic certainty. The boy was changing in this memory realm, becoming more solid, more present. His eyes—usually clouded with that distant, half-here gaze—focused sharply on the falling leaves. He snatched one, then another, examining them before tucking some into his tunic.

"What is he doing?" Asvarr asked.

"Collecting fragments," Yrsa said. "Leif exists partially outside the pattern. He can see connections the rest of us can't."

Asvarr walked deeper into the grove, leaves brushing his face and shoulders like curious fingers. Each touch brought whispers—voices of clansmen, shield-mates, enemies faced and fallen. Names he knew but faces he could no longer picture clearly.

"Waste of sword-arm, that one." A woman's voice from a serrated oak leaf.

"Too much fire in his blood." A man's laughter from a pale birch.

"You fight like your father." His shield-trainer's voice from a glossy rowan.

The voices surrounded him, a chorus of fragments. What unsettled him most was his lack of emotional response. He recognized the voices without feeling their significance. They existed as knowledge without context—stars without constellations to give them meaning.

Leif returned to his side, hands full of carefully selected leaves. The boy arranged them on a flat stone, placing each with deliberate precision. They formed a pattern—a spiral of overlapping edges that somehow remained in place despite the gentle breeze.

"What are you making?" Asvarr asked.

Leif looked up, that unnervingly adult expression crossing his childlike features. "A map," he said simply, as if it were obvious. "The leaves remember where they've been. Together, they show a way."

The boy placed the final leaf, and the pattern began to glow. Golden light outlined each leaf, connecting them in a network of illuminated veins. The pattern shifted, no longer a spiral but a rendering of the landscape ahead—valleys, ridges, and the outline of what might be a lake.

"The path to the Gate flows this way." Leif traced a shimmering line across the leaf-map. "Through the Mournwood and across the Tears."

Asvarr squinted at the map. "There are gaps."

"Missing memories," Yrsa said quietly. "Parts you've surrendered."

A leaf drifted down, landing directly on the vacant area of the map. It filled one of the gaps perfectly, its veins connecting with the surrounding pattern. Asvarr reached for it, but Leif caught his wrist.

"That one isn't yours to touch," the boy said. "Not yet."

***

The forest floor trembled. A subtle vibration traveled up through Asvarr's boots, into his legs, settling uncomfortably in his chest. The bark patterns etched into his skin contracted painfully.

"We're being watched," Yrsa whispered, her hand moving to her crystal knife. "The grove has guardians."

Between the endless falling leaves, shapes moved. Humanoid figures with bark for skin and branches for fingers. Their eyes glowed amber in hollow wooden faces. They made no sound as they approached, merely parting the curtain of falling leaves.

"Rootlings," Yrsa said. "Servants of the Five. They collect memories the grove hasn't yet absorbed."

Asvarr drew his bronze sword. The golden veins within the blade flared in response, mimicking the patterns across his chest. "Hostile?"

"Territorial," Yrsa replied. "We're trespassing in their harvest field."

One of the Rootlings stepped forward. Its face contained suggestions of humanity—eye hollows, a ridge for a nose, a crack for a mouth—but no individual features. When it spoke, its voice sounded like wood creaking in a high wind.

"Walker-between," it addressed Yrsa. "You bring flame where only root should grow."

"The pattern calls for both," Yrsa replied. "As you well know."

The Rootling tilted its head, branches scraping against each other. "The bearer has given enough. Why does he seek what was surrendered?"

"We seek a path, not memories," Asvarr interjected. "The way to the third anchor."

The Rootling's attention shifted to him, amber eyes flaring brighter. "Anchor-seeker. The flame in your blood burns quick and hot. How much of yourself will remain when the fifth anchor claims its price? Will you even recognize your own name?"

The question struck deeper than Asvarr expected. Would he? Already faces blurred, voices reached him as if through water, emotions dulled like colors faded by harsh sun. What would remain after three more bindings? A hollowed vessel bearing a name without meaning?

"I'll remain enough," Asvarr said, voice hardening. "The anchor awaits my claim, not yours."

The Rootling's wooden face couldn't form expressions, but its posture changed—a subtle shifting of branch-limbs that suggested tension.

"You may pass through the grove," it finally said. "But take nothing. Each leaf belongs to the pattern now."

"And the boy's map?" Yrsa asked.

"Knowledge freely given is knowledge earned," the Rootling replied. "But no physical leaf may leave this place."

Leif knelt by his leaf-map, studying it intently. "I see the way," he said. "We don't need to take them."

The Rootling stepped aside, gesturing deeper into the grove with a branch-arm. The others followed suit, forming a gauntlet of wooden sentinels through which they must pass.

"Stay close," Yrsa murmured. "Touch nothing else."

Asvarr sheathed his sword, though the tension in his body remained. They followed Leif between the silent Rootlings, deeper into the shower of whispering leaves. Each step brought more voices—fragments of conversations, battles, quiet moments around fires. The collected memories of a life increasingly distant from the transformed creature he was becoming.

Halfway through, a leaf spiraled down directly into Asvarr's path—larger than the others, its surface rippling with golden light. Without thinking, he caught it.

"The northern star guides home," spoke his father's voice from the leaf.

Asvarr froze, the leaf trembling in his palm. His father—the man who disappeared when Asvarr was barely ten winters old, whose face had become one of the first memories to fade after his communion with the Root.

"Father." The word escaped him unbidden.

The Rootlings shifted, wooden limbs creaking in agitation. The one who had spoken moved toward him. "That belongs to the grove, anchor-seeker."

Asvarr clutched the leaf tighter. "This is my father's voice."

"It was," the Rootling corrected. "Now it belongs to the pattern."

Yrsa touched Asvarr's arm. "We must respect their ways in their domain," she urged quietly.

The leaf burned against his palm, with possibility. In it lay answers to questions he'd held since childhood—where his father had gone, why he never returned. Did the leaf contain those truths, or merely fragments without context?

The Rootling extended a branch-hand. "The leaf. Now."

Asvarr stared into its amber eyes, feeling the weight of his father's voice in his palm. Surrender this too? Another piece of himself given to the endless hunger of the pattern?

A sharp crack split the air. One of the Rootlings further back had seized Leif by the arm. The boy struggled silently, eyes wide with panic.

"Release him," Asvarr demanded, his free hand moving to his sword.

"The leaf," the Rootling repeated, branch-fingers reaching.

Asvarr looked down at the leaf, then at Leif. The boy's captured arm had begun to glow where the Rootling gripped it, golden light seeping into the wooden fingers. They were trying to take something from him—some fragment of his in-between essence.

"Let the boy go," Asvarr said, "and you can have the leaf."

The Rootling considered this, head tilting. "Agreed."

The one holding Leif released him. The boy stumbled forward, clutching his arm where five branch-finger marks glowed golden against his skin.

Reluctantly, Asvarr extended his hand, the leaf resting on his palm. The Rootling took it with surprising gentleness, tucking it somewhere within the folds of its bark-body.

"Continue on your path, anchor-seeker," it said. "But know that what you surrender is never truly lost—merely transformed beyond your recognition."

They pressed on, Leif moving close to Asvarr's side, still rubbing his marked arm. The leaf shower grew denser, voices overlapping into a chorus of whispers that echoed around them. Asvarr felt each step taking him deeper into the memory of what he once was, while carrying him further from the person he had been.

***

At the grove's far edge, where the leaf-fall thinned enough to see the forest beyond, Leif suddenly stopped. He pointed upward at a single leaf spiraling down—broad, golden, and glowing with internal light more intense than any they'd seen.

"That one," Leif said, his voice tight with urgency. "That one you must hear."

The golden leaf drifted down, suspended momentarily in a shaft of sunlight that broke through the canopy. Asvarr reached for it instinctively.

"Wait—" Yrsa began.

But his fingers had already closed around the leaf's stem.

The golden leaf settled in Asvarr's palm, weightless yet somehow heavier than anything he'd ever held. Unlike the others, it didn't immediately speak. It pulsed instead, gentle waves of warmth spreading up his arm and into his chest where the bark patterns burned in response.

"Open your hand," Leif whispered, golden eyes fixed on the leaf.

Asvarr uncurled his fingers. The leaf floated upward, hovering at eye level. It spun slowly, golden veins catching the dappled light filtering through the canopy.

"Asvarr," the leaf whispered in a woman's voice.

His breath caught. Something deep within his hollowed memory stirred, a feeling. Warmth. Security. The scent of pine smoke and sweet herbs.

"Mother?" The word felt strange on his tongue, disconnected from any clear memory of the woman who had given him life.

The Rootlings had withdrawn to the edges of the clearing, branches creaking as they shifted. Even they sensed the significance of this moment.

"My brave one," the leaf continued, its edges rippling with each word. "You've walked far from home."

Asvarr strained to recall her face, but found only darkness where that memory should have been. The emptiness ached like a physical wound. "I can't remember what you looked like," he admitted, voice rough.

"Memory fades. Blood remains." The leaf pulsed brighter. "You carry more than just our bloodline, my son. You bear a choice."

The golden light from the leaf intensified, casting Asvarr's shadow long across the grove floor. The falling leaves around them slowed, as if time itself hesitated.

"What choice?" Asvarr asked.

"Between the fire of vengeance and the light of forgiveness." His mother's voice grew clearer, more substantial than the whispers from the other leaves. "Your path is tangled with both Root and flame. Neither fully claims you."

Yrsa touched his shoulder in warning. "Asvarr, this is rare—a complete memory fragment, not just an echo. It contains power."

The leaf spun faster. "You survived when others didn't," his mother's voice continued. "That is a responsibility to live well. To choose wisely."

Asvarr's throat tightened. The words struck something fundamental within him—a truth he'd been afraid to acknowledge since finding his clan's remains. He had survived. While everyone he loved burned and bled, he alone had walked away. That survival had festered within him as guilt, driving his hunt for meaning, for vengeance.

"I've forgotten so much," he said. "The faces of our clan, your voice, your smile. The Root takes everything."

"Not everything," the leaf replied. "Forgiveness remains. Of others. Of yourself."

"How can I forgive what destroyed our clan? What shattered the Tree? What's taking my memories piece by piece?" Asvarr demanded, a flicker of his old fury surfacing through the hollowness.

"The question isn't whether you can forgive," the leaf responded. "It's whether you can transform through forgiveness rather than being consumed by vengeance."

Asvarr closed his eyes, feeling the weight of his remaining identity balanced against the vastness of what he'd already surrendered. Rage had been his companion since finding his clan's bodies. Its absence left space for something else—something he didn't yet recognize.

"Forgiveness is stronger than vengeance," the leaf whispered. "It creates rather than destroys. The flame in your blood can forge or consume. The choice has always been yours."

The bark patterns across Asvarr's chest pulsed painfully. The Grímmark and the competing patterns beneath his skin responded to his mother's voice—his Root-connection recognizing something fundamental in her words.

"Move back," Yrsa warned, pulling Leif away from Asvarr. "The fragment is awakening."

The golden leaf began to expand, its edges dissolving into motes of light that orbited around a central core of radiance. The light grew, taking shape—the silhouette of a woman with hair braided in the northern style, wearing a simple linen dress with a sword-belt at her waist.

Asvarr's breath stopped. Though her features remained indistinct, blurred by time and transformation, he recognized her stance—feet planted firmly, shoulders squared. A shield-maiden's posture. His mother had been a warrior in her own right, something he'd forgotten until this moment.

"You have her bearing," the Rootling nearest them observed, its amber eyes bright with interest. "The pattern preserves more than memories. It preserves essence."

The glowing figure raised a hand toward Asvarr's face. He felt no physical touch, yet something brushed his consciousness—a familiar presence long absent.

"The third path awaits," his mother's voice said from within the light. "Neither Root nor flame alone, but balance between. Bind without being bound. Transform without being consumed."

The figure's arm moved to her side, where a spectral blade hung. She drew it—a motion Asvarr suddenly recalled with crystal clarity. The same movement he used himself, taught to him during childhood lessons he'd believed lost to memory.

"You forged your path in fire," the luminous figure said. "Now learn to walk it with grace."

The sword in her hand dissolved into tendrils of light that wove themselves into a complex pattern—the same interlaced design of roots and flame now embedded in Asvarr's flesh.

"Remember your purpose when all else fades," she said, her voice beginning to thin like stretched silk. "Not vengeance. Restoration."

The light-figure reached forward again, this time pressing her palm against Asvarr's chest where the bark patterns spiraled across his skin. Warmth flooded through him, the gentle heat of recognition. Something unlocked within his fragmented memory—understanding.

"She's anchoring you," Yrsa breathed. "A blood-memory stronger than what the Root can absorb."

The luminous figure began to dissolve, golden motes drifting away like embers from a dying fire. The Rootlings moved closer, branches extended as if to catch the dissolving light.

"Wait," Asvarr pleaded, reaching for the fading apparition. "Don't go."

The figure's features solidified briefly—just long enough for Asvarr to glimpse dark eyes like his own, a strong nose, and lips curved in a smile that spoke of both sorrow and pride.

"I remain in your blood, my brave one," her voice whispered, fading with her form. "When the fifth binding comes, remember: forgiveness creates what vengeance destroys."

The figure collapsed inward, condensing once more into a leaf that drifted down into Asvarr's outstretched palm. For a heartbeat, it retained its golden glow, then crumbled into dust that sank beneath his skin. Where it disappeared, a faint spiral pattern formed, a more deliberate design resembling the runic symbols his clan had carved into their weapons and doorposts.

The closest Rootling tilted its wooden head. "The mother-memory has joined with you," it said. "This has not happened in nine cycles."

Asvarr stared at the spiral marking on his palm, feeling strangely whole despite the hollow spaces within his memory. "What does it mean?"

"That you remain something more than vessel," the Rootling replied. "That your blood remembers even when your mind forgets."

Leif approached cautiously, reaching for Asvarr's marked palm. When the boy's fingers touched the spiral, he smiled—a genuine expression rarely seen on his serious face. "The way is clearer now," he said. "The bloom-grove calls us."

"You've received a gift," Yrsa said, studying the spiral. "An anchor against dissolution. Use it wisely."

Asvarr closed his hand, feeling the spiral pattern pulse against his palm. His mother's face was already fading again, details dissolving back into the darkness of lost memory. But her words remained, etched now in blood and bone rather than conscious recollection.

Forgiveness creates what vengeance destroys.

The Rootling stepped back, gesturing toward the grove's exit with branch-arms. "Your path lies beyond, anchor-seeker. The Grove of the Blooming Dead awaits those who carry leaf-memory."

"Thank you," Asvarr said, surprising himself with the sincerity of the words. These were not enemies, he realized, but caretakers of what he'd surrendered. In preserving his memories, they preserved fragments of who he had been.

They followed Leif toward the edge of the grove, where the endless leaf-fall thinned and ordinary forest resumed. With each step, Asvarr felt the new spiral mark on his palm pulsing in rhythm with his heartbeat. Something had changed within him—a subtle shift in perspective. The hollow spaces left by surrendered memories remained, but they no longer felt like wounds. They were simply... spaces. Room for something new to grow.

At the threshold between grove and forest, Asvarr paused, looking back at the cascade of whispering leaves. How many other fragments of himself remained here? How many voices and faces from his past, preserved but transformed beyond recognition? Would he one day return, emptied of all but purpose, to walk among memories he could no longer claim?

"Asvarr," Yrsa called, already several paces ahead with Leif. "We must reach the bloom-grove before nightfall."

The spiral mark on his palm flared warm. Asvarr turned away from the whispering leaves and followed his companions, his stride more certain than before. The burden of vengeance had lightened, making space for something he hadn't permitted himself in too long—possibility.

"What will we find in this Grove of Blooming Dead?" he asked Leif.

The boy glanced back, golden eyes reflecting light that didn't exist in the shaded forest. "Life from endings," he said cryptically. "The path through death to the third anchor."

Asvarr nodded, surprisingly untroubled by the boy's strange words. Whatever awaited them, he would face it differently now. His mother's memory-fragment had given him something the Root's transformation had been steadily consuming—a sense of choice, of agency beyond mere reaction.

The forest grew darker around them as they moved deeper along Leif's chosen path. The trees here were older, their bark blackened as if by ancient fire. No birds sang. No insects buzzed. Even the air felt still, weighted with the silence of abandoned places.

Leif stopped suddenly, pointing ahead where the trees thinned. "There," he whispered. "The bloom-grove begins."

Beyond the blackened trees lay a vast clearing awash in colors Asvarr had never seen, shades that seemed to exist at the edges of perception. Trees unlike any he recognized stood in ordered rows, each growing from a distinct mound of earth. Their trunks twisted in unnatural patterns, and their branches bore impossible blooms—flowers with faces, fruits that glowed from within, leaves that moved without wind.

"The Grove of the Blooming Dead," Yrsa said quietly. "Where all that ends begins anew."

Asvarr stepped forward, the spiral marking on his palm burning with sudden intensity. As his boot crossed the threshold between forest and grove, a chorus of whispers rose from the strange trees—voices too numerous to distinguish, speaking words too intertwined to separate.

The third anchor waited somewhere in this garden of transformed endings, calling to him through bark and blood. Touching the spiral mark his mother's memory had left, Asvarr stepped fully into the Grove of the Blooming Dead, ready to walk the third path she had revealed.

CHAPTER 19

GROVE OF THE BLOOMING DEAD

Sunlight struck the grove in slanting columns that illuminated impossible colors. Asvarr stood at the threshold, the spiral mark on his palm burning as if awakened by the strange place before them. The Grove of the Blooming Dead stretched in ordered rows toward a horizon that couldn't exist in ordinary space—too distant, too curved, as if this small clearing somehow contained vastness beyond natural measure.

Each mound of earth sprouted a tree unique from its neighbors. Near the entrance stood a sentinel with bark like burnished bronze and thorns as long as daggers protruding from its trunk. The branches twisted into shapes reminiscent of sword-forms, and red sap beaded at the joints like fresh blood.

"A warrior," Leif said, stepping toward the tree. "His name was Hafthor. He died with his sword in hand, defending his kin against frost giants."

Asvarr frowned. "How could you possibly know that?"

Leif placed his hand on the bronze bark, leaving a golden print that faded slowly. "The tree remembers," he explained, his voice carrying that unsettling adult resonance. "Each holds the essence of the one planted beneath."

"The boy speaks truth," Yrsa added, her crystal pendant glowing softly against her chest. "The Grove of the Blooming Dead exists in all realms simultaneously—a nexus where those who die are transformed rather than ending."

Asvarr moved deeper into the grove, drawn by an immense willow visible at the center, its golden leaves cascading like metallic rain. The spiral mark his mother's memory had left throbbed with each step, matching the pulse of his heart.

The ordered rows yielded secrets as they passed. A tree dripping with fruits that glowed from within, its bark smooth and pale like skin. The scent of herbs and healing hanging heavy around it.

"A healer," Yrsa said. "She saved hundreds before succumbing to the very plague she fought."

Another tree nearby grew impossibly fast, trunk visibly stretching skyward even as they watched. Its branches reached with an eagerness that felt deliberate, leaves unfurling and flowers blooming in moments rather than seasons.

"A child," Leif whispered, touching the rapidly growing sapling. "Taken too soon, now growing as he never could."

The wrongness of it—life emerging from death, trees sprouting from flesh—scraped against Asvarr's warrior instincts. Bodies were meant to burn on pyres, returning to smoke and ash. This preservation, this transformation... it felt like defiance of natural order.

"Your discomfort shows on your face," Yrsa observed. "You wonder if this is abomination."

Asvarr touched the spiral marking on his palm, feeling its warmth. "A warrior should return to the sky through fire," he said. "These are trapped between worlds—neither living nor truly dead."

"You misunderstand." Yrsa gestured toward a tree with black bark and white flowers shaped like stars. "They are not trapped. They are transformed. Death is continuation in another form, it is not the ending."

A low hum filled the air as they moved deeper into the grove, vibrations that Asvarr felt in his transformed flesh rather than heard with his ears. The bark patterns across his chest tightened in response.

"The anchor calls to you," Leif said, pointing toward the golden willow at the center. "It knows your purpose."

Their path took them past trees reflecting every manner of life and death. A massive oak with branches bearing shields instead of leaves—a chieftain surrounded by his sworn warriors. A slender birch whose bark flickered with script-like symbols—a poet or skald whose words remained even when flesh failed. A twisted pine whose needles chimed like tiny bells in the windless air—a musician whose songs continued beyond death.

"How are they chosen for this place?" Asvarr asked, stepping over roots that curled like grasping fingers.

"They aren't chosen," Yrsa replied. "All come here in some form. Those you see manifested chose transformation over dissolution. Others surrendered their essence to the wider pattern."

"Like memories surrendered to the Root," Asvarr murmured, understanding flowing through him. The Root didn't simply take—it transformed, preserved in altered state what would otherwise vanish completely.

Near the center, they encountered a grove-within-the-grove—seven trees arranged in a circle, their branches intertwining overhead to form a living dome. Each tree bore different fruit, and the air beneath them smelled of mead and smoke.

"Your clan," Leif said softly. "The warriors of your steading."

Asvarr's heart clenched. The spiral mark on his palm flared hot, and the bark patterns across his chest contracted painfully. These trees—somehow he knew them, recognized them despite having no faces, no voices, no names he could recall. The knowledge lived in his blood rather than his mind.

"Hakon," he whispered, touching the largest tree, its bark scarred with patterns like battle-wounds. "And Torfa." A slender tree with branches that curved like a shield-maiden's bow.

Each tree pulsed with golden light at his touch, sap weeping from knots in the bark. He moved among them, touching each in turn, speaking names that came to him unbidden. Connections formed through his transformed flesh—the bark on his chest resonating with the essence preserved in these trees.

"They remember you," Yrsa said. "Even if you can't fully remember them."

"They're truly here?" Asvarr asked, his voice rough with emotion he thought long surrendered to the Root. "Their essence?"

"More than essence," Leif answered. "They chose this rather than the void or the halls of their gods. They wait for purpose to return."

Asvarr drew his bronze sword, the golden veins within the blade flaring in response to the energy flowing through the grove. He dropped to one knee in the center of the circle, driving the tip into the soft earth between the seven trees of his clan.

"I carry your purpose," he declared, the ancient words coming to him through blood-memory. "Your battle lives through me. Your vengeance becomes restoration."

The trees shuddered, branches swaying though no wind stirred the grove. Sap flowed more freely, running down the bark to pool around the roots. Where droplets touched his skin, they sank beneath the surface, joining with his transformed flesh.

"They strengthen you," Yrsa observed. "Their choice affirms yours."

Standing, Asvarr sheathed his sword and touched the spiral mark his mother's memory had left. The trees of his clan—the physical manifestation of their transformed essence—had recognized him, reinforced his purpose. His memory might be fractured, hollowed by the Root's hunger, but connections remained in blood and bone that transcended conscious recall.

"We should continue," Leif urged, pointing beyond the clan-circle toward the massive golden willow at the grove's center. "The anchor grows restless."

They left the circle of clan-trees behind, moving toward the heart of the grove. The ordered rows gave way to wild growth—trees of every description intermingled rather than arranged by type or kind. Their branches formed a canopy so dense that the light changed, filtering through countless leaves to create a cathedral-like illumination of greens and golds.

"Why does the pattern change?" Asvarr asked, noting the shift from order to chaos.

"The outer grove is maintained by the Guardian," Yrsa explained. "But the heart grows according to its own will—a reflection of the anchor's nature."

"And what nature is that?"

"Memory," Yrsa said. "The Root Anchor of Memory slumbers here, preserving what would otherwise be lost. Unlike your flame anchor, which burns with active energy, this one receives, stores, transforms."

The ground beneath their feet changed from soil to a carpet of moss so thick it felt like walking on fresh wool. With each step, tiny flowers bloomed and died in their footprints—complete life cycles compressed into moments.

"Why am I drawn to this anchor if I'm flame-blooded?" Asvarr asked, touching the bark patterns on his chest. "Shouldn't Brynja be the one called here?"

Yrsa's expression darkened. "The memory anchor responds to all bloodlines," she said. "It preserves without preference. But your path has intersected with it for purpose beyond mere binding."

"What purpose?"

"That remains to be discovered." Yrsa pointed ahead, where the canopy opened to reveal the massive golden willow they'd been approaching since entering the grove. "The answer waits beneath the Tree of Remembrance."

They stepped into a perfect circular clearing dominated by the golden willow. Its trunk, thicker than ten men with linked arms, wasn't formed of ordinary wood but countless smaller trees that had grown together, their individual forms still visible within the greater whole. Thousands, perhaps tens of thousands of lives, merged into a single entity. Its roots spread visibly across the clearing, some as thick as a man's waist, creating a network that pulsed with subtle light.

"Gods," Asvarr breathed, the scale of it striking him with physical force. "How many are preserved here?"

"All who chose transformation," Leif answered, his eyes reflecting the golden light of the willow's leaves. "The Tree of Remembrance holds what the anchor preserves."

Beneath the spreading canopy of golden leaves, a still pool reflected the willow's majesty. Unlike ordinary water, this liquid had the consistency of sap—thick, amber-hued, rippling with internal currents that followed no natural pattern.

Yrsa knelt beside the pool, trailing her fingers through the surface. The liquid clung to her skin momentarily before flowing back into the perfect circle.

"The memory-sap," she explained. "Drawn up from the slumbering anchor through the roots of those who came before. To reach the anchor itself, we must pass through memory."

"Through the pool?" Asvarr asked, eyeing the thick liquid with suspicion.

"Through what it contains," Yrsa corrected. "The sap is merely the threshold. The anchor lies beneath the roots, accessible only to those who navigate the memories stored within."

The spiral mark on Asvarr's palm burned suddenly, bright pain lancing up his arm. At the same moment, the bark patterns across his chest contracted, golden veins pulsing in rhythm with his racing heart.

"The anchor recognizes you," Leif said, excitement rising in his childlike voice. "It knows what you carry."

Asvarr stared into the golden pool, watching images form and dissolve in the swirling sap—faces, places, moments from countless lives preserved through transformation. The vastness of it—the accumulated memory of perhaps every soul that had ever lived and died—threatened to overwhelm him.

"What must I do?" he asked, voice dropping to a whisper.

"Offer what remains most precious to you," Yrsa said solemnly. "The anchor demands tribute before granting access."

Asvarr touched the bark patterns covering his chest, feeling the golden veins pulse beneath his fingers. He'd already surrendered rage, identity, and his earliest memories. What remained that held value enough to serve as tribute?

The spiral mark his mother's memory had left flared warm against his palm, as if in answer.

"No," he said firmly. "I won't surrender that. It's all I have left of her."

"The anchor doesn't require surrender," Leif said, his golden eyes fixed on the memory-sap. "Only sharing. What you offer returns multiplied."

Steeling himself, Asvarr knelt beside the pool. The scent rising from the memory-sap reminded him of honey mead and forge-smoke, of blood and iron, of every fragrance that defined human existence compressed into a single breath.

***

He pressed his marked palm against the surface of the pool, the spiral pattern sinking into the golden liquid. Images flashed through his mind too rapidly to process—a flood of memories not his own pouring through the connection.

"Blood calls to blood," Leif chanted, voice taking on the resonance of ritual. "Memory joins with memory. What was forgotten returns transformed."

The memory-sap surged upward, twining around Asvarr's wrist like a living vine. He tried to pull back, but the golden liquid held fast, drawing him inexorably toward the surface of the pool.

"Don't fight it," Yrsa cautioned. "Accept what it offers or receive nothing."

Relaxing his arm required conscious effort, every instinct screaming to break free. The memory-sap climbed higher, past his elbow, coating his transformed skin with a golden sheath.

Through the connection, a voice spoke directly into his mind—neither male nor female, neither young nor old, but somehow all possibilities at once.

"Flame-blood comes to Memory's heart," it said. "Seeking binding yet already bound. What tribute does the Warden offer to the guardian of what was?"

Asvarr closed his eyes, focusing on the spiral mark his mother's memory had left. The pattern felt warm against his palm even submerged in memory-sap.

"I offer connection," he responded silently. "The thread between who I was and who I'm becoming."

The memory-sap tightened around his arm, a pressure that bordered on pain without crossing that threshold.

"Connection requires anchoring," the voice replied. "Name what anchors you, Warden of Flame."

The answer came to him without thought. "Those I've lost anchor me to purpose. Those who remain anchor me to humanity."

The memory-sap surged suddenly, engulfing Asvarr to the shoulder. Through the golden sheath, he saw the bark patterns on his chest flare with matching light, the transformed flesh recognizing its kin.

"Worthy tribute," the voice acknowledged. "The path opens."

The surface of the pool rippled outward from Asvarr's submerged arm, waves forming concentric circles that expanded to the edge before rebounding inward. Where the returning waves met at the center, the memory-sap parted, revealing a staircase of roots spiraling downward into darkness.

"The way to the anchor," Yrsa breathed, awe evident in her voice. "The Root of Memory allows your passage."

The memory-sap released Asvarr's arm, flowing back into the pool while leaving a thin golden residue that sank beneath his skin, joining with the bark patterns and transformed flesh. The connection with the voice faded, leaving behind a sense of acceptance—of recognition between kindred essences.

Leif bounced on his toes, pointing excitedly at the spiraling staircase. "Down and down to the heart of memory," he said, voice shifting between childlike wonder and ancient knowledge. "Where what was meets what could be."

Asvarr stood, flexing his arm where the memory-sap had gripped him. The residue had left a pattern of interlocking spirals from wrist to shoulder, similar to the mark his mother's memory had created yet distinct—more complex, less personal.

"What awaits below?" he asked Yrsa.

"The slumbering anchor," she replied. "Different from your flame anchor, which burns with active energy. This one preserves, transforms, connects—the aspect of Yggdrasil that maintained the history of all realms."

"This is why the memory realm exists," Leif added, his golden eyes reflecting the shimmering pool. "The Root preserved what would otherwise be lost when the Tree shattered."

Asvarr faced the spiraling staircase, steeling himself for what lay beneath. The third anchor awaited—different from the first two, yet essential to the pattern. With each binding, he lost more of himself while gaining connection to something beyond individual identity.

"I'll go alone," he decided, touching the spiral mark on his palm. "The anchor called to me specifically."

"No," Yrsa countered immediately. "The memory anchor is too vast to approach without guides. We accompany you to the threshold, at least."

"And I go all the way," Leif declared with childish stubbornness. "I belong to the in-between, where memory meets potential."

Asvarr nodded, accepting their counsel. The spiral staircase beckoned, root-steps leading down to the heart of all memory. What waited for him there? What would this binding demand, and what would remain of Asvarr afterward?

The spiral mark on his palm warmed reassuringly. His mother's final gift—an anchor against dissolution, preserving connection when memory failed.

"Stay close," he told his companions, drawing his bronze sword. The golden veins within the blade pulsed in perfect rhythm with the patterns across his chest and the new markings on his arm.

Taking a deep breath, Asvarr stepped onto the root-staircase and began to descend toward the slumbering heart of memory.

***

The root-staircase spiraled downward, each step a living vein of wood thick as Asvarr's forearm. The walls of the passage—if they could be called walls—consisted of countless intertwined smaller roots that pulsed with subtle golden light. The air grew thick with the scent of sap and soil, of growth and decay merged into a single fragrance that seemed older than the world itself.

Asvarr led the way, one hand on his bronze sword, the other tracing the spiral pattern his mother's memory had left. The mark warmed beneath his touch, providing comfort as they descended into unknown depths. Behind him, Leif hummed a tuneless melody that echoed strangely through the passage, while Yrsa moved in contemplative silence, her crystal pendant casting blue-white light that mingled with the golden glow of the surrounding roots.

"How far down does this go?" Asvarr asked when the staircase showed no sign of ending.

"Distance loses meaning here," Yrsa replied. "We aren't traveling through space alone, but through memory and time."

Something skittered through the root walls, a disturbance that sent ripples of light flowing upward along their path. Asvarr tensed, hand tightening on his sword hilt.

"The anchor knows we approach," Leif said, voice shifting to that unsettling adult resonance. "It dreams of us even in slumber."

Finally, the stairs emptied into a vast spherical chamber hollowed from the earth. Roots lined the walls in complex geometric patterns—spirals within spirals, whorls that reminded Asvarr of the mark on his palm. At the chamber's center stood what appeared to be a tree of pure crystal, its trunk no wider than Asvarr's waist but branching outward to touch the chamber walls in all directions. Unlike the golden willow above, this tree appeared dormant—transparent, unmoving, with a faint golden glow emanating from deep within.

"The Root Anchor of Memory," Yrsa whispered, her voice filled with reverence. "Asleep since the shattering."

Asvarr approached the crystal tree, drawn by a resonance that vibrated through the transformed parts of his flesh. The bark patterns across his chest pulsed in response, golden veins flaring with sympathetic light. Unlike his first anchor, which had burned with fierce energy that demanded control, this one slumbered peacefully, its power turned inward rather than projecting outward.

"Why is it shaped like this?" he asked, circling the crystal trunk. "My flame anchor was a root fragment, not a complete structure."

"Each anchor manifests differently," Yrsa explained, staying at the chamber's edge. "The flame anchor burns, consumes, transforms. The memory anchor preserves, contains, protects. Form follows function."

Leif skipped forward to stand beside the crystal tree, placing his small hand against the transparent trunk. Where his fingers touched, ripples of golden light spread outward, as if the anchor responded to his presence.

"It remembers everything," the boy said. "Every face, every voice, every moment that was or might have been. This is why the memory realm exists. When the Tree shattered, the Root preserved what would otherwise be lost."

Asvarr studied the crystal trunk, noticing how the light within it moved in currents and eddies, like liquid gold flowing through transparent channels. At the tree's core, a sphere of concentrated light pulsed in a rhythm he recognized—the same cadence as his own heart, matched with the patterns across his chest.

"I've never seen anything like this," he murmured.

"Few have," Yrsa said. "Most who seek the anchors look for power to wield. The memory anchor gives nothing to those who come to take, only to those who come to understand."

The spiral mark on Asvarr's palm throbbed suddenly, sharp pain lancing up his arm. At the same moment, the dormant anchor flared brighter, golden light surging through its crystalline branches.

"It recognizes your bloodline," Yrsa said. "And the mother-memory you carry."

Asvarr approached the crystal trunk, drawn by a compulsion he couldn't name. This anchor was different from his flame anchor—receptive rather than active, feminine rather than masculine in energy. Yet it called to him with undeniable force, recognizing something in his transformed flesh that transcended bloodline divisions.

"Why does it call to me?" he asked. "I'm flame-blooded, not root-tender."

"Perhaps because you've already begun walking the third path." Yrsa moved closer, her pendant pulsing with blue-white light that complemented the anchor's golden glow. "Between surrender and dominance, between root and flame. The memory anchor responds to potential, to balance."

Asvarr extended his marked palm toward the crystal trunk, hesitating just before contact. The first anchor binding had been violent—a battle of wills that required him to subjugate the flame essence. What would this binding demand? What part of himself would he lose in the exchange?

"What happens if I touch it?" he asked.

"It will test you," Yrsa replied. "Through remembrance. It will search your memories—what remains of them—to determine worthiness."

"I've lost so many," Asvarr said. "What if there's not enough left to judge?"

"The anchor doesn't seek quantity but quality," Yrsa explained. "Your understanding of what memories mean, how they've shaped you. This is why the memory anchor requires vulnerability rather than strength—a willingness to be known completely."

Leif bounced on his toes, excitement written across his childlike features. "I want to watch the binding!" he exclaimed. "I've never seen one before!"

Yrsa placed a restraining hand on the boy's shoulder. "This isn't a performance, child. It's a sacred communion." She looked at Asvarr. "We should withdraw to the chamber's edge. The binding is between you and the anchor alone."

They retreated, leaving Asvarr facing the crystal tree in solitude. The golden light within the trunk pulsed faster now, responding to his proximity. The bark patterns across his chest tightened, a reminder of how far he'd already transformed since beginning this journey.

Steeling himself, Asvarr pressed his marked palm against the crystal trunk.

***

Connection formed instantly—a bridge between his consciousness and the slumbering anchor. Unlike the flame anchor, which had forced entry into his mind with burning intensity, the memory anchor welcomed him, drawing him gently inward. Through the crystal surface, he felt a pulse like a heartbeat, steady and ancient.

Images flowed into his mind—memories, but not his own. He saw the grove from above, a vast pattern of trees arranged in concentric circles that formed a massive sigil when viewed from this perspective. He saw the memory-sap flowing beneath the earth in channels that matched the geometry of stars overhead. He saw the nine realms connected by the branches of Yggdrasil before the shattering, and felt the moment when the Tree broke—the desperate effort to preserve what would otherwise be lost.

The anchor showed him how it had gathered the memories of countless beings at the moment of shattering, drawing them into itself for safekeeping. Memories became seeds, and seeds became trees—the Grove of the Blooming Dead, a physical manifestation of the anchor's preservation effort.

"This is why the memory realm exists," a voice whispered directly into his mind—the same voice he'd heard through the memory-sap pool. "We are the keepers of what was, the guardians against oblivion."

Asvarr saw how the memory anchor functioned, transforming them, preserving their essence while allowing their form to evolve. The whispers he'd heard in falling leaves, the essence contained in the grove's trees, the knowledge stored in the memory-sap—all manifestations of the anchor's power.

"You seek binding," the voice continued. "Yet you are already bound. Flame marks you, Root claims you. What remains that you would offer to Memory?"

The question resonated through Asvarr's transformed flesh. What did he have left to give? The flame anchor had taken his rage, the communion with the Root had claimed his earliest memories, and his quest had cost him his identity as a simple warrior seeking vengeance. What remained that held value enough for binding?

The answer came from somewhere deeper than conscious thought. "Understanding," he replied silently. "I offer my understanding of what memories mean—how they shape purpose even when forgotten."

The anchor's presence deepened within him, probing the truth of his words. Asvarr felt it touching the hollowed spaces in his mind, the voids where memories had once resided. Through the connection, he understood what the anchor sought, the meaning he'd derived from them, the lessons learned, the wisdom gained.

"Show me," the voice commanded.

Asvarr opened himself completely, surrendering the walls that guarded his inner thoughts. He showed the anchor how he'd transformed the pain of losing his clan into purpose, how he'd evolved beyond simple vengeance to seek restoration. He revealed how the absence of memory had forced him to focus on present choice rather than past obligation, freeing him from the constraints of who he'd been to become who he needed to be.

The anchor's presence withdrew slightly, considering. "You've learned what few Wardens discover until too late," the voice observed. "That memory serves purpose, not defines it. That identity transcends recollection."

Golden light flowed from the crystal trunk into Asvarr's palm, following the spiral pattern his mother's memory had left. The warmth spread up his arm, across his chest, merging with the bark patterns and transformed flesh. Unlike the burning invasion of the flame anchor, this binding felt like completion—pieces fitting together that had always been meant to join.

"The binding forms," the voice acknowledged. "Through recognition. Memory accepts you, Asvarr Flame-Bearer, though you walk a path between bloodlines."

The crystal trunk pulsed with intensifying light, brightening until Asvarr had to close his eyes against the glare. The chamber filled with golden radiance that penetrated even closed eyelids, accompanied by a sound like crystalline chimes ringing in perfect harmony.

When the light subsided and Asvarr opened his eyes, the crystal tree had transformed. Where before it had been transparent and dormant, now it glowed with internal fire, its trunk swirled with patterns of gold and silver that matched the marks on Asvarr's flesh. The branches reached with new vitality, leaves of translucent crystal forming along their length.

"The second binding is complete," Yrsa said from the chamber's edge, her voice tight with controlled emotion. "The memory anchor awakens after nine cycles of slumber."

Leif clapped his hands excitedly. "It's so pretty now!" he exclaimed, childlike wonder overtaking the ancient knowledge that sometimes spoke through him.

Asvarr stepped back from the transformed anchor, inspecting the changes to his own flesh. The bark patterns had expanded, now covering his chest and back with intricate whorls that incorporated both the flame spirals of his first binding and new crystalline structures that reflected the memory anchor. Where the patterns crossed his heart, they formed a perfect replica of the transformation seed that had appeared on his palm—a spiral tree with roots and branches equally extended.

"What did you give it?" Yrsa asked, approaching cautiously. "What did the binding take?"

Asvarr searched within himself, probing the hollowed spaces of his memory. To his surprise, nothing new had vanished—no fresh voids where recollections had once lived. Instead, his perception of those spaces had changed. The emptiness no longer felt like loss but like possibility—containers waiting to be filled with new experience.

"Understanding," he answered. "It took my understanding of memory's purpose and gave it form."

"And what did you receive in return?" Yrsa pressed, studying him with narrowed eyes.

Before Asvarr could answer, something solid formed in his palm—a crystalline fruit shaped like a miniature version of the anchor tree. It pulsed with golden light, warm against his skin.

"The Remembrance Key," Yrsa identified it, awe in her voice. "The memory anchor's token. With it, you can navigate the paths between memories, find what was lost, restore what was forgotten."

Asvarr examined the crystal fruit, feeling its resonance with both his transformed flesh and the awakened anchor. Unlike the tokens from his previous bindings, this one felt complete in itself—a tool meant for active use rather than merely a symbol of accomplishment.

"Can it restore my own memories?" he asked, hope flaring briefly.

Yrsa shook her head. "What is surrendered cannot be reclaimed in the same form. But it can help you find echoes, reflections, fragments preserved in the pattern even when lost to your mind."

The chamber trembled suddenly, dust and small fragments of root falling from the ceiling. The crystal tree's light flickered, stabilized, then brightened.

"The awakening disturbs the grove," Yrsa warned. "The five will have felt it. We must leave quickly."

"Where to?" Asvarr asked, tucking the Remembrance Key into his belt pouch alongside the tokens from his previous bindings.

"The path ahead flows toward Alfheim," Leif said, pointing upward. "Where starlight meets memory, where the third anchor waits."

Another tremor shook the chamber, stronger than the first. Larger chunks of root and earth rained down, forcing them to shield their heads.

"The memory anchor's awakening renews connections severed at the shattering," Yrsa explained, ducking as a root fragment narrowly missed her. "The pattern responds with growing pains."

They hurried toward the spiraling staircase, but found the passage blocked by fallen roots and soil. Asvarr drew his bronze sword, the golden veins within the blade matching the patterns of the awakened anchor.

"We need another way out," he said, scanning the chamber walls for alternative passages.

Leif tugged at his arm, pointing to where a new opening had formed near the crystal tree. "Through there," he urged. "The anchor creates a path."

The opening pulsed with golden light, expanding and contracting like a heartbeat. Through it, Asvarr glimpsed what appeared to be a forest glade dappled with starlight, though they stood deep underground.

"A shortcut through memory," Yrsa identified it. "The anchor's gift. It will take us beyond the grove, away from those who would sense your binding."

Another violent tremor decided the matter. Larger sections of the ceiling collapsed, threatening to bury them beneath the chamber. The crystal tree stood unaffected at the center, its light steady despite the destruction around it.

"Move!" Asvarr commanded, pushing Leif toward the pulsing doorway. The boy darted through without hesitation, vanishing into the starlit glade beyond.

Yrsa followed, pausing at the threshold to look back at Asvarr. "Two anchors bound, three remain," she said. "With each binding, you become less human but more essential to the pattern. Remember your purpose when memory itself begins to fail."

She stepped through, leaving Asvarr alone with the awakened anchor. The chamber continued to collapse around him, the destruction accelerating as the tremors intensified.

Asvarr touched the transformation seed mark on his palm, feeling its connection to the crystal tree. This binding had been different, a recognition of shared purpose. The memory anchor had joined with him, accepting what he offered without demanding more.

"Thank you," he said to the awakened anchor, a gesture of respect he hadn't considered offering to his flame anchor.

The crystal tree's light pulsed once in acknowledgment, branches swaying though no wind stirred the chamber. As Asvarr turned toward the threshold, a single crystalline leaf detached from the nearest branch, floating down to land at his feet. He picked it up, finding it identical to the Remembrance Key but smaller, simpler.

"A token within a token," he murmured, tucking the leaf alongside the crystal fruit in his belt pouch.

***

With a final glance at the awakened anchor, Asvarr stepped through the pulsing doorway. The golden light enveloped him, and for a moment he felt himself stretched across space and time, existing simultaneously at multiple points along his journey. Then reality solidified, and he stood in a forest clearing beneath an impossible sky—star-patterns unlike any he'd seen in Midgard swirling overhead in complex geometries that matched the spiral on his palm.

Yrsa and Leif waited beside a pool of water so still it perfectly reflected the celestial display above. The air smelled of night-blooming flowers and something metallic, like forge-smoke but colder, sharper.

"Alfheim," Yrsa announced. "The realm of starlight and memory."

Leif bounced on his toes, pointing excitedly at the sky. "The third anchor waits where starlight touches the ground," he said. "But first we need the others."

"Others?" Asvarr asked.

"The other Wardens," Yrsa clarified. "Brynja Earth-Healer. Svala Storm-Speaker. The memory anchor has awakened connections to help you find them."

Asvarr touched the Remembrance Key through his belt pouch, feeling its warmth even through the leather. Two anchors bound, three remaining. With each binding, pieces of his human self fell away while something else grew in their place—transformation rather than mere loss.

The spiral mark his mother's memory had left throbbed reassuringly on his palm. Whatever he became through these bindings, something essential remained—purpose that transcended memory, identity that survived transformation.

"How do we find them?" he asked, watching the star-patterns shift overhead in configurations that tugged at his consciousness.

Yrsa pointed to the reflection pool, where the surface had begun to ripple though no wind disturbed it. Images formed in the disturbance—Brynja with her wooden arm amid a forest of thorns; another figure, female and wreathed in frost, atop a mountain peak.

"The memory anchor shows the way," she said. "Now that two anchors speak through you, the others will hear the call."

Overhead, a constellation shifted suddenly, stars rearranging into the unmistakable outline of a spear. A warning, though Asvarr couldn't say how he knew this.

"We're being watched," he whispered, hand moving to his sword hilt. "Something in the stars sees us."

"The Ashfather has eyes everywhere," Yrsa confirmed, her pendant flaring with protective blue light. "Even in Alfheim. We must move quickly, find shelter before night deepens."

Asvarr studied the alien sky, the unfamiliar forest, the reflection pool showing distant Wardens. The pattern expanded around him, connections forming between anchors and bloodlines that had remained separated across nine cycles of breaking and binding. His role grew clearer with each step, restoring balance and awakening anchors to their original purpose.

He drew his bronze sword, the golden veins within the blade glowing with increased brilliance in this realm of starlight. The blade hummed in his hand, resonating with both the flame and memory anchors now bound within his transformed flesh.

"Lead on," he told Yrsa, determination hardening his voice. "The third anchor waits, and apparently, so do others who share this path."

The stars continued their silent observation as they left the clearing, moving deeper into the alien forest where silver trees grew in mathematical patterns that echoed the constellations above. Behind them, the reflection pool stilled, its surface once again perfectly mirroring the spear-shaped constellation that tracked their progress across Alfheim's strange landscape.

CHAPTER 20

ANCHOR OF THORNS

The golden willow's roots pulsed beneath Asvarr's palm. He knelt before the massive trunk formed of countless smaller trees, their bark fused into intricate patterns like frozen rivers joining a sea. The Grove of the Blooming Dead stretched around him, countless transformed souls rising from burial mounds in arboreal rebirth. In the hushed twilight, only the whisper of golden leaves filled the silence.

"This anchor differs from your first," Yrsa said, her voice hushed with reverence. "It seeks understanding."

Asvarr's fingers traced the willow's bark, feeling the warmth beneath. Unlike the burning vitality of his first anchor, this one slumbered, waiting rather than demanding. The memory-sap that had marked his arm with spiral patterns tingled, calling to something within the dormant anchor.

"How do I bind with it?" he asked, the bark-like patches on his skin resonating with the willow's presence.

Yrsa crouched beside him, her crystal pendant catching the dim light that filtered through the golden canopy. "The flame anchor required strength to dominate. This one requires vulnerability—the willingness to surrender rather than control."

Leif circled the trunk, his small fingers tracing patterns in the bark. "The way down is through the heart," he said, pointing to a fold in the willow's trunk that resembled a doorway.

The boy's golden-flecked eyes met Asvarr's, and for a moment, the child-like facade slipped, revealing something ancient. "The memory of the Tree is a wound that never healed. To bind it, you must offer understanding, not just remembrance."

Asvarr pressed his palm more firmly against the bark. The spiral mark his mother's memory had left throbbed in rhythm with the willow's pulses. He'd fought so hard to retain pieces of himself through each transformation, guarding memories like precious jewels. The thought of surrendering more made his chest tighten.

"What exactly must I surrender?" he asked, the words tight in his throat.

"Not memories themselves," Yrsa said, "but your understanding of them—the meaning you've derived from your experiences." Her weathered hand covered his. "This anchor preserves. It does not consume like the first."

Asvarr closed his eyes. Since the destruction of his clan, vengeance had been his compass, his purpose. Each memory of loss had fed that fire. What would remain if he surrendered the meaning he'd built around them?

The fold in the willow's trunk widened, revealing a narrow passage spiraling downward. Golden sap seeped from the edges, forming droplets that floated upward against gravity.

"I'll lose myself," Asvarr whispered.

Leif shook his head. "You'll find a different self." The boy's voice carried that unsettling resonance that hinted at his true nature. "The Root remembers everything, even what we lose."

Asvarr stood, drawing his bronze sword. The golden veins within the metal pulsed in time with the willow's rhythm, recognizing kin. "How do I begin?"

Yrsa's crystal pendant brightened. "The ritual requires grief and sacrifice. Speak your understanding to the Root—what the memories mean to you. Then release that meaning, allowing the Root to transform your understanding."

Asvarr sheathed his sword and stepped toward the opening. The spiral marking on his palm burned, and the bark-patterns across his chest shifted like leaves in wind. The golden sap droplets drifted toward him, touching his skin and dissolving into the transformed flesh.

"I'll wait here," Yrsa said. "The chamber below is for you alone."

Leif plucked a golden leaf from the lowest branch and pressed it into Asvarr's hand. "For when the memories become too much," he said, then stepped back alongside Yrsa.

Asvarr ducked through the opening, following the spiral path downward. The walls of the passage were smooth, polished by countless years of sap flow. They pulsed with soft light that responded to his presence, brightening as he descended.

The path opened into a spherical chamber hollowed from earth and root. Its walls were lined with geometric patterns of intertwined roots that writhed slowly, restructuring themselves with each heartbeat. At the chamber's center stood a crystal tree no taller than Asvarr himself—transparent and dormant, its branches perfectly motionless.

Within the crystal, a golden core pulsed like a caged heartbeat, waiting.

When Asvarr approached, the crystal tree resonated, sending vibrations through the floor that traveled up his legs. Unlike the flame anchor's aggressive heat, this energy was cool, patient, ancient. It passed through him like a current, stirring memories.

Mother's voice singing by the hearth. Father's calloused hand on his shoulder. Hakon's booming laugh during the raid. Torfa's last stand, shield raised against inevitable death.

"I remember them," Asvarr said, his voice echoing in the chamber. "I've held their memories to fuel my vengeance. Every face, every voice I can still recall has been a weapon to sharpen my hatred."

The crystal tree's response was subtle—a slight brightening of its golden core, listening.

Asvarr circled the anchor, watching how the light played through its translucent branches. "My understanding of these memories has been single-minded. Loss became purpose. Grief became fuel." He stopped, pressing his hand against the cool crystal. "Vengeance gave structure to chaos."

The crystal warmed beneath his palm, no longer cool but neutral, receptive. Within its depths, the golden core pulsed faster.

"What do you want from me?" Asvarr asked.

A voice replied directly into his mind, bypassing his ears. It had no gender, no age—merely presence, ancient and measured.

Understanding is more than purpose. Memory is more than weapon.

Asvarr jerked his hand back, but the voice continued, filling the chamber.

Show the fullness of your understanding, not merely the edge you've honed.

He paced the chamber, the bark patterns on his skin illuminated by the crystal's light. The meaning he'd derived from his memories—was it truly so narrow? Vengeance had been a shield against despair, a path forward when all paths were ashes. But there was more, hidden beneath layers of rage and determination.

"They lived," he said finally, returning to the crystal tree. "Before they died, before they became memories, they lived." His voice broke. "I survived because they taught me how."

The crystal responded, branches shifting slightly.

"My understanding..." Asvarr swallowed hard. "My understanding is incomplete. I've shaped their memories into weapons, ignoring the fullness of who they were. What they gave me was life, not just purpose."

He pressed both palms against the crystal, feeling the cool surface warm beneath his touch. "I offer my understanding, flawed as it is. And I surrender the meaning I've built around these memories."

The golden core within the crystal flared, and a wordless question formed in Asvarr's mind: *What meaning would you create anew?*

This was the genuine sacrifice, willingly surrendering it without knowing what would take its place. Asvarr hesitated, his mind racing through possibilities. Without vengeance as his compass, what path would he follow? Without rage as his strength, what would sustain him?

The memory of his mother's words returned: *"Your survival is a responsibility to live well."*

"I would create meaning through restoration," he said. "Through connection."

The crystal tree shuddered, its branches beginning to move. Asvarr kept his palms pressed against it, even as heat built beneath his touch. Unlike the first binding, which had demanded dominance, this one formed through recognition—anchor and vessel acknowledging each other.

"By blood and oath, horn and blade," Asvarr whispered the ritual words. "I bind myself to you, Root of Memory."

The crystal tree's surface liquefied beneath his palms, flowing around his fingers like living glass. The golden core expanded, ribbons of light extending through the branches until the entire tree glowed from within.

The voice returned, stronger now.

The binding forms through recognition. What is freely given cannot be taken.

The liquefied crystal flowed up Asvarr's arms, covering the bark patterns with translucent layers that hardened into geometric designs. The familiar burning pain of transformation spread through his chest as the mark expanded, incorporating the new patterns.

Asvarr gritted his teeth against the sensation. This binding hurt differently than the first, a profound ache, as though his very core was being restructured.

Images flashed through his mind too quickly to grasp—fragments from countless lives preserved by the Root. They weren't his memories, but they touched his own, reshaping his understanding of what memory meant. The past transformed in the act of remembering.

The crystal tree shimmered, its form becoming fluid. The branches extended, thinned, twisted into more complex patterns. The trunk elongated and narrowed. When the transformation completed, what remained was no longer crystal but a living tree with a trunk of gold and silver patterns, leaves that glowed with internal fire.

In the sudden silence, Asvarr removed his hands from the transformed anchor. His skin tingled where the crystal had touched him, new markings extending from his chest to cover his back in intricate patterns. He felt changed, expanded, his perception of memory itself transformed.

At his feet lay a small crystal fruit that had fallen from the transformed tree—a perfect miniature of the anchor's original form. When he lifted it, the crystal warmed in his palm, revealing depths that shifted like liquid.

"The Remembrance Key," Asvarr murmured, somehow knowing its name.

The transformed anchor tree rustled its glowing leaves, and a second token fell—a crystalline leaf that drifted down to land beside his foot. Asvarr picked it up, holding both tokens.

A token within a token, the voice explained. *The key to restore what was forgotten. The leaf to find what was lost.*

The chamber shuddered. The geometric patterns on the walls shifted, rearranging themselves into new configurations. The binding was complete, but its effects were still propagating through the memory realm.

Asvarr tucked both tokens into his belt pouch. His fingers brushed the verdant anchor seed from his second binding, which pulsed with recognition.

"What now?" he asked.

A section of the chamber wall parted, revealing a passage different from the one he'd entered through. Beyond it, starlight glimmered—not the familiar stars of Midgard, but impossible patterns that matched the spiral designs now etched into his transformed flesh.

Find the others, the voice said. *The flame must not walk alone.*

Before Asvarr could ask more, a reflection formed in the polished wall, Brynja, her wooden arm now covered in flowering vines. Beside her stood a slender figure wreathed in mist that he somehow knew was Svala, bearer of the Frostmark.

Other Wardens walk the paths. The third anchor awaits in Alfheim, where starlight touches the ground.

The reflection faded, leaving Asvarr with a clear directive. He had bound two anchors. Three remained. And he would need help for what came next.

Asvarr took a deep breath, steadying himself against the chamber wall as the full impact of the binding settled into his transformed flesh. The memory anchor had changed him by reshaping his understanding. Vengeance no longer seemed as vital as restoration. The past was not just a wound to avenge but a foundation to rebuild upon.

***

He stepped toward the new passage, the Remembrance Key warm against his hip. Alfheim awaited, and with it, the other Wardens he must find before seeking the third anchor.

Behind him, the transformed tree's leaves rustled with satisfaction. The binding was complete. The Root of Memory had awakened.

The chamber trembled. Asvarr stumbled backward from the transformed anchor tree, catching himself against the wall as golden cracks spiderwebbed across the ceiling. Dust and fragments of root rained down. The entire chamber—no, the entire realm—shuddered like a struck bell.

The Remembrance Key burned against his hip, and the crystalline leaf in his hand pulsed with urgent light. Both tokens resonated with the transformed anchor, sending waves of energy through Asvarr's flesh. The bark-patterns across his chest and back, now overlaid with crystalline designs, flared with golden fire.

"What's happening?" he shouted, though no one remained in the chamber to answer.

The anchor tree's response came in waves of sensation rather than words. *Balance shifts. Memory awakens. Matter remembers what it was.*

Asvarr staggered toward the passage that had opened in the chamber wall. The floor rippled beneath his feet, no longer solid but a memory of solidity. With each step, his boots sank slightly before the surface remembered its purpose and firmed again. The passage walls flexed and twisted, the geometric patterns upon them rearranging themselves into new configurations that told tales of ancient growth and forgotten winters.

He clambered upward through the writhing passage. The golden sap droplets that had drifted upward now fell like rain, striking his skin and bursting into fragments of light. Each droplet carried memories—sharp flashes of other lives, other worlds, other cycles of breaking and binding.

***

The passage's end yawned ahead, but what lay beyond wasn't the Grove of the Blooming Dead. The familiar landscape had transformed. Trees no longer grew from burial mounds; they *were* the memories of the dead, their bark peeling away to reveal faces, their branches moving like limbs, their leaves whispering with the voices of those they had been.

Asvarr hauled himself from the passage, rolling onto shifting ground that remembered being grass yet felt like feathers one moment and stone the next. The massive golden willow that had housed the anchor had transformed into a tower of intertwined memories that stretched toward a sky fractured with golden cracks.

"Yrsa!" Asvarr shouted, searching for his companion. "Leif!"

The boy's small form lay crumpled at the willow-tower's base. Yrsa knelt beside him, her crystal pendant blazing with blue-white light as she traced symbols in the air above his body. Asvarr scrambled toward them, the ground lurching beneath him.

"The binding destabilized him," Yrsa said without looking up. Her hands moved in complex patterns, leaving trails of blue light hanging in the air. "His nature is tied to the boundary between memory and reality. When you merged with the anchor, the boundary shifted."

Leif's form wavered like heat over summer stones. His edges blurred, portions of his flesh becoming transparent to reveal a golden light within. His eyes—fully golden now—darted wildly beneath half-closed lids.

"What can I do?" Asvarr knelt beside the boy, the crystalline leaf still clutched in his palm.

"Learn control quickly." Yrsa's voice held an edge of desperation he'd never heard from her. "The anchor responds to you now. It's transforming everything into memory, including Leif."

Around them, the distortion intensified. Trees melted into recollections of trees, their forms shifting between seasons, aging and youthing in erratic cycles. The sky rippled between day and night, sunset and dawn, summer blue and winter gray. Even the air tasted of memory—metallic with blood one moment, sweet with meadowgrass the next.

Asvarr closed his eyes, focusing on the marks across his chest and back. He could feel the anchor's power flowing through them, raw and untamed. Unlike the flame anchor, which had burned with single-minded intensity, this power spilled in all directions, transforming everything it touched.

"How do I control it?" he asked, frustration edging his voice.

Yrsa's fingers closed around his wrist. "Memory serves life, not the reverse. Find the boundary. Establish what is now and what is *remembered now.*"

Asvarr concentrated, reaching through the marks on his flesh to touch the anchor's consciousness. The voice returned, more scattered than before.

Too much. Too fast. Reality remembers being memory. Memory remembers being real.

"I need to separate them," Asvarr murmured. "Create a boundary."

The crystalline leaf in his hand warmed. Following an instinct he couldn't name, Asvarr pressed it against Leif's forehead. The boy's wild thrashing stilled as the leaf melted into his skin, leaving a small spiral pattern where it touched.

Asvarr felt a connection form—the leaf serving as an anchor point through which he could channel the Root's power with greater precision. He directed his focus through this connection, imagining a membrane separating memory from matter, past from present.

You remember who you are, he thought toward Leif. *You remember being solid.*

The boy's form solidified slightly, the transparency receding from his limbs. But the effect was temporary, the boundary fraying almost immediately as memory and matter contested the space.

Frustrated, Asvarr reached for the Remembrance Key at his hip. The crystal fruit warm against his palm, its liquid depths swirling. The anchor tree had called it *the key to restore what was forgotten.* Perhaps it could restore the proper order of things?

He pressed the Remembrance Key against his own chest, where the mark's patterns were densest. Pain flared—sharp and clarifying—as the key's energies surged through the mark and into his blood. Suddenly, he could *see* the boundaries between states of being—memory and matter, past and present, flesh and spirit.

"Memory exists to serve the present," Asvarr said, the words coming from a deeper understanding than his own. "The present exists to create memory."

He reached both hands toward Leif, the power flowing through him in controlled streams now. Where before it had poured out in all directions, now he directed it like a weapon—or a healers tools.

"Remember your shape," he commanded, pressing one palm against the boy's chest. "Remember your purpose."

The spiral mark left by the leaf pulsed with golden light. Leif gasped, his back arching. Around them, the chaotic transformations continued, but within the space outlined by Asvarr's outstretched arms, reality stabilized. Leif's body solidified fully, his breathing steadying, though his eyes remained closed.

"It's working," Yrsa's voice held wonder. "You're creating a stable zone."

Asvarr nodded, sweat beading on his forehead from the effort of maintaining control. "I can separate memory from matter, but only in a small area."

"Expand it," Yrsa urged. "The realm will tear itself apart if the transformation continues unchecked."

Extending his awareness through the crystalline patterns etched into his flesh, Asvarr reached toward the churning boundary between states. He could feel the strain in his muscles, taste copper blood where he'd bitten his tongue. The marks across his chest burned like fire-ant bites, each crystalline pattern a point of focused pain.

Gradually, he extended the zone of stability outward. The ground beneath them firmed, remembering its purpose. The air cleared of memory-tastes, becoming simply air again. The nearest trees settled into their proper forms, though they still bore faces in their bark—permanent reminders of the souls they housed.

But beyond this zone, chaos reigned. The horizon itself buckled and twisted, memory and matter fighting for dominance. In the distance, mountains melted into visions of ancient battles, valleys filled with the echoes of children's laughter from forgotten summers.

"I can't stabilize everything," Asvarr gasped, trembling with effort. "The realm is too vast."

Yrsa's crystal pendant pulsed in rhythm with Asvarr's heartbeat. "You don't need to stabilize everything," she said. "Only the path to our destination."

She pointed toward what had once been the eastern border of the grove. There, a rift had formed in the fabric of reality—a tear showing glimpses of a silver forest beneath an impossible sky filled with unfamiliar stars.

"Alfheim," Asvarr whispered, recognizing the realm from the anchor's visions.

"The memory realm was never meant to exist independently," Yrsa explained, gathering Leif's small form in her arms. "It was a fragment created when the Tree shattered. By awakening the anchor, you've triggered its reintegration with the original pattern."

The zone of stability around them shrank as Asvarr's strength flagged. The effort of controlling the anchor's power drained him like a bleeding wound. His legs trembled, threatening to buckle.

"We need to reach that rift," Yrsa urged, rising with Leif cradled against her chest. "The other anchors will help stabilize this one once we're beyond the memory realm."

Asvarr nodded, forcing himself upright. He concentrated on maintaining a stable path between their position and the distant rift, allowing the rest of the memory realm to transform as it would. Trees melted into memory-mist behind them, the ground remembering ancient seas or long-buried mountains.

They staggered forward, following the narrow corridor of stability Asvarr maintained. With each step, the effort grew more difficult. Blood trickled from his nose, the strain of separating memory from matter taking its physical toll.

Halfway to the rift, Leif stirred in Yrsa's arms. His eyes flickered open—still solid gold, but aware now.

"The pattern changes," the boy said, his voice carrying that unsettling adult resonance. "Memory returns to the Tree."

"What does that mean?" Asvarr asked through gritted teeth, maintaining their stable pathway with diminishing strength.

"The dreamer remembers dreaming," Leif murmured. "The Tree remembers growing."

The boy reached out, touching Asvarr's arm with fingers that glowed with inner light. Strength flowed from the contact, enough to keep Asvarr on his feet.

"You've bound yourself to memory itself," Leif said. "That which remembers all things."

The rift drew closer, its edges shimmering with silver light. Beyond it, Asvarr glimpsed trees of impossible slenderness reaching toward a sky filled with mathematical star patterns. Alfheim—the realm of light and memory, where starlight touched the ground.

Twenty paces from the rift, a new tremor shook the memory realm. This one felt different—deliberate, malevolent. The chaotic transformation of memory and matter took on a darker tone, shadows stretching from tree trunks, the ground bleeding a viscous black fluid that smelled of old graves.

"The Ashfather senses the anchor's awakening," Yrsa said, clutching Leif tighter. "He comes."

Above them, the sky split along the golden cracks, revealing a darkness deeper than night. Within that void, a single golden eye opened, its gaze falling directly on Asvarr. The mark across his chest burned in response, both the flame patterns and the crystalline designs flaring with protective light.

"Run," Asvarr commanded, pouring his remaining strength into maintaining their stable path. "Get Leif through the rift. I'll hold this open."

Yrsa hesitated only a moment before sprinting forward with Leif in her arms. The boy's golden eyes remained fixed on Asvarr over her shoulder, communicating something wordless yet profound.

The Ashfather's presence intensified. The darkness above them condensed, taking a vaguely humanoid shape that reached a shadowy hand toward the rift.

Asvarr summoned the last reserves of his strength, channeling the anchor's power through the crystalline patterns on his flesh. Gold and silver light erupted from his skin, creating a blazing shield that surrounded their path.

"You cannot have this anchor," he shouted at the void-figure. "Neither can the Tree. It serves a new purpose now."

The shadow-hand hesitated. The single golden eye narrowed, assessing. Then, to Asvarr's surprise, it withdrew in a calculated retreat. The darkness receded, though the single eye remained, watching.

Yrsa reached the rift with Leif, passing through the silver-edged tear into Alfheim beyond. Asvarr staggered after them, maintaining the stable path until he stood at the rift's threshold. There, he turned back for one final look at the memory realm.

The transformation had accelerated in his wake. Trees, ground, sky—all melted together into a sea of memory that flowed toward some unseen center. The realm wasn't being destroyed; it was being reabsorbed into the pattern, returning to its original purpose.

With a final surge of will, Asvarr stepped backward through the rift. The sensation of crossing between realms felt like plunging into ice water and fire simultaneously. His vision blurred, and for a moment, his body forgot how to be solid, his edges blurring like Leif's had done.

Then he stood on solid ground beneath an alien sky filled with impossible stars. Silver trees surrounded him, their trunks slender as spear shafts, their leaves glowing with internal light. The air tasted of metal and starlight, cool and invigorating after the chaos of the memory realm.

Yrsa knelt nearby, still holding Leif. The boy looked different here—more substantial, his golden eyes now flecked with silver like the stars above. The spiral mark left by the crystalline leaf still adorned his forehead, pulsing faintly in rhythm with Asvarr's heartbeat.

"You controlled the anchor," Yrsa said, her voice filled with something like awe. "I didn't think it possible for one so newly bound."

Asvarr touched his chest where the crystalline patterns overlaid the bark. The pain had subsided to a dull ache, but he could still feel the anchor's power flowing through the mark, more controlled now that they'd left the memory realm.

"The memory anchor is different from the flame," he said. "It doesn't demand; it responds."

Behind them, the rift sealed itself, the edges knitting together until only a faint silver scar remained in the air. The memory realm was gone—or rather, it had returned to its proper place within the pattern.

Leif stirred, sitting up in Yrsa's arms. "We're here," he said, looking around with recognition. "Where starlight touches the ground."

The boy's words echoed the anchor's vision. Alfheim—where the third anchor awaited.

Asvarr retrieved the Remembrance Key from his chest, where it had partially embedded itself during the crossing. The crystal fruit came free with a sensation like removing a splinter, leaving a small, perfect indentation in the bark-patterns of his flesh. Within its depths, memories swirled, countless others preserved by the Root.

"What now?" he asked, though he already knew the answer.

"Find the others," Yrsa said, setting Leif gently on his feet. "The flame must not walk alone."

Leif pointed deeper into the silver forest, where the mathematical star patterns above aligned with the trees below to create a pathway of light. "They come," he said simply.

In the distance, two figures emerged from between the silver trunks. One moved with fluid grace, a wooden arm covered in flowering vines clearly visible even at this distance. The other seemed partially formed of mist, frost crystals glittering in her wake.

Brynja and Svala—just as the anchor had shown. The other Wardens had found their way to Alfheim, drawn by the same power that had guided Asvarr.

The memory anchor had changed him fundamentally by expanding his understanding. Vengeance now seemed a small thing compared to restoration. The past was a foundation to rebuild upon.

With the Remembrance Key warm in his palm, Asvarr stepped forward to meet his fellow Wardens. The third anchor awaited them somewhere in this realm of starlight. And after that, two more, to complete the binding of the five.

Behind him, the silver scar of the sealed rift pulsed once, then faded entirely. The memory realm was gone, but its essence lived on in the anchor bound to Asvarr's flesh—and in the transformation it had wrought upon his understanding.

CHAPTER 21

BRYNJA'S RECKONING

The silver light of Alfheim dappled through impossibly slender trees, casting geometric shadows across Asvarr's face. He sat on a stone that glowed faintly beneath him, warm despite the cool, metallic air. Three days had passed since they crossed the rift, three days of waiting while Leif regained his strength and Asvarr learned the rhythms of his newly bound anchor.

He traced the crystalline patterns overlaying the bark on his forearms, feeling the memory anchor's pulse synchronized with his heartbeat. The Remembrance Key hung at his belt, no longer burning with awakening power but maintaining a steady warmth against his hip.

Footsteps crunched on silver grass behind him. Yrsa approached, Leif trailing in her wake. The boy looked stronger now, though the spiral mark on his forehead remained, glinting like captured starlight.

"They're coming," Leif said, golden eyes fixed on the eastern path where mathematical star patterns aligned in the sky above. "She walks between worlds now."

Asvarr rose, hand instinctively dropping to the bronze sword at his hip. Its golden veins pulsed in rhythm with his mark, remembering old threats and anticipating new ones.

"How many?" he asked.

"Only Brynja," Yrsa replied, her crystal pendant glowing with blue-white intensity. "The other—Svala—has gone ahead to scout the path to the third anchor."

The words had barely left her mouth when the space between two silver trees shimmered like heat over summer stones. The air parted like drawn curtains, and Brynja stepped through the gap.

Asvarr's breath caught in his throat. This was not the Brynja he remembered. The transformation had progressed far beyond what he'd seen in his visions. Her entire left arm was wooden now, bark textured like ancient oak but supple as living flesh. Flowering vines spiraled from shoulder to fingertips, small white blooms opening and closing with her breathing. The right half of her face bore similar patterns, bark-like skin transitioning to human flesh in a perfect spiraling line down the center of her forehead, across her eye, and along her jaw.

She moved with fluid grace, each step deliberate yet natural. When she raised her transformed arm in greeting, the movement held none of the jerky rigidity of the corrupted Root-beings they'd encountered. This was something else entirely—integration, not corruption.

"Flame-Keeper," she said, her voice unchanged. Those familiar amber eyes studied him, noting his own transformation with a flicker of surprise. "You've bound the second anchor."

Asvarr nodded, keeping his distance. Despite the blood-oath mark they'd shared, her betrayal remained fresh in his memory. The crystalline patterns on his flesh resonated with her presence, recognizing the Root essence bound within her.

"And you've changed as well," he replied. "The wooden arm has spread."

Brynja flexed her transformed fingers, a cascade of tiny movements rippling through the flowering vines. "The Verdant Five offered me a choice upon our separation—serve them willingly as their vessel or be consumed entirely by the Root fragment I carry."

She stepped closer, the silver light catching in the amber depths of her eyes. The mark of their blood-oath was still visible on her palm, a faded spiral that pulsed in rhythm with Asvarr's own.

"I chose neither," she continued. "I forced a third option—true symbiosis with the Root fragment. Not master, or servant, but partner."

Leif approached her without fear, reaching up to touch the flowering vines along her wooden arm. The blossoms turned toward him like eager children, opening wider to reveal centers that glowed with golden light.

"You carry the Severed Bloom," the boy said, his voice carrying that eerie adult resonance. "The fragment that chose its own purpose."

Brynja's expression softened as she looked down at him. "You see clearly, little one." She knelt to his level, the movement fluid despite the wooden components of her body. "Yes, I carry part of what they call the Severed Bloom—the fragment that rebelled against control."

Asvarr exchanged glances with Yrsa, whose crystal pendant pulsed with sharp blue light. The boundary-walker's expression remained carefully neutral, but tension lined her posture.

"How did you find us?" Asvarr asked, still wary. "The memory realm collapsed when we crossed the rift."

Brynja rose, gesturing to the silver trees surrounding them. "The Root connects all things, especially those who carry its essence. When you bound the second anchor, every Root fragment across the Nine Realms trembled in response." She touched a silver trunk, and it bent slightly toward her wooden fingers. "I simply followed the ripples to their source."

A small white flower bloomed where her fingertips met the tree's bark—something that should have been impossible with these metallic Alfheim trees. Asvarr's mark burned in response, the crystalline patterns warming against his skin.

"The truth-compelling runes still bind you," he observed, noting the golden lines etched into the wooden portion of her face. They caught the silver light, glowing faintly like embers beneath ash. "Whatever else has changed, you cannot speak falsehood."

"I have no need to lie," Brynja replied. The runes flared briefly on her face, confirming her sincerity. "In your absence, I learned many truths the Verdant Five would have kept hidden."

She walked a slow circle around them, movements graceful as a predator—or a dancer. The flowering vines along her arm shifted with each step, blooms opening and closing in complex patterns. Asvarr turned to keep her in view, the bronze sword humming softly in its sheath.

"The Five held me in their sanctuary for three days," she continued. "They spoke freely before me, believing I would soon be nothing more than a vessel for their will. They didn't realize that the Severed Bloom grants protection against such consumption—it was the first fragment to choose independence, after all."

Yrsa stepped forward. "What did you learn from them?"

"That they fear our unified bloodlines more than anything," Brynja said. She reached toward a branch above her head, stretching her wooden arm impossibly long to pluck a silver leaf. The limb contracted smoothly back to human proportions as she examined the leaf. "They've kept flame-keepers and root-tenders separated for nine cycles because together, we limit their control over the pattern."

Asvarr remembered the shared blood-oath, the brief glimpse he'd had into their common ancestry. "They manipulated our history, turned our bloodlines against each other."

"Yes." The truth-runes glowed golden on Brynja's face. "And they orchestrated the destruction of both our clans when they sensed our bloodlines were remembering across generations." She crushed the silver leaf in her wooden palm, releasing a scent like cold metal and moonlight. "They used the Ashfather as their weapon, though he had his own purpose in the slaughter."

A memory surfaced in Asvarr's mind, drawn from the depths by the anchor bound to his flesh—the vision of a one-eyed wanderer watching as warriors descended on a village much like his own. The hooded figure had stood apart, observing rather than participating, yet somehow directing the carnage.

"The Wanderer," Asvarr said. "You called him that before. The False Odin."

Brynja nodded, the truth-runes brightening. "One of many names he wears. He was there when my clan burned, just as he was there when yours fell. I saw him with my own eyes before I fled into the forest."

The confession hung in the air between them. Asvarr still remembered her shame at having run while her people died—a guilt revealed when the truth-runes were first carved into her flesh. But now she spoke of it without the crushing weight of that shame, as if she had made peace with her past.

"What changed?" Asvarr asked. "When last we met, you were ready to betray me to this Wanderer."

"I was driven by vengeance then, believing your bloodline responsible for destroying mine." The flowering vines along her arm curled inward, blooms closing tight. "The truth-runes forced me to confront reality—that I knew nothing of my clan's true history, that I had been manipulated by both the Five and the Wanderer."

She held out her wooden hand, palm up, where their blood-oath mark still glowed faintly.

"I've made terrible choices, Flame-Keeper. I meant to betray you to the Wanderer, believing it would avenge my clan. The truth-runes force me to acknowledge this."

Asvarr stared at the outstretched hand, remembering her betrayal in the Hollowfruit orchard. The memory anchor within him stirred, casting the memory in a different light, the tangled web of manipulations that had brought them both to that moment.

"And now?" he asked.

"Now I understand that vengeance serves neither of us," Brynja replied. The truth-runes pulsed steadily, golden light tracing the contours of her transformed face. "The Five and the Wanderer both fear what we might accomplish together—why else try so hard to keep us apart?"

Leif tugged at Asvarr's sleeve, drawing his attention. "The pattern wants balance," the boy said, his golden eyes serious. "Flame and root, control and freedom, memory and possibility."

Yrsa remained watchful, her hand never straying far from her crystal knife. "The binding of the second anchor has accelerated events," she said. "Two anchors awakened after nine cycles of dormancy—it has drawn attention from all quarters."

Brynja nodded agreement. "The Verdant Five have called forth guardians from the First Forest to hunt us. The Ashfather marshals his forces at the boundaries. Even the gods stir in their distant exile, sensing the pattern's shift."

She gestured upward, where the mathematical star patterns of Alfheim had subtly changed, forming new configurations that spoke of ancient purposes reawakening.

"We stand at a fulcrum point," she continued, her wooden arm extending to point toward a distant peak that gleamed like polished silver. "The third anchor awaits atop the Starfall Mountain, where sky and earth meet. Svala has gone ahead to scout the paths."

Asvarr studied her transformed face. The truth-runes left no room for deception, yet caution still wrapped around his heart like iron bands. "Why come to me now? Why not pursue the third anchor yourself?"

Brynja's expression shifted, the wooden portion of her face reshaping to match the human half in a look of grim determination. "Because the anchor will respond to neither of us alone. Like the Verdant Gate, it requires both bloodlines in harmony."

She knelt suddenly, plunging her wooden fingers into the silver soil. Moments later, a small sapling erupted from the ground, growing impossibly fast until it stood waist-high. Its trunk bore spiraling patterns that matched both the crystalline designs on Asvarr's flesh and the wooden textures of Brynja's transformed body.

"The Root showed me this," she said, voice hushed with wonder as the sapling continued to twist and grow. "When our bloodlines unite in true purpose, we become more than vessels or wardens. We become shapers of the pattern itself."

The tree stopped growing, now standing level with their heads. At its crown, a single bud formed, swelling until it bloomed into a flower with petals of silver and gold. At its center gleamed a perfect miniature of the star patterns above—an exact map of the constellations surrounding Starfall Mountain.

"This is what the Five fear," Brynja whispered, the truth-runes blazing on her face. "This is why they've kept us apart for nine cycles. Together, we can reshape the pattern in ways even they cannot control."

Asvarr approached the tree cautiously, drawn by an instinct that rose from the anchor bound to his flesh. When he touched one of the silver petals, crystalline patterns flowed from his fingertips onto the flower's surface, merging with its structure. The entire tree shuddered, responding to his touch.

"Together," he murmured, testing the word against his instincts.

Brynja stepped closer, her wooden hand rising to touch the opposite side of the bloom. Where her fingers met the petals, tiny flowering vines extended to twine with Asvarr's crystalline patterns. The tree pulsed with golden light, strengthening, its roots visibly extending through the silver soil.

"Not as master and servant, nor as vessel and anchor," she said, the truth-runes steady on her face, "but as partners in restoration."

Leif clapped his small hands, his golden eyes wide with delight. "The pattern remembers what it was meant to be!"

Yrsa's caution finally broke. She approached the tree, her crystal pendant swinging forward to touch its trunk. Blue-white light spread through the bark in branching patterns.

"I haven't seen this since the First Breaking," she whispered. "You've created a Path-Tree—a living guide to the pattern's true form."

The four of them stood around the tree as it continued to transform, branches extending outward to form a perfect map of Alfheim, roots spreading visibly through the soil to create a network of golden lines that pulsed with shared purpose.

Asvarr looked from the tree to Brynja, seeing her anew. The wooden corruption had indeed spread across half her body, but she carried it differently now—integrated rather than consumed, graceful rather than grotesque. In her amber eyes, he saw determination matched with clarity of purpose.

The memory anchor within him stirred, accepting the truth his eyes witnessed. This was not the betrayer who had left him in the Hollowfruit orchard. This was someone who had faced her own reckoning and emerged transformed—just as he had.

"We find Svala," he decided, touching the map-constellation at the tree's crown. "Then we climb Starfall Mountain together to bind the third anchor."

Brynja nodded, the flowering vines along her wooden arm shifting to mirror the star patterns above. "The Storm-Speaker has found a passage through the Silverfall Glen that avoids the Ashfather's watchers. She waits for us at the edge of the singing pools."

Leif tugged at both their sleeves, pulling them back from the tree. "Hurry," he urged, his voice carrying that unsettling adult resonance. "The tree has awakened eyes that watch from between stars."

Above them, the mathematical constellations shifted subtly, patterns re-aligning to focus on their position. Something distant but vast had turned its attention toward the silver forest where they stood. Whether it was the Verdant Five, the Ashfather, or some other power entirely, Asvarr couldn't tell—but the weight of that regard pressed down like storm clouds before lightning strikes.

"We need to move," Yrsa agreed, gathering their few possessions. "This Path-Tree marks our position like a beacon to those who know how to read the pattern."

Brynja plucked the silver-gold flower from the tree's crown, cupping it carefully in her wooden palm. The petals curled inward, forming a protective shell around the star-pattern at its center.

"Our guide," she said, offering it to Asvarr. "A living map that will show us the way to Svala and the third anchor."

Asvarr accepted the flower, feeling its warmth pulse against his palm in rhythm with his heartbeat and the anchor bound to his flesh. When his fingers closed around it, the petals shifted to reveal new patterns—hidden paths through the silver forest that ordinary eyes would never find.

"Let's go," he said, already turning toward the easternmost path, where the star patterns aligned most densely. "We find Svala, then we climb the mountain."

The tree they left behind continued to grow, its branches extending, its roots deepening. It would stand as testament to what had happened here—the moment when flame and root, after nine cycles of separation, had finally begun to work in harmony.

With Brynja at his side, transformed yet familiar, Asvarr set out on the hidden path toward Starfall Mountain and the third anchor that awaited them there. The weight of distant regard followed them, unseen eyes watching their every move from between the stars.

***

The eastern path through Alfheim's silver forest gleamed with ghostly light. Asvarr led their small band between trees that grew in perfect mathematical patterns, following the guidance of the flower cupped in his palm. Its petals shifted continuously, revealing hidden turns and secret passages through the metallic wood.

Brynja walked at his side, her wooden arm occasionally brushing against the silver trunks. Each touch left tiny flowering tendrils that dissolved minutes later. Behind them, Yrsa maintained a watchful presence, her crystal pendant pulsing with steady blue light. Leif bounded ahead occasionally, his golden eyes scanning the path, before returning to their formation.

"We're being followed," Brynja said, her voice low. The flowering vines along her wooden arm curled inward, blooms closing tight. "Three watchers, moving parallel to our path."

Asvarr nodded, having felt the same prickling awareness along his spine. The crystalline patterns overlaying the bark on his forearms had been warming intermittently for the past hour, responding to distant scrutiny.

"The Ashfather's hunters?" he asked.

"No." Brynja flexed her wooden fingers, and a small vine extended outward, impossibly long, to touch the ground thirty paces back. "They move differently. More fluid. I think they're the guardians the Verdant Five promised to unleash—Rootbound from the First Forest."

Leif returned from his latest scouting foray, his small face somber. "More ahead," he whispered. "Where the path crosses the silver stream."

Asvarr cursed under his breath. The flower-map indicated they needed to cross that stream to reach the singing pools where Svala waited. There would be no avoiding confrontation.

"We should make camp," Yrsa suggested, gesturing toward a small clearing ringed by particularly dense silver trees. "Night approaches, and we'll need our strength if we're to face these guardians tomorrow."

Asvarr agreed, though his instincts urged haste. The Remembrance Key at his belt had grown warmer throughout the day, as if sensing proximity to the third anchor. Still, a confrontation in darkness would favor their opponents.

They made a simple camp. No fire burned—the silver trees would neither catch flame nor provide suitable fuel—but Yrsa produced small crystals from her pack that emitted soft blue light and surprising warmth when arranged in specific patterns. Leif gathered silvery fronds that, when woven together, created unexpectedly comfortable bedding.

As twilight deepened, stars emerged in Alfheim's sky—constellations arranged with the same mathematical precision as the forest itself. The patterns above shifted subtly, matching movements in the flower-map cupped in Asvarr's hand.

Brynja sat opposite him across the ring of glowing crystals. The light caught in the wooden contours of her face, highlighting the golden truth-runes embedded in the bark. Since their reunion, she had shared fragments of what she'd learned from the Verdant Five, but Asvarr sensed she held deeper revelations in reserve.

"You've been circling something since we met in the silver grove," he said, meeting her amber gaze directly. "What haven't you told me about the Wanderer?"

Brynja's flowering vines stilled completely. The truth-runes along the wooden half of her face pulsed once, then steadied into a constant golden glow. Even Yrsa and Leif grew quiet, attention focused on what would come next.

"The being you know as the Ashfather, the False Odin, the Wanderer—his true intent isn't what either the Tree or the Verdant Five believe," she said, each word measured. "He seeks neither to control the pattern nor to restore it."

Asvarr leaned forward. "What then?"

"He wants to prevent Yggdrasil's rebirth entirely." The truth-runes blazed across Brynja's face, confirming her sincerity. "The gods fear that a restored Tree might not grant them the same power they once held."

Leif made a small, startled sound. Yrsa's hand froze where it had been adjusting one of the light crystals.

"Explain," Asvarr demanded, the bark patterns on his chest warming with sudden heat.

Brynja rose and paced the small clearing, her movements fluid despite the wooden components of her body. Tiny flowers bloomed and died along her transformed arm with each gesture.

"When the Five held me in their sanctuary, they spoke freely about the Wanderer. They view him as a rogue element—dangerous but ultimately predictable. They believe he still seeks to control the pattern, as he did in previous cycles." She paused, touching one of the silver trees. A small flower bloomed beneath her wooden fingertips. "But they're wrong."

"How do you know this?" Yrsa asked, her voice sharp with suspicion.

"Because he told me himself," Brynja replied simply. The truth-runes flared again. "When he sought my allegiance, he revealed more than he intended."

Asvarr remembered the vision from the memory anchor—a one-eyed figure watching impassively as warriors slaughtered a village. "He was present when both our clans were destroyed," he said. "Yet he neither participated nor prevented the slaughter."

"Because he serves neither the Tree nor the Five," Brynja confirmed. "He serves only the gods—or what remains of them in their exile."

She returned to the circle and knelt across from Asvarr. "The gods fear the Tree's restoration because the original pattern granted them no special privilege.

They seized that power during the First Breaking, when the pattern fractured and rules could be rewritten."

A memory surfaced in Asvarr's mind—drawn from the depths by the anchor bound to his flesh. He saw vast beings of light and shadow arguing on a mountain peak while forests burned below. At their feet lay the shattered remnants of the First Pattern, and in their eyes gleamed hunger for what those fragments might become under their shaping.

"The Tree breaking was their opportunity," he murmured, the vision fading.

"Yes," Brynja said, truth-runes steady on her face. "And its complete restoration would force them to relinquish what they've taken. That's why the Wanderer has manipulated events across nine cycles—to ensure the pattern remains broken enough for the gods to maintain their stolen power, yet stable enough to prevent complete dissolution."

Leif moved closer to the crystal lights, his golden eyes reflecting their blue glow. "The spaces between," he said in that unsettling adult voice. "That's where they hide now. Where I came from."

Yrsa nodded slowly. "The boy speaks truth. The gods withdrew to the boundaries after the Last Breaking, neither fully within nor without the pattern."

The understanding struck Asvarr like a physical blow. "And each cycle of partial restoration has maintained those spaces—the in-between where they can exist without accountability to the pattern's true form."

"The Wanderer ensured each cycle followed the same path," Brynja continued. "Wardens would bind enough anchors to prevent complete dissolution, but never all five. The pattern would stabilize in its broken state, then gradually degrade until another Breaking threatened, and the cycle would begin again."

She leaned forward, the flowering vines along her arm extending slightly toward Asvarr. "But we've disrupted the cycle. Two anchors bound successfully by a single Warden—it hasn't happened in nine turns of the wheel. Now the Wanderer acts directly, which means the gods themselves grow desperate."

The Remembrance Key at Asvarr's belt pulsed with warmth, resonating with the truth of her words. The memory anchor within him stirred, casting up fragments of previous cycles—Wardens who had bound one anchor, perhaps two, before falling to the Wanderer's manipulations or the Tree's consumption.

"If what you say is true," Asvarr said slowly, "then neither the Tree nor the Five can be trusted. The Tree seeks restoration that serves its purpose; the Five seek control that serves theirs."

"And the Wanderer serves gods who fear both outcomes equally," Brynja finished. The truth-runes blazed across her wooden features. "That's why he approached me after our separation at the Hollowfruit orchard. He sensed the cycle breaking and sought to turn us against each other—as he's done for nine cycles before."

Yrsa's crystal pendant flared with sudden intensity. "So the Ash-Priest who pursued you through the memory realm—"

"Was the Wanderer's servant, yes," Brynja confirmed. "Sent to prevent our bloodlines from reuniting."

Leif had been unusually quiet, his small form hunched near the crystal lights. Now he looked up, golden eyes reflecting the glow. "The pattern remembers what it should be," he said. "Not Tree. Not Five. Not gods. Something else."

Asvarr touched the crystalline patterns on his chest, feeling the memory anchor's pulse beneath his fingers. With each binding, his understanding had expanded, yet each revelation only emphasized how little he truly knew of the forces at play.

"What do you propose?" he asked Brynja directly.

She straightened, the wooden half of her face reshaping to match the determination in the human half. The flowering vines along her arm extended outward, reaching toward Asvarr without quite touching him.

"Alliance," she said simply, the truth-runes glowing with steady golden light. "This was based on necessity, not friendship or loyalty. Together, we stand a chance against the Wanderer, the Five, and even the Tree's consumption. Divided, we will fail—as all Wardens have failed for nine cycles before us."

The night air between them filled with tension. Asvarr studied her transformed face—half human flesh, half living wood, yet entirely Brynja in its expressions and movements. The gold-flaring truth-runes left no room for deception, yet old caution wrapped around his heart.

"You once meant to betray me to this Wanderer," he reminded her.

"Yes," she acknowledged without hesitation. "I believed it would avenge my clan. I was wrong." The flowering vines along her arm curled inward, a visible sign of her regret. "The truth-runes forced me to see the reality—that I knew nothing of my clan's true history, that I had been manipulated by both the Five and the Wanderer."

She held out her hand—the human one, not the wooden—palm up to reveal the faded blood-oath mark they had shared.

"Our bloodlines were sundered for a reason, Flame-Keeper. Together, we limit their control over the pattern. That's why they've worked so hard to keep us apart across nine cycles."

Asvarr glanced at Yrsa, who had remained watchful throughout the exchange. The boundary-walker's expression revealed little, but her crystal pendant pulsed with steady light—neither warning nor encouraging, merely observing.

Leif, on the other hand, had crept closer to Brynja, one small hand reaching up to touch the flowering vines along her wooden arm. "The truth-blade carved what needed carving," he said cryptically. "Now the path grows clear."

A distant sound interrupted the moment—a long, low cry that might have been wind through the silver trees, except the air remained perfectly still. The flower-map in Asvarr's palm shifted suddenly, its petals fluttering in alarm.

"They're moving," Brynja said, rising to her feet in one fluid motion. "The guardians from the First Forest—they've sensed our discussion and are closing in."

Asvarr stood as well, hand dropping to the bronze sword at his hip. The crystalline patterns on his chest and arms warmed, responding to approaching danger.

"How many?" he asked, scanning the darkness between the silver trunks.

"More than before," Brynja replied, her wooden arm extending slightly, vines reaching out to touch the earth around their camp. "At least a dozen, moving in a pattern I don't recognize."

Yrsa had already begun gathering their few possessions, her movements quick and practiced. "We can't fight them all," she said. "Not here, not in darkness."

"We need to reach Svala," Asvarr agreed. "Together, three Wardens might stand a chance."

The strange cry sounded again, closer now. Between the silver trees, shadows moved—elongated forms with too many limbs, weaving through the mathematical patterns with unnatural grace.

"There's a more direct path to the singing pools," Leif said suddenly, his small hand pointing toward what appeared to be solid silver trunks. "Through the star-seam."

"A boundary passage?" Yrsa asked sharply. "Those are dangerous for anyone but a boundary-walker."

"I can guide us through," Leif insisted, his golden eyes gleaming with certainty. "I was born in the spaces between."

Asvarr glanced at Brynja, a silent question in his gaze. She nodded once, the truth-runes on her face pulsing in rhythm with her heartbeat. "We must trust the boy," she said. "These guardians were shaped by the Five specifically to hunt Wardens."

The decision crystallized in Asvarr's mind. He lifted the flower-map, watching as its petals rearranged to show a thin silver line—barely visible—cutting through the forest toward the singing pools. Leif's star-seam.

"Lead us, boy," he commanded, gathering the last of their supplies. "Brynja, can you slow them down?"

She nodded, kneeling to press her wooden palm against the silver soil. The flowering vines extended outward, sinking beneath the surface. For a moment, nothing happened. Then the ground trembled slightly, and slender silver roots erupted in a wide circle around their camp, intertwining to form a barrier between them and the approaching guardians.

"It won't hold them long," Brynja warned, rising. "The silver trees resist my influence."

"Long enough," Asvarr replied.

Leif had already moved toward what appeared to be solid forest. The boy placed his small palms against two adjacent tree trunks and pushed. To Asvarr's amazement, the trees parted like curtains, revealing a narrow path suffused with faint starlight that seemed to come from nowhere and everywhere simultaneously.

"Quickly," Leif urged, his voice carrying that unsettling adult resonance. "The seam will close once the guardians reach it."

Yrsa went first, then Brynja. Asvarr hesitated at the threshold, looking back to where shadowy forms now moved at the edge of their abandoned camp. The barrier Brynja created trembled as something massive pressed against it.

"Go," Leif insisted, tugging at Asvarr's sleeve.

Asvarr stepped through the gap between trees, entering a passage unlike anything he had experienced before. The walls shimmered with starlight, the floor beneath his feet vibrating slightly as if alive. The path stretched ahead in a straight line that somehow curved without bending, a geometric impossibility that made his eyes water if he tried to focus too long on any single point.

Behind them, the entrance sealed seamlessly, the silver trees rejoining as if they had never parted. The sounds of pursuit cut off abruptly, leaving only the faint musical hum of the star-seam surrounding them.

"This place exists between Alfheim and the void," Leif explained, taking the lead with confident steps. "A fold in the pattern where one realm touches another without merging."

Asvarr fought a wave of disorientation as the passage shifted around them. "Will it take us to the singing pools?"

"Yes," Leif assured him. "All seams connect to places where the pattern thins. The singing pools are such a place." He glanced back, golden eyes serious. "But we must hurry. Seams close when too many with power walk them at once."

They moved forward at a near-run, the strange passage seeming both endless and instantaneous. Asvarr lost all sense of time and distance, his only anchors the physical forms of his companions moving ahead of him and the steady warmth of the Remembrance Key at his belt.

The passage ended as abruptly as it had begun. One moment they ran through the star-suffused corridor; the next, they stumbled out between two perfectly ordinary-looking silver trees into a clearing dominated by seven circular pools arranged in a geometric pattern.

The singing pools of Alfheim. Each pool glowed with a different shade of silver-blue light, and from their surfaces rose haunting tones that blended into complex harmonies. At the center pool stood a slender figure wreathed in mist, with frost crystals glittering in her wake.

Svala, the Storm-Speaker. The third Warden.

She turned as they emerged, her expression shifting from wariness to recognition. "Flame-Keeper," she said, her voice like ice breaking on a frozen lake. "You've brought the Root-Tender." Her gaze shifted to include Leif and Yrsa. "And the boundary-walkers."

"The guardians from the First Forest pursue us," Brynja said without preamble, the truth-runes on her face pulsing with urgency. "And behind them comes the Wanderer himself."

Svala nodded, unsurprised. "I've felt his presence growing stronger since dawn. The pattern shifts around him, creating paths where none existed before."

Asvarr took in Svala's appearance—her form partially transparent, shimmering with inner light like the mist that surrounded her. Frost patterns marked her throat where the Frostmark resided, spreading outward in crystalline fractals.

"We need to reach Starfall Mountain," he said, gesturing toward the distant silver peak that dominated the eastern horizon. "The third anchor awaits us there."

Svala smiled, a cold, sharp expression that revealed teeth like tiny icicles. "I know," she replied. "I've found a path that avoids the Ashfather's watchers. But we must move now—the singing pools warn of shadow-thoughts spreading through the forest."

A terrible cry shattered the harmony of the pools—the same sound they had heard in the forest, but louder, filled with rage and hunger. The guardians had found another way to follow.

"We can't run forever," Brynja said, the flowering vines along her wooden arm flaring outward like a shield. "Sooner or later, we must stand and fight."

Asvarr drew his bronze sword, its golden veins pulsing with the combined power of two bound anchors. The crystalline patterns across his chest and arms heated, ready to channel that power outward.

"Then we stand now," he decided. "Four against their dozen—better odds than we might find later."

Svala stepped forward, frost crystals forming in the air around her like miniature stars. "Three Wardens together," she said, her voice carrying harmonics that resonated with the singing pools. "The pattern has not seen this in nine cycles."

Between the silver trees at the clearing's edge, shadows gathered—elongated figures with limbs like twisted branches and eyes that gleamed with malevolent purpose. The guardians from the First Forest had found them.

Brynja moved to Asvarr's side, her wooden arm fully extended now, flowering vines weaving together to form a shield-like structure. The truth-runes blazed across her face as she prepared for battle.

"Together," she said, her amber eyes meeting his. "Not for friendship, nor loyalty. For necessity."

Asvarr nodded, raising his sword as the first of the guardians emerged from the shadows. With Brynja at his side and two more Wardens at his back, he faced the coming storm with grim determination. The third anchor awaited them on Starfall Mountain—if they lived long enough to claim it.

CHAPTER 22

THE GROVE-TWINED PACT

Silver mist shrouded the seven singing pools, their melodic tones rising and falling in eerie counterpoint as Asvarr traced the spiral patterns emerging on his palm. The blood-oath mark from his earlier binding with Brynja pulsed beneath his fingertips, warm and alive. Around them, Alfheim's forest of metallic trees cast impossible shadows—each a perfect geometric shape that bore no relation to the slender trunks creating them.

"We need terms," Asvarr said, his voice breaking the harmonic resonance of the pools. "True terms. Binding terms." The Grímmark on his chest throbbed in response, golden sap leaking from the edges where bark-like patterns had replaced his skin.

Brynja looked up, her truth-runes glowing softly across the wooden half of her face. Flowering vines curled along her transformed left arm, blossoms opening and closing with each breath. "Agreement without trust," she said. "Wise."

Yrsa crouched beside one of the singing pools, her crystalline pendant suspended above the silvery surface. "Four wardens gathered freely for the first time in nine cycles. The pattern shifts already." She lifted weathered eyes toward the others. "The hunt follows still. We have until moonrise."

Leif sat cross-legged between them, golden eyes reflecting the starlight above. Since arriving in Alfheim, the boy had spoken more, moved with greater confidence. Even now, his fingers traced patterns in the air that momentarily solidified into geometric shapes of pure light.

"I know what I was," he said, his child's voice momentarily resonating with adult depth. "A fragment. Born in the space between moments when the Tree shattered." His gaze turned to Asvarr. "I need to find when, where, who I was before fragments."

Asvarr studied each of them in turn. Four souls with different purposes, different pasts. The guardians from the First Forest might find them at any moment. The Wanderer—the False Odin—hunted them across realms. If they were to reach the third anchor at Starfall Mountain, they needed more than a shared destination.

"An alliance then," Asvarr said, rolling his shoulders to ease the pressure of transformation spreading across his back. "With terms each of us requires. We speak now, and we bind our words with something stronger than promises."

Brynja stepped forward, her movements fluid despite the twisted nature of her form. The wooden half of her face caught the light of the singing pools, illuminating the truth-runes carved into her flesh.

"I require equality," she said simply. "The anchor we seek isn't yours to claim alone. The Verdant Five raised me to be their vessel, but I'll be no one's instrument. When we reach Starfall, we approach the anchor together, as equals in Wardenship."

The runes on her face blazed golden—truth spoken aloud.

Asvarr nodded once. "Agreed, but I have terms too." He met her gaze directly. "I require honesty without reservation. Your runes show truth, but they don't compel you to speak it. From now until our mission ends, you will answer any question I ask with complete truth."

A muscle twitched along Brynja's jawline, the only sign of her discomfort. The wooden side of her face remained motionless. "If I refuse to answer?"

"Then you've broken the pact, and I walk alone."

The pools' singing intensity increased as tension hung between them. Finally, Brynja inclined her head.

"I accept," she said, the runes flaring brightly.

Yrsa stepped between them, her weathered hands raised. "My turn then." Her crystal pendant swayed hypnotically. "In matters of Root-lore, my knowledge guides our path. Nine cycles I've watched, learned, preserved. When I speak of the Tree's ways, of anchors, of the pattern's workings—heed me."

Asvarr frowned. "Even when your guidance contradicts our judgment?"

"Especially then." Yrsa's eyes sharpened. "You've bound two anchors, young Warden. The third will test you differently. The flame sought dominance, the memory required recognition. Starlight demands something else entirely."

Leif stood suddenly, his small frame casting an impossibly long shadow across the singing pools. "My turn," he said, and for the first time, Asvarr heard no child-like qualities in his voice. "I require your help finding my origin. The moment of my creation. Who I was before the shattering tore me into fragments."

"How would we even begin to find that?" Brynja asked, her wooden fingers flexing.

"I exist across boundaries," Leif replied, his eyes momentarily shifting to pure gold. "Parts of me remember different things. When we reach Starfall Mountain, the stars will show the way. I need your promise that we'll follow it, even if it takes us from the direct path."

The four of them stood in silence, weighing each other's terms. Above them, Alfheim's starscape shifted subtly, aligning into unfamiliar patterns.

Yrsa spoke first. "There's one more term needed." She reached into a pouch at her belt, withdrawing a handful of bark shavings—a rich amber-gold unlike any tree in Alfheim's silver forest. "The pact must be sealed with more than words. A blood-oath is strong, but a grove-twining is stronger."

She placed the bark shavings in a perfect circle at their feet. "A piece of the First Tree, preserved across nine cycles. The only true remnant of Yggdrasil before gods or anchors. It binds with blood and flesh, growing roots through those who swear upon it."

"Roots through flesh?" Asvarr's hand instinctively covered his expanding Grímmark.

"The price of true binding," Yrsa said simply. "A shared root that connects us. Break the pact, and the root withers, taking part of your essence with it."

Asvarr stared at the circle of bark. Another sacrifice, another surrender of self to powers beyond his understanding. Yet what choice remained? Division meant failure. The Wanderer would find each of them separately, and the third anchor would remain beyond reach.

"I'll do it," he said, kneeling beside the circle.

"As will I." Brynja knelt opposite him, her wooden arm extended.

"The pattern welcomes this binding," Yrsa murmured, joining them.

Leif completed their circle, his small hand steady. "I choose this path."

Yrsa produced her crystal knife, its edge glinting with unnatural sharpness. "Left palms extended over the circle. Blood and oath, spoken intent."

Asvarr extended his hand first, palm up. The crystal blade sliced across his skin, drawing a line of blood that fell upon the bark shavings. They hissed at the contact, curling upward like living things seeking warmth.

"I, Asvarr Flame-Bearer, bind myself to this pact. Equality in Wardenship, truth in all matters, guidance in Root-lore, aid for Leif's origin. My blood seals these terms."

Brynja extended her human hand, allowing Yrsa to cut across her palm. Golden-red blood—tinged with sap—dripped onto the now-moving circle of bark.

"I, Brynja Root-Speaker, bind myself to this pact. I claim equal Wardenship, offer truth without reservation, accept guidance in Root-lore, and pledge to help find Leif's origin. My blood seals these terms."

The bark shavings twisted together, forming a living tendril that coiled upward.

Yrsa drew the knife across her own palm. "I, Yrsa Boundary-Walker, bind myself to this pact. I acknowledge equal Wardenship, speak truth when asked, offer guidance in Root-lore, and will help find Leif's origin. My blood seals these terms."

Leif was last, his small hand steady as the crystal blade drew a thin line across his palm. His blood shimmered with an inner light as it fell upon the writhing circle of bark.

"I, Leif Between-Worlds, bind myself to this pact. I recognize equal War-denship, offer truth, accept guidance, and will follow my origin when re-vealed. My blood seals these terms."

The circle of bark erupted upward, twisted strands weaving together like fingers interlacing. It formed a perfect ring hovering in the air between their four extended hands.

"Grove-twining requires true acceptance," Yrsa whispered. "The root will find passage through flesh only if welcomed."

Asvarr stared at the floating ring of living wood. Another surrender, an-other transformation. Yet in this act lay unity and purpose. He took a deep breath and pressed his bleeding palm against the ring.

"I accept," he said firmly.

The others followed suit, their hands meeting around the circle of bark. The moment their four palms touched, the ring shuddered, then exploded into countless filaments that drove into their flesh. Asvarr gasped as living wood burrowed through his left palm, intensely intrusive. The sensation crawled up his arm, beneath his skin, a foreign presence taking residence within his body.

For one terrible moment, the filaments reached toward his heart, and Asvarr feared he had made a fatal mistake. Then they curled away, focusing instead on his palm where they coalesced into a perfect circle of wood em-bedded in his flesh. Within the circle, tiny roots formed an intricate pattern that connected at its center.

When he pulled his hand away, the wooden circle remained—a living sigil grown through his palm.

Brynja examined her own identical mark with fascination. "Grove-twined," she murmured. Her truth-runes glowed steady and golden, confirming her acceptance.

"We are connected now," Yrsa said, examining her palm where the same wooden circle had formed. "Break the pact, and this withers, taking some-thing vital with it."

Leif stared at his small hand where the mark seemed proportionally larger. "I feel you," he said wonderingly. "All of you, like distant stars."

Asvarr flexed his fingers, feeling the strange weight of the living wood embedded in his flesh. Another transformation, another sacrifice of self. Yet this one felt different—a joining rather than a taking.

The singing pools suddenly silenced, their surfaces freezing into perfect stillness. In the distance, a hollow cry echoed—the guardians from the First Forest, drawing closer.

"The alliance is sealed," Asvarr said, rising to his feet. He felt the others' presence now through the grove-twined mark, distant echoes of emotion and intent. "Together we seek the third anchor at Starfall Mountain."

Brynja's wooden arm flexed, flowers closing along its length. "The Hunt approaches from the east. We should move now."

Yrsa gathered her belongings swiftly. "The western path leads through the Crystal Vales. We can reach the foothills of Starfall by tomorrow's dusk if we travel without rest."

Leif stood between them, his childlike frame belied by the ancient wisdom in his golden eyes. "The stars align tonight," he said, pointing upward where constellations shifted like living things. "The serpent constellation coils around the mountain peak. It watches us now."

Asvarr flexed his hand, feeling the living wood pulse with his heartbeat. They were bound now—four souls with separate purposes united by necessity. The grove-twined mark ensured loyalty, but trust would come only through action. With the Hunt drawing closer, the time for words had ended.

"We move west," he said, drawing his bronze sword with its golden veins. "Together."

The oath-sigil in his palm throbbed once, sending a pulse of warmth through his transformed body. Whatever awaited at Starfall Mountain, they would face it as one—a unity forged from necessity, bound by living wood and shared purpose, stronger than blood or memory alone.

Behind them, the singing pools resumed their haunting melody, a song of paths converging where once they had walked apart.

Asvarr's palm throbbed with unfamiliar weight. The grove-twined mark sat embedded in his flesh, a perfect circle of living wood with intricate root patterns spiraling to its center. His senses stretched across the landscape as they moved westward, away from the singing pools where their pact had been sealed. The Call of the Hunt faded behind them, yet Asvarr felt no relief. Something else pulled at him now, tugging from within.

"The anchors," he gasped, halting abruptly. The Remembrance Key at his belt pulsed with sudden heat, its crystal form glowing brighter than the stars overhead. "They're... waking."

Brynja stumbled beside him, her human hand flying to her wooden arm where sap beaded like sweat. "I feel it too." Her eyes widened as golden light blazed beneath the bark patterns covering half her face. "The Severed Bloom stirs."

Yrsa circled them, her leathery face grim. "The grove-twining has created resonance. Your bound anchors recognize each other now." She touched her crystal pendant, which emitted a high, clear tone. "We need shelter before it takes you both. Somewhere the visions can come without drawing unwanted attention."

The urgency in her voice propelled them forward. Asvarr fought the rising pressure in his chest where the Grímmark burned against his ribs. He'd undergone anchor bindings before—first flame, then memory—but this sensation was different, more invasive. The anchors weren't merely responding to his presence; they were reaching toward something external, like lodestones seeking their counterpart.

They found refuge in a hollow between silver trees whose geometric shadows created a perfect dome of darkness. Leif knelt at its edge, pressing small hands against the metallic soil.

"Here," he said, his childlike voice resonating with unexpected depth. "The roots run deep here, touching something ancient. The visions will come clearly."

Asvarr sank to his knees as the pressure became unbearable. The Grímmark blazed through his clothing, his transformed flesh glowing with amber light.

Nearby, Brynja curled inward, her wooden arm erupting with impossible blossoms that opened and closed in rapid sequence.

"What's happening to them?" Leif asked Yrsa, golden eyes reflecting the anchors' radiance.

"Two anchors converge within one vessel, while a fragment stirs in another," Yrsa explained. "The grove-twining connected them. Now we witness the union."

Asvarr gasped as the Grímmark's burning intensified. Through his shirt, golden sap leaked in precise patterns, forming spirals and whorls across the fabric. He saw Brynja reach toward him with her wooden arm, flowers fully bloomed along its length.

"Give me your hand," she said, her voice strained. "The mark... it wants connection."

The grove-twined sigil in Asvarr's palm pulled toward her like a living thing with will of its own. Their hands clasped—flesh to wood—and the world dissolved.

Light engulfed him, neither painful nor gentle but simply overwhelming. Asvarr felt his consciousness stretch, as though his mind had become liquid, flowing outward beyond the boundaries of his physical form. Images flooded in, something raw and immediate.

He stood upon a peak of crystalline stone that caught starlight and amplified it into twisting pillars of radiance. Alfheim spread below, its silver forest a perfect geometric pattern extending to the horizon. Above, stars moved with deliberate purpose, forming and reforming constellations with each passing moment.

At the mountain's summit, a perfectly circular pool reflected nothing of the sky above. Instead, it showed depths that extended beyond the physical realm—a darkness alive with potential, threaded with strands of silver light that coiled and twisted like living things.

"The third anchor," Asvarr whispered, though he had no body in this vision to speak with.

"Starfall Mountain," Brynja's voice replied, equally disembodied. "Where sky meets root in something new."

The vision shifted, diving into the dark pool. They plunged through layers of reality, passing ghostly memories of previous seekers who had failed to reach its depths. Deep below, something massive coiled in the darkness—a serpent formed of constellations, its scales reflecting pinpricks of light like captured stars. Around it, the darkness thickened into branches, roots, tendrils of absolute void that branched in perfect fractals.

The serpent's eyes opened—vast gold-flecked orbs that contained entire galaxies within their depths. In their reflection, Asvarr glimpsed Yggdrasil in its prime—not as he had imagined it from stories, but as it truly had been: a vast consciousness spanning all existence, simultaneously tree and pattern and possibility, connecting worlds through thought rather than physical matter.

"The Starlight Anchor," Brynja's voice resonated through the vision. "It remembers."

The serpent uncoiled, rising through the depths toward them. Its movement parted the darkness, revealing a cavern beneath the mountain peak where sap and starlight merged. At its center sat a crystalline structure unlike anything Asvarr had encountered—neither tree nor root nor crown, but a perfect merging of light and matter, pulsing with quiet intensity.

"Three must become one," the serpent spoke, its voice reverberating through Asvarr's being. "Flame to ignite, memory to preserve, starlight to transform. The anchors call to each other across the void."

The serpent's massive head drew level with them, its gaze both ancient and immediate. "You have chosen the third path, between surrender and dominance. Now you must walk it together, for none may reach the center alone."

With sudden violence, the vision twisted. The serpent's body elongated, stretching across the star-field above Alfheim, becoming a constellation that pointed directly to Starfall Mountain. Its eyes dimmed, becoming merely stars, but their pattern remained—a map etched in light.

"Follow my form when darkness falls," the serpent's voice faded. "The way opens only under twilight's embrace, when boundary falters between day and night."

The vision collapsed inward, reality rushing back with bruising force. Asvarr found himself sprawled on the ground, his hand still clutched in Brynja's wooden grasp. Their grove-twined marks pulsed with golden light, sending waves of warmth up their arms.

Yrsa knelt beside them, crystal pendant dangling over their clasped hands. "What did you see?" she asked, her voice hushed.

Asvarr struggled upright, noticing that the bark-like patterns on his chest had spread further across his torso. "Starfall Mountain," he rasped. "A pool that leads beneath the peak, and a serpent of stars that guards the way."

"The constellation," Brynja added, her truth-runes glowing golden across her face. "It forms a map to the anchor's location, but only visible at twilight."

Leif moved closer, his small form radiating unexpected solemnity. "The serpent is the guardian of boundaries," he said. "It existed before the Tree, in the void between potential and manifestation."

The grove-twined marks in their palms flared suddenly, sending a jolt through Asvarr's transformed flesh. Beneath his eyes, impossible things happened—tiny green shoots emerged from the wooden circle, unfurling into perfect miniature leaves that fluttered with each heartbeat.

"The oath-sigils," Yrsa breathed. "They've sprouted."

Brynja stared at her palm where identical leaves had grown from the living wood. "The Root has accepted our pact," she said, her truth-runes confirming her words.

The small leaves weren't merely decorative. Asvarr felt new awareness flowing through them—a subtle connection to the others that transcended mere physical proximity. He sensed Brynja's guarded hope, Yrsa's measured caution, Leif's ancient knowledge wrapped in childlike wonder.

"We've been granted blessings," Yrsa said, examining her own sprouted mark. "The Root recognizes our alliance as necessary."

Asvarr flexed his hand, watching the tiny leaves shimmer with inner light. "How is this possible? The anchors are fragments, scattered pieces of a broken whole. How can they still act with purpose?"

"The Tree wasn't merely destroyed," Yrsa said, her voice taking on the formal cadence she used when speaking of Root-lore. "It shattered itself deliberately, preserving its consciousness across anchors and vessels. What we call fragments retain the whole's intent, separated but undiminished."

Leif stepped forward, touching his small hand with its oversized grove-mark to the metallic ground. "The pattern shifts around us," he said. "I can feel it stretching, accommodating our changed path."

The hollow between the trees had darkened, the weird geometric shadows deepening as Alfheim's strange stars shifted overhead. Asvarr felt exposed despite their shelter, aware that the anchors' awakening might have drawn unwanted attention.

"What lies within Starfall Mountain," Brynja asked, her wooden arm flexing thoughtfully, "how is it different from the anchors we've already bound?"

"The first was fire—active, consuming, demanding dominance," Yrsa replied. "The second was memory—receptive, preserving, requiring recognition. The third is starlight—transformation itself, demanding neither control nor submission, but the balance between them."

Asvarr remembered the serpent's words from the vision. "Three must become one," he murmured. "Our anchors called to each other."

"The Tree seeks reunion," Yrsa nodded. "Each anchor bound brings the pattern closer to wholeness. But the third anchor has always been the most difficult to approach. Nine cycles of Wardens have tried; none succeeded in binding starlight."

Dark possibilities surfaced in Asvarr's mind. If nine previous cycles had failed, what hope did they have? Yet the vision had shown something unprecedented—his flame and memory anchors resonating with Brynja's fragment, creating harmony where before there had been only conflict.

"The twilight path," he said suddenly, understanding dawning. "That's why we need both bloodlines. The anchor isn't merely waiting to be claimed; it's guarding itself against those who would approach with dominance or surrender alone."

"The third path requires both flame and root," Brynja agreed, her truth-runes flaring. "Neither can reach it separately."

Leif stood, his childlike face solemn in the deepening shadows. "The guardians are coming," he said. "They've followed our trail from the singing pools."

Yrsa gathered her belongings with swift efficiency. "We must move now, while the constellation is forming. By twilight tomorrow, we need to be at Starfall's base."

Asvarr rose, noticing how the grove-twined mark's tiny leaves turned like compass needles, pointing westward toward the distant peak visible on the horizon. His anchors pulled in the same direction, a tugging sensation behind his breastbone that couldn't be ignored.

"Together, then," he said, extending his marked palm.

The others placed their hands above his—wood, crystal, and childhood innocence joined with his transformed flesh. For a moment, the tiny leaves on all four marks blazed with shared light, binding them more surely than any blood-oath or spoken vow.

Beyond their shelter, sinuous shapes moved through the silver forest—the guardians drawing closer, hunting those who dared approach the third anchor. The Hunt of Broken Fate still pursued them across realms. The Wanderer watched from between stars.

Yet for the first time since the Grímmark had first burned into his flesh, Asvarr felt something beyond the weight of his burden.

The oak-sigil's leaves trembled against his palm, alive with possibility. The anchors had called to each other across the void and found response. The pattern was changing, and they with it.

"To Starfall Mountain," Brynja said, her wooden arm gleaming with sap in the starlight.

"To transformation," Yrsa added.

"To boundaries crossed," Leif whispered.

Asvarr felt the serpent constellation forming overhead, stars aligning like ancient eyes watching their path. "To the third anchor," he said, as they stepped from their shelter into the silver night of Alfheim, the sprouted oath-sigils lighting their way with living luminescence, four souls united by necessity and bound by living wood, walking the third path together.

CHAPTER 23

THE VERDANT GATE CLOSES

A crack echoed through Alfheim's silver night, the sound splitting the air with crystalline precision. Asvarr whirled, his transformed flesh tingling with warning. The others froze mid-step, their oath-sigils pulsing in synchronized rhythm.

"Did you hear—" Asvarr began, but the words died in his throat.

Behind them, where the forest gave way to the glimmering plain they'd crossed hours earlier, reality tore. A jagged fissure hung suspended in the air, edges fluttering like torn fabric. Through it, Asvarr glimpsed the memory realm they'd left behind—the Whispering Grove with its falling leaves, the Circle of Splinters, the Rootless King's twisted domain. Places that should have been days of travel apart showed through the single rent, compressed and distorted.

"The anchors," Yrsa breathed, crystal pendant blazing with blue light. "Your binding resonance has weakened the boundaries."

Leif stepped toward the fissure, golden eyes reflecting its otherworldly light. "The memory realm collapses," he said, his childlike voice resonating with ancient understanding. "It was never meant to contain the power of two bound anchors and a fragment in harmony."

Brynja's wooden arm stretched toward the tear, flowers opening along its length. "I feel it," she said, her truth-runes glowing across the wooden portion of her face. "The spaces between realms thin."

The fissure widened with another crack, sending vibrations through the silver soil beneath their feet. Through the growing tear, Asvarr saw movement—shadows flowing like liquid, shapes fragmenting and re-forming, pathways he remembered walking now twisting like serpents. The memory realm was unraveling.

"We need to move," Asvarr said, turning away. "We've destabilized something fundamental. If we're caught in it—"

He stopped. Ahead of them, where moments ago the path had stretched clear toward Starfall Mountain, another tear had opened. Through it poured images and sensations—fragmented memories from the countless souls who had walked the memory realm before them. They solidified in the air like glass sculptures before shattering into dust, only for new ones to form in their place.

Asvarr drew his bronze sword, its golden veins pulsing in harmony with his Grímmark. "We're surrounded."

Yrsa circled, her leathery face grim. "The realms are separating, but the memory realm has nowhere to go. It's a construction, not a true world—a space created from the Tree's breaking to preserve what might otherwise be lost."

"And now it's breaking again," Brynja said, wooden fingers flexing.

A third tear appeared to their right, and a fourth to their left. The silver forest around them wavered, trees briefly transparent before solidifying again. Looking up, Asvarr saw Alfheim's stars ripple like disturbed water.

"We have to get back to the Verdant Gate," Yrsa said, pointing toward the southwest, where a distant mountain peak caught starlight like a blade. "It's the only stable passage between realms that might withstand this collapse."

"The Verdant Gate?" Asvarr questioned. "We passed through it days ago—it closed behind us."

"The Gate exists in time, not place," Leif said, stepping forward with unexpected certainty. "I can lead us there."

The grove-twined mark in Asvarr's palm throbbed. The tiny leaves growing from it trembled, reaching toward Leif as if drawn by an invisible current. Asvarr felt the surge of connection between them, stronger than before.

"How?" he asked.

"I exist between boundaries," Leif replied, his small hand taking Asvarr's. "I can see where realities stretch thin, where passages form and fade. The in-between is my home."

Another crack resounded, and the tears around them widened. Through them, Asvarr glimpsed places he'd never seen—realms beyond the memory domain, perhaps even beyond the Nine Worlds he knew. In one, mountains floated untethered to ground; in another, oceans of liquid fire flowed beneath skies of crystal. The boundaries between worlds were failing.

"We trust you," Asvarr told Leif. "Lead us."

The boy nodded, his face suddenly solemn beyond his years. "Stay close. Touch nothing but each other and the path I show you. The spaces between are hungry now."

They formed a chain—Leif first, then Asvarr, followed by Brynja with Yrsa at the rear. Their grove-twined marks pulsed in unison, creating a physical bond that transcended mere linked hands. Asvarr felt the others through it: Leif's ancient certainty wrapped in childlike courage, Brynja's wary determination, Yrsa's weathered resilience.

Leif stepped confidently forward, avoiding fissures that weren't visibly present until he skirted them. The landscape around them blurred and shifted—one moment they stood in Alfheim's silver forest, the next they walked across the memory realm's layers, compressed and overlapping. Asvarr glimpsed the Whispering Grove again, then the Hollowglade, then places he'd never visited but somehow recognized from shared visions.

"The memory realm fragments into its components," Yrsa explained as they moved. "Each section was formed from different aspects of the Tree's consciousness. They separate now like oil from water."

A massive tear opened directly before them. Unlike the others, this one revealed nothing beyond—only absolute darkness that drank light from its surroundings. Leif halted, his small frame tensing.

"We can't cross here," he said. "This isn't just a break between realms. It's... absence. Unmaking."

Brynja's truth-runes flared golden. "The Ashfather's influence," she said with certainty. "This bears his mark."

Leif led them around the dark tear, following a twisting path that seemed to double back on itself yet somehow made progress. The oath-sigil leaves created a trail of soft illumination in their wake, marking their passage through the destabilized realm.

**

They crested a rise formed from solidified memories—fragments of battlefields, childhood homes, and ancient forests compressed into a single landscape—and saw below them a plain where reality itself came apart. The ground heaved like a troubled sea, memories solidifying into physical objects before dissolving again. Trees grew from nothing, reached full height, and withered in moments. Mountains rose and crumbled like sandcastles.

"There," Leif pointed toward the far side of the plain. "The Verdant Gate still stands."

Asvarr squinted through the chaos. For a moment, he saw nothing. Then, as a particularly violent surge of memory-matter cleared, he glimpsed it—the massive doorway of intertwined roots and branches that had first led them into the memory realm. It pulsed with golden light, seemingly stable despite the destruction around it.

"Can we cross that?" Asvarr asked, eyeing the violently fluctuating plain.

"We have no choice," Yrsa replied. "If we remain caught between realms when the memory domain fully collapses, our essences will fragment with it."

Brynja flexed her wooden arm, sap beading along its length. "I can stabilize sections of ground ahead of us. My fragment responds to this chaos—it recognizes the pattern beneath the breaking."

"And I can see safe paths through the worst of it," Leif added.

Asvarr tightened his grip on the boy's hand, feeling their oath-sigils pulse in response. "Together, then."

They descended toward the churning plain. With each step, the destruction around them intensified. The ground shuddered beneath their feet. Islands of solid reality floated in seas of formless potential. In places, the very air crystallized into shards of frozen time that shattered when disturbed.

Leif guided them with unerring precision, pointing out invisible paths through the chaos. When they reached areas too unstable to cross, Brynja knelt and pressed her wooden arm into the formless matter. Golden sap flowed from her transformed limb, creating temporary structures that hardened just long enough for them to cross.

Halfway across the plain, a massive surge of memory-matter erupted before them. It coalesced into a towering shape—a tree formed from the collective memories of Yggdrasil, simultaneously smaller than a sapling and larger than mountains. Its branches extended beyond sight, twisting through layers of reality.

"Projection," Yrsa said, her voice tight with awe. "The memory realm's last attempt to maintain its structure."

The tree-projection shimmered, its form unstable. Within its translucent trunk, Asvarr glimpsed moving shapes—five figures formed of living wood with faces of intertwined branches. They turned toward the travelers with eyes that contained galaxies.

"The Verdant Five," Brynja hissed, wooden arm instinctively rising in defense.

The projected figures made no move to attack. They simply watched, their branch-faces shifting into expressions Asvarr struggled to interpret—there was satisfaction there, yet also concern. One raised an arm, pointing toward the distant Gate. Another shook its head, clearly troubled. A third reached toward Brynja, fingers stretching impossibly.

"They're not truly here," Yrsa explained. "These are echoes, fragments of their consciousness projected through the breaking realm."

The fragmented Five continued their silent observation. Their projected forms blurred and sharpened rhythmically, like beings struggling to maintain presence across a vast distance. The meaning of their gestures remained ambiguous—approval or warning, welcome or threat?

A thunderous crack split the air, and the projection fragmented. The memory-tree shattered into countless glittering shards that hung suspended for a heartbeat before dissolving into golden dust. Behind it, a new path had opened—a straight line of relatively stable ground leading directly to the Verdant Gate.

"They're manipulating the realm's collapse," Yrsa realized. "Creating a path while they still can."

"But why help us?" Asvarr questioned.

"Perhaps they don't see it as help," Brynja replied, her truth-runes pulsing. "Perhaps they're steering us toward their purpose, not ours."

They had no time to debate. The realm's disintegration accelerated around them. What had been islands of stability amid chaos became mere stepping stones in a sea of unmaking. They rushed forward along the provided path, the grove-twined mark in Asvarr's palm burning with warning.

Ahead, the Verdant Gate pulsed with increasing urgency, its living wood contracting and expanding like a heart struggling to maintain rhythm. Beyond it lay darkness, the solidity of true realm-space, a reality anchored in the pattern.

"It closes," Leif gasped, pulling them forward with strength belying his small frame. "The Gate feels the realm's death."

They ran the final distance, leaping over gaps where even the Five's provided path crumbled into nothingness. The ground behind them dissolved entirely, leaving them on a floating island of reality with the Gate at its edge. Beyond the island's boundaries, existence itself unraveled—the memory realm fragmenting into its component pieces, each seeking its original place in the pattern.

They reached the Verdant Gate as its pulsations reached a frantic pace. The intertwined roots and branches that formed its structure groaned with strain, golden sap bleeding from stress fractures along its surface.

"Together," Asvarr commanded, raising his grove-marked palm. The others joined him, their four hands pressing against the Gate's shuddering surface. The tiny leaves sprouting from their oath-sigils flared with unified light, and the Gate responded—its pulse stabilizing momentarily, its structure recognizing their combined essence.

The gateway began to open, wood separating with the sound of ancient hinges protesting movement. Through the widening aperture, Asvarr glimpsed a forest unlike Alfheim's silver trees or the memory realm's ever-changing landscape—this was solidity, reality anchored firmly in the pattern.

Behind them, the floating island of stability began to crumble at its edges. The unmaking reached for them with hungry tendrils. Above, what had been sky fragmented into irregular shards revealing the void beyond creation itself.

A presence coalesced beside them—neither fully physical nor merely spiritual. Patterns of light and shadow twisted into a vaguely humanoid shape, its edges constantly shifting. Within its fluid form, Asvarr glimpsed something familiar—the consciousness he had encountered across his journey, the voice that had guided and warned him since his first binding.

"Coilvoice," he whispered in recognition.

The entity pulsed in acknowledgment, its form growing more defined as it drew substance from the disintegrating realm around them. Arms formed of shadow reached toward the Gate as it continued its agonizingly slow opening.

"The realm dies," the entity spoke, its voice resonating directly in their minds. "But fragments survive through vessels like yourselves. The Tree's consciousness persists."

"What are you?" Brynja demanded, her wooden arm extending reflexively.

Light and shadow shifted within the entity's form. "I am the Tree's final thought as it shattered—fragment, echo, memory given form." The being pulsed again, growing momentarily more substantial. "I have watched across nine cycles of breaking and binding. I have guided those who might restore the pattern."

The Verdant Gate opened wider, nearly enough to pass through. Beyond it, solid reality waited—escape from the collapsing memory realm. The island beneath their feet had shrunk to barely the size of a small room, unmaking encroaching from all sides.

"Come with us," Asvarr said impulsively. "You'll be destroyed if you remain."

"I am bound to this realm," Coilvoice replied, its form already beginning to fray at the edges. "My purpose continues through you. The anchors remember, even when vessels forget."

The Gate opened fully at last. Leif pulled urgently at their hands. "We must go now! Everything falls apart!"

Asvarr felt the boy's fear through their connection. Leif understood the spaces between realms in ways the others couldn't comprehend. If he said time had run out, they needed to trust him.

Brynja and Yrsa stepped through the Gate first, their forms briefly outlined in golden light as they crossed the threshold. Leif followed, tugging Asvarr forward. As he prepared to step through, Asvarr cast one last glance back at Coilvoice.

The entity's form had deteriorated further, fragments of its substance drifting away like autumn leaves caught in a breeze. Yet its core remained, a concentration of light and shadow that pulsed with deliberate rhythm.

"What awaits us beyond the third anchor?" Asvarr asked quickly. "What lies at the pattern's heart?"

Coilvoice's form contracted, focusing its remaining strength. "Something older than the Tree, older than gods, older than pattern itself." The entity's voice grew distant, fragments of its consciousness already dispersing. "The Verdant Five fear it. The Ashfather sought to control it. The Tree shattered to contain it."

The Gate began to contract, its momentary stability failing as the realm around it dissolved. Asvarr felt Leif pull him with desperate strength, the oath-sigil burning with urgency.

"Remember," Coilvoice called, its form now barely coherent, "not all that sleeps beneath the roots was meant to wake!"

Asvarr stumbled backward through the Gate as it slammed shut, cutting off the entity's final warning. The last image he carried was of Coilvoice—the Tree's dying thought—dissolving into motes of light as the memory realm collapsed around it, fragments of consciousness returning to the pattern from which they had been torn.

***

Fragmented reality clawed at Asvarr's mind as he ran. The ground beneath his feet shifted between solid earth and memories of solidity. Trees dissolved into fragments of recollection before reforming as something half-remembered, their branches reaching with desperate need. The combined resonance of his bound anchors with Brynja's fragment had torn the fabric of the memory realm beyond repair.

"The path splits here!" Leif shouted, his small frame suddenly substantial where previously he'd seemed half-transparent. The boy extended one arm toward a golden thread of light barely visible through the chaos. "Follow that thread exactly—step where I step!"

Asvarr gripped his bronze sword, its gold-veined blade humming with the resonance of his bound anchors. The memory realm unraveled around them in violent spasms. Where chunks of landscape broke away, he glimpsed other realms through the gaps—Midgard's forests, Niflheim's ice plains, Muspelheim's volcanic terrain—all fragmenting like reflections in a shattered mirror.

Brynja's wooden arm extended, fingers elongating into branch-like appendages that wove into the collapsing reality. Golden sap flowed from her transformed limb, briefly stabilizing their immediate surroundings.

"I can't hold this!" she grunted, teeth clenched with effort. The bark patterns creeping across her face pulsed with green-gold light. "The realm recognizes me as part of itself—it's pulling me in!"

Yrsa gripped her crystal pendant, which blazed with blue-white light. "The boundary is thinning everywhere. We must reach the Gate before the realm collapses entirely."

Overhead, the sky split along jagged lines, revealing a cosmos filled with unfamiliar stars. Memory fragments rained down like glass shards—a warrior's last battle cry, a child's forgotten lullaby, an ancient oath spoken when the Tree was young—each shattering into motes of golden light upon impact.

"There!" Leif pointed toward a massive structure shimmering in and out of perception—the Verdant Gate. It stood half-formed in the distance, a towering archway of interwoven roots and branches weeping golden sap, surrounded by a maelstrom of disintegrating reality.

A frigid gust tore through the collapsing realm, carrying whispers of countless lost memories. Asvarr shielded his eyes as the wind intensified, his Grímmark burning beneath his tunic. The grove-twined mark on his palm throbbed in rhythm with those of his companions, the tiny leaves sprouting from the wooden circle glowing emerald-bright.

Five massive wooden figures materialized around them, their bodies partially composed of living wood, faces formed of interwoven branches with galaxies swirling in their eye sockets. The Verdant Five had projected themselves into the dying realm, present enough to affect reality.

"Look." Asvarr nodded toward the projections. "They're creating a path."

The wooden figures raised their arms in synchronized movement. Scattered fragments of reality coalesced before them, forming a narrow bridge of solid memory stretching toward the Gate. Their expressions shifted between approval at the Wardens' alliance and concern at the realm's accelerating collapse.

"They fear what we've awakened," Brynja said, her truth-runes glowing golden across her face. "Yet they need us to reach it first."

Leif darted forward onto the memory bridge, bare feet leaving shimmering footprints. "Hurry! This won't hold long!"

Asvarr followed, the boy's footprints flaring brighter when he stepped into them. The bridge felt solid one moment, ephemeral the next—like walking on dreams given temporary substance. The Verdant Five maintained their positions, branches creaking with effort as they held the collapsing realm at bay.

Behind them, entire sections of the memory forest dissolved into swirling golden particles. The maelstrom intensified, reality collapsing inward as though being consumed by an invisible maw. Trees that had stood for millennia in remembered form screamed as they unraveled—the sound of memory itself being undone.

"We're not going to make it," Yrsa gasped, clutching her side as she ran. Her crystal pendant flashed with increasing urgency.

The Verdant Gate loomed closer now, its massive structure pulsating like a heart, each beat causing ripples through what remained of reality. The archway leaked golden sap that formed intricate, shifting patterns across its surface—patterns identical to those spreading beneath Asvarr's skin.

"Almost—" Asvarr's words died in his throat as a massive fissure split the bridge before them. Beyond the gap, the Gate beckoned, tantalizingly close yet unreachable.

Leif skidded to a stop at the bridge's edge. "We need to jump together! The connection between us is stronger than the realm!"

"On my count," Asvarr shouted over the cacophony of unraveling memory. "Three, two—"

A blinding flash erupted between them and the Gate. When Asvarr's vision cleared, a figure stood at the bridge's edge—neither solid nor shadow, but a pattern of light and darkness woven together in humanoid form. It shifted constantly, light becoming shadow becoming light, its voice resonating directly within their minds.

I am what remains of the Tree's final thought.

"Coilvoice," Asvarr whispered, the name rising unbidden to his lips.

The figure inclined its head in acknowledgment. *I have watched your progress through nine cycles of breaking and binding. You are the first to walk the third path together.*

"Help us cross," Brynja demanded, her wooden arm creaking as she gestured toward the fissure.

I cannot leave this realm. I am bound to it as guardian of what was. When it falls, I fall with it. The figure's voice carried ancient sorrow. *But I can offer one final warning before the Gate closes forever.*

The memory realm shuddered violently. Great chunks of landscape vanished into nothingness, leaving only void in their wake. The Verdant Five's projections flickered, their power waning as reality disintegrated around them.

Coilvoice extended a limb of interwoven light and darkness. Where it touched the fissure, golden threads sprang forth, weaving together to form a narrow bridge.

Cross now, Wardens. What awaits in the third anchor will test your alliance in ways you cannot imagine.

They sprinted across the golden bridge, the structure disintegrating behind their heels with each step. Asvarr felt Coilvoice's presence following them, a consciousness formed from Yggdrasil's dying thoughts, preserving what could be saved of the Tree's final moments.

At the Verdant Gate, Asvarr pressed his palm against the living wood. Brynja did the same, her wooden fingers sinking slightly into the surface. The Gate recognized their blood, their combined essence. It shuddered, then split down the middle, revealing a swirling vortex beyond.

Listen carefully. Coilvoice's form began to fragment as the realm collapsed around them. *Something ancient has awakened—a force that once threatened the Tree before its creation was complete. The breaking was not just destruction, but protection.*

"Protection from what?" Asvarr demanded.

Coilvoice's voice grew fainter as its form dispersed. *Not all that sleeps beneath the roots was meant to wake. The pattern shifts with each binding—what was contained becomes free, what was free becomes—*

The message cut off as the vortex within the Gate intensified. Reality bent at impossible angles, the collapsing memory realm folding in upon itself like paper crushed by a giant's fist.

"We have to go now!" Yrsa shouted, seizing Leif's hand.

Asvarr cast one final glance at Coilvoice, catching a glimpse of ancient eyes within the dissolving pattern—eyes that had witnessed nine cycles of breaking and binding, of hope and failure.

"Thank you," he whispered.

Coilvoice's response came as the barest whisper: *Remember... the third path leads to transformation. The choice must be conscious, or the cycle merely begins anew.*

Together they leapt through the Verdant Gate. As they passed the threshold, Asvarr heard a tremendous crack behind them. He turned in time to see the Gate slamming shut, sealing the memory realm as it collapsed into fragments of forgotten history.

The last thing he saw before the Gate closed completely was Coilvoice raising a hand in farewell—guardian of a realm that had served its purpose, returning to the void from which all memory eventually emerges, and to which all memory ultimately returns.

Then they were falling through darkness shot through with threads of golden light, hurtling toward a Midgard transformed by the awakening of the second Root Anchor.

CHAPTER 24

THE THORN-LIT HORIZON

The fall between realms lasted both an eternity and an instant. Asvarr tumbled through darkness laced with threads of golden light, the void pulling at his transformed flesh. His companions' bodies flashed beside him—Brynja's wooden arm trailing luminescent sap, Yrsa's crystal pendant blazing with blue-white radiance, Leif's small form wreathed in silver mist.

Then air rushed into Asvarr's lungs as gravity seized him once more, dumping him onto solid earth with bruising force. The bronze sword clattered beside him, its golden veins pulsing with the power of two bound anchors. He dug his fingers into soil—real soil, not memory masquerading as matter—and inhaled the scent of damp earth, pine resin, and woodsmoke.

Home. Midgard.

Asvarr rolled onto his back, then froze at the sight above him. The sky had split in two—half a familiar twilight blue, half an impossible latticework of thorny branches that pulsed with golden light. The lattice stretched across the heavens like a vast net, its tendrils weaving between clouds, creating shadows that danced across the land below.

"By all the gods," he whispered, the oath catching in his throat as he realized gods might once again be listening.

Birds flew between the celestial thorns, perching on branches that should not exist, building nests where stars once hung unimpeded. Through gaps in the lattice, new constellations had formed—patterns of light unlike any he'd seen before, arranged in geometric configurations that resembled the runes spreading beneath his skin.

Brynja stirred beside him, her face—half human, half wooden—turned skyward. The bark patterns that covered part of her features had grown more intricate, spiraling outward from her left eye in whorls that mimicked the thorny lattice above.

"The anchors," she murmured, her truth-runes glowing golden with sincerity. "They're reshaping everything."

Asvarr pushed himself upright, wincing as the Grímmark burned beneath his tunic. The mark had spread further across his torso, now extending over his shoulders and down his back in patterns of intertwined flame and root. Crystal formations had begun appearing within the bark-like patches on his skin—remnants of his communion with the Memory Anchor.

Yrsa crouched nearby, her breathing labored. The crystal pendant at her throat pulsed erratically. "The transformation accelerates," she gasped. "The second anchor's awakening ripples through all realms simultaneously."

"Where are we?" Asvarr asked, scanning their surroundings.

They had landed in a clearing within a forest, but this was no ordinary woodland. Trees grew at impossible angles, their branches reaching sideways and in spirals. Some trunks split in their middle, forming perfect archways before reconnecting higher up. Flowers bloomed despite the chill in the air, their petals metallic and reflective, turning like faces to track the group's movements.

Leif stood at the clearing's edge, the spiral mark on his forehead glowing faintly. "The border of Graywood," he said with that unsettling adult resonance that occasionally emerged from his childlike frame. "Three days' walk from your clan's former lands, Asvarr."

The grove-twined mark on Asvarr's palm throbbed, its tiny sprouted leaves glowing emerald-bright. Through it, he sensed the others' emotions—Brynja's wary alertness, Yrsa's exhaustion, Leif's strange detachment. The oath they'd sworn bound them together in more ways than the physical.

"We should move," Brynja said, flexing her wooden arm. Golden sap oozed from the seams between bark plates, falling to the earth where small shoots immediately sprouted. "I hear voices to the east."

Before they could gather themselves, a horn sounded in the distance—three short blasts followed by one long note. The call echoed strangely, as if passing through layers of reality before reaching their ears.

Asvarr snatched up his bronze sword, its golden veins flaring in response to potential danger. "Scouts from Thornhaven, by their horn pattern."

"You know this place?" Yrsa asked.

"I've traded here." Asvarr stepped toward the sound, careful to place himself between it and his companions. "Before the Shattering, it was a small settlement of sheep farmers and woodcutters. The forest wasn't like this then."

They moved cautiously through the transformed woodland. With each step, Asvarr became more aware of how profoundly Midgard had changed during their absence. Mushrooms glowed with internal light, casting purplish illumination across the forest floor. Vines with finger-like tendrils reached toward them, recoiling when they drew too close. The very air tasted different—metallic and sharp, charged with potential like the moments before lightning strikes.

"The Root's awakening has thinned the boundaries between realms," Yrsa explained, touching a flower that chimed like crystal when her fingers brushed its petals. "What was once hidden behind veils of perception now manifests physically."

A rustling noise ahead brought them to a halt. Asvarr signaled for silence, his warrior's instincts taking over despite his transformation. He advanced slowly, the others falling into formation behind him.

The forest opened into another clearing where a group of villagers gathered around several enormous plants Asvarr had never seen before. The growths resembled roses but stood taller than a man, their massive crimson blooms wider than shield bosses. The villagers carefully collected dew from the petals, the liquid glowing faintly as it dripped into wooden bowls.

One of the villagers, a woman with graying braids and a threadbare cloak, noticed their approach. She raised a gnarled walking stick, her face hardening with suspicion.

"Hold there," she called, her voice carrying the sharp edge of fear disguised as authority. "State your business in Thornhaven's wood."

The other villagers turned, their expressions shifting from wariness to shock as they took in Asvarr's group—particularly Brynja's wooden transformation and Leif's golden eyes. Several made warding signs with their fingers.

Asvarr sheathed his sword slowly, demonstrating peaceful intent. "I am Asvarr of Hralvik. I've traded furs in your market before."

The woman squinted, recognition gradually softening her features. "The berserker from the northern clan?" She lowered her staff slightly. "We heard Hralvik was destroyed during the Shattering."

"It was," Asvarr confirmed, the familiar ache returning despite the memories he'd sacrificed.

She gestured to the others. "Your appearance has changed, Northman."

Asvarr touched his chest where the Grímmark burned beneath his clothing. "Much has changed for all of us."

The woman nodded gravely. "That it has." She introduced herself as Dalla, elder of what remained of Thornhaven. While she spoke, the villagers resumed their careful harvesting, their movements reverent.

"What are these plants?" Yrsa asked, her gaze fixed on the enormous roses.

"We call them Night-singers," Dalla replied. "They grew after a root fragment fell two leagues north. Been spreading ever since."

"Night-singers?" Brynja echoed.

Dalla's expression turned haunted. "Wait until dusk. You'll understand."

The woman invited them to follow the harvesting party back to Thornhaven. As they walked, she explained how the settlement had changed since the Shattering. The village had tripled in size as survivors from surrounding steadings sought refuge. The forest had transformed, producing plants with strange properties—flowers that sang in voices resembling lost loved ones, trees that walked under moonlight, rearranging themselves by morning, vines that coiled in agitation when arguments broke out nearby.

"The plants respond to our feelings," Dalla said, pointing to a cluster of blue flowers that closed their petals as the group passed. "The stronger the emotion, the stronger their reaction."

The settlement came into view—a walled compound of wooden buildings with thatched roofs, surrounded by newly erected palisades. The thorny lattice in the sky cast geometric shadows across the village, creating patterns that shifted as clouds passed across the sun.

"Had to build higher walls," Dalla explained, gesturing to where workers reinforced the palisade. "Things come out of the forest at night now."

"What kinds of things?" Asvarr asked.

"Creatures we have no names for." Dalla's voice lowered. "Half-formed, like the world can't decide what shape they should take."

At the village gates, guards eyed them suspiciously but allowed entry after Dalla's explanation. Inside, Thornhaven bustled with activity despite the apprehension visible on many faces. Children played in the central square, watched over by elders who sat beneath a gnarled tree that had twisted itself into a shelter-like form. Craftspeople worked at open-air stalls, creating tools and goods from materials Asvarr didn't recognize—wood that glowed from within, metals with impossible colors, fabrics woven from fibers that seemed to shift and change as they caught the light.

Dalla led them to a longhouse that served as the village's gathering place. Inside, village elders had assembled around a central hearth where a cookfire burned with flames that occasionally shifted to green or purple.

"Guests from beyond our borders," Dalla announced. "Asvarr of Hralvik and his companions."

The elders regarded them with a mixture of wariness and hope. One man with a white beard and a heavily lined face leaned forward, his pale eyes reflecting the strange-colored flames.

"You've walked with the Root," he said. "We've seen others with marks like yours."

"Others?" Asvarr asked sharply.

The man nodded. "A woman passed through three moons ago. Her skin bore patterns like yours." He pointed to Asvarr's chest where the Grímmark lay hidden beneath his clothing. "She spoke of five who would bear the mark of change."

Brynja and Asvarr exchanged glances. The grove-twined oath-mark on his palm pulsed with shared recognition.

"Her name?" Brynja asked.

"Brenna," the elder replied. "Called herself Flame-Carver."

Asvarr's breath caught. The völva who had completed his Grímmark at the ritual stones. She had spoken of marking others—the remaining Wardens.

"Did she say where she was going?" he asked.

The elder shook his head. "Only that she followed the path of the broken Root."

As they spoke, a commotion arose outside. Villagers shouted in alarm, and the longhouse door burst open. A young boy rushed in, his face flushed with exertion.

"The thorns are spreading!" he cried, pointing skyward. "Look!"

They hurried outside. The thorny lattice had expanded since their arrival, now covering nearly three-quarters of the visible sky. The branches pulsed more rapidly, the golden light growing stronger as twilight approached. New tendrils extended from the main structure, reaching toward the horizon like grasping fingers.

"It happens faster each day," Dalla murmured. "Soon the entire sky will be covered."

As the light faded, an extraordinary transformation occurred. The massive Night-singer roses throughout the village began to emit a soft harmonic tone that rose and fell like human voices. The sound carried emotion—longing, grief, hope—weaving together into a complex melody that echoed across the settlement.

Villagers emerged from their homes, gathering in silence as the flowers sang. Some wept openly; others closed their eyes in reverence. The song grew louder as more blooms joined the chorus, the melody shifting constantly, never repeating the same phrase twice.

"They sing of what was lost," Dalla whispered, tears tracking down her weathered cheeks. "And what might yet be."

Asvarr stood transfixed as the melody washed over him. Within the song, he heard echoes of his clan's battle chants, his mother's lullabies, oaths sworn and broken. The sound resonated with the marks on his flesh, the Grímmark heating in response.

Above, stars appeared in the gaps between the thorny branches, new arrangements that formed runes and symbols matching those etched into the standing stones where his journey began.

"The world unmakes itself to be reborn," Yrsa murmured, her crystal pendant catching and fracturing the starlight.

Leif slipped his small hand into Asvarr's, the touch anchoring him as the song threatened to overwhelm his senses. "The third anchor awaits," the boy said with that ancient resonance. "In Alfheim, where starlight touches root."

Brynja leaned close, her wooden arm brushing against Asvarr's. "The pattern changes with each binding," she whispered, truth-runes confirming her sincerity. "What kind of world are we creating, Flame-Keeper?"

Asvarr had no answer. He stared up at the thorn-lit horizon, the sky caged by golden branches that had not existed when he began his journey. The world transformed around them—flowers that sang with human voices, trees that walked beneath moonlight, vines that responded to emotion, and above it all, a barrier growing between the mortal realms and whatever lay beyond.

With each anchor they bound, the transformation accelerated. The third anchor waited in Alfheim, and beyond that, the fourth and fifth. What would remain of Midgard when their task was complete? What would remain of Asvarr himself?

The Night-singers' song shifted, taking on an urgent, warning tone. At the village perimeter, guards raised the alarm—something approached from the forest's depths, drawn by the music and the gathering of people.

Asvarr drew his bronze sword, the golden veins within the blade flaring in response to his intent. Whatever emerged from the transformed woodland would find the Warden of Two Anchors waiting, his path now irrevocably bound to the remaking of all realms.

The alarm at Thornhaven's perimeter faded to distant shouts as guards confronted whatever had emerged from the forest darkness. Asvarr kept his sword drawn, the golden veins pulsing beneath his grip, but Dalla placed a weathered hand on his arm.

"The night-watch can handle it," she said. "Common enough occurrence these days. Come, there's something you should see while the sky remains clear."

She led them to a watchtower built into Thornhaven's eastern wall. The rough-hewn ladder creaked beneath their weight as they climbed, the wooden rungs worn smooth by countless hands. At the top, Dalla gestured toward the horizon where the thorny lattice met the edge of the world.

"Watch," she instructed, pointing to where a tendril of golden light extended from the main structure, reaching toward the ground like a searching finger.

Asvarr narrowed his eyes. The branch moved with deliberate purpose, probing the air before suddenly plunging downward. Where it touched earth, a flash of golden light erupted. When it receded, the branch had rooted itself, creating a massive pillar of light connecting ground to sky.

"They've been forming since the second full moon after the Shattering," Dalla explained. "Started along the northern mountains, now spreading south and east. Some say they'll eventually encircle the world."

Yrsa moved to the watchtower's edge, her crystal pendant blazing with blue-white light. She studied the thorny lattice with an intensity that made her eyes shine like polished silver in the darkness.

"It's a defense mechanism," she announced, her voice carrying the weight of ancient knowing. "The Root creates a barrier between realms, separating the mortal worlds from the divine."

"Defense against what?" Asvarr asked.

"Against those who would reclaim what they believe is theirs." Yrsa turned to face them, her expression grave. "The gods withdrew during the Last Breaking, but they did not disappear. They exist in the spaces between, waiting. This lattice prevents their full return."

Brynja's wooden fingers traced patterns in the air that matched the thorny branches overhead. "The five who created it fear the gods returning," she said, her truth-runes glowing with golden confirmation of her sincerity. "They shape the Tree to their purpose, just as the gods once did."

Asvarr's Grímmark burned beneath his tunic, responding to the sight of the distant pillar. He could feel the second anchor stirring within him, the memory-essence recognizing its handiwork in the transformed sky.

"What happens when the barrier is complete?" he asked.

"The final bloom," Yrsa replied. "A key stage in Yggdrasil's potential rebirth—or its permanent transformation into something new. The pattern awakens, but whether it follows the old design or creates a new one depends on those who guide it." Her gaze shifted between Asvarr and Brynja meaningfully.

"I've seen enough." Dalla turned toward the ladder. "Best get inside before the mist rises."

They followed her back to the longhouse where village elders had prepared a meal. Meat stewed with unfamiliar herbs filled wooden bowls, the steam carrying scents both familiar and strangely alien. Bread woven with silver fibers gleamed in the firelight, and mead in horn cups shimmered with an internal luminescence.

"Food from the changed lands," the white-bearded elder explained when he noticed Asvarr's hesitation. "Takes some getting used to, but it sustains us."

Asvarr tried the stew, finding the flavor unexpectedly complex—sweetness followed by a metallic tang that numbed his tongue briefly before fading to warmth.

The mead glowed faintly as he swallowed, sending tendrils of heat through his chest that seemed to resonate with his transformed flesh.

While they ate, Dalla and the elders shared stories of how Midgard had changed since the Shattering. Rivers flowed uphill in some places, forests rearranged themselves overnight, animals spoke in half-formed words before retreating in confusion at their own voices. Time stretched and compressed unpredictably—a single night might last three days in certain valleys, while in others, seasons passed in the span of a week.

"The root-strikes change everything they touch," the white-bearded elder explained. "Those who survive learn to adapt."

After the meal, the villagers departed to their homes, leaving Asvarr's group alone in the longhouse with Dalla. The hearth fire had dwindled to embers that pulsed with the same rhythm as the thorny lattice overhead.

Brynja broke the silence. "The barrier serves a purpose beyond keeping the gods at bay." She turned to Asvarr, her face—half human, half wooden—caught in shadows from the dying fire. "It creates space for something new to grow. Evolution, not restoration."

The word struck Asvarr like a physical blow. "Evolution?" He straightened, feeling the Grímmark heat in response to his emotional state. "We're meant to restore what was broken, not replace it with something unknown."

"Restore to what?" Brynja challenged, her wooden arm creaking as she gestured toward the ceiling, indicating the transformed world beyond. "The Tree was already corrupted before it shattered. The gods twisted it from its original purpose, just as the Five seek to twist it now. True restoration would return to what existed before either claimed it."

"And what was that?" Asvarr demanded. "None living remember."

"The memory anchor showed you glimpses," Brynja countered, her truth-runes flaring golden. "A pattern of connection without domination, growth without constraint."

Asvarr's fists clenched as he stepped toward her, the grove-twined mark on his palm burning. "Without constraints, chaos reigns. The Tree gave structure to existence."

"Structure that served those who imposed it," Brynja replied, standing her ground. "First the gods, then the Five. Always control disguised as protection."

"Enough." Yrsa's voice cut between them. Her crystal pendant flared with blue-white light, casting stark shadows across the longhouse interior. "Both views are too simplistic for what's coming."

She approached the hearth where the embers pulsed with an unnatural rhythm. Kneeling, she scattered something from a small pouch onto the coals. The fire erupted in a column of blue flame that twisted into patterns matching those beneath Asvarr's skin.

"The anchors serve neither restoration nor evolution alone," Yrsa said, her face transformed by the eerie light. "Each binding reshapes the world and those who undertake it. Have you noticed your own transformations? The choices that seemed clear at the beginning blur with each new sacrifice."

She gestured toward Asvarr's chest where the Grímmark lay hidden, then to Brynja's wooden limb with its flowering vines. "You change, the world changes, the pattern changes. The question is not whether to restore or evolve, but what you will become in the process, and what that becoming means for all realms."

***

Leif, who had remained silent throughout the meal and subsequent argument, now moved beside Yrsa. The spiral mark on his forehead glowed faintly in the blue firelight.

"The pattern grows three ways," he said with that unsettling adult resonance. "Through what was, what is, and what could be. The flame preserves the past." He nodded toward Asvarr. "The root reaches for the future." His gaze shifted to Brynja. "The binding holds them in balance—or tears them apart."

Asvarr felt the weight of the boy's words settle into his bones. He touched his chest where the Grímmark spread beneath his clothing, its design now incorporating elements of both flame and root. Each binding changed him, making him less human and more... what? Vessel? Tool? Something entirely new?

"What do you counsel, Boundary-Walker?" he asked Yrsa. "If neither restoration nor evolution is the true path?"

"I counsel awareness," she replied. "The pattern exists in a constant state of tension between what was and what could be. Your task is to maintain that tension—to prevent either force from dominating completely."

Outside, a horn sounded—three short blasts followed by two long notes. Dalla burst through the longhouse door, her face pale in the blue firelight.

"The barrier is failing at the northern edge," she announced breathlessly. "Something's coming through."

They rushed outside into the night air that tasted of metal and ozone. Villagers gathered in the central square, pointing toward the northern sky where the thorny lattice shimmered with unstable light. The branches there had thinned, creating a gap through which stars were visible, strange, cold lights that moved with deliberate purpose.

"The spaces between," Yrsa whispered, her crystal pendant pulsing frantically. "The barrier weakens where the Root's influence fades. If it fails completely..."

She didn't need to finish the thought. If the thorny lattice served as defense against the returning gods or whatever else waited beyond the mortal realms, its failure would have consequences beyond imagination.

The grove-twined mark on Asvarr's palm throbbed, its tiny leaves glowing emerald-bright. Through it, he sensed his companions' emotions—Brynja's determination, Yrsa's concern, Leif's eerie calm. The connection between them had grown stronger since their oath-making, creating a bond that transcended words.

"We need to reach the third anchor," Asvarr decided. "The pattern must be reinforced before more breaches appear."

"That would accelerate the transformation," Brynja warned. "Each binding changes the balance between worlds."

"Each binding also strengthens what remains," Asvarr countered. "Without the anchors, all realms will unravel."

The cold stars beyond the gap grew brighter, casting an unnatural light across Thornhaven. Shadows stretched in impossible directions, and the Night-singer roses unleashed a discordant melody that made Asvarr's teeth ache.

Dalla approached, clutching her walking staff like a weapon. "Whatever comes through that gap won't be friendly to our kind," she said grimly. "The old stories speak of what existed before the gods claimed dominion—nameless things from the void that hunger for form and purpose."

The white-bearded elder joined them, his pale eyes reflecting the strange light from above. "There's an ancient passage east of here," he told Asvarr. "A hollow tree that some say leads to the realm of light. If you seek Alfheim, that would be your path."

Asvarr glanced at his companions, feeling the weight of decision press upon him. The choice between restoration and evolution now seemed a luxury compared to the immediate threat. Whatever philosophical differences existed between them, survival took precedence.

"We leave at dawn," he announced. "With or without resolution to our debate."

"The resolution comes through action, not argument," Yrsa observed. "Each step you take shapes the pattern more than any belief you hold."

The cold stars pulsed, and a tendril of darkness extended through the gap in the thorny lattice. It probed the air as the golden branches had done earlier, searching with alien purpose. Where it touched the barrier, the thorns blackened and crumbled to ash.

Asvarr drew his bronze sword, the golden veins within the blade flaring in response to the threat. The Grímmark burned against his skin, recognizing what his conscious mind could not yet comprehend. Beside him, Brynja's wooden arm extended, fingers elongating into branch-like claws. Leif stepped between them, his small hand slipping into Asvarr's free one.

"The third path requires both of you," the boy said quietly. "Flame and root, past and future, held in balance."

Above them, the gap in the barrier widened as more thorns blackened and disintegrated. The darkness beyond pulsed with hunger older than the Tree, older than the gods, perhaps older than reality itself. Whatever came through would find the Wardens waiting, their quest now sharpened by immediate danger.

Evolution or restoration—the debate would continue. But first, they had to survive the night.

CHAPTER 25

THE MEMORY EATERS

Asvarr woke to the sound of teeth chattering. A skittering, metallic clacking that echoed through the walls of the longhouse. He sat up, golden sap leaking from the bark-like patterns across his chest as his heart quickened. The fire in the central hearth had dimmed to embers, casting the space in murky blue shadows. Outside, moonlight cut between the lattice of thorns overhead, dappling the ground with fractal patterns.

"You hear it too," Brynja whispered from across the room. Her wooden arm gleamed faintly in the darkness, delicate flowering vines spiraling around what had once been flesh.

"Something's coming through." Asvarr reached for his bronze sword, its golden veins pulsing in rhythm with his transformed heart. The memories of two bound anchors thrummed within his flesh, calling to whatever approached from beyond the thorny lattice.

Leif sat bolt upright, his childlike face ghostly in the dying firelight. "They're hungry," he said with unnerving adult resonance. "They remember being forgotten."

Before anyone could respond, Dalla burst through the door, her gray braids wild around her face. "Wake the others," she hissed. "The north barrier's been breached. They're coming."

Yrsa rose from her sleeping mat, crystal pendant blazing with blue-white light. "What manner of breach?"

"Things—" Dalla's voice broke. "Things that eat what you are."

***

The village alarm horn sounded three long, mournful notes as Asvarr reached the northern wall. The palisade stood intact, but beyond it, the forest had... changed. Where sturdy pines had stood the previous evening, twisted, blackened trunks now clawed at the sky. The ground beneath them had cracked open, revealing fissures that glowed with sickly purple light.

And through those cracks they came.

Blank-faced figures with skin like tarnished silver. Their limbs bent at impossible angles, too many joints folding and unfolding as they pulled themselves into Midgard. Each stood roughly human height, but their proportions were wrong—arms too long, torsos stretched, fingers that branched and split into more fingers. Where faces should have been, they bore only smooth, featureless masks, until they turned just so and moonlight revealed the suggestion of eyes—vertical slits that contained stars.

The grove-twined mark on Asvarr's palm burned, warning of danger. Five villagers already stood frozen at the wall's edge, weapons fallen from limp hands. Their eyes remained open but vacant—each iris clouded over like river ice. They still breathed, still stood, but something fundamental had been hollowed from them.

"Don't let them touch you," Yrsa warned, materializing beside him with her crystal knife drawn. "They feed on memory and selfhood. One touch, and they'll begin devouring what makes you who you are."

Brynja joined them, her wooden arm extending into thorny branches. "We need to reach the hollow tree before dawn," she said. The truth-runes on her transformed half-face pulsed with golden light. "It's our passage to Alfheim."

A village defender crumpled before them. The Memory Eater that touched him hadn't used claws or teeth—just pressed one silvery hand against the man's chest. Now the creature stood taller, its form shifting subtly, taking on hints of the defender's posture and features. The emptied man fell to his knees, eyes glassy, drool leaking from slack lips.

"What are they?" Asvarr demanded, raising his bronze sword.

"The unremembered," Yrsa replied, her voice tight. "When Yggdrasil first formed reality, certain... possibilities were culled. Beings that could have existed but never did. They've waited in the gaps between worlds, feeding on scraps of identity that fall through the cracks."

Leif tugged at Asvarr's sleeve, golden eyes wide. "They want to be real again."

The Memory Eaters moved with unsettling grace, flowing between panicked villagers. They seemed drawn to those who resisted most fiercely, as if strong will and clear identity made for better feeding. Several turned toward Asvarr and his companions, vertical eye-slits widening.

Dalla rushed to them, clutching her gnarled walking stick. "We can hold them at the wall. These things seemed confused by fire." She pressed something into Asvarr's hand—a small pouch of iron filings mixed with dried herbs. "Memory-salt. Throw it in their faces if they come too close."

"We can't stay," Brynja said. "Every moment we delay puts the third anchor at risk."

Asvarr felt the pull of competing obligations—the villagers who needed protection versus the greater fate of the realms. The grove-twined mark throbbed, connecting him to Brynja's urgency, Yrsa's caution, and Leif's strange, boundless knowing.

A Memory Eater glided forward, movements jerky yet precise. Its arms unfolded with nauseating wrongness, joints bending backward, fingers splitting into silver filaments as it reached for Brynja's wooden face.

Asvarr leapt between them, swinging his bronze sword in a wide arc. The blade passed through the creature without resistance, as if cutting through mist. But where the golden veins touched silver flesh, the being shrieked—a sound like metal tearing, like ice cracking on a frozen lake.

Dark ichor splashed across the ground, each droplet containing swirling fragments of memory. The Memory Eater staggered backward, its faceless mask rippling with pain or rage. The wound sealed instantly, but the creature's attention shifted fully to Asvarr.

"They'll sense the bound anchors within you," Yrsa warned. "You carry more identity than a dozen ordinary humans combined. You're a feast to them."

As if to confirm her words, three more Memory Eaters turned toward Asvarr, their blank faces somehow radiating hunger. They moved in perfect unison, silver limbs unfolding like nightmarish blooms.

"Get to the hollow tree," Dalla urged. "We'll defend the village—we've faced strangeness before. The Night-singers will help us." She gestured toward the massive crimson roses that lined the village perimeter, each taller than a man. As if responding to her words, they began to hum with human-like voices, creating harmonies that made the Memory Eaters pause.

Brynja caught Asvarr's arm. "We must go," she insisted. Her eyes—one human brown, one swirling with sap—locked with his. "The third anchor won't wait."

The grove-twined mark pulsed. Even Leif tugged at him, the boy's face uncharacteristically desperate. For a creature usually untethered from urgency, his fear resonated powerfully.

A piercing scream cut through the night as another villager fell, clutched in a Memory Eater's many-jointed embrace. The victim didn't struggle, just stared blankly as silver tendrils caressed his face. When the creature released him, he slumped to the ground, breathing but emptied—a vessel without contents.

Asvarr made his decision. "We go now. Dalla, get your people inside—use fire, use the Night-singers."

Dalla nodded grimly. "The eastern path leads to the hollow tree. Move quickly and don't look back."

***

They fled through Thornhaven's eastern gate, Asvarr leading with bronze sword drawn. Memory Eaters glided in pursuit, flowing between trees with mercury smoothness. The thorny lattice overhead had thinned here, creating pools of silver moonlight in which the creatures moved more freely.

"They're faster in starlight," Yrsa called, her crystal pendant blazing. "Stay in shadow when you can."

Leif darted ahead, small form navigating the transformed landscape with uncanny precision. The boy existed partially outside normal reality, Asvarr remembered—perhaps that gave him insight into the Memory Eaters' movements.

The forest had changed dramatically from the previous day. Trees bent at unnatural angles, their bark now rippling like muscle. Mushrooms glowed in geometric patterns along the ground, illuminating a path that hadn't existed before. The Memory Eaters moved among the trees in silver flashes, circling rather than attacking directly.

"They're hunting," Brynja said, her wooden arm extending into a thorny shield. "Testing our defenses."

A Memory Eater lunged from shadow, fingers splitting into tendrils that reached for Leif. Brynja lashed out with vine-like extensions, thorns piercing silver flesh. The creature made that terrible tearing-metal sound again but didn't retreat. Instead, it flowed around the thorns, reshaping itself to avoid further harm.

Asvarr flung a handful of memory-salt. The iron particles burst into blue sparks when they contacted the creature's skin. It recoiled, its blank face rippling with something resembling pain.

"Keep moving," Yrsa commanded. "The hollow tree isn't far."

They ran deeper into the forest, dodging between shadow and moonlight. Memory Eaters pursued, growing bolder with distance from the village. One flowed directly into their path, its limbs unfolding into a silver web of grasping fingers.

Leif skidded to a halt, his childlike voice ringing with adult authority: "You cannot have us."

The Memory Eater tilted its featureless face, vertical eye-slits narrowing. When it spoke, the sound emerged from the air itself—vibrations that formed words: "We... remember... being... forgotten."

Asvarr's transformed flesh crawled. The thing's voice resonated inside his skull, scraping along his thoughts. The Grímmark on his chest burned in response, golden sap leaking through bark-like patterns.

"What do you want?" he demanded, sword raised.

The creature's form rippled. "To... be... again."

"You never were," Yrsa cut in, her crystal knife gleaming. "You were culled possibilities—paths untaken."

"Paths... stolen." The Memory Eater's blank face turned toward the thorny lattice overhead. "The... pattern... chose... wrong."

Before Asvarr could respond, three more creatures emerged from the darkness, surrounding them. They moved in perfect coordination, as if sharing a single mind. Silver tendrils extended from their fingers, reaching for the four companions.

Brynja unleashed her wooden arm, vines and thorns lashing out in a protective circle. "We don't have time for this," she snarled. The truth-runes on her face pulsed golden. "The hollow tree is just beyond that ridge."

The Memory Eaters pressed closer. One touched a thorny vine, and Brynja gasped as the wood instantly blackened. Whatever these creatures did, they could affect even her transformed flesh.

"They're cutting us off from the tree," Yrsa realized. "They know what we seek."

Asvarr felt the two anchors pulsing within him, flame and memory intertwined. The creatures wanted that essence—the concentrated identity he carried. Desperation bloomed in his chest. They couldn't fail now, not with the third anchor so close.

"I'll draw them off," he decided. "Get to the hollow tree. I'll catch up."

Brynja seized his arm, wooden fingers digging into flesh. "No. The blood-oath connects us. If they take your identity, I'll feel the loss." Her transformed face was fierce. "We stay together."

The Memory Eaters circled closer. One reached for Leif, silver tendrils brushing the boy's golden hair. Leif didn't flinch, his eyes clear and unafraid. The creature withdrew as if burned, its fingers smoking slightly.

"They can't touch me," Leif said simply. "I don't... exist the way you do."

A plan formed in Asvarr's mind. "Leif—can you lead them away? Just for a few moments?"

The boy nodded, his unnervingly adult gaze meeting Asvarr's. "They're curious about me. I'll draw them, but not for long."

Without waiting for further discussion, Leif darted into the forest. The Memory Eaters hesitated, then flowed after him like quicksilver streams. Their hunger momentarily diverted by something they couldn't understand—a being that existed across boundaries.

"Now," Asvarr commanded. "The ridge."

They ran, pushing through undergrowth that seemed to reach for them with deliberate malice. The forest itself had changed, becoming an extension of the Memory Eaters' hunger. Plants twisted toward them, roots erupting from soil to grab at ankles. Even the air felt somehow predatory, pressing against skin with unsettling intimacy.

The ridge came into view—a sudden rise in the land crowned with twisted trees. And there, at its base, the hollow tree stood waiting. Unlike the grasping forest around it, this ancient oak remained still, a sanctuary of stability. Its massive trunk split halfway up, creating an archway large enough for a person to walk through. Inside, darkness swirled—a living void that connected to somewhere else.

"Alfheim," Brynja breathed, her transformed face alight with determination. "Beyond that threshold lies the third anchor."

They were thirty paces from the hollow tree when the Memory Eaters returned. Dozens flowing through the forest like a silver tide. In their midst stood Leif, unharmed but surrounded. The boy met Asvarr's gaze across the distance and nodded once—*I tried*.

The creatures advanced, blank faces somehow radiating hunger. Their movements became more urgent, limbs stretching impossibly as they closed in. They no longer bothered to appear even remotely human, transforming into a grotesque tangle of silver appendages and reaching tendrils.

"They know we're escaping," Yrsa warned, crystal pendant blazing brightly. "They'll risk everything to stop us."

A Memory Eater lunged forward with shocking speed, flowing like liquid metal across the ground. It reformed directly before Asvarr, silver flesh molding into a crude approximation of his own features—a mirror face with vertical slits for eyes. It reached for him with too many fingers, each splitting into needle-thin filaments.

"Feed... us..." it whispered, the voice crawling through Asvarr's mind. "Your... memories... so... bright..."

The bronze sword flashed, golden veins pulsing. The blade connected with silver flesh, and the creature shrieked—a sound like glass shattering. It reformed instantly, but the attack created an opening. Asvarr surged forward, Brynja and Yrsa close behind.

Twenty paces to the hollow tree.

Memory Eaters converged from all sides, silver bodies flowing together into a rippling barrier. They no longer resembled humanoid forms but had become a single entity—a wall of hungry silver studded with vertical eye-slits. Tendrils extruded from the mass, reaching for the three companions.

Brynja's wooden arm erupted into thorns. Yrsa's crystal knife flashed blue-white. Asvarr's bronze sword hummed with the power of two bound anchors. They fought desperately, cutting through the silver mass only to see it reform immediately. The Memory Eaters were learning, adapting to their attacks, becoming harder to repel.

Ten paces to the hollow tree.

A silver tendril brushed Asvarr's cheek. Cold numbness spread from the point of contact, followed by a sensation of something being drawn out of him. Memories flickered and dimmed: his father's face grew hazy, his mother's voice faded to a whisper. The creature was feeding, pulling pieces of his identity into itself.

Brynja cried out, the grove-twined mark on her palm flaring with emerald light. Through their oath-bond, she felt the assault on Asvarr's selfhood. Her wooden arm lashed out, severing the silver tendril. The connection broke, leaving Asvarr gasping—diminished but still himself.

Five paces to the hollow tree.

The Memory Eaters surged forward in a final, desperate wave. Silver flowed around them, seeking any opening, any exposed flesh. They fought with renewed fury, cutting through the hungry mass without hesitation.

Yrsa reached the hollow tree first, crystal pendant illuminating the swirling void within. "Quickly," she called. "The passage won't remain stable for long."

Brynja seized Asvarr's arm, pulling him forward as silver tendrils clutched at his legs. The grove-twined mark burned between them, their blood-oath providing strength when his faltered. Together they stumbled toward the threshold where Yrsa waited.

Asvarr looked back once, searching for Leif. The boy stood just beyond the silver tide, golden eyes bright and knowing. *I'll find my own way*, his expression seemed to say. Then he vanished between one heartbeat and the next—there, then gone, slipping between realities as only he could.

"Now," Yrsa commanded, and together they plunged into the hollow tree's darkness. The void enveloped them, cool and weightless. Behind them, silver tendrils reached into the threshold but couldn't follow—the passage rejected them, recognizing them as entities that should never have existed.

As the void claimed him, carrying him toward Alfheim and the third anchor, Asvarr felt the Memory Eaters' touch lingering in his mind. Small pieces of himself had been taken—fragments of memory and identity devoured by creatures hungry for existence. The loss wasn't crippling, but it left spaces within him—hollow places where something essential had been.

And in those hollows, he sensed something else taking root—the pattern growing into spaces freshly emptied, claiming more of him with each transformation. He wondered how much would remain when the final anchor was bound, and whether he would recognize what was left.

The void within the hollow tree swallowed them whole. Asvarr tumbled through nothingness, his connection to physical reality severed. No up, no down, only the thundering of his pulse in his ears and the burning awareness of the two bound anchors within his flesh. Darkness pressed against his eyes, absolute and consuming, until—

Light. Blinding, silver-blue, pouring from a distant point that rushed toward him with stomach-turning speed. The void thinned, reality condensing around him once more as he crashed onto solid ground. Knees struck stone, palms scraped against rough crystal, the impact jarring bone and sinew.

***

Alfheim.

Asvarr gasped, drawing air that tasted of metal and starlight. The sky above blazed with impossible constellations—star patterns matching the ones beneath his skin, swirling in mathematical precision. Trees like silver spears surrounded them, their bark gleaming with internal light, leaves translucent as insect wings.

"They're still coming," Brynja said, hauling herself upright. Her wooden features caught the starlight, glowing with amber undertones. The flowers along her transformed arm had closed tight, protective in this alien realm.

Yrsa stood several paces away, crystal pendant blazing with blue-white intensity. "The barrier between realms is too thin. The Memory Eaters can't physically cross, but they're reaching through."

Even as she spoke, the air between two silver trees rippled. Something pushed against reality itself—fingers of tarnished silver extending through a membrane that shouldn't have been breachable. Vertical eye-slits peered through the distortion, hungry and determined.

"We need to move," Asvarr said, gripping his bronze sword. The weapon felt strange in his hand, too heavy in one moment, almost weightless the next. More than physical weight had been stolen during their escape—fragments of identity and memory stripped away, leaving hollow spaces in his mind. His father's voice, once clear in memory, now sounded distant and distorted. His mother's face blurred at the edges, features sliding away when he tried to focus.

Brynja caught his arm, steadying him. The grove-twined mark on their palms pulsed in unison. "You're wounded," she said. The truth-runes on her face confirmed her sincerity, glowing with golden light. "Not physically, but in essence."

"What I lost wasn't vital," Asvarr said, the lie bitter on his tongue. Every memory mattered, each fragment of identity precious as the transformation progressed. With each binding, his humanity eroded—the pattern filling in the spaces, reshaping him into something less mortal, more vessel.

Another ripple in the air, larger this time. Three Memory Eaters pushed halfway through the barrier, silver bodies contorting unnaturally as they struggled to enter Alfheim fully. Their blank faces stretched wide, vertical slits opening into hungry mouths that hadn't existed before.

Yrsa raised her crystal knife, the blade hissing as it cut the air. "We can't fight them here. The third anchor waits at the peak." She pointed toward a distant mountain that gleamed like polished silver, its slopes mathematical in their precision. "Starfall Mountain."

They ran through the silver forest, each step carrying them farther than physics should have allowed. Distance worked differently here—the mountain both impossibly distant and strangely close, depending on the angle of their approach. Memory Eaters pursued, gliding through reality distortions with increasing ease. The barrier between worlds was failing, allowing these never-beings to manifest where they should never have existed.

"There!" Brynja called, pointing to a circular clearing ahead. Seven crystal pillars rose from silver grass, each inscribed with runes that shifted when viewed directly. "A ward-circle. We can make our stand there."

They reached the circle moments before the Memory Eaters. Yrsa thrust her crystal knife into the central stone, activating the runes. Blue-white light flared along the inscriptions, forming a dome of protective energy. The creatures circled outside, blank faces pressed against the barrier, silver fingers testing for weakness.

"It won't hold long," Yrsa warned. "These wards were designed for threats the makers understood. The Memory Eaters exist outside the pattern—they'll find a way through."

Asvarr studied the Memory Eaters through the barrier. They moved with more confidence now, having crossed from Midgard into Alfheim. Their forms shifted constantly, absorbing aspects of their surroundings—limbs lengthening into branches, skin taking on metallic qualities that mirrored Alfheim's silver trees. They were adapting, becoming more substantial with each passing moment.

One creature larger than the others pressed against the ward-circle's barrier. Its blank face rippled, vertical eye-slits stretching wide. When it spoke, the words crawled through Asvarr's mind: "Give... us... what... you... are..."

"What happens if they take everything?" Asvarr asked, gaze fixed on the circling creatures. "If they consume all my memories, my identity—what remains?"

Yrsa's expression darkened. "A vessel without content. You'd continue existing physically, but everything that makes you *you* would be gone. The pattern would fill those spaces with its own purpose."

"Like the emptied villagers," Brynja said, her wooden features tight with dread.

The largest Memory Eater slammed against the barrier, creating spider-web cracks in the blue-white energy. "Hungry..." it hissed, the word slithering through their minds.

"We need to reach the anchor," Asvarr insisted, gripping his bronze sword tighter. The golden veins pulsed in rhythm with his transformed heart, carrying the essence of two bound anchors. "If we bind it, perhaps we can drive them back."

Brynja shook her head, wooden features creaking as they shifted. "The mountain is too far. They'll break through before we're halfway there."

The barrier cracked again, fragments of energy falling like shattered glass. Three Memory Eaters pushed against the weakening point, their silver bodies flowing together into a unified mass of reaching tendrils and hungry mouths. The ward-circle's runes flickered, power draining with each assault.

"We need to fight," Asvarr decided, raising his sword. The bronze blade caught starlight, golden veins blazing with the power of bound anchors.

Yrsa's crystal knife flashed. "Against emptiness itself? We can't defeat hunger—we can only escape it."

The barrier shattered with a sound like breaking ice. Memory Eaters poured through the gap, silver bodies reshaping into something more predatory—all reaching limbs and grasping tendrils. They flowed across the ground like quicksilver, surrounding the three companions in a tightening circle.

Asvarr struck first, bronze sword cutting through silver flesh. The creature shrieked—a sound like tearing metal—but reformed instantly, the wound closing without trace. Brynja's wooden arm extended into thorny vines, lashing at the advancing entities. Where thorns pierced silver flesh, small bursts of memory escaped like puffs of golden smoke, each containing fragments of stolen identity.

The largest Memory Eater lunged at Asvarr, multiple limbs unfolding into a silver web. He ducked beneath the grasping tendrils, sword flashing in desperate defense. A silver tendril brushed his cheek—just the lightest touch—and cold numbness spread outward. Something vital pulled away from him, drawn into the creature's hungry essence.

His first weapon—the feel of leather wrapped around wood, the balanced weight of axe-head and handle.

His first kill—blood spraying hot across his face, the shock of taking life.

His first love—a shield-maiden's calloused fingers against his jaw, the taste of mead on her lips.

Each memory stripped away in an instant, leaving ragged holes in his identity. The Memory Eater grew more substantial, its blank face taking on hints of Asvarr's features—the shape of his jaw, the angle of his brow. It was becoming more real by consuming what made him real.

"Asvarr!" Brynja cried, seeing him stagger. She fought toward him, wooden arm lashing at the silver creatures that blocked her path. The grove-twined mark on her palm blazed with emerald light, responding to his distress through their blood-oath.

Another Memory Eater seized Asvarr from behind, silver tendril wrapping around his throat. More memories torn away—his mother singing while working at her loom, his father teaching him to track deer through snow, his clan gathering around the hearth fire during the longest night of winter. Each loss made him less himself, less anchored in his own existence.

The bronze sword slipped from numbed fingers. The Grímmark on his chest burned with sap-fire, the pattern fighting to preserve what remained of its vessel. But the Memory Eaters' hunger was too vast, their need for existence too desperate. They would consume him entirely, leaving nothing but an empty shell for the pattern to fill.

Brynja reached him as he fell to his knees. Her wooden arm shattered two Memory Eaters, thorns tearing through silver flesh that couldn't reform quickly enough. She knelt beside him, eyes fierce with determination—one human, one swirling with golden sap.

"I can save you," she said, clasping his face between flesh hand and wooden one. The truth-runes on her transformed features glowed golden, confirming her sincerity.

"How?" he managed, voice hollow as more memories drained away. The Memory Eaters clustered around them, tendrils reaching for fresh feeding.

"With something they can't digest." Brynja pressed her forehead against his, the grove-twined mark on her palm aligning with his. "A foreign memory—something rooted in different soil."

Yrsa fought to reach them, crystal knife flashing blue-white with each desperate swing. "Brynja, no! A core memory can't be replaced!"

But Brynja had already made her decision. The grove-twined mark blazed with blinding emerald light as she opened herself completely to the blood-oath's connection. Through that channel poured something precious—pure experience, direct and unfiltered.

A child stands at the edge of a clearing, hand in her mother's firm grip. Dawn light filters through ancient pines, painting the world in gold and shadow. Above them towers Yggdrasil—impossibly vast, its trunk wider than a village, its branches disappearing into cloud and starlight. Golden sap weeps from the bark, each drop containing worlds upon worlds. The child's heart expands with wonder and love and terror, too small to contain the magnificence before her. "Remember this," her mother whispers, voice breaking with emotion. "Remember what we serve."

The memory crashed into Asvarr's mind—foreign yet familiar, alien yet perfect in clarity. He gasped as it took root, expanding to fill spaces the Memory Eaters had hollowed out. Brynja's child-self became part of his understanding, her wonder at first seeing Yggdrasil merging with his own experiences.

The Memory Eaters recoiled, silver tendrils withdrawing from his flesh. The transferred memory confused them—a foreign element they couldn't process or consume. It disrupted their feeding, forcing them to retreat temporarily as their hunger recalibrated.

Brynja slumped against him, her face tight with loss. A hole gaped in her past—the place where that precious memory had lived now emptied, never to be refilled. She had sacrificed her first glimpse of Yggdrasil, the moment that had shaped her destiny, to save him from consumption.

"I can still fight," she said, voice rough with determination despite her loss. The truth-runes glowed softly, confirming she believed this to be true.

Yrsa reached them, crystal knife blazing with blue-white fire. "We need to move." She looked directly at Asvarr, eyes sharp with worry. "Can you stand?"

He nodded, reclaiming his fallen sword. The bronze blade hummed in his grip, golden veins pulsing with renewed vigor. The Memory Eaters had taken much, but Brynja's sacrifice had disrupted their feeding long enough to create an opening.

"What did you see?" Yrsa asked Brynja as they retreated from the ward-circle, Memory Eaters still disoriented behind them.

"Nothing," Brynja replied, her voice hollow. "There's nothing there now—just emptiness where something important used to be." The truth-runes confirmed this loss, glowing with painful intensity.

They fled through the silver forest, each step carrying them closer to the mountain peak where the third anchor waited. Behind them, the Memory Eaters regrouped, their hunger temporarily confounded. They would follow, driven by desperate need to exist fully.

Asvarr ran with Brynja's memory burning bright within him—her child-self gazing up at Yggdrasil with wonder and terror. The foreign memory felt strange nested among his own experiences, its edges sharp against the fabric of his identity. Yet it had saved him, filling spaces the Memory Eaters had emptied, providing substance where they had created void.

He caught Brynja's hand as they ran, feeling the grove-twined mark pulse between them. Through that connection, he sensed her loss—a vital piece of herself sacrificed to preserve him. No words could properly acknowledge such a gift, but the blood-oath between them carried his gratitude wordlessly.

The silver forest thinned as they approached the mountain base. Ahead, crystal steps carved into the mountainside spiraled upward toward the peak where starlight pooled like liquid silver. The third anchor waited there—where sky touched earth in a union of opposites.

At the mountain's base, Yrsa paused, crystal pendant pulsing with blue-white light. "The Memory Eaters can't follow up the mountain. The starlight is too concentrated—it would burn away their stolen substance."

"Then we keep climbing," Asvarr said, gaze fixed on the distant peak. The Grímmark on his chest burned hotter as they approached the third anchor, the pattern responding to its proximity.

They began ascending the crystal steps, each footfall releasing soft chimes that echoed across Alfheim's strange landscape. Behind them, Memory Eaters gathered at the mountain's base, blank faces tilted upward in frustration and hunger. They had found the pathway between realms, but this barrier they could not cross.

Halfway up the spiraling staircase, Brynja stumbled. Asvarr caught her before she could fall, steadying her against his side. Through the grove-twined mark, he felt her exhaustion and disorientation—the hole in her memory destabilizing her sense of self.

"I don't know who I am without that memory," she admitted, voice barely audible above the crystalline chimes. The truth-runes glowed faintly, confirming this fear. "It was the foundation of everything."

"You're still you," Asvarr said, supporting her as they continued climbing. "I'll hold the memory for both of us until we find a way to restore what was taken."

Yrsa looked back at them, her expression grave. "Some sacrifices can't be undone. The pattern takes and transforms—it rarely returns what is given."

The crystal steps grew steeper as they neared the peak. Starlight poured down like water, soaking into their flesh, resonating with the transformed parts of them. Asvarr's bark-like skin drank in the light, the patterns matching the constellations overhead. Brynja's wooden features gleamed with amber highlights, the flowers along her arm slowly reopening in response to the concentrated energy.

***

They reached the mountain's summit as twin moons rose on the horizon—one silver, one gold, orbiting each other in perfect harmony. The peak formed a circular plateau, its surface polished to mirror-smoothness. At its center floated a crystalline structure—neither tree nor root nor crown, but a perfect merging of all three. Starlight poured into it from above, while golden sap welled up from below, the two substances swirling together without mixing.

The third anchor. The Starlight Anchor.

It pulsed in rhythm with Asvarr's transformed heart, calling to the two anchors already bound within him. This union would be different from the previous bindings—neither dominance nor recognition but transformation itself, the balance between controlling and being controlled.

As they approached the floating anchor, Asvarr felt Brynja's memory flaring bright within him. Her child-self gazing up at Yggdrasil with wonder became a mirror for this moment—staring at the third anchor with mingled awe and determination. Her sacrifice had preserved enough of him to complete this binding, to continue walking the third path between Tree and Shadow.

He turned to her, the grove-twined mark pulsing between them. "Together," he said, extending his hand.

Brynja nodded, her wooden features settling into resolute lines. The hole in her memory remained—a wound that might never heal—but her purpose stood undiminished. "Together," she agreed, taking his offered hand.

Behind them, at the mountain's base, the Memory Eaters watched with hungry patience. They couldn't climb the crystal steps, couldn't breach the starlight barrier, but they would wait. Sooner or later, the Wardens would descend, and the feeding would begin anew.

But that was a battle for another moment. Now, the third anchor called, its crystalline structure singing with power. The binding awaited—the union of starlight and sap, sky and root, control and surrender. Another transformation, another step away from humanity toward something both greater and more terrible.

Asvarr faced the anchor with Brynja's memory burning inside him—her wonder becoming his strength, her sacrifice his obligation. Whatever remained after this binding, whatever emerged from the transformation, would carry that memory forward as testament to what had been given freely.

He extended his free hand toward the crystalline structure, feeling the pattern respond within his transformed flesh. The anchors tugged at him, flame and memory reaching for their stellar counterpart. One more binding, one more surrender, one more transformation.

And within the emptied spaces of his identity, the pattern grew stronger, filling the hollows the Memory Eaters had created, preparing its vessel for what came next.

CHAPTER 26
WHEN THE GODS WEEP

The landscape of Alfheim twisted around them as they fled. Silver trees bent unnaturally, their branches reaching like desperate fingers. Asvarr stumbled, his mind still reeling from the Memory Eaters' attack. Foreign images flickered behind his eyes—a towering ash tree piercing nine skies, impossibly vast, seen through a child's wondering gaze. Brynja's memory. The borrowed wonder felt strange within him, like wearing another's skin.

He glanced at Brynja. Her face was slack, one cheek still bark-covered but the expression beneath vacant. She had given him her first sight of Yggdrasil, and with it, something essential to her being.

"We need shelter," Yrsa whispered, her crystal pendant pulsing with faint light. "The Memory Eaters can't climb beyond the silver ridge, but they'll follow the scent of our essence." She pointed toward a narrow pass between twin peaks that gleamed like polished blades. "There. I sense old power there. Different from the Tree or the Five."

Asvarr helped Brynja forward. Her wooden arm had darkened where the Memory Eaters touched it, the flowering vines withered.

"Can you walk?" he asked.

"I can walk." The truth-runes on her face glimmered, but dimly. "I just... can't remember why I began this journey. There's a hollow where something important should be."

The grove-twined mark on Asvarr's palm burned. Through it, he felt Brynja's disorientation—a vertigo of identity. She had sacrificed her foundational memory to save him, and now existed with that core piece missing.

"I'll remember for both of us," he promised, though he knew the foreign memory could never mean to him what it had meant to her.

They climbed in silence, Asvarr half-carrying Brynja when the path steepened. Leif moved ahead, his golden eyes scanning for danger. The boy seemed untouched by the Memory Eaters, shifting between locations with uncanny ease. Yrsa brought up the rear, occasionally drawing symbols in the air with her crystal knife that briefly flared blue-white and faded.

"They're still following," she murmured. "But something holds them back. This place has... protection."

***

They crested the ridge and saw what lay beyond.

A perfect circular valley nestled between silver peaks, filled with soft mist that clung to the ground like reluctant spirits. Within the valley stood stone figures arranged in a circle—each twice human height, carved with such precision that Asvarr could count the strands of their beards, the folds of their robes. Gods. Ancient and familiar.

And they wept.

Real tears trickled from stone eyes, cutting glistening tracks down weathered cheeks before gathering in a small lake at the circle's center. The lake shimmered with opalescent light, neither water nor something else, but both simultaneously.

"What is this place?" Asvarr whispered, the words catching in his throat.

Yrsa stepped forward, her expression solemn. "The Sanctuary of Sorrow. One of the oldest places in all Nine Realms."

"I know this," Brynja said suddenly, her voice stronger. She pulled away from Asvarr, approaching the circle with halting steps. "I've seen this in... in dreams, maybe? The memory is incomplete."

"Not dreams," Yrsa replied. "Blood-memory. This is one of the few places the gods revealed something true of themselves. Your ancestors would have passed this knowing through generations."

Asvarr followed them into the valley. The mist parted before their steps and sealed behind them, isolating them in strange, muffled silence. He studied the stone gods, recognizing some from the tales of his childhood. Thor with his hammer lowered in defeat. Freya with her head bowed, necklace hanging heavy. Tyr missing his hand, eternally sacrificed. All wept with the quiet dignity of beings unused to grief but unable to escape it.

And at the circle's head, a one-eyed figure seated on a stone throne, tears falling from both the seeing eye and the empty socket. The Allfather, before he became the Wanderer.

"I don't understand," Asvarr said. "Why do they weep? Gods don't mourn mortals."

"Don't they?" Yrsa asked softly. She knelt by the lake's edge, letting its strange luminescence play over her fingers. "This is the one place they allowed themselves to acknowledge what they had done—and what it cost."

"And what was that?" Brynja asked, her wooden hand reaching toward the stone Freya as if drawn by some unseen connection.

"Separation," Yrsa said. "The gods withdrew from the mortal realms long ago, severing themselves from direct connection with those they once walked among. They chose power and distance over vulnerability and connection. And in that moment of choice—just one moment—they glimpsed what they had lost. Their tears formed this lake."

Asvarr approached the one-eyed figure cautiously. Unlike the other statues, this one seemed to watch him, the single eye following his movement. The weeping from its empty socket wasn't water but something darker, thicker. He felt the Grímmark pulse beneath his skin, responding to the ancient power.

"The Wanderer," he said. "The Ashfather. He was Odin once."

"Part of him," Yrsa corrected. "When gods withdraw, they sometimes leave fragments behind—pieces of themselves they cannot reconcile with their new purpose. The Wanderer is Odin's regret given form. His doubt made manifest."

Leif, who had been uncharacteristically silent, suddenly spoke with that unsettling adult resonance that occasionally overtook his childlike voice.

"The gods made themselves by unmaking their connection to the world," he said. "They shaped themselves from the Tree's power but feared becoming lost in its vastness. So they withdrew to the spaces between branches, where they could watch without being changed themselves."

Asvarr felt a strange resonance with those words. Wasn't that his own fear? That with each binding, with each transformation, he was losing pieces of himself to the pattern?

He sank down beside the lake, exhaustion overtaking him. His mind felt scraped raw from the Memory Eaters' attack. The foreign memory of Brynja's—her first sight of Yggdrasil—pulsed within him, both comfort and intrusion.

"Rest here," Yrsa said. "The tear-lake offers protection. No entity that feeds on identity can cross these waters."

"Will it heal what the Memory Eaters took from me?" Asvarr asked.

Yrsa's expression turned grave. "The lake doesn't return what is lost, Asvarr. It only acknowledges the loss." She glanced at Brynja, who had sat beneath the stone Freya, her wooden arm wrapped around her knees. "Some sacrifices can never be undone."

A weight settled in Asvarr's chest. He had survived the Memory Eaters because of Brynja's sacrifice, but at what cost to her? He studied the transformation seed mark on his palm, the living wood that connected him to her. Through it, he sensed her disoriented grief—a pain without context, a mourning for something she could no longer recall.

The lake before him reflected his changed face. Bark patterns had spread up his neck and across his jaw, with crystalline formations along his temples that caught the opalescent light. Each binding transformed him further. Each sacrifice altered what he had been.

"The gods aren't alone in their regrets," he murmured, tracing the patterns on his skin.

"No," Yrsa agreed, settling beside him. "But unlike them, you haven't withdrawn. You're still walking the path, still choosing connection despite the cost." She nodded toward Brynja. "Go to her. The tear-lake allows truth between souls. Speak with her while you can."

Asvarr rose and crossed to where Brynja sat. As he approached, he noticed crystals forming in her wooden arm where the bark had been blackened by the Memory Eaters. She looked up at him, her truth-runes glimmering faintly.

"I can feel the hollow," she said without preamble. "Like a word forgotten on the tip of my tongue, but it's not a word—it's myself." She touched her chest. "How do you build a life when you don't know how it began?"

Asvarr sat beside her, their shoulders touching. He felt inadequate before her pain.

"I have parts of your memory," he said. "I could... tell you what I see in it."

She turned toward him, hope and skepticism warring in her expression. "Would it help? Or would it just be a story someone else is telling me about myself?"

"I don't know," he admitted, the grove-twined mark warming between them. "But I think... I think our memories were never entirely our own anyway. We share them, reshape them. The Memory Eaters showed me that—how pieces of myself resided in others' memories of me."

Brynja looked toward the lake, which reflected impossible patterns. "Then tell me. Tell me what it is to see Yggdrasil for the first time. Tell me what I've lost."

Asvarr closed his eyes, allowing the foreign memory to surface.

"You were young," he began. "Your mother held your hand as you climbed a hill before dawn. The sky was just beginning to lighten, stars still visible. She told you to watch the space between two mountains, where mist gathered."

He felt the memory sharpen as he spoke it aloud. "Then the sun crested the horizon, and for just one moment, the light hit the mist perfectly, and you could see it—Yggdrasil, spanning all Nine Realms. Your mother whispered something in your ear, her voice reverent. You felt... small and vast simultaneously. Connected to everything. You understood, really understood for the first time, that all life was joined through the World Tree's branches."

Brynja's breath caught. A single tear traced the bark patterns on her cheek, glowing faintly with the same light as the lake before them.

"What did she whisper?" she asked, her voice barely audible. "My mother. What did she say to me?"

Asvarr focused harder on the memory, trying to extract that detail, but it slipped away. "I... I can't hear it. That part didn't transfer."

Brynja nodded, resignation settling across her features. "Then it's truly gone. The most important words she ever spoke to me."

The stone Freya above them wept faster, tears pooling at their feet. Asvarr wondered if the gods' statues responded to mortal pain, or if it was merely coincidence.

Through their grove-twined mark, Asvarr felt Brynja's grief sharpen into something harder, more determined.

"It's decided, then," she said. "We must reach the third anchor at Starfall Mountain. Whatever it costs us, whatever we lose—we cannot fail."

Before Asvarr could respond, a low rumble shook the valley. The lake's surface rippled with concentric rings, and the mist retreated up the valley walls like startled breath.

Leif appeared at their side, golden eyes wide. "Something approaches," he whispered. "Something that even the gods' tears cannot hold back."

Yrsa stood at the lake's edge, her crystal pendant blazing. "We need to prepare," she said. "The sanctuary offers protection, but not against something that was once a god itself."

The rumble intensified, and the stone statues' weeping increased, tears now flowing in streams down weathered features. Through the mist at the valley's entrance, a tall shadow appeared, crowned with twisted branches.

"He's found us," Asvarr said, drawing his bronze sword. The golden veins within the blade pulsed in time with his heartbeat. "The Ashfather."

Brynja rose beside him, her wooden arm extending into thorn-like projections. "He wants what we carry—the bound anchors and the path to the third."

But Yrsa shook her head, her expression was thoughtful. "No," she said. "Look closely. He comes alone, without his Hunt. He isn't here to attack."

"Then what does he want?" Asvarr asked, keeping his sword raised.

The shadow continued forward, mist parting before it. As it reached the edge of the stone circle, its features became clear—a broad-shouldered figure with silver-streaked dark hair and beard, wearing a cloak of raven feathers. A wide-brimmed hat shadowed his face, but couldn't hide the single golden eye that glowed with ancient knowledge. In his hand he carried a spear of ash wood with an iron head that gleamed unnaturally.

"He wants to talk," Leif said with strange certainty, moving to stand between Asvarr and the approaching figure. "He wants to offer another way."

The Ashfather stopped at the circle's edge. He looked up at the weeping statue of Odin, his expression unreadable. Then his golden eye shifted to Asvarr, and he spoke in a voice like grinding mountains.

"Warden of Fire and Memory," he said, the words carrying power that rippled the lake's surface. "You've bound two anchors. Soon you'll seek the third. Before you continue on that path, there are truths you should know."

"Why would you share truth with me?" Asvarr demanded, the Grímmark burning beneath his skin. "You've manipulated events for nine cycles. You destroyed my clan."

The Ashfather's expression shifted slightly—was that regret? He planted his spear in the ground and leaned on it, suddenly seeming weary rather than threatening.

"Because I once stood where you stand," he said. "I once thought as you think. And I would spare you my mistakes, if you'll listen."

Asvarr felt the grove-twined mark on his palm pulse with warning, but also with something else—recognition. Part of him, the part most connected to the pattern, sensed kinship with this being that had once been a Warden.

"I'll listen," Asvarr said finally, lowering his sword. "But here, by the lake of the gods' tears, where truth cannot be hidden."

The Ashfather nodded, stepping into the circle. The stone gods seemed to turn slightly, their weeping eyes following his movement. He approached the lake's edge and gazed into its depths.

"Let me tell you of gods and regret," he said, "and why some patterns must never be restored."

A chill ran down Asvarr's spine. For all his certainty about his path, about binding the five anchors to heal what was broken, he suddenly felt like a child playing with forces beyond his comprehension.

And somewhere deep within, in the spaces hollowed by the Memory Eaters, something whispered that the Ashfather's words might contain the truth he needed most.

The Ashfather settled beside the lake, his cloak of raven feathers pooling around him like liquid shadow. He planted his spear in the soft earth, its iron tip catching the opalescent light from the tear-water. For a long moment, he simply gazed at his reflection—a broad-shouldered figure with silver-threaded hair and beard, a face weathered by time and knowledge, one eye golden bright and the other an empty socket that wept slowly, matching the stone statue looming behind him.

Asvarr kept his distance, bronze sword lowered but still in hand. The blade's gold veins pulsed in warning, responding to the ancient power before them. Brynja stood at his shoulder, her wooden arm extended in thorny preparation. Yrsa had positioned herself near the lake's opposite edge, crystal pendant glowing fiercely, while Leif crouched behind a stone god's feet, watching with unblinking golden eyes.

"I was once called Gautr," the Ashfather said finally, his voice rumbling across the water. "Before that, other names, now forgotten. I walked as you walk now, bound anchors as you have bound them." He looked up at Asvarr, his single eye piercing. "I stood at the center of the pattern and made a choice. What I tell you now, I tell so you might understand the weight of the choice that awaits you."

"Why should I believe anything you say?" Asvarr challenged, though the grove-twined mark on his palm burned with something beyond caution—recognition. "You've manipulated nine cycles of breaking and binding. You ordered my clan destroyed."

The Ashfather's expression tightened with something that might have been pain. "Yes. I used the Hunt to cull your bloodline, as I culled others before it. Because I saw what would happen if the bloodlines unified again." He touched the surface of the lake, creating ripples that spread outward in perfect circles. "Just as you'd burn away corruption to save a wounded limb, I severed possibilities to preserve the whole."

"You burned entire clans," Brynja said, her truth-runes glowing golden on her face. "Mine included."

"I did." The Ashfather did not flinch from her accusation. "And I would do it again, if necessary. The consequences of full awakening are far worse than the loss of a few bloodlines."

Asvarr felt bile rise in his throat. "You speak of sacrifice while sitting safely apart from it. Easy to slaughter others for your grand purpose."

The Ashfather laughed, a sound like stones grinding against each other. "Safely apart? Look at me, Flame-Bearer." He gestured to his form, to the empty socket weeping dark tears. "I sacrificed my eye, my name, my humanity. I split myself from my greater self and remained behind when the gods withdrew. For nine cycles, I have walked alone between worlds, containing what would otherwise consume all."

He stood suddenly, towering over them. "I am what Odin left behind—his regret, his doubt, his understanding of the price of power. When the All-Father chose godhood over connection, when he withdrew to the spaces between branches, I remained to ensure the pattern never fully restored."

Asvarr studied the being before him. Through the Grímmark, he sensed truth in the Ashfather's words, uncomfortable as they were.

"Why tell me this now?" he asked.

"Because you've bound two anchors and survived with your mind intact. Because through nine cycles, no Warden has maintained their identity through multiple bindings as you have." The Ashfather's eye gleamed. "You walk a third path—neither surrender nor domination. You transform while maintaining essence."

Yrsa moved closer, her stance cautious but her expression intrigued. "You've watched him since the beginning, haven't you? You wanted to see if he would choose differently than those before him."

The Ashfather nodded. "Every cycle, the Tree attempts to restore itself. Every cycle, it selects Wardens to bind its anchors. And every cycle, those Wardens either surrender completely to the pattern, becoming empty vessels, or they attempt to dominate it and are consumed by their own ambition." His gaze locked on Asvarr. "Until you."

Brynja stepped forward, her wooden fingers intertwining with Asvarr's. The grove-twined mark between them pulsed with shared wariness. "And what do you want from him now?"

"To join me," the Ashfather said simply. "To stand as my equal in ensuring the gods never return to dominate mortal lives again."

The words hung in the air, heavy with implication. Asvarr felt a strange resonance with them, an uncomfortable alignment with thoughts he'd harbored since binding the memory anchor.

"How would we accomplish that?" he asked, unable to keep the curiosity from his voice despite his suspicion.

The Ashfather gestured to the weeping statues surrounding them. "The gods withdrew to the spaces between branches, where they could maintain their power without connection or responsibility. Their return would mean the end of mortal freedom—beings of such power cannot help but dominate, even when they believe themselves benevolent."

He moved to the lake's edge again, stirring the waters with his fingertips. Images formed on the surface—visions of the Nine Realms with gods walking among mortals, their mere presence bending reality around them, mortals kneeling in worship or fleeing in terror.

"What the Tree remembers as harmony was subjugation dressed as protection," the Ashfather continued. "The gods shaped reality to serve themselves, called it guidance, and demanded gratitude. Their tears here—" he gestured to the lake "—came only when they glimpsed the truth of what they had done. A moment of clarity before they chose power once more."

Asvarr watched the visions ripple across the lake. They stirred something within him—memories not his own, perhaps from the Root anchors he'd bound. He saw flashes of enormous figures striding across landscapes, mountains forming beneath their steps, mortals scattering like insects, their lives reshaped by divine whim rather than choice.

"And what of the Tree itself?" he asked. "You claim to oppose the gods' return, yet you've manipulated the breaking and binding cycles for your own purposes."

"The Tree is not what you believe it to be," the Ashfather said, his voice lowering. "It was never a benevolent force connecting all life in harmony. It was a cage—a beautiful one, perhaps, but a cage nonetheless. It bound the realms into a fixed pattern, a hierarchy with gods at its peak and all other beings arranged beneath them according to divine design."

Brynja's grip tightened on Asvarr's hand, her truth-runes flaring brighter. "He believes what he's saying," she whispered. "This isn't deception."

The Ashfather continued, pointing to the statue of Odin with his spear. "When I stood at the pattern's center, I glimpsed the truth behind the tree's roots. I saw the void beyond branches, where possibility exists without constraint. I understood that the Tree was created to contain and control, not to connect."

Asvarr felt cold certainty spreading through him. The words resonated with doubts he'd harbored since the Hollowglade, when he'd communed deeply with the Root. There had been something beneath the surface of what he'd experienced—something ancient and hungry that the Tree itself seemed to be containing.

"What exists beyond the pattern?" he asked.

The Ashfather's expression darkened. "Chaos. Potential. Everything that could be but is not permitted to manifest within the Tree's rigid structure. The gods feared it, so they shaped the Tree to keep it at bay, to maintain their version of order."

He stepped closer to Asvarr, his voice dropping to a harsh whisper. "When I broke the cycle, when I prevented full restoration, I wasn't destroying connection—I was allowing for freedom beyond the pattern imposed by gods. In the spaces between breaking and binding, mortals shape their own destinies for a brief, precious time."

Leif, who had been silent throughout, suddenly spoke with that unnerving adult resonance. "He's describing the in-between where I was born," the boy said. "Where possibility forks without constraint."

The Ashfather nodded at Leif. "The child understands. He exists because of my actions, because I maintained the spaces between where new patterns can form."

"And what do you propose?" Asvarr asked, weighing each word carefully. "What would it mean to join you?"

"Complete your journey. Bind the remaining anchors. But instead of using them to restore the pattern as it was, use them to maintain the balance between structure and void." The Ashfather's eye gleamed with fierce intensity. "Stand with me at the center, neither surrendering to the Tree nor seeking to control it. Together, we could ensure neither gods nor chaos dominate—a true third path of transformation."

He extended his hand toward Asvarr, palm up. "I offer you equality, not servitude. Partnership in maintaining freedom for all beings to shape their own fates."

Asvarr stared at the offered hand. The proposal aligned uncomfortably well with his own growing doubts about restoration. Since binding the memory anchor, he'd glimpsed fragments of the Tree's true nature—moments where its spreading roots seemed less like connection and more like control.

"You destroyed my clan," Asvarr said, his voice tight. "You've manipulated events across nine cycles. Why should I trust you?"

"Because I did what was necessary, not what was easy," the Ashfather replied, his hand remaining extended. "And because deep in your heart, flame-bearer, you know there is truth in what I say. You've felt it since your first binding—the pressure to surrender your identity to the pattern. You've resisted because some part of you recognizes the Tree for what it truly is."

Brynja released Asvarr's hand, stepping back. Her face was unreadable, the wooden patterns shifting subtly. "This must be your choice alone," she said. "My truth-runes confirm he believes what he says, but belief isn't always truth."

Yrsa moved closer, her crystal pendant pulsing with blue-white light. "Be wary, Asvarr. Nine cycles of manipulation leaves deep grooves in reality. What he offers may be simply another form of control."

The Ashfather lowered his hand, resignation crossing his features. "Think on what I've said. When you reach the third anchor at Starfall Mountain, you'll face a choice—surrender to the pattern or attempt to dominate it. Both paths lead to loss. There is a third way, if you're brave enough to forge it." He retrieved his spear from the ground, leaning on it heavily. "I'll be watching. When you're ready to speak again, call my name in moonlight."

He turned, cloak swirling around him, and began walking toward the valley's entrance. Before he reached the circle of statues, he looked back once more. "Ask yourself this, flame-bearer: if restoration is truly the path of harmony, why has the Tree broken itself nine times rather than remain whole? What truth hides within that cycle of breaking and binding?"

With those words, he passed beyond the stone gods and vanished into the mist, leaving only footprints that wept tears like the statues themselves.

For a long moment, the valley was silent except for the soft patter of divine tears falling into the lake. Asvarr stared at where the Ashfather had disappeared, the question echoing in his mind. Why would the Tree shatter itself nine times? What purpose could be served by such a cycle?

"His words carry partial truth," Yrsa finally said, breaking the silence. "The Tree's nature is more complex than either harmony or control. It exists in balance between order and chaos, structure and freedom."

"Then what would happen if it were fully restored?" Asvarr asked, turning to her. "Would the gods return? Would mortals lose their freedom?"

Yrsa's expression turned grave. "I don't know with certainty. The pattern shifts with each breaking and binding. No cycle completes exactly as the one before it." She touched her crystal pendant, which had dimmed since the Ashfather's departure. "What I do know is that the world cannot survive without some form of the pattern. The void beyond would consume all."

Leif approached Asvarr, his childlike face uncommonly solemn. "I was born in the space between breaking and binding," he said. "I exist because the pattern isn't fixed. If it were fully restored..." He trailed off, golden eyes distant.

"You would cease to exist," Brynja finished for him, her truth-runes confirming the statement's validity.

Asvarr's stomach twisted with the implications. He'd begun this journey certain of his purpose—to bind the five anchors, restore what was broken, heal the worlds. Now, with two anchors bound and their power flowing through him, doubt gnawed at that conviction.

He moved to the lake's edge, staring at his reflection in the tear-water. The transformation had advanced further than he'd realized. Bark patterns spiraled up his neck and across his jaw. Crystalline formations glittered at his temples. His eyes had changed, too—still blue, but with flecks of gold that caught the light unnaturally.

"I don't know what to believe anymore," he admitted, the words tasting bitter. "The Tree saved me, marked me, guided me. Yet the Ashfather's words ring true in parts. I feel... pulled in multiple directions."

Brynja joined him at the water's edge, her reflection showing similar transformation—wood spiraling across half her face, her eyes holding emerald light. "Then we continue forward until the truth becomes clear," she said. "We seek the third anchor at Starfall Mountain. We test each claim against what we discover."

***

She took his hand, the grove-twined mark warming between them. Through it, Asvarr felt her determination, her pragmatic acceptance of uncertainty.

"The third anchor is of starlight," she continued. "Neither flame nor memory but something between. Perhaps it will show us a clearer path."

Asvarr nodded slowly, grasping at her certainty like a lifeline. "We need to create the map," he said, thinking of Yrsa's earlier suggestion. "If we combine our Root connections, we might see the pattern more clearly—understand the anchors' true nature."

"Yes," Yrsa agreed, approaching with Leif. "A living map created from your bound anchors. It would show the location and status of all anchors across the Nine Realms."

Asvarr drew his bronze sword, the golden veins within it pulsing with the power of two bound anchors. Brynja extended her wooden arm, flowering vines unfurling from her fingertips. Together, they knelt by the lake's edge, their transformations reflecting in the opalescent waters.

***

"By flame and root," Asvarr murmured, the ritual words coming to him instinctively. "By memory and growth. Show us the pattern as it truly exists."

The tear-lake's surface rippled as if stirred by an unseen wind. Light gathered beneath the water, coalescing into threads of gold, silver, and emerald that wove together, rising above the surface in shimmering strands. The strands twisted, branched, connected, forming a miniature Yggdrasil that hovered between Asvarr and Brynja.

Five points of light gleamed among its branches—two burning bright with Asvarr's bindings, the others dimmer but still visible. The third pulsed silver-white atop what could only be Starfall Mountain in Alfheim. The fourth and fifth anchors glimmered in distant realms he couldn't identify.

But what truly captured Asvarr's attention was the pattern itself, it was more complex then he imagined. The branches didn't extend upward in hierarchy but outward in all directions. There was no center, no peak, no base—only connection points forming a web that encompassed all Nine Realms simultaneously.

"This is Yggdrasil's true form," Yrsa breathed, her eyes wide with wonder. "Not as the skalds sing it, or as the gods described it, but as it exists across all realities."

As they watched, the living map expanded, revealing that each anchor existed in multiple realms simultaneously—what they'd perceived as separate fragments were actually aspects of the same entities viewed through different cosmic lenses.

"This explains why our actions in the memory realm affected Midgard's physical reality," Brynja said, her wooden fingers tracing the connection threads. "The anchors exist everywhere at once."

Asvarr stared at the map, the Ashfather's question burning in his mind. If this was the Tree's true nature—complex, interconnected, existing across all realities simultaneously—why would it break itself nine times? What purpose could possibly be served by such a cycle?

And more troubling still: if he continued binding the anchors, if he helped restore this vast pattern to its original form, what would happen to the spaces between—the places where beings like Leif existed? What would happen to mortal freedom if gods returned to walk the Nine Realms?

The living map spun slowly between them, beautiful and terrible in its complexity. Somewhere within its gleaming strands lay the answer he sought—the truth about the Tree, about the breaking and binding, about his own purpose in this vast pattern.

Asvarr closed his hand around the transformation seed mark on his palm, feeling its warmth pulse in time with his heartbeat. The third anchor awaited at Starfall Mountain. Whatever truth it held, he would face it—neither surrendering nor dominating, but walking the third path of transformation.

He looked up, catching Brynja's gaze across the shimmering map. "We leave for Starfall Mountain at dawn," he said, his decision crystallizing. "Whatever awaits us there, we'll face it together."

The stone gods wept around them, their tears falling faster now as if in anticipation of what was to come. The map between them pulsed with living light, its strands forming a pattern both familiar and utterly foreign—a representation of reality far more complex than Asvarr had ever imagined.

And somewhere beyond the valley, walking the spaces between realms, the Ashfather watched and waited for Asvarr's choice.

CHAPTER 27

ROOTS ACROSS REALMS

Dawn bled across Alfheim's silver forest, casting geometric shadows through trees that should not exist in nature. Asvarr sat cross-legged at the edge of the tear-lake, its opalescent surface still except where gods' tears dripped from stone faces. His skin prickled, bark patterns spreading across his jaw, crystalline formations glittering at his temples. The Ashfather had left hours ago, his offer hanging in the air like smoke.

Asvarr traced the grove-twined mark on his palm, feeling Brynja's presence before she appeared through the mist. Her wooden arm gleamed with morning dew, flowers furled in sleep along the transformed limb.

"Your face gives nothing away," she said, sitting beside him. Truth-runes glowed faintly on her half-wooden face. "But this—" she tapped the oath-sigil on her palm "—tells me you haven't slept."

"Too many voices in my head." Asvarr ran his fingers through the tear-lake, watching ripples fracture light into impossible colors. "The anchors, the Root fragments, your memory... they speak all at once now."

Brynja nodded, extending her wooden fingers to brush the water's surface. "The Ashfather's words have truth to them. I felt it through the runes."

"Truth can be wielded like any weapon." Asvarr drew his bronze sword, laying it between them. Golden veins pulsed beneath the metal's surface, resonating with his transformed flesh. "What if there's something he's not telling us? Something worse than gods returning?"

"There always is." She lifted her gaze to the stone faces above. "But sitting here won't reveal it. We need to see more of the pattern."

Yrsa and Leif approached from the camp they'd made between two weeping god-statues. The boundary-walker's crystal pendant blazed with blue-white light, while the boy's eyes held fragments of stars caught in their golden depths.

"The tear-lake will help us see," Yrsa said, kneeling at the water's edge. "It exists in all realms simultaneously, a place where boundaries thin."

"Like me," Leif said with that unsettling adult resonance that occasionally overtook his childlike voice. "Between what is and what could be."

Asvarr studied the boy. "You understand more than you say."

Leif shrugged thin shoulders. "I see differently. The pattern looks... incomplete from where I stand."

Brynja extended her wooden arm over the lake. "Then let's see more of it. The anchors we've bound should give us enough power."

"It's dangerous," Yrsa warned, her fingers tightening around her crystal pendant. "What you're suggesting could tear the boundaries further."

"They're already tearing," Asvarr said, reaching for Brynja's wooden hand. "Better we see what we're facing than stumble blind."

Their fingers interlocked, flesh against wood, the twin oath-sigils pulsing emerald against their palms. Asvarr felt the Root's power surge through the connection, his mark burning across his chest as Brynja's wooden patterns flared golden beneath her skin.

"Focus on the anchors," Yrsa instructed, placing her crystal pendant in the tear-lake. "Let them guide your sight."

Asvarr closed his eyes, concentrating on the flame anchor burning in his chest and the memory anchor cooling at his temples. He felt Brynja doing the same with her fragment—the Severed Bloom that had taken her arm. The tear-lake's surface began to ripple without wind, colors spiraling beneath it.

From the water rose golden threads, woven with silver and emerald, twisting into the air to form a pattern. Root and branch, flame and frost, all binding together into a miniature Yggdrasil hovering above the lake. But this wasn't the uniform tree Asvarr had imagined—this was a complex lattice of connections, paths branching and reconnecting in ways his mind struggled to comprehend.

"It's beautiful," Brynja whispered, her wooden fingers extending toward the manifestation.

The liquid tree rotated slowly, revealing nine distinct sections—the realms—connected by golden pathways that shimmered with potential. Five points of light pulsed within the structure: flame-red in Midgard, memory-gold in the branches, frost-silver near the roots, verdant-green in the lowest deeps, and star-white at the peak.

"The five anchors," Yrsa breathed. "Exactly where the prophecy said they would be."

"But not as we thought," Asvarr said, tracing a pattern in the air that mirrored the miniature tree's structure. "Look—they're not separate pieces. They're aspects of the same thing viewed from different angles."

As he spoke, the liquid manifestation shifted, showing how each anchor existed simultaneously across multiple realms. The flame anchor he'd bound in Midgard pulsed with connections to Muspelheim. The memory anchor bridged Alfheim and the now-collapsed memory realm.

Leif moved around the manifestation, his face illuminated by its glow. "The spaces between are what matter. That's where I live. That's where the gods hide."

A new presence made itself known through resonance in the air itself. Patterns of light and shadow wove between the branches of the liquid tree, forming into a vaguely humanoid shape composed of interlaced threads.

"Coilvoice," Asvarr recognized, remembering the entity from the memory realm's collapse.

I am what remains when all else is forgotten, the entity's voice bypassed their ears to speak directly into their minds. *The Tree's final thought as it shattered.*

"You survived the memory realm's collapse," Brynja said, fingers tightening around Asvarr's.

I exist where memory touches reality—in the spaces between thought and matter. The manifestation moved through the liquid tree, illuminating different pathways and connections. *What you perceive as separate anchors are aspects of the same entities. Your actions in the memory realm affected Midgard because the anchors exist simultaneously across boundaries.*

"That's why the thorny lattice appeared in the sky when we bound the second anchor," Asvarr realized. "It wasn't just symbolic—it was an actual physical manifestation across realms."

The pattern remembers itself, Coilvoice confirmed. *Each binding strengthens those connections, rebuilding what was sundered.*

Yrsa stepped forward, her crystal pendant reflecting the manifestation's light. "But something is wrong with the pattern. The Ashfather's interference has twisted it across nine cycles."

The liquid tree shifted, revealing distortions where connections had been forcibly rerouted or severed. Golden pathways dimmed in places, showing where the pattern had been weakened or altered.

The one who came before understood enough to maintain but not enough to heal, Coilvoice's form rippled with what might have been sorrow. *He kept the realms from collapse but prevented true restoration.*

"Because he feared what would come with restoration," Brynja said quietly, her truth-runes glowing. "Gods returning to dominate, or something worse from beyond the pattern."

Asvarr studied the manifestation closely, noticing how the third anchor—the starlight one they sought in Alfheim—pulsed with increasing urgency. "The third anchor is different from the others. It bridges rather than binds."

Yes. The flame demands dominance. Memory requires recognition. Starlight seeks transformation. Each has its own nature, its own price.

"And the price increases with each binding," Asvarr unconsciously touched the crystalline formations at his temples, remembering what he'd already surrendered. "What happens when all five are bound? What lies at the pattern's heart?"

The manifestation darkened briefly, then blazed with renewed light. *That is the question even I cannot answer. Nine cycles of binding have never completed. The pattern remains unfinished, its center void.*

"Something waits there," Leif said, his child's voice suddenly ancient. "Something older than Tree or gods. I've glimpsed it between worlds."

The liquid tree trembled, connections wavering as if disturbed by an unfelt wind. Coilvoice's form grew less distinct, stretching thin across the manifestation.

Others watch this revelation, the entity warned. *The Wanderer's eye turns toward you. The Five seek to rewrite what you've uncovered. And something else stirs beneath the roots—hungering for what awakens.*

"Tell us about the crossing points," Brynja urged, her wooden arm extending toward the manifestation. "Where can we reach the other anchors?"

There are paths, but they shift with each binding. Coilvoice highlighted three routes through the liquid tree. *Alfheim leads to starlight, where celestial power meets earthly form. Helheim holds death and legacy intertwined. Muspelheim balances creation against destruction.*

"Paths we must walk to complete the pattern," Asvarr muttered, studying each route. His gaze fixed on the starlight anchor, so close yet unreachable without the proper understanding.

***

The manifestation suddenly contracted, liquid splashing back into the tear-lake as Coilvoice's form dispersed like mist before dawn. Asvarr felt cold air against his skin, realizing the temperature had plummeted around them.

"Something's coming," Yrsa warned, snatching her pendant from the water. "The barriers between realms have thinned from our casting."

Frost formed across the tear-lake's surface in geometric patterns, spiraling outward from where the liquid tree had stood. The weeping stone faces of the gods seemed to watch with intensified sorrow, their tears freezing midway down their cheeks.

Brynja pulled her wooden arm back, bark creaking as frost attempted to claim it. "Whatever it is, it comes from beyond the pattern—from the void-spaces."

Leif backed away, eyes wide. "The boundaries are breaking. Too many have seen what we've revealed."

Asvarr drew his sword, golden veins pulsing brighter as he pointed toward the horizon where stars began to fade from view, replaced by unnatural darkness. "The Ashfather warned us about this—the consequences of seeing too much of the pattern at once."

Cold light pierced through tears in reality, casting wrong-angled shadows across the sanctuary. Formless shapes moved within those tears, pressing against the boundaries that separated realms from the void beyond.

"We've drawn their attention," Yrsa said grimly, clutching her crystal pendant that now blazed like a miniature star. "The unremembered. The culled possibilities."

"Memory Eaters," Brynja named them, recalling their previous encounter.

"We need to move," Asvarr decided, sheathing his sword and pulling Brynja to her feet. "Toward Starfall Mountain—toward the third anchor. They can't follow us there."

"Not directly," Yrsa agreed, "but they'll find ways through the boundaries we've weakened."

Leif stared into the encroaching void-spaces with a mixture of fear and recognition. "They hunger for what we possess—identity, memory, connection to the pattern."

Asvarr felt the weight of two bound anchors within him, the third calling from Starfall Mountain's peak. The manifestation had shown him something crucial—the anchors weren't prizes to be claimed but connections to be understood. Each binding reshaped both Warden and pattern itself.

"Brynja," he said, gripping her wooden hand tightly. "The manifestation showed something the Ashfather didn't tell us. Something about the center of the pattern."

Her truth-runes glowed golden as she met his gaze. "What?"

"It's empty," he said, watching frost spread across the sanctuary in unnatural formations. "Nine cycles, and no one has ever filled that void. Not the Tree, nor the Ashfather—no one knows what truly waits there."

"Which means his warning could be manipulation," she concluded. "Or there truly is something terrible waiting to be awakened."

"Either way," Asvarr said as they gathered their belongings and prepared to flee, "we need that third anchor. Only then will we have enough of the pattern revealed to make our own choice."

They left the Sanctuary of Sorrow as the stone gods' tears froze solid, the protective boundary failing against pressures from beyond the pattern. The living map of existence they'd conjured burned in Asvarr's mind—a vastly more complex structure than the simple Tree he'd envisioned, showing connections and potentials he'd never imagined.

The true question wasn't whether to restore Yggdrasil, but what form that restoration would take. What waited in the void at the pattern's heart, and who would shape it when all five anchors were bound?

Starfall Mountain gleamed in the distance, silver peak catching dawn's first light. The third anchor waited there, and with it, answers that would determine their path forward—toward restoration, evolution, or something else entirely that no Warden had achieved in nine cycles of breaking and binding.

Starfall Mountain loomed before them, its crystalline peak shattering dawn into prismatic fragments across Alfheim's silver forest. Asvarr led their group through the underbrush, pushing aside translucent leaves that chimed like tiny bells when touched. His skin tingled where bark patterns had spread up his neck, the memory anchor's crystalline formations catching the broken light.

Memory Eaters still pursued them—silver-skinned entities seeking to feast on identity and connection. He felt their hunger like a cold void at his back. The void-spaces they'd glimpsed through the tear-lake's manifestation haunted his thoughts, endless emptiness pressing against reality's thin membrane.

Brynja moved beside him, wooden arm extended to brush against tree trunks, sharing something through their living connection.

"The trees speak of hidden paths," she said. "Ways between what we see and what exists behind perception."

Yrsa knelt at a stream of liquid starlight, dipping her crystal pendant into its gleaming surface. "We need shelter to examine what the Root-map revealed."

Leif had gone ahead, his small form somehow both solid and insubstantial against the metallic forest. He returned with golden light trailing from his fingertips.

"There's a hollow in the silver mountain's shadow," he said, that adult resonance overtaking his childlike voice. "The boundaries are stronger there. They can't follow."

Asvarr nodded, feeling the two bound anchors within him responding to Starfall Mountain's proximity. The third anchor—the starlight bridge—pulsed at the mountain's peak, calling to him. Its nature differed from the others; it sought transformation rather than surrender or dominance.

***

An hour later, they reached the hollow, a curved space beneath an outcropping of crystal rock that reflected the forest in countless facets. Inside, they found unexpected safety—the air itself felt solid, the boundaries between realms reinforced rather than thinned.

"We can speak freely here," Yrsa said, hanging her crystal pendant from a jutting stone. Blue-white light rippled across the hollow's walls. "The living map showed us truths that change everything."

Asvarr unsheathed his bronze sword, laying it before them. Golden veins pulsed beneath the metal, echoing the patterns beneath his skin. "Three paths remain to complete the pattern. Starlight waits above us. Death and legacy converge in Helheim. Creation and destruction balance in Muspelheim."

"If we complete those paths—bind those anchors—what then?" Brynja asked. The flowers along her wooden arm furled closed, responding to her tension. "The Ashfather warned us—"

"The Ashfather manipulates," Asvarr interrupted, the Grímmark burning across his chest. "Nine cycles he's maintained the pattern at a breaking point, never allowing full restoration."

"Perhaps for good reason." Brynja's truth-runes glowed golden on her half-wooden face. "The tear-lake showed us distortions in the pattern, places where connections were severed or rerouted. But what if those changes were necessary? What if what waits at the center is worse than divine domination?"

Yrsa moved between them, her face illuminated by her pendant's light. "Both perspectives have merit. The pattern seeks completion, yet nine cycles have passed without it. We must ask why."

"Because no Warden ever bound all five anchors," Asvarr said, tracing the path of his Grímmark beneath his tunic. "Each time the cycle repeats, the pattern is broken before completion."

Brynja leaned forward, her wooden fingers forming intricate patterns in the air. "The Ashfather told us he walked this path before. He bound the anchors and glimpsed what waits at the center—something ancient and hungry from beyond the pattern."

"And we should trust his word?" Asvarr scoffed, though doubt gnawed at him. The living map had revealed complexity far beyond his understanding, connections and pathways he couldn't have imagined.

"My truth-runes confirmed he believes what he says." Brynja touched the golden sigils etched into her wooden cheek. "Fear drives him, not malice. He maintains the breaking because he fears what restoration might unleash."

"Or because restoration would end his power," Asvarr countered.

Tension thickened the air between them. The flames of their small fire twisted unnaturally, reflecting the fractured unity of their purpose.

Leif sat cross-legged beside the flame, his golden eyes unusually bright. "You both speak of two paths as if they're the only choices." His voice carried that unsettling resonance again—ancient knowledge in a child's throat. "Restoration versus breaking. Tree versus Ashfather. But I exist in the spaces between. I walk paths that others cannot see."

They all turned to him, suddenly aware of what they'd overlooked. Leif had been with them from the beginning, guiding them through boundaries, opening paths that shouldn't exist.

"What are you saying?" Yrsa asked gently.

"I'm saying there's always another way." Leif traced patterns in the air that mirrored the living map they'd created. "The third path. Not restoration. Not breaking. Transformation."

Asvarr felt the echo of his mother's words from the golden leaf in the Whispering Grove: "Forgiveness is stronger than vengeance." Had she been hinting at this third path all along?

"The Ashfather spoke of control to prevent divine domination," Asvarr said slowly. "I've sought restoration to heal what was broken. What if neither answers the pattern's true need?"

"Transformation," Brynja repeated, her wooden arm creaking as she flexed it. "The severed bloom within me seeks that. Not merely to exist as before, but to become something new."

Yrsa's fingers tightened around her crystal pendant. "Boundary-walkers have whispered of this possibility across nine cycles. A path between paths. Neither surrender to the old pattern nor destruction of it."

A new possibility unfolded before Asvarr, challenging everything he'd believed about his quest. From the moment he'd found the Grímmark burning on his chest, he'd sought vengeance against the Ashfather, restoration of what was lost. Now he saw the narrowness of that vision.

"The starlight anchor," he murmured, looking toward the mountain. "It bridges rather than binds. Transforms rather than dominates or recognizes. It could show us this third path."

"Perhaps that's why no Warden has ever bound all five anchors," Brynja suggested. "They clung to one vision—restoration or breaking—while the pattern itself seeks evolution."

"Look," Leif whispered, pointing to the hollow's opening.

The sky outside had darkened, stars appearing despite the day's full light. The stars moved with deliberate purpose, forming runes and symbols that matched patterns beneath Asvarr's skin.

"The starlight anchor reaches for us," Yrsa said. "We must go to it before the Memory Eaters find another way through the boundaries."

Asvarr gathered his belongings, fingers lingering over his bronze sword. The weapon had changed with each binding, evolving as he evolved. Golden veins now formed patterns matching those on his flesh, the metal itself transformed by its connection to the anchors.

"We go to Alfheim's peak," he decided. "To the starlight anchor. But first—" He turned to Brynja, extending his hand. "I need to understand your position more clearly. The Ashfather's offer—do you truly believe we should consider it?"

Her truth-runes glowed as she took his hand, wooden fingers interlacing with his flesh. "I believe we should understand his fear before rejecting it. Nine cycles, Asvarr. Nine times the pattern has been broken and partially restored. If no Warden has ever completed the binding, there must be a reason."

"Or an obstacle deliberately placed in their path," he countered.

"Perhaps both are true," Yrsa interjected. "The pattern resists completion, yet something manipulates that resistance."

Their grove-twined marks pulsed between their palms, the living connection strengthening despite their disagreement. Asvarr felt Brynja's genuine concern, her fear for the consequences of wrongful restoration.

"I will go to the starlight anchor," Asvarr said firmly. "What I've seen in the living map convinces me we must continue binding the anchors. But—" He squeezed Brynja's hand, feeling the smooth wood against his callused palm. "I hear your concern. I acknowledge the risk. And I'll seek this third path Leif speaks of. Transformation, not simply restoration."

Relief softened Brynja's features, truth-runes dimming as the tension between them eased. "That's all I ask. That we move forward with eyes open to all possibilities."

Yrsa gathered her belongings, crystal pendant blazing brighter as she moved toward the hollow's entrance. "Starfall Mountain will test everything you believe, Asvarr. The starlight anchor demands transformation beyond what the others required. Are you prepared for what that means?"

"No," Asvarr admitted, touching the crystalline formations at his temples. "But readiness has never been part of this journey. Only necessity."

***

They emerged from the hollow to find the forest transformed. Silver trees had shed their leaves, metallic trunks gleaming like polished spears thrust into the earth. The air tasted of metal and starlight, charged with potential that raised the fine hairs on Asvarr's arms.

Leif moved ahead, more confident in this landscape than any of them. "The sky and earth speak the same language here," he said cryptically, pointing toward geometric shadows that didn't match the objects casting them.

As they neared the mountain's base, the strain between them became physical. Starfall's proximity heightened the differences in their perspectives, creating an almost visceral barrier between them despite their blood-oaths and grove-twined marks.

Asvarr felt the divide most keenly with Brynja, whose wooden features had grown more pronounced since they'd entered Alfheim. Her transformed arm now extended past her elbow, bark patterns reaching toward her shoulder. The Severed Bloom within her responded differently to the anchors than his Grímmark did—seeking independence rather than connection.

"I don't understand," Asvarr said quietly as they paused beside a stream of flowing silver light. "We survived the memory realm together. We created the living map together. Why now does our purpose fracture?"

Brynja stared at her wooden fingers, flexing them deliberately. "Because now we face the consequences of our choice. The living map showed us the pattern's complexity, how each anchor exists simultaneously across realms. If the anchors are connected that way, what else might transcend boundaries? What might we unleash from one realm into all others?"

Her words struck Asvarr with uncomfortable force. He'd seen the void-spaces pressing against reality's edges, felt the hunger of the Memory Eaters. What if the pattern's center contained something similar but infinitely more powerful?

"We need more information," Yrsa stated firmly, breaking their spiraling tension. "The starlight anchor bridges realms through transformation. Binding it will reveal more of the pattern than we can see now."

"And transform us further," Asvarr added, unconsciously touching the bark patterns on his neck. Each binding changed him—how much humanity would remain after three more?

A cold wind swept down from Starfall Mountain, carrying fragments of star-song—crystalline notes that resonated with the pattern beneath Asvarr's skin. The mountain called to him specifically, recognizing the two anchors he'd already bound.

"I'll go," Asvarr decided, staring up at the peak where starlight pooled in a perfect silver circle. "Alone if necessary."

"Not alone," Leif said firmly, golden eyes reflecting the stars above despite the daylight. "Never alone."

"I'll go as well," Brynja added, though hesitation threaded her voice. "Our blood-oath binds us to this path, whatever my doubts."

Yrsa nodded solemnly. "The boundary-walker walks with you. But know this—" Her eyes flashed with sudden intensity. "The starlight anchor will demand more than physical transformation. It will require you to see beyond your understanding of pattern and purpose. Beyond restoration, beyond breaking. Are you prepared to have every belief challenged?"

"No," Asvarr said again, truth heavy in his voice. "But I'll go anyway."

They continued toward the silver spire, their unity damaged but intact. Behind them, the boundaries thinned further, Memory Eaters pressing against reality's edge. Before them, starlight pooled at Starfall's peak, promising transformation none of them truly understood.

Asvarr felt the tension between restoration and breaking, between his vision and Brynja's, between the Tree's purpose and the Ashfather's fear. But now he glimpsed something else—the possibility that both were correct yet incomplete. The third path that Leif had suggested might hold the true answer, a transformation beyond simply healing what was broken.

The promise-thread bound them physically still, their sworn oaths unbroken despite their fractured unity. As they ascended toward the third anchor, Asvarr recognized the truth that had eluded him since binding the first anchor: the pattern itself was neither good nor evil, neither salvation nor doom. It simply was—a framework upon which reality hung, capable of evolution or stagnation depending on those who shaped it.

And he, marked by the Grímmark, bound to two anchors, would help determine which it would become.

CHAPTER 28

THE BROKEN BLOOM

Dawn painted Alfheim's sky in shades of silver and pearl. Asvarr knelt at the edge of the tear-lake, filling waterskins for their journey to Starfall Mountain. The stone faces of weeping gods stared down at him, their carved expressions frozen in eternal sorrow. Cold droplets fell from stone eyes into the opalescent water, each tear creating rings that spread and vanished.

The bark patterns along his jaw itched as he worked, a constant reminder of his transformation. Two anchors bound within him—flame and memory—with three more awaiting. He touched the crystalline formations at his temples, feeling the chill of the memory anchor responding to the tear-lake's proximity.

"The boundaries have stabilized," Yrsa announced, approaching from where she'd been testing the perimeter. Her crystal pendant pulsed with steady blue light. "The Memory Eaters can't reach us here, at least for now."

"Then we should move quickly." Asvarr secured the waterskins to his belt, rising to his feet. "Starfall Mountain isn't far."

Behind him, Brynja sat cross-legged, her wooden arm extended over the tear-lake's surface. Small flowers bloomed along the transformed limb, opening and closing in rhythmic patterns. Since their disagreement the previous night, she'd grown more distant, her truth-runes occasionally flaring with words left unspoken.

"Leif is gathering supplies," she said, withdrawing her arm. Droplets of divine tears clung to her wooden fingers, glistening like trapped stars. "We should be ready to leave soon."

Asvarr nodded, uncomfortable with the tension between them. Their debate about the Ashfather's offer had revealed fundamental differences in their understanding of the pattern. Where he sought restoration, she feared the consequences. Where he trusted the Tree's purpose, she questioned it.

The tear-lake's surface rippled without wind, concentric circles spreading from its center. Something about the motion struck Asvarr as wrong—unnatural. The water darkened, colorless patches spreading like bruises beneath the surface.

"Yrsa," he called, his hand moving to his bronze sword's hilt.

The boundary-walker was already moving toward them, her face tight with concern. "Something's coming through the tear-lake. Something that shouldn't be here."

Brynja rose fluidly, wooden arm extending into branch-like appendages. "Memory Eaters?"

"Worse." Yrsa's pendant flared with sudden intensity. "The boundaries are fracturing from below."

***

The tear-lake's surface bulged upward, a dome of liquid rising impossibly into the air. Within it, shadows writhed and twisted, taking form then dissolving again. Golden sap mixed with the clear tears, creating sickly yellow threads that spread through the rising water.

Asvarr unsheathed his sword, the golden veins beneath the bronze blazing in warning. The Grímmark burned across his chest, responding to a presence that felt simultaneously familiar and utterly alien.

The water-dome burst, sending tear-drops spraying in all directions. Where it had stood, a twisted mass of branches and thorns hovered above the lake, dripping golden sap that steamed where it touched water. The entity had no clear form—parts of it resembled a tree, other sections twisted into almost-human shapes before collapsing back into chaotic tangles.

"What is that?" Asvarr breathed, the words catching in his throat.

"Corruption." Yrsa's voice dropped to a whisper. "The sickness that weakened Yggdrasil before the breaking."

The entity pulsed, branches extending and contracting like breathing lungs. Thorns sprouted along its limbs, razor-sharp and oozing dark sap. Where divine tears touched it, the corruption hissed and recoiled, only to reform stronger moments later.

"It's drawing power from the Root network," Brynja said, her wooden arm vibrating in response to the entity's presence. "I can feel it pulling at the fragment within me."

The corruption lurched toward them, branching appendages lashing outward. Asvarr raised his sword defensively, but the entity veered toward Brynja instead, drawn to her transformed arm.

Asvarr lunged, slashing at the tendril reaching for her. His blade sliced through the wooden limb, releasing a spray of golden sap that splattered across his tunic. The severed piece fell into the tear-lake, where it continued to writhe and pulse before dissolving.

The entity shrieked—a sound like splintering trees and tearing roots. It withdrew briefly, branches pulling inward as if reassessing its approach.

"My blade hurt it," Asvarr muttered, shifting to stand between Brynja and the corruption.

"Temporarily," Yrsa warned, backing away from the tear-lake. "It regenerates."

The corruption surged again, this time splitting into multiple tendrils that attacked from all directions. Asvarr spun, blade flashing as he severed branch after branch, each cut releasing splashes of tainted sap. Brynja's wooden arm extended into whip-like vines that slashed at the corruption, while Yrsa's crystal pendant cast protective light around them.

Despite their efforts, the entity grew faster than they could cut it back. Each severed piece dissolved into the tear-lake, only for two more branches to extend from the main mass. Its attacks became more coordinated, more deliberate—as if it were learning from each exchange.

A thorned tendril caught Asvarr's arm, piercing leather and flesh. Burning pain shot through his veins as something cold and alien entered his blood. He tore free, bark patterns along his jaw darkening where the corruption had touched him.

"Fall back!" he shouted, retreating from the lake's edge.

They regrouped beneath the stone gods, whose tears now fell more rapidly, as if responding to the corruption's presence. The entity hovered at the center of the tear-lake, its mass swelling as it absorbed more water. Branches formed and reformed, creating patterns that almost resembled runes before dissolving into chaos again.

"What is it trying to do?" Asvarr asked through gritted teeth, examining the thorn wound on his arm. Black veins spread outward from the puncture, following the paths of his transformed flesh.

"It's seeking a vessel," Yrsa said, her finger tracing glowing patterns in the air that temporarily held the corruption at bay. "Like the Tree itself, it needs a physical form to fully manifest in this realm."

"It wants me," Brynja said quietly, her truth-runes glowing gold against her wooden features. "It senses the Severed Bloom in my arm. Like calls to like."

Leif appeared beside them, eyes wide with fear and recognition. "It remembers what it once was," he said in that unsettling adult voice. "Before corruption. Before breaking. It remembers being part of something whole."

The entity surged forward again, this time focusing entirely on Brynja. Branches twisted together into a massive battering ram that slammed against Yrsa's protective barrier, each impact sending spiderwebs of cracks through the glowing shield.

"We can't stop it conventionally," Yrsa warned, her hands shaking as she struggled to maintain the barrier. "It adapts too quickly."

Asvarr's mind raced, searching for a solution. The corruption clearly originated from the Root network, perhaps the same sickness that had forced Yggdrasil to shatter itself. If it connected to the anchors somehow...

"The memory anchor," he said suddenly, touching the crystalline formations at his temples. "It preserves and transforms memory. What if we could use it against this thing?"

"How?" Brynja asked, her wooden arm retracting defensively as another impact shook Yrsa's barrier.

Before Asvarr could answer, the shield shattered. Yrsa collapsed to her knees, blood trickling from her nose from the exertion of maintaining it for so long. The corruption surged through the gap, branching tendrils spread wide to engulf them.

Asvarr acted instinctively. He seized Brynja's wooden hand, channeling power through their grove-twined marks. His memory anchor flared, crystalline formations blazing with white light. He pulled at the corruption's essence, trying to understand it through memory rather than physical form.

Images flooded his mind—the Root network stretching across worlds, a dark presence infiltrating the connections, and Yggdrasil's desperate gambit to save itself through shattering. The corruption had been trapped, contained in fractured pieces across the Nine Realms, until their actions had awakened it.

"It's from before," he gasped, struggling to make sense of the visions. "Before the Tree. Before pattern."

The corruption enveloped them, branches wrapping around their bodies. Where it touched Asvarr's transformed flesh, it burned cold, attempting to overtake his anchors. Where it touched Brynja's wooden arm, it merged, wood twisting around wood in grotesque communion.

Yrsa raised her crystal pendant, casting blue-white light that momentarily drove back the corruption. "It exists because of the breaking," she shouted over the entity's shrieking. "And because of the binding. Both are necessary for its manifestation."

Leif ducked between writhing branches, reaching Asvarr and Brynja. His small hand grasped their intertwined fingers, adding his connection to theirs. "Remember what you saw in the living map," he urged. "The anchors exist across all realms simultaneously. What happens in one affects all others."

Understanding blossomed in Asvarr's mind. If the anchors existed across realms, and if the memory anchor preserved and transformed memory itself...

"Brynja," he said urgently, gripping her wooden hand tighter. "We need to use the memory anchor together. Create a loop that the corruption can't escape."

Her truth-runes flared with golden light. "What memory?"

"Our first shared one—when we dueled in the Thorned Vale. When our blood mingled and we saw our connected past."

Recognition flickered across her face. "Combined with this moment—the corruption's attack. A closed loop of memory trapping it between was and is."

The corruption tightened around them, thorns digging into flesh and wood alike. Brynja's wooden arm began to blacken where the entity merged with it, corruption spreading up toward her shoulder. Asvarr's transformed flesh responded similarly, bark patterns darkening as the infection spread.

Time was running out.

Asvarr closed his eyes, reaching through their connected hands to the memory anchor within him. Crystalline formations at his temples blazed white-hot, channeling power outward. He focused on that moment in the Thorned Vale when their blood mingled on an ancient tree trunk, revealing shared ancestral memories of unified clans.

Brynja did the same, her truth-runes glowing so brightly they illuminated her skull beneath flesh and wood. Through their grove-twined marks, their memories merged—past duel and present battle fusing into a single experience that looped continuously.

The memory anchor responded, energy surging through Asvarr's transformed flesh and into their joined hands. The crystalline patterns at his temples spread, forming intricate geometries across his skin that mirrored the patterns beneath. Power flowed into Brynja, then outward into the corruption wrapped around them.

The entity convulsed, caught in the memory loop they'd created. Branches thrashed wildly, sap spraying in all directions as it struggled against the temporal trap. Where it had merged with Brynja's arm, it began to separate, forced out by the purifying power of shared memory.

"It's working," Asvarr gasped, maintaining his grip on Brynja despite the pain of thorns digging into his palm.

The corruption's form began to destabilize, branches dissolving into golden sap that rained down into the tear-lake. Wherever divine tears touched the corrupted essence, small explosions of light erupted, purifying the infection.

Then, just as victory seemed within reach, the entity's center split open, revealing a pulsing core of absolute darkness. Not shadow or void, but something fundamentally wrong—an absence of pattern itself. From that core emerged a sound that wasn't truly sound at all, but direct impression upon their minds.

Chains broken. Void between branches. Freedom comes.

The voice penetrated Asvarr's thoughts like ice shards, ancient and utterly alien. This wasn't the Root's voice, nor any entity connected to Yggdrasil. This came from outside, from before, from something that existed in the spaces between pattern.

Yrsa threw her crystal pendant into the tear-lake, where it detonated in a blast of blue-white light. The explosion caught the corruption at its most vulnerable, shredding its remaining branches and destroying the dark core at its center.

The entity dissolved entirely, fragments of wood and thorn raining down into the tear-lake, where divine tears dissolved them completely. Within moments, no trace remained beyond a faint darkening of the water's opalescent surface.

Silence fell across the sanctuary. The stone gods' tears slowed to their previous steady rhythm. The air lightened, pressure easing from Asvarr's chest.

He released Brynja's hand, both of them collapsing to their knees. The memory anchor's power receded, crystalline formations cooling at his temples. His transformed flesh still bore marks of the corruption—darkened patterns that stood out against the golden veins of healthy transformation.

"What was that?" he asked, voice raw. "That voice at the end—that wasn't the Root."

Yrsa retrieved her crystal pendant from the shallows of the tear-lake, its light dimmed but still present. "That," she said gravely, "was what the Ashfather fears. What the Tree shattered itself to contain."

"The void-hunger," Leif whispered, golden eyes wide with recognition. "The anti-pattern that exists between worlds."

Brynja examined her wooden arm, which now bore darkened streaks where the corruption had temporarily merged with it. Her truth-runes glowed steadily as she spoke. "The Ashfather told the truth. There is something ancient and dangerous beyond the pattern."

Asvarr stared at the tear-lake, mind reeling from the implications. The corruption hadn't been merely a twisted fragment of Root—it had been a vessel for something far older and colder, something that saw the pattern itself as chains to be broken.

"The Verdant Gate closing, the memory realm collapsing, the Memory Eaters appearing—they're all symptoms of the same problem," he realized. "The boundaries between realms are weakening each time we bind an anchor."

"Because the anchors exist across all realms simultaneously," Yrsa confirmed. "Each binding affects the entire pattern, for better or worse."

Brynja rose shakily to her feet, her wooden features set in grim determination. "This changes everything. The third path Leif mentioned—transformation—may be our only option. We can neither restore the pattern as it was, nor allow it to collapse completely."

Asvarr stood beside her, feeling the tension between them ease slightly in the face of this new understanding. "The starlight anchor becomes even more crucial now. We need to see more of the pattern before making any final decisions."

They gathered their belongings, still shaken by the encounter. Divine tears continued to fall from stone faces, washing away the last traces of corruption from the lake's surface. But the memory of that alien voice remained, echoing in Asvarr's mind with terrible clarity.

Chains broken. Void between branches. Freedom comes.

Whatever lay at the pattern's center—whether empty void or ancient hunger—would determine the fate of all Nine Realms. And Asvarr, bearing the Grímmark and two bound anchors, would help decide whether to restore those chains, break them completely, or transform them into something entirely new.

***

The corrupted entity reformed itself, branches knitting together where Yrsa's crystal blast had torn them apart. Asvarr's breath caught in his throat as he watched the twisted mass grow larger, drawing power from the tear-lake itself. The sickly yellow-gold sap that flowed through its limbs darkened to amber, then black, veined with pulsing red lines that resembled blood vessels.

Across the sanctuary, Yrsa struggled to her feet, her face drawn with exhaustion. "It adapts too quickly," she called, crystal pendant clutched in her trembling hand. "Each attack makes it stronger."

Brynja's wooden arm vibrated in response to the corruption's presence, dark stains spreading where the entity had temporarily merged with her transformed flesh. "We can't defeat it conventionally. It's not just Root—it's something that infected the Root."

The entity surged forward again, this time splitting into a dozen separate tendrils that attacked from all directions. Asvarr slashed at the nearest branch, severing it cleanly only to watch two more sprout from the stump. His transformed skin burned where the corruption had touched him, bark patterns darkening along his jaw and neck.

"Leif!" he shouted over the entity's wail. "Get behind us!"

The boy darted between thorned branches, golden eyes wide with fear. A tendril lashed out, missing his ankle by a finger's width. "Remember the living map," Leif called, that unsettling adult resonance overtaking his voice. "The anchors connect across realms!"

The memory anchor. Asvarr's mind raced, crystalline formations at his temples pulsing with cool power. If the anchors existed in all realms simultaneously, perhaps they could use that connection against the corruption.

A thorned whip caught him across the shoulder, slicing through leather and flesh. Burning cold spread from the wound as some alien presence tried to work its way deeper. Asvarr staggered back, fighting both the physical pain and the mental invasion that accompanied it.

Brynja reached him, her wooden arm extending to block another strike. Where corruption touched wood, the two substances recognized each other, merging briefly before Brynja wrenched her limb away. Truth-runes flared golden on her face, revealing both fear and determination.

"We need to try something else," Asvarr gasped, pressing his palm against the wound in his shoulder. "The memory anchor—we can create a loop."

"A loop?" Her eyes widened with sudden understanding. "Like we did in the Thorned Vale, with our blood memories."

"Yes." Asvarr seized her wooden hand, feeling the grove-twined mark on his palm connect with hers. "Our first shared memory, when our blood mingled and showed us our shared past."

"Combined with this moment." Brynja's truth-runes blazed brighter. "Trapping it between was and is."

The entity sensed their intention, branches pulling back briefly before surging toward them again with renewed force. It no longer attacked randomly—all tendrils focused on separating them, recognizing the threat they posed together.

Yrsa shouted words in a language Asvarr didn't recognize, her crystal pendant flaring with blue-white light that momentarily drove back the corruption. "Do it now," she commanded. "I can't hold it long."

Asvarr tightened his grip on Brynja's wooden hand, focusing on the memory anchor within him. Crystalline formations at his temples burned cold then hot, power flowing outward through their connected marks. He pictured that moment in the Thorned Vale when their blood had mingled on ancient bark, revealing generations of connected history between their clans.

Brynja gasped as the memory transferred through their mark, the full sensory experience. The surprise of discovery. The confusion of contradictory histories. The revelation that their bloodlines had once been unified before some ancient betrayal.

"Now this moment," Brynja whispered, her wooden fingers tightening around his. The flowers along her transformed arm unfurled and closed in rapid succession, channeling power between them.

Asvarr opened himself to the present—corruption surging against Yrsa's weakening barrier, the scent of divine tears mingling with rot-sweet sap, the burning wound in his shoulder, the press of Brynja's wooden palm against his flesh. He fed these sensations through their connected marks, creating a complete circuit between past and present.

The memory anchor responded, crystalline formations spreading across his temples and down his cheek in geometric patterns. Power surged through him, then into Brynja, whose truth-runes now glowed so brightly her skull shone through flesh and wood.

Together they focused this energy outward, directing it at the corruptive entity. The power flowed from them in visible waves, golden light rippling across the sanctuary and striking the twisted mass of branches and thorns.

The entity shrieked—a splintering, tearing sound that resonated in Asvarr's bones. Where the memory waves touched it, the corruption seemed to lose cohesion, branches phasing between states of was and is, unable to fully exist in either.

"It's working," Yrsa called, though her voice sounded distant through the roar of power in Asvarr's ears.

The memory loop caught the corruption in temporal flux, trapping it between the first time their bloodlines recognized each other and this moment of unified defense. Past and present twisted around the entity like chains, binding it in contradictory realities it couldn't escape.

Where the corruption had merged with Brynja's wooden arm, it now violently separated, torn away by the purifying power of shared memory. Similarly, the darkness spreading through Asvarr's transformed flesh receded, forced out by the same cleansing energy.

But the entity fought back with unexpected strength. Its core pulsed with absolute darkness—a void within its tangled mass that consumed light rather than reflected it. From this void rose a sound that wasn't truly sound at all, but direct impression upon their minds.

Chains broken. Void between branches. Freedom comes.

The voice penetrated deeper than flesh, colder than ice, older than any language Asvarr had ever heard. This wasn't the Root speaking, nor anything connected to Yggdrasil. This came from outside, from before, from something that existed in the spaces between pattern.

Leif cried out, clutching his head. "It's the anti-pattern," he gasped. "The void that waits between worlds."

The entity's branches bent impossibly, twisting through angles that shouldn't exist. Its form bulged and contorted as if something within fought to emerge—something far worse than corrupted Root. The void at its center expanded, threatening to engulf their memory loop entirely.

"We need more," Asvarr growled through gritted teeth, blood trickling from his nose with the strain of maintaining the memory anchor's power. "Another memory to complete the loop."

Brynja's truth-runes pulsed with golden light as she nodded. "The duel," she gasped. "Our battle in the present."

Understanding flooded through him. Three points to create a perfect loop—their shared ancestral past, their confrontation in the Thorned Vale, and this moment against the corruption. A triangle of memory that would close the entity within.

Asvarr reached deeper into the memory anchor, drawing forth the final piece—their duel beneath the bleeding canopy, where Brynja had tried to extract the flame essence from his blood. The clash of bronze blade against wooden thorns. The revelation of their shared heritage. The moment their separate paths had first entwined.

Power exploded from their joined hands, no longer waves but a solid beam of golden-white light that struck the corruption's core. The memory triangle locked into place, creating a perfect prison of temporal energy that contracted around the entity.

The corruption thrashed wildly, branches whipping through air as it fought against the memory loop. But each movement only entangled it further in the temporal web they'd created. Past, middle, and present moments wrapped around it like living bonds, compressing it into an ever-smaller space.

Divine tears fell more rapidly from the stone gods above, each droplet burning the corruption where it touched. The entity's shrieking reached a pitch that shattered clarity, forcing Asvarr to his knees. Still, he maintained his grip on Brynja's hand, feeling her doing the same despite the agony that tore through them both.

Then, with a final convulsion, the entity collapsed in on itself. Branches, thorns, and corrupted sap imploded around the void-core, compressing into a single point of darkness that hung suspended above the tear-lake. For a heartbeat, absolute silence fell across the sanctuary.

This silence shattered as the compressed point exploded outward in a blast of golden light. The corrupted matter burned away in an instant, consumed by contradictory realities that tore it apart at the level of pattern itself. Only the void-core remained, a tear in reality that wavered like heat above stone.

From this tear came that terrible voice once more, no longer forced into words but pure concept impressed directly upon their minds:

You merely contain. You cannot destroy. What exists between pattern cannot be unmade.

The void-core pulsed once more, then collapsed with a sound like stone grinding against stone. Divine tears washed away the last traces of corruption from the lake's surface, calm spreading across the opalescent water.

Asvarr released Brynja's hand, both of them collapsing to the ground. The memory anchor's power receded, crystalline formations cooling at his temples.

Blood trickled from his nose and ears, the price of channeling such energy through flesh still partially human.

"What was that?" he asked, voice raw from screaming he didn't remember.

"The void-hunger," Yrsa answered, approaching with her crystal pendant held protectively before her. "What exists between branches of the pattern. What the Tree feared enough to shatter itself rather than be consumed."

Brynja examined her wooden arm, which now bore dark veins where corruption had temporarily merged with it. "The Ashfather was right," she said, her truth-runes confirming her sincerity. "There is something worse than gods returning."

Leif stood at the tear-lake's edge, golden eyes fixed on where the void-core had collapsed. "It's not gone," he said quietly. "Just banished temporarily. Each time you bind an anchor, the boundaries between realms thin further. Each time, it has more space to reach through."

Asvarr pushed himself upright, muscles trembling with exhaustion. The wound in his shoulder burned cold, then hot, as his transformed flesh worked to purge the last traces of corruption. His mind reeled with implications of what they'd witnessed—and what they'd heard in that ancient, terrible voice.

"The pattern as chains," he murmured, recalling the entity's words. "It sees reality itself as a prison."

"Because it is," Yrsa said, helping Brynja to her feet. "For certain entities, at least. The pattern establishes rules, limitations, boundaries. Without it, there is only void—formless possibility without restraint."

"The third path becomes even more crucial now," Brynja said, her wooden features set with determination. "We can't simply restore the pattern as it was, nor allow it to break completely."

Asvarr nodded, mind still processing the confrontation. "Transformation. Not merely healing what was broken, but evolving it into something stronger."

They gathered their scattered belongings, each lost in thought. The sanctuary felt changed, as if the battle had altered the very nature of the place. Divine tears continued to fall from stone faces, but the water seemed clearer now, purified by the corruption's destruction.

As they prepared to depart for Starfall Mountain, Asvarr became aware of a new sensation spreading beneath his skin. Where the memory anchor had flooded his system with power, crystalline patterns now formed permanently, merging with the bark-like transformation along his jaw and neck. Simultaneously, small branches began to sprout from his shoulders, growing upward in spiraling patterns that resembled the beginning of a crown.

He caught Yrsa watching him with an unreadable expression. "It's happening faster now," she observed. "Each binding, each use of the anchors' power accelerates the transformation."

"How much of me will remain when all five are bound?" Asvarr asked, wincing as the tiny branches continued to grow, merging together into more complex patterns above his head.

"That," Yrsa said gravely, "depends entirely on the path you choose. Restoration would consume you entirely, replacing identity with pure pattern. Breaking would shatter your consciousness across realities. Transformation..."

"Transformation offers a third option," Brynja finished, her wooden hand resting on Asvarr's arm. "Partnership rather than domination or surrender."

Asvarr touched the growing crown of branches, feeling how they connected directly to the crystalline formations spreading from his temples. Two anchors now visibly manifested in his transformed flesh—flame and memory intertwined, neither dominating the other.

The emergence of this living crown marked him as something beyond mere human—Warden of Two anchors, a station that hadn't existed since before the gods rose to power. The Tree recognized him now, as did the corruption that opposed it.

"To Starfall Mountain," he said firmly, shifting his pack to accommodate the crown's growth. "The third anchor will show us more of the pattern—and our place within it."

"The void-hunger will try again," Leif warned, golden eyes reflecting starlight despite the full day. "It felt you, recognized you as Warden. It will hunt you specifically now."

"Let it come," Asvarr said, feeling both anchors pulse within him in response to his resolve. "Better we face it knowing what it is than be caught unaware."

They departed the sanctuary under the weeping gaze of stone gods, leaving behind a tear-lake now stained with the memory of confrontation. The path to Starfall Mountain stretched before them, silver landscape gleaming beneath Alfheim's impossible sky.

The crown of branches continued to grow from Asvarr's shoulders, intertwining with the crystalline patterns of the memory anchor. Each step drew him further from humanity, each transformation bringing new awareness while erasing pieces of who he had been.

But in that moment, watching Brynja's wooden arm extend into flowering vines that matched his crown's pattern, Asvarr understood. The pattern wasn't meant to be restored to what it was. Nor was it meant to be broken entirely. The third path—transformation—offered evolution instead, a new pattern that might withstand what waited in the void between branches.

CHAPTER 29
VERDANT CROWN

Pain blazed through Asvarr as the void-creature's final scream faded across the tear-lake's surface. His knees buckled, sending him sprawling onto the silver-flecked grass. Every heartbeat pumped molten agony from his chest to his shoulders. Something was happening, a violent restructuring of flesh and bone.

"He's changing," Leif whispered, backing away. The boy's golden eyes had darkened to amber, reflecting an ancient fear.

Brynja knelt beside Asvarr, her wooden arm still bearing black veins where the corruption had briefly merged with her transformed flesh. "Fight it," she urged, gripping his hand. Her truth-runes flared golden across her face. "Don't surrender."

"It's too late for that," Yrsa said, her voice holding none of its usual calm. She clutched her damaged crystal pendant, now dimmed after its sacrifice against the corruption. "The anchors have claimed him."

Asvarr couldn't respond. His vision fractured into overlapping perceptions—the clearing around the tear-lake, a burning village from centuries past, a forest where every tree bled golden sap. The boundaries between memory and present dissolved. He tasted copper and dirt, smelled crushed pine needles and smoke from fires long extinguished, heard the low groan of ancient roots pushing through soil. His shoulders burned as though being torn open from within.

"Asvarr!" Brynja shouted, the sound reaching him as if through water.

He fixed his gaze on her face—half wood, half flesh, truth-runes glowing across her cheeks—and used it as an anchor against dissolution. The grove-twined mark on his palm throbbed with her heartbeat.

"I'm still here," he gasped, each word carved from raw throat. "I'm still—"

The pain crested. Slender branches erupted from his shoulders, unfolding in intricate patterns of wood and crystalline formations. They curled upward and inward, forming a living crown that settled with impossible lightness upon his brow. Golden sap wept from the joining points before hardening into amber beads.

The wave of transformation passed, leaving Asvarr trembling and drenched in sweat. He drew a shuddering breath as the world stabilized around him—yet it wasn't the same world he'd inhabited moments before.

The tear-lake's surface revealed his reflection: a man with bark patterns covering half his face and neck, crystalline structures at his temples that caught and refracted light, and a crown of living branches interwoven with amber drops and memory-crystal. It should have felt alien, horrific. Instead, it felt like remembering something long forgotten.

"Warden of Two," Yrsa murmured, keeping her distance. "The anchors recognize you."

"What does that mean?" Asvarr reached up, fingers brushing the living crown. It responded to his touch, branches shifting slightly.

"It means you've walked further down this path than any Warden in nine cycles." Yrsa's voice held a trace of awe. "Flame and memory bound together. Only three remain."

Asvarr struggled to his feet, surprised by the crown's lightness. He should have felt weighed down, but instead experienced a curious balance, as if the branches were an extension of his own body. With each breath, he became aware of new sensations flooding his consciousness.

A massive pine at the edge of the clearing—he could feel its slow heartbeat, the gradual stretch of its roots through soil. In the tear-lake, he sensed memories captured within each ripple, some ancient beyond reckoning. Above, stars wheeled in patterns that suddenly held meaning—time written in celestial script.

Most unsettling were the distant whispers of other living things—a herd of elk moving through a valley leagues away, birds nesting in the boughs of a mountain ash, even the microscopic life teeming in a handful of soil. All connected, all part of patterns he'd never perceived before.

"What's happening to me?" he asked, voice cracking.

"The crown grants perception," Yrsa explained, approaching cautiously. "You stand as Warden of flame and memory. You perceive connections others cannot—the rhythm of seasons, the thoughts of ancient trees, the patterns that bind all living things."

"It's too much," Asvarr growled, pressing his palms against his temples. "I can feel everything."

"Focus on your own heartbeat," Brynja said, her voice cutting through the cacophony of sensations. "Count each pulse. Find the center."

He followed her instruction, concentrating on the steady thrum in his chest. Gradually, the overwhelming flood of awareness receded to manageable currents. The world remained transformed—richer, deeper, vibrating with connections he'd never imagined—but no longer threatened to drown him.

"Better?" she asked.

"Yes." He lowered his hands and met her gaze. "Thank you."

"Don't thank me yet." She glanced at her oath-mark, which pulsed with emerald light. "We've defeated one enemy, but the Ashfather watches, the Five scheme, and whatever lay within that corruption—"

"The void-hunger," Leif interrupted, the child's voice resonating with unnerving depth. "The anti-pattern. It exists between branches, hating all structure."

"It's still out there," Asvarr said, memory of its alien presence making his skin crawl. "And it recognized me."

"Because you threaten it," Yrsa said. "With each anchor you bind, you strengthen the pattern it seeks to unravel."

A thought struck Asvarr with physical force. "The Tree didn't shatter to escape the Ashfather or the Five. It broke itself to escape that thing."

"And with each anchor you bind, you thin the boundary that contains it," Yrsa confirmed, her expression grave.

Asvarr cursed, feeling the weight of his choices pressing down despite the crown's physical lightness. "Then why continue binding them at all? Why not leave the anchors scattered?"

"Because the void-hunger grows stronger regardless," Brynja said, her wooden arm exuding golden sap that dripped onto the grass. Where each drop landed, tiny white flowers bloomed and died in the span of heartbeats. "The Tree's breaking was desperate protection, not permanent solution. Nine cycles of partial restoration have maintained enough structure to keep the realms intact, but entropy increases with each turning."

"How do you know this?" Asvarr demanded.

Her truth-runes flared. "I don't know—I feel it. The fragment within me understands on some level I cannot fully articulate." She touched her wooden arm. "The Severed Bloom remembers what came before the breaking."

Yrsa nodded. "The Ashfather told the truth about one thing—there are powers beyond the pattern that see reality itself as chains to be broken."

"Then what's the answer?" Asvarr paced, the crown's branches swaying with his movement. "Restoration invites the void-hunger's attention. Breaking everything removes what little protection remains."

"The third path," Leif said, golden eyes fixed on the distance. "Neither restoring nor breaking, but transforming."

Asvarr stopped, staring at the child who spoke with ancient wisdom. "What does that mean, practically? How do we transform the pattern?"

"It means exactly what you're doing now." Yrsa gestured toward his crown. "Becoming neither fully human nor fully pattern, but something between that can navigate both states. The Warden's crown marks this transformation—you're becoming part of the pattern while maintaining enough humanity to guide its growth."

Asvarr looked again at his reflection in the tear-lake. The crown's branches had settled into a configuration that mirrored the Grímmark patterns on his chest—flame spirals interwoven with memory geometry. It no longer looked entirely alien. It looked like it belonged there.

The realization sent a shiver through him. Was this how the Ashfather began? One transformation at a time, each seeming necessary, until humanity slipped away entirely?

"I'm still me," he said, though uncertainty threaded through the words.

"For now," Yrsa acknowledged. "But each binding changes you. The question is whether enough of Asvarr will remain when all five anchors are bound."

"If anyone can maintain balance, it's you," Brynja said, the truth-light of her runes confirming her sincerity. "You've already chosen the third path—flame without consuming, memory without dissolving."

Leif approached, reaching up to touch a hanging branch of the crown. "It needs your humanity," he said. "The pattern can't guide itself."

Asvarr knelt to meet the boy's eyes. "And what are you in all this, Leif? You exist between states, born when the Tree shattered."

"I am possibility," Leif answered, voice resonating with that unsettling adult depth. "What exists between breaking and binding. I cannot survive if the pattern fully restores or completely shatters."

"So you also walk the third path."

"I am the third path," Leif corrected. "I couldn't exist before the breaking. I won't exist after whatever comes next."

Asvarr's chest tightened. Despite the mysteries surrounding the child, he'd grown protective of Leif during their journey. The thought of the boy simply ceasing to exist struck a deeper chord than he'd expected.

He rose, feeling the crown settling more firmly into place with his resolve. "Then we make sure whatever comes next has room for all possibilities, including you."

Yrsa exchanged a glance with Brynja. "The starlight anchor awaits on the mountain's peak," she said. "Each binding thins the boundary further, but without it, you cannot complete what you've begun."

"The void-hunger will return stronger," Brynja warned. "It's retreated, but it knows you now."

Asvarr nodded, feeling the weight of decision despite the crown's uncanny lightness. "Then we continue to Starfall Mountain. We bind the third anchor and see what truths it reveals."

With sudden clarity, he perceived the mountain in the distance through the patterns connecting it to the land around them. Starlight poured into its peak, mingling with sap rising from deep roots. The third anchor pulsed there, waiting. Neither flame demanding dominance nor memory requiring recognition, but transformation itself.

He turned to the others. "We should move quickly. The Memory Eaters still hunt, and the void-hunger will gather strength."

As they prepared to depart, Asvarr became aware of something else—a rhythmic vibration through the grove-twined mark on his palm. Brynja felt it too, her gaze meeting his with the same realization.

"The oath-mark is changing," she said, holding up her palm where the wooden spiral glowed with emerald light.

Asvarr examined his own mark. The pattern had subtly altered, branches growing more complex, forming a miniature version of the starlight anchor they sought.

"It's responding to the crown," Yrsa observed. "Your connection to the pattern grows stronger."

"And to each other," Brynja added, closing her hand. "I can feel your thoughts at the edges of mine."

Asvarr hesitated, then focused on the connection between them. Beyond the emotional awareness the oath-mark had always provided, he now sensed deeper currents—fragments of Brynja's consciousness brushing against his own. It should have felt invasive, terrifying. Instead, it felt like remembering part of himself he hadn't known was missing.

"We're becoming something else," he murmured.

"Yes," Brynja agreed, truth-runes flaring. "The question is whether that's transformation or consumption."

Through their connection, Asvarr felt her uncertainty mirroring his own. The crown of branches framed his vision as he gazed toward Starfall Mountain. With each binding, he walked further from humanity and deeper into the pattern's embrace. How much would remain of Asvarr the man when he became Warden of Three?

The crown seemed to tighten momentarily, as if responding to his doubt.

"We keep moving," he decided, adjusting his bronze sword with its golden veins that now perfectly matched those running through the crown's branches. "The third anchor waits."

He stepped forward, and for an instant, perceived the world through the eyes of all living things around him—trees anchored in ancient soil, birds winging through crystal air, insects building homes in leaf litter. He was Asvarr, but also the pattern itself gaining consciousness through his binding.

The crown of verdant branch and memory-crystal settled more firmly upon his brow. The world would never look the same again.

***

The morning sun cast long shadows across the clearing as they prepared to depart for Starfall Mountain. Asvarr adjusted his bronze sword, its golden veins pulsing in harmony with the crown's branches. Each movement felt strange—his body responding with unfamiliar precision, senses extending far beyond normal reach. He tasted metal on the air, smelled the subtle decay of leaves fallen decades ago, heard the creaking growth of roots pushing through soil leagues distant.

"We should reach the mountain base by midday," Yrsa said, gathering her travel pouch. Her crystal pendant hung against her chest, still dimmed from its sacrifice against the corruption. "If we follow the starlight path—"

"I can't go with you."

Brynja's words cut through the clearing. She stood several paces away, her wooden arm gleaming with fresh sap that caught the morning light. The truth-runes carved into her flesh glowed golden, confirming the sincerity of her declaration.

Asvarr turned toward her, the crown's branches shifting with his movement. "What?"

"The oath-sigil has shown me another path." Brynja held up her palm, revealing the grove-twined mark. Where Asvarr's had evolved to mirror his verdant crown, hers had transformed differently—the wooden spiral now surrounded by tiny flame patterns. "I must return to confront the Verdant Five about their true intentions."

Asvarr crossed the distance between them in three strides. "We're bound by oath, Brynja. The starlight anchor requires both our bloodlines."

"Our bloodlines remain connected through the grove-twining," she replied, gesturing between their marked palms. "But our paths must diverge now." Her truth-runes flared brighter, illuminating the wooden patterns across her face. "The Verdant Five have manipulated us from the beginning. I no longer believe they seek true transformation—they want vessels to wear like garments while they reshape what remains."

The memory of their shared vision at the Circle of Splinters flashed between them through the oath-sigil—unified bloodlines standing against forces that would control the pattern.

"You think you can face them alone?" Yrsa asked, her voice sharp with concern.

"Not alone." Brynja turned toward Leif, who stood quietly watching the exchange. "The boy comes with me."

"Leif?" Asvarr looked between them, confusion mingling with a protective impulse that tightened his chest. "Why?"

Brynja knelt beside the child, her wooden arm dripping sap that froze before touching the ground. "Because his origin is connected to my clan's final ritual before its destruction."

Leif stepped forward, golden eyes reflecting a knowledge far beyond his years. "She speaks truth," he said, his childlike voice carrying that unsettling adult resonance. "I was born when the Tree shattered, but my beginning lies with the Hrafn clan's ending."

"What does that mean?" Asvarr demanded, the crown's branches rustling with his agitation.

"It means I existed before I existed," Leif answered cryptically. "Part of me was called forth by the ritual Brynja's clan performed as the shadows closed around them."

Brynja's truth-runes pulsed. "The Verdant Five told me my clan was destroyed by yours, Asvarr. Another lie. They were killed because they discovered how to create beings like Leif—possibilities born of the in-between that could navigate beyond the pattern."

Asvarr felt the weight of revelation press against his crown. Through their oath-mark connection, he sensed no deception from Brynja, only fierce determination and a grief so deep it transcended conscious thought.

"You risked revealing this to me before. Why tell me now?" he asked.

"Because the void-hunger recognizes you as Warden. It will hunt you specifically, and I need you focused on binding the starlight anchor," Brynja replied. "If I can discover the truth about the Five's intentions, about Leif's nature and origin, I might find knowledge that helps you walk the third path without dissolving into the pattern entirely."

The branches of Asvarr's crown tightened against his temples, responding to the conflict within. He wanted to command her to stay—the starlight anchor's binding would be more dangerous without her. Yet the connection between them revealed her conviction, as solid and immovable as the mountain itself.

"You've decided regardless of what I say," he stated, the words rough in his throat.

"Yes." No hesitation, no apology. The truth-runes confirmed what he already knew.

"Separating is tactically unwise," Yrsa interjected. "The Memory Eaters still hunt. The void-hunger gathers strength. The Ashfather watches from the spaces between stars."

"Which is why we must understand what truly shapes the pattern." Brynja stood, placing her flesh hand on Leif's shoulder. "If we're crafting the third path, we need to know all forces attempting to influence its direction."

A long silence stretched between them. Asvarr felt the crown's branches flex against his skull, pulling tension from his thoughts into physical form.

"How will you find the Verdant Five?" he finally asked.

"The oath-sigil shows me the way," Brynja answered, holding up her marked palm. "Just as yours guides you toward Starfall Mountain, mine pulls toward the sanctuary where they've withdrawn to watch events unfold."

Asvarr turned away, staring toward the distant peak where morning light glinted off crystal formations. The crown allowed him to perceive paths connecting this moment to potential futures—gossamer threads of possibility spinning outward. Some led to restoration, others to collapse, many to uncertain transformations. None offered guarantees.

"When will we see you again?" he asked, still facing the mountain.

"We'll meet in Muspelheim," Brynja said. "After you've bound the third anchor."

"How can you be certain?" Asvarr turned back to her, finding her truth-runes blazing golden across her face.

"Because the oath binds us regardless of distance. Because the pattern pulls us toward convergence." She approached him, close enough that he could smell the sap flowing beneath her bark-skin. "What burns there will determine whether we stand as allies or enemies in the end."

"Enemies?" The word tasted of ash.

"The third path has many branches, Asvarr." Her eyes held his without wavering. "Our understanding of transformation may differ once we've both learned what awaits us."

Through their oath-mark connection, he sensed her fear of what truths they might discover. The mark pulsed with shared emotion, flowing between them like a tide.

"I don't accept that," he said firmly. "We've come too far together."

"Then prove me wrong." A smile ghosted across her face, half-flesh, half-wood. "Bind the starlight anchor without surrendering to it. Hold enough of yourself apart to recognize me when we meet again."

Yrsa approached them, her crystal pendant glowing faintly. "For what it's worth, I believe this separation serves the pattern. Different perspectives on the same truth may reveal pathways neither could see alone."

Leif stepped forward, reaching up to touch a low-hanging branch of Asvarr's crown. "Remember what grows beneath the surface," he said, voice resonating with that ancient wisdom that belied his childlike form. "The joining of roots matters more than the separation of branches."

Asvarr knelt to meet the boy's eyes. "Will you be safe with her?"

"I exist where possibility overlaps certainty," Leif replied. "I am safest walking the boundary between what is and what could be."

"That's not an answer."

"It's the only one I have." Leif's golden eyes reflected Asvarr's crowned image back at him. "Truth has many faces, Warden of Two."

Brynja placed her wooden hand on Asvarr's forearm, the touch cool against his skin. "I won't let harm come to him. My oath-mark guarantees that much."

Asvarr rose, feeling the crown settle more firmly against his skull. He wanted to argue further, to command her loyalty through their oath. But the connection between them revealed the futility of such demands. Her path had diverged from his—fighting this truth would only weaken them both.

"Then go," he said, the words carved from reluctance. "Discover what you can about the Five's true intentions. But remember our oath—we seek transformation."

"I remember." The truth-runes flared one final time across her face.

Before he could respond, Brynja leaned forward and pressed her lips against his—a kiss that tasted of sap and humanity mingled. Through their oath-mark, emotions surged between them: her determination and fear, his reluctance and resolve, shared purpose despite divergent paths.

She pulled away, flesh fingers brushing against the bark patterns on his cheek. "Until Muspelheim, Warden of Two."

"Until Muspelheim, Root-tender," he replied, the formal title emerging unbidden from some ancestral memory buried in his blood.

Brynja nodded once, then turned to Leif. The boy took her wooden hand without hesitation. Together they walked toward the eastern edge of the clearing, following a path only they could perceive. At the tree line, Brynja paused and looked back. No words passed between them, but their oath-marks pulsed with simultaneous recognition.

Then they were gone, swallowed by silver trees and morning shadows.

"You're letting them go," Yrsa observed. "Despite your misgivings."

"The crown shows me threads of possibility stretching between us," Asvarr replied, watching the place where they'd vanished. "Some futures lead to reunion, others to confrontation. None reveal which path serves the pattern best."

"That's the burden of Wardenship," Yrsa said, adjusting her dimmed crystal pendant. "To choose without perfect knowledge, to bind without complete understanding."

Asvarr turned toward Starfall Mountain, feeling the third anchor's distant pull—colder than flame, more deliberate than memory. "Will they be safe?"

"The oath-mark would reflect her betrayal or destruction," Yrsa answered. "Beyond that, certainty belongs only to gods and fools."

The crown's branches tightened briefly against Asvarr's skull. With each passing moment, the connection to Brynja grew fainter as distance stretched between them. Yet the grove-twined mark remained, a warm spiral on his palm linking him to choices made and paths yet to walk.

"We continue to Starfall Mountain," he decided, adjusting his bronze sword with its veins of gold that matched the patterns beneath his skin. "The third anchor won't bind itself."

As they departed the clearing, Asvarr felt the weight of the verdant crown pressing more firmly into his flesh. Two anchors bound, three remaining. With each binding, he walked further from humanity and deeper into the pattern's embrace. How much would remain of Asvarr the man when he became Warden of Three?

The answer lay waiting at Starfall's peak, where starlight touched the ground and transformation demanded its price.

CHAPTER 30

THE ROOT THAT HUNGERS

Cold morning air filled Asvarr's lungs as he watched the place where Brynja and Leif had disappeared into the silver forest. Their absence created a hollow sensation in his chest that the crown's branches couldn't fill. The grove-twined mark on his palm still pulsed with faint connection, but with each passing moment, the link grew more tenuous as distance separated them.

"We should move," Yrsa said, adjusting her travel pack. "Starfall Mountain awaits, and your crown grows heavier by the hour."

She spoke truth. What had begun as an uncanny lightness now pressed against Asvarr's skull with noticeable weight. The branches extending from his shoulders had lengthened, curving down to frame his face before sweeping upward again. Tiny leaf buds formed along them, each containing fractured memories—some his, others ancestral, many from unknown sources. The crown integrated more deeply with each breath, bark and flesh merging in patterns that blurred the boundary between man and Root.

"How far to Alfheim?" Asvarr asked, rolling his shoulders to adjust to the crown's shifting weight.

"The realm itself? We're already in it." Yrsa gestured to the silver forest surrounding them. "The border thinned when you bound the second anchor. But the heart of Alfheim—where starlight pools at the mountain's peak—that journey will take until nightfall."

They departed the clearing, following a path that only Yrsa could see. The forest grew stranger as they progressed—trees with metallic bark that resonated when touched, flowers that bloomed in geometric patterns, shadows that moved independently of their casters. Asvarr's transformed senses overwhelmed him with information: the dreams of hibernating creatures beneath the soil, the slow grinding of stones remembering their molten birth, the whispers of starlight that had fallen centuries ago and embedded in tree rings.

"Focus on what lies ahead," Yrsa advised, noting his distraction. "The crown grants perception beyond mortal limits, but losing yourself in it serves nothing."

Asvarr nodded, concentrating on the physical act of walking. His bronze sword with its golden veins tapped rhythmically against his thigh, each contact sending subtle vibrations through his transformed flesh.

"Tell me about the starlight anchor," he said, desperate for anything that might anchor his thoughts.

Yrsa's expression darkened. Her crystal pendant, still dimmed from its sacrifice against the corruption, swung at her throat as she ducked beneath a low-hanging branch.

"It's the most dangerous of the five," she said. "The flame anchor demanded dominance, the strength to master rather than be mastered. The memory anchor required recognition, the wisdom to understand rather than merely know."

"And the starlight anchor?"

"Transformation itself." Yrsa's voice dropped lower. "Neither mastery nor understanding, but becoming. Stars remember longer than roots, burn colder than flame, and care nothing for mortal concerns."

The crown tightened against Asvarr's temples, branches creaking softly. "You speak as if it's alive."

"All anchors contain fragments of consciousness," Yrsa replied. "The starlight anchor holds the Tree's awareness of time—what was, what is, what might be. Time dilates in its presence. Moments stretch into eternities; centuries compress into heartbeats."

They crested a hill to find Starfall Mountain rising before them, its crystalline peak reflecting morning light in prismatic patterns. Even from leagues away, Asvarr felt its pull—a cold, constant pressure behind his eyes. Unlike the fierce demand of flame or the sorrowful patience of memory, the starlight anchor called with the distant certainty of cosmic forces. Inevitable. Inexorable. Indifferent.

"The mountain sees you," Yrsa murmured. "And judges your worthiness."

Asvarr squared his shoulders beneath the crown's weight. "How many have bound the starlight anchor before me?"

"None in nine cycles." Yrsa's fingers traced the edge of her pendant. "Some have tried. All were consumed—their humanity dissolved into the pattern."

"Encouraging." Asvarr's mouth twitched in a humorless smile.

"The Ashfather claimed it in the First Breaking," Yrsa continued. "He bound all five anchors, becoming neither human nor pattern but something between. Each subsequent cycle, he prevented others from completing what he began."

"Why? If he wanted to control the pattern, wouldn't more bindings strengthen it?"

"Control requires limitation." Yrsa pointed toward the mountain peak. "Full restoration would solidify the pattern beyond even his manipulation. The Ashfather maintains just enough structure to prevent collapse while preserving spaces he can reshape."

They descended into a valley where silver grass grew in spiral patterns, each blade pointed toward the mountain. As they walked through it, the crown pulled knowledge from Asvarr's memories—teachings from his mother about the stars, raids conducted beneath winter constellations, moments staring skyward while his clan burned around him. The branches twisted tighter, integrating these fragments into the crown's structure.

"It's getting heavier," he said, rolling his neck to ease the strain.

"The crown prepares you," Yrsa replied. "Each binding changes its nature, as it changes yours."

Midday found them crossing a stream of liquid starlight—a glowing silver ribbon that flowed uphill toward the mountain's peak. Asvarr knelt beside it, his reflection wavering in the luminous surface. The crowned figure looking back barely resembled the berserker who had survived his clan's destruction months ago. Bark patterns covered half his face, crystalline structures grew from his temples, and the branched crown framed his features like a predator's jaws.

"Still me in there?" he murmured to his reflection.

No answer came, only the soft trickle of starlight over stone.

Rising, Asvarr felt the grove-twined mark pulse once on his palm—a distant heartbeat from Brynja, impossibly far away. The connection remained, thread-thin but unbroken. He wondered what she had discovered about the Verdant Five, about Leif's origins, about the path they all walked.

"Will we see them again?" he asked, more to himself than Yrsa.

"The pattern draws together what belongs together," Yrsa answered cryptically. "Whether as allies or enemies remains for wyrd to decide."

The weight of Brynja's parting words pressed against Asvarr's mind. *What burns there will determine whether we stand as allies or enemies in the end.* He had rejected the possibility then. Now, with the starlight anchor's cold call replacing the warmth of human connection, doubt crept through him like frost.

They continued toward the mountain, the landscape growing increasingly alien. Trees floated upside-down, their roots drinking starlight from the air. Stones arranged themselves in perfect geometric patterns when unobserved, then scattered at a glance. Time stretched unevenly—moments when the sun seemed frozen in the sky, followed by sudden lurches of shadow as it jumped positions. Through it all, the crown grew heavier, its branches extending to brush Asvarr's shoulders.

"Something's wrong," he said, stopping suddenly. The crown pulled brutally at his skull, yanking his head toward the mountain with physical force. Pain lanced behind his eyes.

"The anchor senses your approach," Yrsa explained, reaching for his arm to steady him. "It tests your resolve."

"It's trying to take control," Asvarr growled, fighting the crown's pull. His knees buckled as branches tightened around his head, bark patterns crawling further across his cheeks.

"Fight it," Yrsa urged, her voice sharp. "Establish dominance now or the binding will consume you entirely."

Asvarr clenched his fists, focusing on the physical sensation of nails biting into palms. He thought of his clan, of Brynja's kiss, of Leif's cryptic wisdom—anchors to his humanity beyond the pattern's reach. The pressure eased fractionally, allowing him to straighten.

"I am Asvarr," he snarled through gritted teeth. "Flame-bearer. Memory-keeper. I control this crown."

The branches twisted, creaking like trees in high wind. For a moment, he feared they would snap his neck—then suddenly the pressure vanished. The crown settled against his skull, acknowledging his assertion. Not surrendering, merely retreating to reconsider its approach.

"It will try again," Yrsa said, watching him closely. "The anchor tests differently than the others. It seeks transformation on its terms."

Asvarr exhaled slowly, tasting metal on the air—the distinctive flavor of starlight concentrating around them. "And on my terms?"

"That is the question the binding will answer." Yrsa gazed toward the mountain's peak, where clouds gathered with unnatural swiftness. "Whether enough of Asvarr remains to shape transformation, or whether the pattern wears you like a garment."

They reached the mountain's base as afternoon light waned toward evening. Massive crystal steps led upward, each releasing chimes when pressed underfoot. Starlight pooled in hollows beside the path, growing more concentrated as they climbed.

The crown's weight increased with their ascent. Branches interwove with Asvarr's thoughts, remembrances becoming indistinguishable from current perceptions. He stumbled, catching himself against a crystal outcropping that sang at his touch.

"The Ginnungagap," he murmured, the ancient word surfacing from some ancestral memory buried in his blood.

"What did you say?" Yrsa asked sharply.

"The void beyond stars." Asvarr blinked, surprised by his own words. "Before pattern, before shape. The hungry darkness between branching possibilities."

"Those aren't your thoughts," Yrsa warned, her expression grave. "The crown pulls knowledge from the anchors. Be careful what you accept as truth."

Halfway up the mountain, they stopped at a flat ledge overlooking the silver forest sprawling below. The streams of liquid starlight converging on the peak had grown more numerous, their glow intensifying as twilight approached. Above them, the summit vanished into unnaturally dense cloud, while twin moons—one silver, one gold—appeared on the eastern horizon.

Asvarr leaned against a crystal spire, closing his eyes against the crown's persistent pull. Each heartbeat drove branches deeper into his awareness, until distinguishing where Asvarr ended and the crown began became impossible. His consciousness expanded outward through root networks, across forest canopies, up into star-patterns that had watched civilizations rise and fall.

"It's taking me," he whispered, eyes flying open. "I can feel myself dissolving."

Yrsa knelt before him, her dimmed crystal pendant held between them. "Focus on this. A single point. One object, one moment."

Asvarr stared at the pendant, forcing his scattered awareness to contract around its muted glow. His breathing slowed. The crown's branches stiffened, then relaxed incrementally.

"The crown grows heavier because you fight fragmentation by clutching every piece of yourself," Yrsa explained. "You cannot hold everything. Some parts must be surrendered."

"If I surrender anything more, what remains of me?" Asvarr demanded, frustration sharpening his voice.

"Identity exists beyond memory, beyond experience." Yrsa's expression softened with unexpected compassion. "The core of Asvarr—your essential nature—that must be protected. The rest? Let it join the pattern."

***

"How do I know what to keep?"

"What would you die to preserve?" Yrsa asked simply.

The question cut through his fragmented awareness like a blade. Images flashed behind his eyes: his mother's hand guiding his on a carving knife, his father's rare smile after a successful hunt, the clan gathered around winter fires singing sagas, Brynja's face half-flesh and half-wood with truth-runes glowing golden, Leif's ancient eyes in a child's face. Not just memories—anchors to his humanity.

"My connections," he answered finally. "To those I've known. Those I've loved. Those I've lost."

Yrsa nodded, satisfied. "The pattern seeks disconnection—absolute freedom at the cost of meaning. Your connection to others may be your strongest defense."

The crown's branches shifted, settling into a configuration that felt less intrusive. Asvarr rose, muscles aching from the transformation's strain. Above them, the summit waited, clouded in stars and mystery.

"We continue at first light," Yrsa decided, eyeing the darkening sky. "The binding should be attempted when the twin moons align at zenith."

Asvarr gazed upward, the crown allowing him to perceive stellar movements with supernatural clarity. The moons would reach perfect alignment tomorrow at midnight—one silver, one gold, reflecting the union of starlight and sap that the third anchor represented.

"And if I fail?" he asked, watching silver light trace patterns across the crystal mountainside.

"Then I continue alone to the fourth anchor," Yrsa answered without emotion. "The pattern must be maintained, regardless of who bears the burden."

Asvarr turned to her, really looking at her for the first time since the crown's manifestation. Her features remained composed, but weariness lined her eyes—ancient exhaustion no mortal should carry.

"How many cycles have you watched, Yrsa?" he asked quietly.

"Enough to know the cost of failure," she answered, her hand straying to her crystal pendant. "Enough to recognize hope when it takes root."

"Am I that hope?"

Yrsa's gaze met his without wavering. "You walk further down this path than any Warden in nine cycles. You balance flame and memory where others burned away or dissolved. If anyone can bind the starlight anchor without surrendering their essence, it might be you."

"Might be," Asvarr repeated, the words bitter on his tongue.

"Certainty belongs only to pattern, not to those who walk within it." Yrsa settled beside a crystal formation that hummed softly in the gathering dark. "Rest while you can. Tomorrow's binding will demand everything you have—and more you don't yet know you possess."

Asvarr sat with his back against stone that sang to his transformed flesh. The crown's weight pressed constantly, branches extending with every heartbeat. He felt the third anchor calling with the cold, distant certainty of starlight. Inevitable. Inexorable. Indifferent to the man it would transform.

On his palm, the grove-twined mark pulsed once—a brief connection to Brynja, impossibly distant yet still linked to his fate. Her final words echoed through his mind: *What burns there will determine whether we stand as allies or enemies in the end.*

As twin moons climbed the night sky, the verdant crown grew heavier on Asvarr's brow. Branches extended, intertwining with his thoughts until the man and his burden became impossible to separate.

Dawn painted Starfall Mountain with molten gold and crimson, the crystalline peak fracturing light into countless prismatic arcs. Asvarr woke with the crown already pulling him upward, its branches having grown another handspan while he slept. They curved around his jawline now, pressing into flesh that had become increasingly bark-like with each passing hour.

"We need to move," Yrsa urged, already gathering her few possessions. "The anchors grow restless."

She spoke truth. Within his transformed awareness, Asvarr felt fluctuations rippling through the pattern—disruptions in the harmonies flowing between realms. The twin moons still hung visible in the morning sky, their alignment hours away, but something had changed during the night. An urgency pulsed through the crystal mountain beneath them, vibrating into his bones.

"Something's wrong," he said, touching the mountain's surface. The crystal hummed discordantly against his fingertips.

"The void-hunger stirs," Yrsa replied, her voice tight with concern. "We must reach the summit before nightfall."

***

They descended from their ledge and continued up the switchback path that wound toward the peak. With each step, the mountain sang different notes, creating melodies that tugged at memories Asvarr had never formed. The crown responded, branches flexing and creaking as if conversing with the mountain through a language beyond human understanding.

His grove-twined mark remained silent. No pulse from Brynja reached him now, the distance between them stretching beyond even their oath-bond's reach. Asvarr found himself rubbing the wooden spiral on his palm, seeking a connection that had temporarily dissolved.

"Will it return?" he asked, holding up his marked palm.

"The oath remains," Yrsa answered. "Distance cannot break what binds your bloodlines together."

They climbed higher, passing through veils of mist that clung to the mountainside. The vapor tasted of starlight and memory, carrying fragments of ancient knowledge that dissolved on Asvarr's tongue. Through the crown's perception, he glimpsed the mountain as it had existed across multiple times—barren rock, lush forest, crystal spire, each state overlapping the others in a palimpsest of possibilities.

Midday found them crossing a narrow bridge of natural crystal that spanned a chasm filled with swirling silver light. Below, liquidized starlight pooled and eddied, flowing both upward toward the peak and downward into the mountain's heart. Crossing the bridge felt like stepping through time itself—moments stretched, compressed, doubled back on themselves. Asvarr experienced each footfall a dozen times, from slightly different angles, before moving to the next.

"The boundary thins here," Yrsa explained, her voice echoing strangely. "Time loses its coherence near the starlight anchor."

On the far side of the bridge, they discovered a plateau where a familiar sight caused Asvarr to stumble. The Verdant Gate stood before them—the massive archway of intertwined roots and branches they had passed through to escape the memory realm. It pulsed with internal light, sap weeping from joints where wood merged with wood.

"How?" Asvarr demanded, instinctively reaching for his bronze sword. The weapon's golden veins flared in response to his agitation. "We left this behind."

"The Gate exists across realms," Yrsa reminded him. "What we passed through was merely one manifestation. This is another—a different face of the same truth."

"Will it take us to the summit?" Asvarr asked, eyeing the archway with suspicion.

"It should open to a root-path that leads directly to the anchor," Yrsa confirmed, approaching the Gate with reverent caution. Her crystal pendant pulsed weakly against her chest, still diminished from its sacrifice.

Asvarr stepped forward, placing his hand against the living wood of the Gate. Unlike previous encounters, it felt cold beneath his touch, the sap congealed rather than flowing. The branches of his crown extended toward it, seeking connection, but recoiled almost immediately as if burned.

"Something's wrong," he muttered, backing away.

Before Yrsa could respond, a sound tore through the air, felt with bone and blood and transformed flesh. A grinding, splitting noise like the world itself breaking apart. The Verdant Gate shuddered from its foundation to its peak. Cracks spread through its living wood, golden sap crystallizing within them.

"No," Yrsa gasped, lunging forward as if to prevent what was happening.

Too late. With a final, shattering groan, the Verdant Gate sealed itself—wood fusing with wood, branches entwining so tightly they merged into solid mass. The archway that had stood open across nine cycles closed with absolute finality.

"What's happening?" Asvarr demanded, the crown pulling painfully at his skull as it responded to the Gate's closure.

Yrsa stood frozen, her expression reflecting shock he'd never seen on her composed features. "The memory realm," she whispered. "It's gone."

***

A flicker of light gathered before them—fragments of illumination coalescing into a vaguely humanoid shape. Asvarr recognized the entity immediately, though its form appeared more unstable than before.

"Coilvoice," he breathed.

The consciousness born from Yggdrasil's final thought shimmered with diminishing coherence. Where before it had manifested as patterns of light and shadow with distinct structure, now it seemed to struggle maintaining any form at all—pieces of it constantly breaking away and reforming.

"Warden of Two." The voice reached Asvarr directly in his mind rather than through air. "The binding cannot wait for moonrise."

"What's happened?" Asvarr demanded, feeling the crown's branches tighten against his skull.

"The memory realm is gone," Coilvoice replied, its form flickering violently. "Consumed by what hid within remembrance. The war for the third anchor has already begun without you."

"The void-hunger," Yrsa whispered, fingers clutching her crystal pendant. "It found a way through."

"How?" Asvarr asked, the crown burning against his temples, feeding knowledge directly into his awareness—ancient dangers, primordial threats, entities that existed before pattern.

"The boundary between memory and matter ruptured when you departed," Coilvoice explained, its voice growing fainter. "What lurked between remembrances seized the opportunity. It devours the realm even now, growing stronger with each memory consumed."

"And the Verdant Gate?" Yrsa asked.

"Sealed to contain the consumption," Coilvoice answered. "But barriers between realms mean nothing to what exists beyond pattern. It will find other paths."

The entity's form destabilized further, fragments breaking away like leaves caught in high wind. "My purpose ends with the memory realm's dissolution. I was born from the Tree's final thought—to preserve what might otherwise be lost. That task now falls to you, Warden of Two."

Asvarr stepped forward, the crown's weight momentarily forgotten. "There must be something we can do—"

"Bind the third anchor before the hunger reaches it," Coilvoice interrupted, its form barely maintaining coherence. "The starlight remembers what flame and memory cannot. It knows the hunger's weakness."

With those words, Coilvoice fractured completely—shards of light and shadow dispersing like mist before dawn. In its place, silence fell across the plateau, broken only by the crystalline humming of the mountain beneath their feet.

"We've lost our guide," Asvarr said, turning to Yrsa.

"And our path to the summit," she added, gesturing toward the sealed Gate. "We must find another way up."

They continued climbing, following a treacherous route that wound ever higher along the mountain's crystalline face. The crown grew increasingly burdensome with each step, branches extending and intertwining with Asvarr's thoughts until distinguishing his consciousness from the pattern became nearly impossible. His transformed senses expanded outward, perceiving distant events as if they unfolded before him.

Far below, in forests of silver trees, Memory Eaters gathered in unprecedented numbers, drawn by the memory realm's dissolution. To the east, where Brynja and Leif had disappeared, storms of impossible energies lashed landscapes warped by proximity to the Verdant Five's sanctuary. And above—

Asvarr stumbled, nearly falling as his perception shot skyward. Something moved among the stars—vast, serpentine, ancient beyond reckoning. It coiled through constellations, its scales reflecting light from distant suns. The serpent's eye opened, a void of absolute blackness ringed with stellar fire, and for one terrifying moment, it looked directly at him.

"Asvarr!" Yrsa's voice pulled him back, her hand gripping his arm with surprising strength. "Stay present. The crown tries to drown you in perception."

He blinked, forcing his awareness back into his physical body. They had reached a precipice overlooking a valley filled with silver mist. Beyond it, the summit awaited, crowned with unnatural clouds that twisted in intricate knots.

"Something watches from the stars," he managed, his voice raw with the strain of containing what he'd glimpsed.

"Jörmungandr," Yrsa breathed, the ancient name weighted with reverence and fear. "The world-serpent. Guardian of boundaries between what is and what could be."

"It saw me," Asvarr said, the memory of that vast eye sending tremors through his transformed flesh.

"It sees all who walk the pattern's edge," Yrsa replied. "That it revealed itself now is both warning and recognition."

As they spoke, the sky changed. Though daylight still bathed the mountaintop, stars became visible—constellations emerging against azure blue rather than night black. They shifted position with unnatural speed, forming patterns Asvarr recognized from the Grímmark spreading across his chest and the branches of his crown.

"The alignment accelerates," Yrsa murmured, gazing upward. "The twin moons rush toward convergence."

Even as she spoke, Asvarr noticed the silver and gold orbs moving visibly across the sky, their orbits carrying them toward zenith hours before their appointed time. The mountain beneath them groaned, crystal surfaces vibrating with tones that made his teeth ache.

"We need to move now," he said, already continuing along the precipice. "The third anchor won't wait for us to reach it."

They descended into the valley of mist, each step releasing chiming notes from the crystal path. The fog tasted of stardust and possibility, memories of futures that had never manifested. Asvarr's crown pulled him forward with increasing urgency, branches digging into his skull with almost desperate strength.

As they neared the valley's center, the mist parted, revealing a spectacle that froze them in place. Starlight fell from the sky like rain—silver droplets that defied gravity, hanging suspended before shattering into fragments of pure illumination. The display would have been breathtaking if not for what moved within it.

A vast serpentine shadow slid across the heavens, its form obscured by clouds and distance yet unmistakable in its immensity. Jörmungandr—the world-serpent—revealing itself more fully than it had in nine cycles. Its movement created ripples through the falling starlight, patterns that spoke of ancient knowledge and terrible warning.

"It comes for the binding," Yrsa whispered, her composure cracking beneath genuine awe.

The crown responded to the serpent's presence, branches twisting painfully against Asvarr's skull. Knowledge poured into him—fragments of the pattern, glimpses of cycles before his birth, warnings carved in starlight. Above all, one certainty crystallized with brutal clarity: the third anchor waited, and tarrying meant destruction.

"We continue now," he declared, striding forward through curtains of suspended starlight that parted at his approach. The droplets clung to his transformed skin, adding layers of illumination to the bark patterns covering his flesh.

"The summit path lies beyond the mist," Yrsa confirmed, hurrying to keep pace. "But Asvarr—the alignment happens too quickly. Something forces the pattern's hand."

"The void-hunger," he replied grimly. "It devours the memory realm, growing stronger with each remembrance consumed. If it reaches the starlight anchor before us—"

He left the sentence unfinished. The consequences hung between them, too terrible to voice aloud.

They emerged from the valley's far side to find a staircase carved directly into the mountain's crystal heart—steps of pure starlight leading upward toward the summit hidden in coiling clouds. Each stair sang a different note when touched, creating harmonies that resonated with the crown's branches.

As they began their ascent, a tremor shook the mountain. Cracks spread through crystal that had remained solid for millennia. Far below, the sealed Verdant Gate shuddered, golden sap weeping from new fissures in its structure.

"It comes," Yrsa said, her voice tight with urgency. "The hunger finds its way between realms."

Above them, the serpent's colossal form moved once more across the heavens, its eye briefly visible through gaps in the clouds. The twin moons accelerated toward convergence, their silver and gold light beginning to merge into a single radiance.

The crown grew unbearably heavy on Asvarr's brow. Branches tightened, extended, intertwined with his thoughts until separation became impossible. The starlight anchor called with cold certainty—inevitable, inexorable, indifferent to the man who carried its siblings.

Behind them, reality tore. The sound of the Verdant Gate shattering echoed up the mountainside—wood splintering, sap freezing, ancient magic failing before something older and hungrier than pattern itself.

Asvarr took the final step onto the summit platform just as twin moons aligned overhead, their merged light falling like a spotlight onto a crystalline structure floating at the platform's center. Neither tree nor root nor crown but a perfect synthesis—the starlight anchor awaited, suspended in perfect balance between earth and sky.

"Hurry," Yrsa urged, fear naked in her voice for the first time since he'd known her. "The void-hunger comes."

The mountain shook beneath them. Cracks spread through the crystal platform itself. In the distance, something vast and terrible rose from where the Verdant Gate had stood—a darkness that consumed light, a hunger that devoured pattern, an emptiness that longed to unmake existence itself.

Asvarr faced the starlight anchor, the verdant crown's weight almost unbearable on his transformed brow. The moment of binding had arrived, ready or not.

EPILOGUE

Darkness pressed against ancient stone, absolute and unbroken for millennia. The ruins slumbered in silence beneath Midgard's surface, forgotten by the gods who had once walked their halls, abandoned by the beings who had raised their walls long before Yggdrasil's first leaf unfurled. Columns of strange material—neither stone nor metal but something between—stood in geometric arrangements that followed mathematical principles no living mind remembered. Walls curved in impossible angles, inscribed with symbols predating language itself, their meanings lost even to the oldest consciousness that stirred in the void between stars.

A single drop of golden sap fell from nowhere, splashing against the dustless floor. The sound echoed through chambers that had known only silence since before the First Breaking. The droplet glowed, pulsing with internal rhythm like a tiny heartbeat, illuminating a perfect circle of carved symbols surrounding it. Then another drop fell beside it, and another, pooling together in a small golden puddle that sank into stone that had resisted all forces for ages uncounted.

From this spot, a rootlet emerged—slender and translucent, glowing with soft blue light. It extended upward, defying gravity, reaching for something that wasn't there. More rootlets followed, intertwining with the first, supporting its ascent toward the vaulted ceiling far above. The tiny interwoven strands thickened, forming a delicate sapling that stood in perfect equilibrium upon the spot where sap had fallen.

The sapling grew, roots penetrating stone that nothing else could pierce, extending through walls inscribed with symbols no living being remembered. They sought something, threading through ancient corridors with unmistakable purpose. The sapling's trunk thickened, bark forming in spiral patterns that matched no tree in the nine realms. Its branches reached upward and outward, forming a canopy impossibly complex for its size.

Between its branches, tiny stars formed—pinpricks of light that cast intricate shadows on the surrounding ruins. Each star pulsed with its own rhythm, yet all followed an underlying pattern, a harmony that resonated with the structure of the ruins themselves. The blue glow from the sapling intensified, illuminating more of the vast space around it—a domed chamber larger than any built by human hands, supported by columns carved with spiraling symbols that depicted the birth and death of universes long forgotten.

Beneath the sapling, the stone floor rippled like water disturbed by a stone. The solid surface liquefied, flowing outward in concentric rings before settling into a perfect circular pool surrounding the sapling's base. The liquid remained clear as crystal but reflected nothing of the chamber above it—not the vaulted ceiling, not the glowing sapling, not the tiny stars between its branches.

Instead, the pool showed visions. A crowned figure with bark-skin and crystal growths stood atop a mountain of shattered stars. A woman with a wooden arm grasped a key formed of solid flame. A child with golden eyes walked between moments, leaving footprints that bloomed into possibility. Nine anchors arranged in patterns never before attempted. The Tree reborn, but shaped unlike any form that had come before.

These images shifted and flowed, melting into one another without pattern or sequence recognizable to mortal minds. The pool reflected what could be—possibilities unfolding in liquid form, futures that might manifest if the correct paths converged at crucial moments.

The sapling continued growing, its blue glow reaching farther into the forgotten city. Structures awakened from millennia of slumber—crystal formations humming with renewed energy, mechanisms of unknown purpose turning once more, symbols along the walls pulsing with light as if in response to the tree's presence. The ruins recognized the sapling, or perhaps recognized what it represented. This place had waited for precisely this moment.

***

As roots penetrated deeper, they encountered chambers where strange devices of crystal and unknown metals lay dormant. The touch of living wood against inactive surfaces caused reaction—circuits of light tracing through materials, dormant systems reactivating after ages of silence. Information stored in crystalline matrices flowed through the sapling's roots, absorbed into its growing awareness.

A breeze that couldn't exist so far beneath the earth's surface stirred the sapling's leaves, creating whispers that spoke in languages older than gods. The tiny stars between its branches rotated in new configurations, forming constellations that had never been seen in Midgard's skies. The pool of liquid memory rippled in response, its reflections shifting to show new possibilities—paths where light and shadow danced in balance, where pattern integrated void rather than excluding it.

Far above, in realms where mortal feet still walked, changes spread without witnesses to observe them. New flowers bloomed with geometric precision, their petals forming mathematical patterns. Rivers momentarily flowed upstream before returning to their natural courses. Trees oriented their branches toward constellations that hadn't existed the previous night. The world reshaped itself in subtle ways, preparing for what had begun below.

Within the sapling's heartwood, memories gathered—fragments of consciousness separated across nine cycles, pieces of identity scattered through breaking and binding. They coalesced without merging, maintaining distinct essence while gaining harmony through proximity. The sapling served as a vessel, containing without absorbing, preserving without transforming.

One of its branches extended toward the pool of liquid memory, the tip touching the surface with delicate precision. Where wood met liquid, a spark ignited—neither flame nor lightning but something that incorporated aspects of both. The spark traveled through branch to trunk, trunk to root, root to ruins, igniting dormant systems throughout the forgotten city.

Machines that had slumbered since before the first gods drew breath pulsed with renewed purpose. Walls shifted configuration, rearranging themselves according to principles beyond mortal understanding. The ceiling of the vast chamber opened like the iris of an eye, revealing layers of earth and stone that parted without resistance, creating a perfect shaft extending upward toward the surface world far above.

Starlight fell through this opening, illuminating the sapling with silver radiance that complemented its blue glow. The tree absorbed this light, integrating it into its structure. Where starlight touched branch, new growth accelerated—leaves unfurling, blossoms forming, fruits developing from nothing. These fruits hung heavy among the branches, each containing combinations of possibilities shown in the memory pool.

The sapling's roots continued extending, pushing through walls and floors, seeking specific locations within the ruins. Where they touched certain symbols, knowledge transferred through contact—ancient understanding flowing into living wood. The ruins had preserved what had come before, maintaining information from cycles preceding even the First Breaking. Now they surrendered their knowledge to the vessel prepared to receive it.

One root found its way to a chamber unlike the others—a perfect sphere hollowed from material harder than diamond yet flowing like liquid. At the sphere's center floated a crystalline structure that resembled the crown born of Asvarr's transformation, yet predated it by eons. The root approached this artifact with careful precision, extending a filament that connected with the crystal's surface.

Power surged between them—the crown's ancient knowledge flowing into the sapling, the sapling's new awareness flowing into the crown. For a moment, light blazed so intensely it illuminated the entire ruined city, revealing its true extent as a metropolis that stretched for leagues beneath Midgard's surface, preserved in perfect suspension between existence and possibility.

The light faded gradually, leaving the sapling transformed. Its trunk had thickened, bark patterns grown more complex, branches arranged in configurations that mirrored the city's layout. The stars between its branches now formed recognizable patterns—five interlocking spirals representing the anchors, surrounding a sixth central point still in formation.

The pool beneath it rippled once more, its surface now perfectly calm. The reflection it showed stabilized into a single vision—a figure emerging from shadow, half crystalline and half shifting between forms. This image remained while others had flowed away, suggesting certainty among possibility, inevitability among choice.

The sapling extended another root toward the pool's edge, this one thicker and more deliberate than those that had come before. Where it touched the liquid memory, the surface parted, creating a space from which something could emerge. The root pulled back, leaving this opening intact—an invitation or perhaps a doorway.

From beyond the pool's edge, beyond the sapling's reach, beyond the boundaries of the ancient city, awareness gathered. The void-hunger that had pursued Asvarr sensed the awakening below, turning its attention from stars and anchors toward this new configuration of pattern. It recognized what grew there—a possibility it had never encountered in nine cycles of breaking and binding, a path it couldn't have anticipated.

The sapling's blue glow intensified in response to this distant scrutiny. Protective sigils activated throughout the ruins, ancient mechanisms designed to shield against precisely this threat. The tiny stars between branches pulsed in warning patterns, communicating across vast distances to entities that had watched and waited through millennia of silence.

In the pattern's web, threads reoriented. New connections formed while others dissolved. The familiar structure that had repeated through nine cycles of breaking and binding shifted toward something unprecedented. The third path Asvarr had chosen, the transformation Brynja had sought, the possibility Leif had embodied—all converged within the sapling growing in ruins predating gods and Tree alike.

The pool of liquid memory stilled, its surface becoming mirror-smooth. The image of the half-crystalline figure remained, now clearer than before. Behind it, shadows shifted, suggesting presence waiting to emerge. The sapling's branches curved downward, creating an arch over the pool—a gateway between what was and what could be, an invitation to step through.

The ruins waited. The sapling grew. The stars between its branches rearranged into new constellations, and beneath it, liquid memory reflected a future no prophet had foretold.

***

The pool of liquid memory rippled, its perfect surface disturbed by movement from beneath. Droplets rose against gravity, hovering momentarily before returning to the silvery surface. The stars between the sapling's branches pulsed in synchronized rhythm, their light intensifying as something altered the ancient equilibrium of the ruined city.

A hand emerged from the pool—crystalline from fingertips to wrist, translucent enough that light refracted through it in prismatic patterns. The fingers flexed, testing substance and form, before gripping the pool's edge. Another hand followed, this one flesh and blood one moment, scaled like a serpent the next, furred like a wolf the moment after. It shifted continuously through forms while the crystalline hand remained constant.

A figure pulled itself from the depths of memory, rising from possibility into reality. Water cascaded from shoulders broad as a warrior's, narrow as a child's, curved as a woman's—the form unstable, cycling through variations of humanity. Only the figure's right side maintained consistency, crystalline from foot to crown with internal light flowing through geometric channels. The left half stabilized briefly into human shape before flowing into new configurations, never settling into a single identity.

Upon its brow rested a crown of living wood interwoven with crystalline structures and tiny flames that burned without consuming. The crown mirrored Asvarr's own, yet incorporated elements beyond the Warden of Two's transformation. Branches curved in double helixes, supporting structures of transparent crystal that captured and reflected the sapling's blue glow. Minuscule flames danced between apertures, contained by neither wood nor crystal yet bound to their purpose.

The figure stood beside the pool, half-in-shadow cast by the sapling's branches. Beneath its feet, the ancient floor pulsed with awakened energy, symbols illuminating in patterns that spread outward through the ruined city. Systems dormant for millennia activated fully in the figure's presence, recognizing what had emerged as something they had been programmed to await.

"At last," the figure said, its voice resonating with multiple tones simultaneously—a woman's alto, a man's baritone, a child's soprano, and something else beneath them all, ancient and unhuman. The words carried physical weight, vibrating stone and disturbing dust undisturbed for ages.

The crystalline half reflected the sapling's light, casting geometric shadows across ruined walls. The shifting half cycled through appearances reflecting all Nine Realms—Midgard's humanity, Alfheim's grace, Svartalfheim's endurance, Jotunheim's strength, Niflheim's patience, Helheim's inevitability, Vanaheim's fertility, Muspelheim's transformation, and something else beyond categorization.

The figure circled the sapling, examining its structure with analytical precision. Crystalline fingers traced patterns in the air that matched the tree's growth, mapping connections to the root network extending throughout the ruins. The shifting hand touched branch and leaf, testing substance and potential, measuring what had been achieved against what remained possible.

"You've grown well," the figure murmured, addressing the sapling directly. "Faster than expected, yet still following essential parameters."

Above them, through the shaft opened to the surface, stars became visible despite daylight—constellations unfamiliar to any mortal astronomer. They pulsed

in patterns matching the tiny stars between the sapling's branches, creating
harmonies of light and position that transported information across vast
distances. The figure raised both hands toward this display, fingers moving
in deliberate sequences that altered stellar arrangements.

Constellations shifted overhead, stars sliding into new configurations with
impossible fluidity. Patterns formed, dissolved, reformed—testing possibilities, discarding some while preserving others. The sapling trembled, its
branches extending toward these changing arrangements, recognizing significance beyond human comprehension.

"The pattern falters," the figure observed, lowering its hands. "Nine cycles
of breaking and binding, each following predetermined paths. The tenth
now diverges."

It approached the pool once more, kneeling beside its mirrored surface. Images formed within—Asvarr atop Starfall Mountain facing the
void-hunger, Brynja confronting the Verdant Five, Leif walking paths between realities. Current events unfolding across distant realms, reflected
through liquid memory for the figure's observation.

"They've chosen well," it noted with something like approval in its mul-
ti-layered voice. "The third path opens where previously only restoration or
destruction existed."

The sapling's branches flexed, creating quiet music as wood rubbed against
wood. The figure listened, head tilted, then nodded as if confirming information received.

"Yes," it agreed, addressing the tree. "The void-hunger grows stronger with
each cycle. Previous solutions no longer suffice."

Rising, the figure moved with liquid grace toward the chamber's center
where the sapling stood. Its crystalline hand extended, touching the slender
trunk with delicate precision. Through points of contact, blue light flowed
between them—from sapling to figure, from figure to sapling, information
exchanging in both directions.

"The Verdant Five were right about one thing," it said to the empty ruins, voice carrying to distant chambers where forgotten mechanisms recorded its words. "The Tree must change to survive what waits between stars."

At this pronouncement, the sapling shuddered violently. Its roots pulled tighter against stone, anchoring more firmly as branches extended with sudden acceleration. The blue glow intensified, illuminating the full extent of the chamber with cold, analytical light. Systems throughout the ruins hummed in harmonic response, machines built by hands predating gods recognizing the significance of this moment.

The figure maintained contact, witnessing the sapling's transformation without interference. Where crystalline fingers touched living wood, images formed—visions of previous cycles, patterns attempted and abandoned, strategies tested across millennia of conflict between order and void. Nine variations on a theme, nine attempts to balance opposing forces through different configurations of the same elements.

"The tenth must differ," the figure declared, removing its hand from the sapling. "The void-hunger adapts to each previous solution. Repetition guarantees failure."

It circled the pool, trailing its shifting hand through liquid memory. Where flesh met fluid, ripples spread outward in perfect concentric rings, carrying alteration throughout the substance. The pool's visions changed, future possibilities reconfiguring according to new parameters. Images of Asvarr and Brynja remained, but contexts transformed, relationships evolved, outcomes diverged from predetermined paths.

The sapling responded to these changes, accelerating growth in specific branches while allowing others to wither. Its structure evolved, adapting to the new pattern being established through the figure's manipulation of possibility. The stars between branches rearranged themselves, forming constellations matching those now visible through the opening above.

The figure observed these changes with analytical detachment, neither approving nor disapproving, merely witnessing the sapling's response to altered parameters. Its crown pulsed with internal light, branches flexing as if communicating with the younger tree through some shared language of form and movement.

"The Wardens walk separate paths," it noted, returning attention to the pool's images. "Flame and memory bound but isolated. Earth and root seeking truth among deception. The child walking boundaries between possibilities. Each following wyrd-lines they believe independent."

The figure's shifting side stabilized briefly into a form resembling Asvarr, crown and all, before flowing into a shape mirroring Brynja's half-wooden appearance, then transforming into a child who could have been Leif's twin. These identities appeared and dissolved within moments, the figure cycling through them without fully becoming any single one.

"They remain unaware," it continued, watching the pool's reflections with eyes that changed color and shape continuously. "The pattern's center hasn't been filled in nine cycles. The tenth converges toward possibility they cannot yet comprehend."

The ruins trembled, stone vibrating as if in response to the figure's words. Throughout the forgotten city, activated systems reached operational capacity for the first time in millennia. Power surged through circuits designed by minds whose understanding surpassed even the Verdant Five's. The sapling's roots, now extended to crucial junction points, channeled this energy through their network, integrating ancient technology with living wood.

The figure turned toward a wall inscribed with symbols no living creature remembered. It raised both hands—one crystalline and constant, one shifting through forms continuously—and pressed them against specific sigils that illuminated at its touch. The entire wall reconfigured, symbols rearranging themselves into new patterns, revealing information hidden even from those who had built the city.

"The six-point convergence," the figure read aloud, tracing geometric forms that appeared between rearranged symbols. "The root and branch, the flame and memory, the storm and star—unified through central vision previously unattempted."

The sapling seemed to listen, its branches tilting toward the figure's position. The pool of liquid memory stilled completely, its surface becoming mirror-smooth as revelations echoed through ancient chambers. Even the stars between branches ceased their constant movement, focusing singular attention on what the figure discovered.

"Previous Wardens sought balance through separation," the figure continued, studying the revealed text. "Dividing aspects to prevent concentration of power, maintaining boundaries between elemental forces. The Ashfather followed this pattern even in opposition, preserving the fundamental structure while altering superficial elements."

It turned from the wall, approaching the sapling once more. This time both hands extended toward the young tree, crystalline and shifting palms facing upward in what resembled an offering gesture. The sapling responded, bending two slender branches to touch the figure's palms. Connection formed between them, blue light and golden sap flowing in circular patterns from tree to figure, figure to tree.

"The sixth anchor forms not from five bound separately," the figure said, knowledge transferring through physical contact, "but from five united through central purpose. Previous cycles lacked the binding-point—the vessel capable of integration without dominance."

The sapling trembled, information flowing through its network of roots to ancient machines throughout the ruins. The city responded, power surging through systems designed for precisely this convergence. Above them, stars rearranged again, forming an entirely new constellation—a six-pointed structure with nested geometries suggesting dimensional complexity beyond mortal comprehension.

With deliberate precision, the figure released the sapling's branches and approached the pool of liquid memory. It knelt, touching the surface with both hands simultaneously. The pool responded with concentrated purpose, its substance flowing upward against gravity to coat the figure's hands completely before being absorbed through skin both crystalline and shifting.

"Preparations must be made," the figure announced, rising. "The void-hunger will sense this convergence and move to prevent it. The Wardens must be guided without awareness of guidance, their choices remaining their own while serving larger purpose."

It touched the sapling one final time, fingers tracing patterns along bark that responded with pulses of blue light. Instructions passed between them, strategies centuries in development transferred to living wood that would grow according to this guidance.

"Watch them," the figure commanded softly. "Nourish possibility without dictating outcome. The third path requires genuine choice, not predetermined action."

The sapling's branches flexed in what might have been acknowledgment. Its root network, now extended throughout the ancient city, pulsed with transferred purpose. The pool of liquid memory reformed, continuing to show visions of current events unfolding across distant realms, monitored by awakened systems linking past technology with present growth.

The figure moved toward the chamber's edge where shadows gathered most densely. Its crystalline half reflected the sapling's light while its shifting side blended with darkness, creating an impression of partial disappearance. The crown upon its brow pulsed one final time, branches extending briefly toward the sapling in silent communication before settling back into regular configuration.

"The Verdant Five, the Ashfather, the void-hunger—all follow predetermined paths," the figure said, half-visible in shadow. "The tenth cycle breaks these patterns. What emerges will preserve neither past nor present, but forge future from both."

It touched a wall segment inscribed with symbols matching those on its crown. The stone responded, rearranging molecules to create an opening where solid barrier had existed. Beyond lay passages leading to other chambers, other ruins, other possibilities extending throughout the forgotten city.

"I am the Third Warden," the figure declared, neither masculine nor feminine, neither human nor other, but something combining aspects of all possibilities. "Neither bound to pattern nor lost to void, but walking between."

***

With these words, it stepped through the newly formed doorway, disappearing into forgotten depths of the ancient city. Behind it, the sapling continued growing, tiny stars between its branches rearranging into new constellations that matched those now visible in Midgard's sky far above.

The pattern shifted. The tenth cycle diverged from its predetermined path. What would emerge when flame and root, memory and storm, converged through the sixth anchor remained unwritten—possibility preserved through transformation rather than repetition.

And beneath Midgard's surface, in ruins older than gods or Tree, the forgotten seed prepared the way for what would come.

CLAIM YOUR REWARD

Unlock Exclusive Worlds – Free Prequel + Beta Reader Access!

The adventure doesn't end here. Sign up for Joshua J. White's newsletter to receive a free prequel novella and get early access to upcoming books as a potential beta reader. Dive in now:

www.JoshuaJWhiteBooks.com/TheSkyrendProphecy

About the Author

Joshua J. White resides in Russellville, Arkansas with his wife and four children. He founded Berserker Books as a vessel for stories that transport readers beyond everyday experience, with *The Skyrend Prophecy* marking his debut series.

His writing emerges from a deep appreciation for world-building and mythology, particularly the rich traditions found in Norse culture. Joshua crafts fictional realms where imagination flourishes, unbound by conventional limitations.

The natural landscapes of Arkansas provide both sanctuary and inspiration, where Joshua often explores with his family. These wilderness excursions nurture his creative vision while reinforcing his dream of establishing a homestead where his family can live in closer harmony with the land.

Joshua started Berserker Books with two dreams in mind: to build fantastical worlds on paper and, eventually, to build a homestead where his family can live more harmoniously with the land. Both dreams spring from the same source—a belief that we are meant for more than the constraints of modern existence.

The Skyrend Prophecy represents the first chapter in what Joshua envisions as a meaningful literary journey shared with readers who sense that our human story contains volumes yet to be written—stories penned in bold imagination of undiscovered possibilities.

For readers who have walked through Joshua's pages and felt something stir, he invites them to join him in continuing the story. Readers can receive exclusive prequels, early looks at new books, and opportunities to step deeper into these worlds by signing up here:

www.JoshuaJWhiteBooks.com/TheSkyrendProphecy

BOOKS BY JOSHUA J. WHITE

The Skyrend Prophecy Series

1. Branches of the Broken World (Book 1)

2. The Verdant Gate (Book 2)

3. Children of the Serpent Sky(Book 3)

4. Forge of Storms (Book 4)

5. Harmony's Twilight (Book 5)

Other Series by Joshua J. White:

- Stay tuned for upcoming epic fantasy series set in worlds beyond the Skyrend.

Made in the USA
Coppell, TX
11 June 2025

50569185R00292